The day **Maggie Cox** saw the film version of *Wuthering Heights*, with a beautiful Merle Oberon and a very handsome Laurence Olivier, was the day she became hooked on romance. From that day onwards she spent a lot of time dreaming up her own romances, secretly hoping that one day she might become published and get paid for doing what she loved most!

Now that her dream is being realised she wakes up every morning and counts her blessings. She is married to a gorgeous man and is the mother of two wonderful sons. Her two other great passions in life—besides her family and reading/writing—are music and films.

USA TODAY bestselling author **Olivia Gates** has written over forty books in action/adventure, thriller, medical, paranormal and contemporary romance.

Her signature is her uber-alpha male heroes. Whether they're gods, black-ops agents, virtuoso surgeons or ruthless billionaires, they all fall in love once and for life with the only women who can match them and bring them to their knees. She loves to hear from readers always, so don't hesitate to email her at oliviagates@gmail.com.

Broken Resolutions

MAGGIE COX
OLIVIA GATES

MILLS & BOON

® and ™ are trademarks owned and used by the trademark owner and/or its licensee. Trademarks marked with ® are registered with the United Kingdom Patent Office and/or the Office for Harmonisation in the Internal Market and in other countries.

First Published in Great Britain 2018
by Mills & Boon, an imprint of HarperCollins*Publishers*
1 London Bridge Street, London, SE1 9GF

BROKEN RESOLUTIONS © 2018 Harlequin Books S. A.

A Rule Worth Breaking © 2014 Maggie Cox
The Man She Can't Forget © 2014 Maggie Cox
Billionaire Boss, M.D. © 2016 Olivia Gates

ISBN: 978-0-263-26799-0

05-0618

MIX
Paper from
responsible sources
FSC
www.fsc.org   FSC™ C007454

This book is produced from independently certified FSC™ paper to ensure responsible forest management.

For more information visit: www.harpercollins.co.uk/green

Printed and bound in Spain
by CPI, Barcelona

A RULE WORTH BREAKING

MAGGIE COX

To Joy
You were and always will be one of the true lights of
my life. With love and affection,
Maggie x

CHAPTER ONE

'WHAT DO YOU think?' Unable to suppress the disagreeable sense of disappointment that was churning in his gut, Jake Sorenson glanced up at the stage at Rick—his 'partner in crime'—who was all but wearing out the floor, pacing back and forth in his worn Cuban-heeled boots. *The auditions weren't exactly going well.*

Rick abruptly stopped pacing to spear an exasperated hand through his dull gold hair. Studying Jake, he snapped, 'What do I think? I think that Rosie Rhys-Jones, or whatever her name is, just isn't good enough. God knows Marcie is a hard act to follow, but *Rosie...*'

'Josie.'

'Josie. Whatever...' Scowling, Rick folded his muscular arms across his leather waistcoat and continued. 'The woman would be fine on a cruise ship, entertaining folk with more money than taste, but she's not lead vocalist material and that's a fact. Bottom line is, Jake, I can't see any of the singers we've heard so far fronting a potentially great band like Blue Sky—can you?'

In answer, Jake stared off into the distance. Mentally reviewing the past few auditions, he couldn't help but agree. He returned his arresting blue gaze to his friend and the characteristic dimple that highlighted a rare smile appeared at the side of his mouth.

'You're right, of course. We'll just have to keep on looking.'

Jake rarely elaborated. Not unless he absolutely had to.

But he knew that when it came to making a decision ulti-mately the final say would be his. Although Rick had been in the music business even longer than he had—at the height of his career Jake had been one of the most successful re-cord producers in the business—he knew that the other man valued his expertise and judgement.

'Is there anyone left outside to see?' Yawning as he rose to his feet, Jake stretched his arms high above his head. The movement made his shirt ride up several inches to reveal a taut flat stomach tapering into lean hips and long-boned thighs, currently encased in faded dark blue denim.

At the same time Rick expertly jumped off the stage and ambled across the dusty wooden floor to join him. 'Not un-less they're lurking in the graveyard out there' he joked.

He feigned an exaggerated shiver, his bemused expres-sion conveying exactly what he thought about conducting auditions in an obscure village hall deep in the heart of rural England. But Jake knew that doing things this way at least afforded them a certain amount of privacy that wasn't al-ways possible in London.

The music press and tabloids were always keen to know what he was up to. He was the man who had famously brought several acts from the UK to prominence. But at the height of his career he'd been caught up in a destructive scandal that had cut short his seemingly unstoppable rise to the top when it hit the headlines. After that Jake had dropped out of producing and promoting bands to lick his wounds, reassess his life and reflect on what he might do instead.

For a few years following his very public fall from grace he'd become a perpetual nomad, travelling the world. And while he'd thought he would never entertain the idea of work-ing in the music industry again, when he'd been travelling he'd begun to listen to and study the ethnic music of other cultures and realised that he couldn't leave music alone. It had always been and still was his abiding interest—the thing that made life worth living. And when he'd finally brought his explorative sojourn to an end he'd returned to the UK and made the decision to go back to his roots.

He'd started out managing a band long before he'd become a producer and now, after fifteen years in the business, had come full circle to manage Blue Sky.

Glancing down at his watch, he grimaced. 'Anyway, I think I've heard enough to know that we haven't found our singer yet. Want to call it a day?'

Dropping his hands to his hips, Jake glanced across at the three band members who were waiting expectantly for him to make a decision about what they were going to do next.

'No doubt these guys have had enough, too. So let's go get a hot pie and a beer. We can make an early start in the morning. There's a girl from Birmingham that might be a possibility. She's lead vocalist in a band that have attracted quite a following in her home town'

Despite trying to sound hopeful, Jake knew his downbeat tone conveyed that the girl from Birmingham was more than likely another no. What he was looking for—what they were *all* looking for—was someone extraordinary, a girl who stood out from the crowd, who could hold her own fronting a band that had been on the brink of major success before Marcie's sudden and abrupt departure.

It was a crying shame that the woman should have decided at the eleventh hour that she'd rather marry her childhood sweetheart and go and cultivate grapes in the Dordogne than front a rock band. But that, as they said, was showbiz. Still, if anyone could work a miracle Jake knew that *he* could. All he needed to prove it was to find an amazing singer.

A door slammed loud and hard and the shock in the room was tangible. The sound reverberated round the vaulted high-ceilinged hall like a cannon exploding. *What the hell...?*

Jake was taken aback when he saw the perpetrator. Tall, slim and dark-haired, she was struggling with the belt of her raincoat, which he could see had become trapped between the hall's back doors when they'd slammed shut. His transfixed gaze worked its way up from long black suede boots to slim toned legs clad in sheer black hosiery. For a long moment he was fixated by a shapely knee, where its smooth flesh peeped intriguingly through a frayed tear the size of a small coin. As she struggled to free her belt the girl emitted a breathy little sound that might have been a curse.

Briefly turning his head, Jake found Rick grinning. *He knew it wasn't just because the girl had got herself in a fix.* When she finally extricated the belt and lifted her head to murmur a blushing apology he felt as though all the air had just been punched out of his lungs. *She was absolutely stunning.* Even at a distance he could see that her eyes were the most dazzling emerald-green he'd ever seen in his life. Add to that apple cheeks, and full, luscious lips stained the colour of ripe cherries, and Jake sensed all the testosterone in the room heave a collective sigh—his own included.

Rick was the first to recover. 'Hi. Can I help you?' he called out cheerfully.

'This is where the auditions are being held, isn't it?'

Glancing nervously round her, the girl took in the five men standing there, as well as the stacked plastic chairs lining the walls, the dusty floor and the lofty ceiling with its yellowing cracked plasterwork. Her expression was definitely bemused, as if she couldn't quite believe where she'd landed. She still hadn't moved any further away from the door.

'Am I too late? I'm sorry I couldn't get here a bit earlier but I've been stocktaking' Swiping a hand down her short black skirt, she tugged the edges of her raincoat together in front of it, as if she might have inadvertently displayed more than she wanted to.

'Stocktaking, you say?' Rick's wolfish grin grew even wider. 'You can check *my* stock any time you want to, honey.'

Time to take charge, Jake thought with a flash of irritation. The girl might be easy on the eye, but she was more than likely another time-waster or wannabe—and God knew he'd auditioned enough of them in the past four days to be honestly weary of hearing any more.

To make matters worse, he'd *lived* with a girl just like that and she'd all but broken him with her relentless desire for fame and fortune. Not to mention what she'd been prepared to do to get it. *In any case, the girl in front of him probably couldn't sing for toffee.*

But even as his cynical gaze surveyed her he felt a hot flash of desire throb through him. He was almost dizzy with the power of it, and in that moment he saw it as a warning to steer well clear—because something told him that, given the chance, the allure of this incredible beauty would be too hard to resist.

The realisation that he might be tempted honestly scared him. Temptation was never a simple option. In Jake's book it equalled weakness, and he was a man who liked to be in control. From a young age he'd quickly intuited that if he didn't take care of himself and instigate boundaries then he was damn sure no one else would.

'Actually, you're too late.'

But even as the words left his lips he immediately belied them. Helplessly drawn, he found himself moving towards the bewitching woman, and somehow the necessity to get her to leave…and *quick*…melted clean away. All his instincts told him to take the chance to admire her beauty while he could. After all, it wasn't every day that a veritable *angel* presented herself in front of him…

'What I mean to say is' he went on 'is that you're too late for the auditions today but you can come back tomorrow if you're serious. If not, then all I can do is thank you for your interest and wish you well.'

'You're questioning if I'm serious or not? If I'm not serious about auditioning then why do you think I'm here?'

Surprised that she would come back at him like that, Jake sighed. His innate instinct was for self-preservation, and his mind scrambled to give her a legitimate reason why he couldn't let her audition today.

'Well, if that's the case, then you won't mind coming back tomorrow, will you? We've been auditioning since early this morning and we could all use a break,'

Watching her wrestle with the emotion his words must have wrought, he saw her hand tuck her hair behind her ear, then free it again as if she wasn't quite sure what to do next.

'I was really hoping you could hear me tonight. The thing is, I won't be able to make it tomorrow'

'Then you can't be that serious about auditioning, can you?'

Hot colour suffused her apple cheeks—but not because of embarrassment, Jake guessed. His cutting rejoinder had infuriated her.

Not wanting to be swayed by her angelic face and big green eyes, he told himself to stand firm. Nonetheless, he heard himself ask, 'What's your name?'

'It's Caitlin. Caitlin Ryan.'

'Well, Caitlin...' Folding his arms across his chest, he let his light-coloured gaze flick an interested glance up and down her figure, simply because it was too irresistible to ignore. 'Like I said, if you're serious about auditioning then you'll come back tomorrow, when it's more convenient for us to hear you. Shall we say around eleven-thirty?'

'I'm sorry...' The woman's incandescent emerald gaze was immediately perturbed. 'I don't want to be a nuisance, but I honestly can't make it tomorrow. A close friend—the manager of the shop where I work—is having her wisdom teeth removed, and I'm the only one who can stand in for her while she's away'

Jake fought down a compelling urge to laugh out loud. Of all the answers he might have expected her to furnish him with, the imminent removal of a friend's wisdom teeth hadn't been one of them!

He could almost sense Rick's laughter bubbling up behind him. *Damn*. It was going to be pretty hard to refuse this beauty anything when she was staring back at him like some little girl lost, those big green eyes of hers reflecting equal measures of hope and disappointment.

'Give the girl a break, man.' As he planted himself beside Jake Rick's amiable features creased into a persuasive smile. 'The band is still set up, so what have we got to lose?'

My sanity, for one thing, thought Jake, with grave misgiving. If Caitlin Ryan looked like a little lost puppy now, before he had even heard her sing a note, God only knew what she was going to look like when he told her *Sorry... don't give up the day job.*

Expelling an aggrieved sigh, he dragged his fingers impatiently through his mane of dark hair and stared at her.

'Okay,' he drawled, his tone painfully resigned, 'I'll give you ten minutes to show me what you can do.' *Or, more to the point, what you can't.* He couldn't pretend he was expecting very much.

Caitlin's heart beat double-time. *Okay, I can do this, she told herself. Singing is second nature to me.*

But her morale-boosting self-talk didn't seem to be having a great deal of effect as she nervously made her way across to the stage. The three young men already there ambled casually back to their instruments and she wondered how many singers they'd already auditioned—because frankly they weren't looking too impressed.

Registering the band's name on the large bass drum in front of the drum kit, and privately acknowledging that she'd never heard of it, she somehow made her lips shape a smile. The lead guitarist introduced himself first. Telling Caitlin that his name was Mike, he extended his hand to help her as she negotiated the final step of the wooden staircase that led onto the stage. He had an open, friendly face she noted, unlike *Captain Ahab* down there, who looked as if he'd just as soon as take a bite out of her rather than throw away a smile on someone who was clearly a time-waster.

Why, oh, why had she thought this was a good idea? Just because she loved to sing, it didn't mean that she had any-where *near* enough talent to make it her career...

'By the way, I'm Rick. The man who told you to come back tomorrow is the head honcho. Aren't you going to take off your coat?'

At the foot of the stage the fair-haired man who'd per-suaded his boss to give her a chance grinned up at her, with a teasing twinkle in his dancing hazel eyes that was in com-plete contrast to the reception Caitlin had received from his stony-faced colleague.

As his dark, brooding friend stayed ominously at the back of the hall she noticed he was staring back at her, as if to say, *Your performance is going to have to be exceptional if you're going to impress me.* He was regarding her as if he fully expected her to disappoint him. *Who was he anyway? Caitlin wondered?* He might be the man in charge of the auditions, but although he'd asked for her name he hadn't volunteered his own.

In answer to Rick's comment about removing her coat, she answered, 'I'd rather keep it on, if you don't mind. I'm feeling a little bit chilly.'

Her hand curved round the mike stand as if to anchor her to something solid. *Oh, why had she worn this stupid short skirt?* Because her friend Lia had told her she should make an effort to 'look nice' for the audition, that was why. Caitlin should have stuck to her preference of wearing jeans and a T-shirt.

Raising his voice so that she could hear him clearly, Rick asked, 'So what are you going to sing for us?'

Caitlin told him. It was a song that was regarded as a clas-sic in the annals of rock culture. Although it had a driving, pulsing beat, there was also great passion and pathos in the lyrics and she loved it.

'Good song choice.'

She couldn't help colouring at the approval in his voice and turned her head towards the band so that he wouldn't see he'd unsettled her. 'Is that okay with you?' she asked them.

The blond bearded drummer, who'd introduced himself as Steve Bridges, answered her with a precise drumroll, and to Caitlin's right the stocky Scottish bass player, whose name was Keith Ferguson, played a couple of chords on his guitar.

'Let's rock and roll, then, shall we?' Rick gave her a mock salute. 'It's all yours, honey. Take it away.'

I can do this, Caitlin told herself dry-mouthed as she waited for the band to play her in.

For a couple of seconds she squeezed her eyes shut tight. If she wanted to stay strong she wouldn't glance at Mr Tall, Dark and Foreboding, lest one disapproving look from those strangely light blue eyes of his smothered the small vestige of courage she had left. But as the music struck up around her fear helpfully receded, replaced by her desire to sing.

She knew this particular number inside out. What she *wouldn't* admit to the present company was that she'd only sung it in the bath or in the privacy of her bedroom. *Oh, and once to Lia.* Her lack of experience would really freak them out if they knew about it before they heard her. Suppressing a suddenly uncharacteristic urge to grin, she listened for her cue, then opened her mouth and launched into the vocal.

Electricity shot through Jake's system with all the power of a lightning bolt. His stomach muscles clenched hard as excitement and shock suffused him. As he listened to the honey-eyed, sexy vocal emanating from the raven-haired beauty onstage he knew they'd struck gold. He didn't even have to let her finish the song to know it, but of course he would.

Caitlin's classy vocals melded with the rich, tight sound the band had worked so hard to attain as though they'd been made for each other. Her performance was stand-out amazing…knee-buckling.

Catching sight of the exchanged grins between the band members, he also saw Rick's silently mouthed '*Eureka*' as he turned round to give Jake the thumbs-up. There wasn't one girl Jake had heard sing in the past four days who came even remotely close to the talent of Caitlin Ryan. Hell…there wasn't one girl he'd heard sing in the past couple of *years* who was even in her league. The woman delivered a song as if she was born to it. *Damn*.

He moved his head in wonder as he watched her, her body moving in a naturally sexy sway to the beat of the music, her shapely legs drawing his appreciative gaze despite her strange insistence on keeping her coat on. With the right clothes and make-up this girl would be sit up and beg gorgeous. As good a singer as Marcie had been, she couldn't hold a candle to Caitlin Ryan in the looks department. He didn't wholly go along with the idea that a singer needed to be attractive, but good looks certainly didn't hurt in this business.

Suddenly his desire for sustenance at the local pub dissipated like snow in the desert. Jake was excited again. Enthused. When the mood was on him he could work twenty-four hours a day without a break if he wanted to, and he would willingly do so to get this band on the road again, expecting nothing less than the same commitment from everyone else.

As the last chords of the music died away Caitlin inhaled a relieved breath to steady herself. Then she reluctantly released the microphone.

Behind her, Steve Bridges blew an appreciative whistle. 'That was incredible. You absolutely killed it.'

Feeling her face grow warm at the compliment, she was taken aback when the two men who had been watching her vaulted onto the stage.

'What other bands have you been in?' Jake demanded.

Glancing back into his mesmerising eyes—eyes the colour of blue ice melting under steam—Caitlin's heart bungee-jumped to her toes. 'I—I haven't been in any other bands,' she admitted softly.

'You're kidding me.' Rick looked completely nonplussed.

Startled that he didn't believe her, she widened her eyes in surprise.

'I wouldn't pretend about something like that. The truth is I've only ever sung for my own amusement and because I'm compelled to. I just love music. I'm passionate about it.'

The rock-hard muscles in Jake's stomach compressed tightly. *He could tell she had passion...had it in spades, he thought.* That was the major difference between her and the instantly forgettable *wannabes* he'd recently auditioned.

'So you've never sung professionally before?' he queried.

'No. I haven't.' Her huge green eyes were absolutely guileless. Gazing back into their depths was like looking down to the bottom of a clear unsullied lake on a hot summer's day.

'So, what do you do to keep body and soul together?'

'You mean for a living?' Caitlin sighed. 'I'm a shop assistant. Remember I told you I had to stand in for the manager earlier today?'

'And where is the shop?'

'It's here in the village, of course.'

Jake was honestly stunned. They'd been auditioning girls from as far afield as Scotland, and this girl—this incredible find of theirs—came from the very village they were auditioning in. It was altogether ludicrous.

Laughing out loud, Rick slapped his leather-clad thigh. 'Well, if that doesn't beat it all! You mean for the past four days now we've been tearing our hair out trying to find a singer and you've been here all the time?'

'I only found out about the auditions when I saw the ad in the post office. I couldn't believe it. Nothing as exciting as that ever happens in the village. It seemed...' she flushed a little '...it seemed like a sign.' Tucking some silky strands of ebony hair behind an ear, Caitlin smiled self-consciously. 'Anyway…thanks for hearing me and giving me the chance to sing for you. Whatever happens, I really enjoyed it.'

She turned away to climb back down from the stage and leave, but was taken aback when Jake held up his hand, a distinctly puzzled crease straining his handsome brow.

'Where do you think you're going?'

'I've got to get back to work. I—I told you…we're stock-taking. I don't suppose we'll finish until late tonight.'

'Do you want to sing with this band or not?' he demanded, hardly able to believe what he was hearing.

'Do you mean…? Are you saying…?'

The stunned look on her face would be almost comical if Jake had a mind to laugh—which he absolutely *didn't*.

'On the strength of the performance we've just heard, I think I'd be a fool not to offer you the chance of singing with the band. I think we're all in agreement that you're just what we're looking for.'

Even though he directed a meaningful glance towards Rick and the others, Jake barely needed confirmation of his decision. Not when the final say categorically rested with him.

Eyes narrowing, he continued, 'But if we take you on you do realise that there's a hell of a lot of work ahead of you? You may be able to sing, Miss Ryan, but there's a lot to learn before we let you loose onstage in public. Have you honestly never sung professionally before?'

He didn't believe her. As exciting as the prospect of singing with the band was, Caitlin knew instinctively that if she accepted the job her relationship with this man was never going to be one made in heaven.

She nervously cleared her throat. 'I was in a school band from fifteen to eighteen, but I've done nothing since then. We only played local functions. Events like Christmas parties, special birthdays and anniversaries…stuff like that'

'And you were the lead singer?'

'No. That is…we all sang. There were six of us altogether. But I occasionally played piano and guitar.'

Rick's eyebrows flew up to his hairline. 'You're a musician as well?'

'Yes. That is, I read music and play a little. I practise whenever I can…at least on my guitar. I no longer have a piano.'

No wonder she knew instinctively exactly where to come in with the vocal, Jake mused. Only someone who was a competent musician or had a natural ear for music could pull that off without rehearsal.

He saw his astonishment reflected back at him when his glance collided with Rick's.

'Sweetheart, as far as I'm concerned there's not the slightest doubt in my mind that you're the right singer for this band.' The American smiled, his hand enthusiastically shaking Caitlin's. 'By the way, my full name is Rick Young— I'm Blue Sky's official dogsbody and general "helper-outer". That means I organise the gigs, make sure the band shows up on time, and most importantly collect the fee at the end of the show. The man standing beside you with the poker face is Jake Sorenson—well-known record producer and the band's manager. You must have heard of him? Anyway, he's going to make us all rich one day, like him. You can count on it. If anyone can work miracles round here, Jake can. He's been in the business so long he's probably due for a plaque in the Rock and Roll Hall of Fame.'

'Very funny.'

Jake didn't put out his hand for Caitlin to shake. *Right then he had the strangest feeling that if he did he wouldn't want to let it go.* If this venture was going to work at all then he needed to maintain the requisite professionalism at all times. The last thing he needed was to get personally involved with Little Miss Hole in her Stocking. The band had been through enough upheaval and disappointment with Marcie walking out. No… If they were going to work together then he was going to play strictly by the rules. He *had* to, no matter how irresistible the temptation. And if he should at any time forget that vow then all he had to do was remember the scandal that had near crushed him and killed his career.

Taking a sidelong glance at Rick, and seeing that his friend's avidly appreciative gaze was all but glued to Caitlin, as if only a madman would want to look anywhere else, Jake firmed his resolve. 'Strictly by the rules' went for Rick and the guys, too. And, by God, he'd make sure that they knew it.

As the band welcomed Caitlin he saw that their pleasure was absolutely sincere. He also saw how her lovely face lit up at their enthusiastic welcome, how a faint flush of pink stained her cheeks as she strove to handle it, and something told Jake she was definitely an innocent compared to the rest of them. *That too could be a sticking point, he reflected*...especially in the dog-eat-dog world that was the music business. But, that said, it made a refreshing change to meet someone with hope and enthusiasm in their eyes— someone who wasn't old and jaded before their time as he probably was...

'Come into my office, Miss Ryan,' he invited her. 'We need to talk in private.'

Vaulting off the stage, Jake strode to the end of the hall, the sound of his boot heels echoing loudly in his wake.

After eagerly helping Caitlin down from the stage, Rick hurried to catch up to his enigmatic boss. 'Hey, don't you want me there too?' he called.

Turning, Jake shook his head, a muscle flexing in the side of his hollowed cheek. 'Not at the moment, my friend. There'll be time enough to go over the timetable for rehearsals when we talk later. We'll have a group meeting tomorrow afternoon so that we can discuss everything. Right now I just want to have a private chat with Miss Ryan'

'Miss Ryan?' Rick frowned. 'What's wrong with Caitlin?'

Ignoring the comment, Jake turned and opened his office door.

Her trepidation mingling with excitement, Caitlin followed him. The whole experience felt strangely surreal to her. The office that Blue Sky's charismatic manager was using was a room not much bigger than a generously-sized broom cupboard, she saw. All it contained were two grey plastic chairs and an upturned orange box masquerading as a table. One small window allowed just a paltry glimpse of sky.

Moistening her lips, Caitlin sucked in a breath. Somehow being in such close proximity to Jake Sorenson was ten times more testing than any audition she could imagine. He had the kind of highly charged aura round him that would stir the senses of a blind woman, she mused nervously.

'Take a seat,' he instructed.

Feeling undeniably overwhelmed, she complied. When she sat, her knees unavoidably pressed up against the rough wood of the orange box as she strove to make herself more comfortable. Adjusting her coat as she waited for Jake to carry on speaking, she felt her anxiety definitely intensify.

'You've already told me that you have a job. I presume that's full-time?' Flipping open the black notebook on top of the box, he started writing inside it.

'That's right.'

'You said you work in a shop? What kind of shop?' Lifting his head, Jake pinned her to the seat with his pale blue eyes.

'It's a shop called Morgana,' she told him. 'It specialises in esoteric and personal development books, but we also sell things like incense, Native American jewellery, ambient music and crystals.'

And I love working there, she silently reflected. She shifted in the hard plastic chair. It would be a real wrench to leave that job, but what was the point in having a passion in life if you weren't planning on doing anything about it? Her friend Lia knew just how much Caitlin loved music, how she loved to sing. And then Caitlin had told her that she'd seen an ad in the post office

Versatile female singer aged twenty to thirty wanted to front established band specialising in soft rock.

Auditions were being held in St Joseph's church hall, in the very village where they lived, and Lia had encouraged her to go for it.

'It must be clear to you that if you want to sing with this band you can't work full-time in a shop as well?'

Jake didn't take his eyes off of her as he addressed Caitlin, and the blatant directness of his unsettling blue gaze made her feel as if someone had just curtailed her oxygen supply.

'Rehearsals start tomorrow afternoon and will continue every day after that for the next three weeks before the band performs in public. After that we'll be all over the country for an initial three-week tour. Are you ready to commit to such a schedule, Miss Ryan?'

'I hadn't really thought about much beyond the audition,' she confessed honestly, 'but I realise whoever gets the job will have to be prepared to do regular gigs and eventually tour. So, yes, I am ready to commit, Mr Sorenson. I've never wanted anything more.'

'And you know that means giving up your present job to do so?'

'Of course.'

Although she hadn't hesitated to answer in the affirmative Jake didn't miss the slightly perturbed frown between her elegant brows, and once again he had the distinct impression that Caitlin was a relative innocent when it came to the type of worldly experience that the rest of them had.

'Does that worry you?' he asked.

Lifting her chin, she was intent on holding his gaze and not shying away from it, he saw.

'I'd be a liar if I said it wasn't daunting to leave something I'm so familiar with for something much more challenging, but I want to rise to that challenge. Especially if it's going to help me realise my dream of becoming a professional singer. Besides…change is inevitable, isn't it? Nothing stays the same.'

'You don't have to make it sound like it's something to fear. There's many a singer who'd give their eye-teeth to have the opportunity I'm offering you. Blue Sky may have lost their lead vocalist but they're still an established band. Just before Marcie left they were invited to play on one of the top music shows on television.'

And the guys had been gutted when they'd had to cancel the engagement. It might have been the big break they'd been praying for…

'Please don't think that I'm ungrateful.'

Shifting self-consciously in her seat, Caitlin snagged her stocking on a splinter from the orange box. As she picked at it to free herself she blushed scarlet, because Jake's gaze was suddenly focused on her knee instead of on her face. The very air between them seemed to throb with heat and a disturbing prickle of perspiration slid worryingly down her spine.

'I think I'm still in shock,' she admitted, 'I didn't expect to get as far as this. I'm still trying to take it all in.'

'Well…' Reluctantly withdrawing his glance from her knee, Jake strove to remain businesslike. 'I'm not asking you to sign on the dotted line tonight. But that doesn't mean I'm giving you the chance to change your mind. When I've decided that I want something, Caitlin, I won't rest until I get it. So be here tomorrow at five. We'll be rehearsing until late in the evening. Do we have a deal?'

She bit down on her lip. 'Yes—yes, we do. But can I make it five-forty-five instead? I have to close the shop at five-thirty. I won't be any later. I can be here in just ten minutes if I drive.'

'Five-forty-five it is, then. And before you leave you'd

better give me your address and mobile phone number, just in case.'

Caitlin gave him the information and watched warily as Jake scribbled it down in his black notebook. Then he threw down his pen and got to his feet. She followed suit, her heart racing as he towered over her. She was five foot seven in her bare feet, but his physical domination of the tiny space seemed to make the already diminutive room even smaller.

Her fingers shaking, she fastened a couple of her coat buttons and managed a tentative smile. 'I'll see you tomorrow then, Mr...?' She had a moment of panic because she'd somehow forgotten his surname.

'You can call me Jake.'

To her utter surprise and secret delight a dimple appeared as if by magic at the corner of his very sexy mouth. Caitlin's insides knotted painfully.

'Right.'

'There's just one more thing before you go.'

'What's that?'

'I'd better explain one of the most important house rules, and that is there's to be no fraternising after hours with members of the band—and I'm not talking about a few drinks backstage after a gig. Am I making myself clear?'

Now Caitlin's face really *did* burn. She tried to look anywhere but straight at Jake. If he seriously thought she would—that she might— Of course he could have no idea that she'd sworn off men for good, she realised. But after what she'd been through with her ex-boyfriend Sean she'd rather trek through the Sahara Desert with a fur coat on than risk another soul-destroying relationship with a man... however brief.

'All I want to do is sing. I'm not interested in anything else. I can positively assure you of that.'

Jake couldn't help wondering why. He'd glimpsed pain and fury in those pretty green eyes of hers just now, as if even the suggestion that she might find herself attracted to a member of the opposite sex was tantamount to contemplating suicide.

He sighed. 'Okay, then. There's just one other thing.'

'What's that?'

This time Caitlin's wary gaze met his in pure defiance, as though she dared him to transgress one more inch into her private life.

Jake ventured a teasing smile. 'I'd seriously think about investing in a new pair of stockings, if I were you'

'How did you know they were—?'

'How did I know that they were stockings and not tights?' He gave her a shameless grin. 'Put it down to long experience...' he drawled, pretty sure that if he told her he'd had a tantalising glimpse of her stocking-tops when she'd first sat down she'd exit so fast he wouldn't see her for dust. 'You can't beat the genuine article.'

'Is that so? Well, anyway...I didn't know you could tell.' With a disturbed frown Caitlin tried to remember to breathe. Sheer embarrassment made her babble. 'The trouble is I seem to have an unhappy knack of snagging them whenever I wear them. They're not really practical. I normally wear jeans.'

'Take it from me...' Jake's voice dropped down a discernible notch or two, making his tone arrestingly smoky '...stockings are better...'

CHAPTER TWO

THE DOORBELL JANGLED and the wind chimes that hung liberally from the lilac-painted ceiling tinkled prettily in the ensuing draught. As far as Caitlin knew, Nicky, their part-time help, was around somewhere, and should have registered the fact that they had customers, but she must have absented herself to go to the bathroom.

Sighing softly, she didn't look round, in the belief that the other girl would appear any minute now, and instead continued to scrub at the particularly stubborn patch of dirt she'd found on the lowest shelf of the temporarily emptied bookshelf. When the stain didn't respond to her increased scrubbing with a damp cloth Caitlin scratched at it with her fingernail, a spurt of annoyance shooting through her when she realised it was the horrid remains of someone's chewing gum.

Of all the… She was immediately affronted on Lia's behalf. How dared someone come into this beautiful space and foul it with chewing gum? Some people just didn't have any respect. Some people just—

'Hi, there.'

Caitlin froze at the sound of that smoky bass voice. Still tense, she turned her head and glanced up to meet Jake Sorenson's indisputably amused glance. Had it really been just a day since she'd last seen him? Was it possible she could have so easily forgotten how dangerously attractive the man was, or that his mere presence had the power to erase anything else from her mind?

Irritated by her purely female response to his tall, dark good looks, she realised she was gaping up at him. What was even worse, he'd caught her wearing an old and tatty pair of jeans that had shrunk in the wash and now adhered to her thighs like a second skin. Caitlin had opted to wear them because she knew she'd be undertaking some general cleaning that day and hadn't wanted to risk ruining any of her good clothes. What made things worse was that she'd also elected to don a favourite old red T-shirt that had also seen better days, and it clung where it didn't ought to cling, possibly inviting too much unwanted attention...like *now*, when Jake's disturbing light blue eyes were making a slow and deliberate inventory of her body.

Heat crawled up her spine...*sexual* heat. It completely undid her. Just what was he *doing* here? Couldn't he have telephoned if he'd needed to speak to her? He had an unfair advantage, taking her by surprise like this.

Leaving her cloth on the bookshelf, she abruptly turned and got to her feet. Long strands of glossy black hair escaped her loosely tied ponytail to drift down gently over her flushed cheeks, and there was a smudge of dust on her nose. She struggled to get her greeting past her lips.

'Hi. I'm sorry, but you've caught me at a rather awkward moment. I was...'

'Let me guess...stocktaking?' Jake drawled softly.

She swallowed hard. The man could read a technical pamphlet on assembling flat-pack furniture out loud and it would still make her hot. 'Cleaning. I was just cleaning. Stocktaking was yesterday.'

'It's nice to see such dedication to the task. You looked like you were giving it your all.' Smiling faintly, he glanced round him. 'Interesting shop,' he remarked, sliding his hands into the back pockets of his jeans and nodding to himself as his gaze made another leisurely reconnaissance.

The heady scent of sandalwood incense perfumed the air and Caitlin wondered for the first time ever if it wasn't just a tad overpowering. Why she should suddenly be concerned about such an inconsequential thing, she didn't know. All she knew was that she wanted Jake to get a good impression of her workplace and not judge it adversely.

Jake's interested glance narrowed as he examined some of the titles on the bookshelves either side of the ones Caitlin had been cleaning. He glimpsed. *Living Your Destiny* and other esoteric titles and permitted himself a smile. He'd known many hippies in his time, who had loved this kind of stuff. He looked up. From the painted ceiling dangled a myriad of wind chimes and crystals, and the music of some Native American drums pulsed gently. But, as eye-catching and diverting as the room furnishings were, he had no trouble bringing his gaze straight back to Caitlin.

He hadn't forgotten how pretty she was, and he was certain that the shape that had been intriguingly hidden behind her coat yesterday would be equally arresting...especially as he'd already been treated to the sight of her long slim legs in those tantalising black stockings. But nothing had quite prepared him for the mouth-wateringly feminine curves that he was looking at now.

Her scarlet T-shirt was at least one size smaller than she needed and it clung sexily to her voluptuous breasts, with the light stretchy fabric hugging her delectable shape like a second skin. Hell, he was on fire—uncharacteristically caught off-guard by his acute reaction to the green-eyed temptress in front of him. There was a tense knot in the pit of his stomach as he tried to tamp down the forceful desire that gripped him.

As he stared helplessly he registered the distinct outline of Caitlin's nipples beneath her bra—and was it his fevered imagination or had they just puckered a little tighter? He'd already been treated to the tempting sight of her delightful derriere as she'd crouched down, cleaning the bookshelf, and God help him, why did he have the distinct feeling that Christmas had arrived early? Because it wasn't just Caitlin's vocal talent that would put Blue Sky on the map. The woman's stunning beauty would put some serious icing on the Christmas cake too.

'My friend Lia owns the shop.'

Folding her arms protectively across her chest, because she'd mortifyingly caught Jake's gaze straying there, Caitlin silently berated herself for wearing that particular shirt today of all days. But then how was she to have known that Jake would pay an impromptu visit?

'As I told you, she's at the dental hospital today, otherwise I'd introduce you.' Her gaze automatically gravitated to the counter, missing the familiar sight of a diminutive slim blonde with elfin features and soft brown eyes.

Nicky must be taking a bathroom break. Caitlin couldn't help wishing that the girl's timing had been better. Just my luck, she thought. If Nicky had been around she could have somehow diverted Jake's attention. But he surely hadn't visited the shop to browse…

'Anyway, what can I do for you?' she asked.

Jake stared at her in bemusement. *You wouldn't believe how creative I could get about that,* he thought, and then gave himself a harsh mental shake. Where were his brains, for goodness' sake? He had a perfectly legitimate reason for seeking out their new vocalist and yet he was standing there gawping at her like some horny teenager hoping to get laid. The realisation was sobering.

'About the rehearsals this afternoon,' he started, 'I just wanted to let you know that we'll be working quite late tonight—perhaps into the early hours of the morning. If you have a boyfriend I hope he's the understanding type. If not, we're all in trouble.'

'There's no boyfriend.'

'Good.'

Caitlin frowned. Rubbing her hands briefly up and down her bare arms, she glanced back into Jake's arresting blue gaze. The man had the kind of reined-in sexuality and physicality that couldn't help but put her on her guard. It didn't help matters that he had a 'bad boy' smile that was surely reserved for a woman's wildest fantasy...*if* she was in the market for such a fantasy—which she most definitely wasn't.

Still, the hard honed body outlined by his black T-shirt, jeans and fashionably battered leather jacket would surely be a thing of beauty without clothes. There was not so much as a hint of surplus flesh on that taut, streamlined physique. The man clearly kept himself in good shape. She couldn't prevent the small shiver of appreciation that ran up her spine. But it wasn't just the commanding, easy-on-the-eye physique that made Caitlin so intimately aware of him. Something told her that Jake Sorenson didn't take any prisoners. When he told her that they would be working late tonight she was certain he meant it in the fullest sense of the word.

What if I've made a terrible mistake? she fretted. *It's the thing I want to do more than anything else in the world, but what if I'm really not cut out to be a singer in a band?*

Her mind slipped into panic mode, as it was apt to do when she was hit by a sudden attack of self-doubt.

He must have read her mind just then. 'Don't look so terrified,' he cautioned, amusement lurking in the steamy blue depths of his mesmerising eyes. 'I promise not to drive you too hard on your first night. But after that I'm afraid you'll just have to roll with the punches like everybody else. Anyone who wants to pursue a dream has to make sacrifices, and the music business is a hard game, Caitlin. It's notoriously competitive and cut-throat, and that's an almost conservative description. If you want to be a success in this game you have to grow a fairly thick skin. Blue Sky have played all over the country in the past two years, trying to establish themselves, and they've gained a loyal following. When their lead singer Marcie walked out it was a huge shock. More than that it was a betrayal. But I owe it to the rest of the band to make good on my promise to take them to the top—and, trust me, I'm going to do exactly that. Failure is just not an option in my book. Do you understand what I'm saying?'

Caitlin did. *Signing up for commando training with the SAS would probably be easier.* She tried for a smile but couldn't help the nervous little quiver that hijacked her lips instead. Was the man always so serious, she wondered?

'I'll try my best not to let you down...Jake.' She added his name because she reasoned she should start being less formal, and couldn't help savouring the taste of it on her tongue— like an enticing new flavour she'd never sampled before.

He scowled.

'That's not good enough. Say, *I won't let you down, Jake.* Not, *I'll try.*'

Flustered, Caitlin pushed a stray strand of hair away from her suddenly burning cheek. 'I *won't* let you down, Jake.'

'That's better. Now, come here.'

Before she'd gleaned what he intended he firmly drew her towards him then gently erased the smudge of dust she'd inadvertently acquired on her nose. Her senses were immediately bombarded by the warm sexy tang of leather mixing provocatively with the alluring masculine scent of the man himself.

If someone could bottle it, they'd make a fortune, Caitlin thought. She felt more than a little off-centre as she stepped away, especially when she saw that he was smiling. A deep, sensual tug registered low in her belly.

'Thanks. I'm probably covered in dust and looking a right mess, aren't I?' she remarked nervously.

The words were out before she could check them. She could have kicked herself, because now Jake would think she was fishing for a compliment—which was absurd when she did honestly believe she must resemble something the cat had dragged in.

But with a charismatic quirk at a corner of his lips Jake elected not to comment. Instead he walked to the door, opened it and gave her a brief salute. 'I'll see you tonight. Five-forty-five. Don't be late.'

As he stepped out onto the pavement Caitlin had a distinct sense of being dismissed. More to the point, she felt bereft, as if he'd somehow taken a part of her with him. The bell jangled as the door swung back on its hinges and she released a long slow breath, as though she'd been holding on to it for nothing less than a lifetime.

The realisation that she was late, even though she had a perfectly legitimate reason, made Caitlin furious with herself. Parking her car on the gravel drive that led up to the sombre-looking Victorian church hall, she bit back a ripe curse, fumbling to organise her car keys and purse as she shut the car door behind her. To add insult to injury, a light rain had started to fall.

She glanced down at her watch and her anxious gaze once more registered the time. *Six-fifteen*... She wasn't just late—she was *very* late. But how was she to have known that a customer would walk in the door at exactly a minute before five-thirty? She could hardly turn the girl away—especially when she'd tearfully told Caitlin that she'd just broken up with her boyfriend and someone had recommended she get some rose quartz to help her.

Lia had often teased her friend that she was a magnet for the heartsick, but Caitlin's naturally compassionate nature wouldn't allow her to stand back and do nothing when someone was hurting. When push came to shove, though, however she explained her tardiness to Jake Sorenson something told her it wasn't going to cut any ice.

Summoning every scrap of courage she could muster, she pushed open the creaky wooden door that led into the porch, wrinkling her nose at the pall of mustiness and damp that clung to the air, her heart bumping against her ribs at the sound of instruments tuning up.

Behind the door that led into the cavernous hall Jake was testing the microphone in the familiar time-honoured way of performers the world over: 'One two, one two...'

Murmuring a briefly fervent prayer, Caitlin pushed open the door. The overhead lights were dimmed, she noticed, and the three members of the band on stage continued to play as Rick Young melted out of the shadows to position himself in front of her. Despite his serious expression, at least his hazel eyes were twinkling, she saw.

'You're late, pretty lady. Not a good start, just thought I'd warn you.'

He jerked his chin towards Jake as Blue Sky's enigmatic manager jumped off the stage, his long jeans-clad legs carrying him purposefully towards Caitlin. It didn't take a genius to deduce that he wasn't happy. *Blast!*

Her chilled fingers curled over the car keys in her pocket and held them tight. It wasn't as if she was late deliberately. She honestly wanted to take this amazing opportunity they were offering her. But right now, judging by the fierce scowl on Jake's handsome face, it might just be about to be taken away from her.

'I'm sorry I'm late. I just—'

'What was the last thing I said to you?' he barked.

Startled, Caitlin glanced across at Rick. His expression conveyed that he'd witnessed similar scenarios too many times before to be at all perturbed.

'Don't be late?' she ventured, her teeth anxiously clamping down on her lip.

'And didn't I also tell you to be here at five-forty-five? It's now twenty past six. You're thirty-five minutes late. That's not acceptable, Miss Ryan. It's not acceptable at all.'

Jake was shifting restlessly from one black-booted foot to the other, a muscle ominously flinching in the side of his lean, unshaven jaw. Caitlin didn't dare quip that his watch must be fast, even though it clearly *was*. The fact that he was unshaven made him look edgy and dangerous—as if anything could happen and probably would.

'A customer came into the shop just as I was getting

ready to leave—' the words came out in a heated rush as she gripped even more tightly onto her car keys.

'Couldn't you have turned whoever it was away and told them to come back tomorrow?' he snapped.

Affronted, Caitlin widened her eyes.

'I *never* turn customers away. People don't just come into our shop to buy things, Mr Sorenson. Many of them come in for healing of one kind or another. The girl that I saw was distraught. She'd just broken up with her long-term boy-friend and was looking for something that might help ease her distress. I'm not so cold-hearted that I would tell her in her hour of need to come back tomorrow.'

Jake was so taken aback by this answer that the red mist of anger that had threatened when Caitlin had walked in late dissipated like ice beneath the sun. Sucking in his cheeks, he blew out a long, slow breath, shaking his head and taking a moment to compose himself. *I must be losing my grip*, he thought irritably.

Caitlin proffered a hesitant smile. Jake's bemused glance collided with hers just as one corner of her pretty mouth nudged a very sexy dimple. Something hitched in his heart... not to mention below his navel.

'Well, we've wasted enough time as it is,' he growled. 'Take off your coat and get yourself up on stage. We've got a hell of a lot to get through tonight and we may well be here until breakfast—so be warned.'

After making her apologies to the other band members, seeing that Jake's attention had suddenly been claimed by Rick, Caitlin fell into animated conversation with them about music. Did they write all their own songs? Did they ever do any covers? And, finally, did they have a playlist for to-night's rehearsals that she could look at?

The young men were only too pleased to answer her questions, interspersing their answers with jokes and anecdotes and generally going out of their way to help put her at ease. Mike Casey, the lead guitarist, with his tousled dark hair and rather serious brown eyes, explained that he added the harmonies to several of the songs and he and Caitlin would need to spend some time together working on them. Then he told her that he and the others had rented a house in the village for the duration of their stay and she'd be more than welcome to come over and work on them there.

'Caitlin?'

She spun round at the sound of her name, folding her arms across the blue chambray man's shirt that she'd thrown over the too-revealing red T-shirt she'd been wearing earlier. The long shirt-tails skimmed her bottom in her tight jeans and helped her feel a little less vulnerable than she had done in the shop, when Jake's toe-curling glance had all but consumed her with its frank and hungry intensity.

She was staring into the same hauntingly blue depths now as he looked up at her from the foot of the stage. Her mouth dried. He handed her a sheet of paper with music and lyrics on. Accepting it without comment, she let her gaze fall eagerly on the title. It was another great rock standard that she knew by heart.

The lyrics were passionate and heart-rending, and she'd sung it with genuine feeling when she'd first learned it because she'd empathised with the sentiment of the song only too well. It was about a girl whose dreams had been cruelly shattered when the man she loved had used her and ill-treated her and had consequently robbed her of every bit of self-confidence she had...

But now... Her glance quickly perused the musical arrangement and her heart skipped a nervous beat, because the time had come for her to really prove to both the band and their enigmatic manager that she could deliver what they hoped she could. It was one thing to conquer her fear of an audition—quite another to front a band for the first time ever and do it well. This was where things started to get serious.

'You know the tune? We can choose something more contemporary if you prefer?'

Jake's blue eyes honed in on the roomy chambray shirt Caitlin had donned over the sexy red T-shirt and once again he sensed that she wasn't at all at ease with her body. *Why else had she covered up?* And how would she cope when she had to perform on stage in front of a crowd he wondered?Would she be self-conscious then?

She was a naturally beautiful woman, and the sensual aura she exuded when she walked into a room was a killer. It was a given that her looks would be a big asset to the band, and he didn't want her to try and hide that sensational body behind oversized clothing. Still, there was plenty of time for that particular discussion. Right now Caitlin had to prove to them that she was a worthy replacement for Marcie.

'The song is fine' she told him. 'I know it well.'

'Good. Take it away, guys.'

As the band started to play the introduction Caitlin listened carefully, curving her hands round the microphone stand in readiness and staring towards the back of the hall rather than at Jake. Her body was tense as a sprinter's at the start of the most important race of her life, but she didn't need to glance at the lyrics as she waited for her cue to come in. The words were etched on her soul.

There was no need for her to imagine that she was the woman she was singing about because she *was*. She'd been used, hurt and scorned by a man she'd once loved and trusted, and the devastating experience had taught her to keep her guard up. Adversity had taught her a huge lesson and, hard as it was, it had helped her to grow stronger.

I'll put steel round my heart that your poison arrows can't dent
And I'll be the phoenix rising that you never saw coming...

Those were the lyrics.

Suddenly her eyes flew open and Caitlin's glance fell on

Jake. He was attired from head to toe in black, and his con-
centrated expression was utterly serious as he watched her
performance. Minutes later, when she came to the end of
the song, she was glad, because she desperately needed to
suck in a steadying breath. Her heart was thumping hard at
the painful memories the words had evoked. *Yet, meeting
Jake's gaze once again, she didn't immediately withdraw
when it hit her that he had seriously begun to fascinate her.*

It was probably just hormones, she thought irritably. She
certainly wasn't looking to take things further than a working relationship. Apart from it being against the rules, she
wasn't looking for a man. Just like in the song, Caitlin had
had the relationship from *hell* with one particular man and
it had nearly destroyed her. She certainly wasn't going to
entertain the idea of being with someone who could twist
her insides into knots merely by looking at her.

'Not bad,' he said grudgingly.

Her fervent hope had been that she'd done much better than just 'not bad', and Caitlin's heart plummeted. Still,
Jake was the boss, and she wasn't there simply in search of
praise. Her ambition was to earn her living as a bona fide
singer—never to be dependent on anyone either for love,
self-esteem or security.

That was why seeing the ad for the auditions had excited
her. It really had seemed like a sign that she should step up
to the plate and start to fulfil her destiny. Staying at the
shop and 'playing safe' just didn't feel like the right option
any more. Her family had moved on and so should she. *It
wasn't the possibility of fame that interested her...far from
it.* Her passion was the music itself—the potential to experience joy in doing what she loved to do and to share it with
anyone who cared to listen.

So she would bow to the man's far greater experience in
such matters and give her all to improve. She prayed her efforts would be enough.

'Wow! Honey, you'll never be poor with a voice like that,' Rick told her as he went to stand next to his friend.

The contrast between the two men was striking. Rick's longish tousled hair was tinted a sun-kissed blond, while Jake's was a dark chestnut-brown, and their physiques were markedly different too. Jake was broad-shouldered and lean, his body supremely fit and toned, while Rick was shorter and more muscular. But, whatever the contrast in appearance, Caitlin sensed the two men were firm friends. There was a definite camaraderie between them that suggested their association had been born out of knowing each other for a very long time.

'She was fantastic,' Rick commented, turning towards Jake. 'I felt every ounce of emotion she put into the song… she made it her own.'

'That may be true,' Jake responded, his cool glance deliberately sliding away from Caitlin's. 'But it won't belong to her until she knows it intimately, inside and out. Let's do it again, guys. Then you can do some of your own material.'

It was three hours later when Caitlin was finally able to take a breather. Perched on the edge of the stage, with her long slender legs dangling over the side, she was attempting to eat her portion of the Chinese take-away that Rick had ordered. Her throat ached, her head throbbed and she could have fallen asleep standing up.

The band's charismatic manager hadn't let up for one minute in his efforts to get the best out of her vocal performance and she felt as if she'd done twelve rounds with a prize fighter. Whilst she was perfectly aware that singing was a very physical occupation, even if a person was blessed with a good voice, nothing could have prepared Caitlin for the sheer effort that Jake demanded.

During the past three hours she'd survived admonition after admonition to, 'Try again!' 'Put your heart into it, woman!' 'Hold back a little on that note…drop down a

key…' *'Damn it, Caitlin! You're just not trying hard enough!'*
Now she could barely summon up the energy to eat, despite
the fact that the shrimp chop suey and bamboo shoots with
Chinese mushrooms looked and smelled delicious.

'Not hungry?'

Her tired glance fell on Jake's long jeans-clad legs as he
dropped down beside her. Her heart skipped a beat. Lifting
her gaze, she looked up into the hauntingly misty depths of
his soulful blue eyes. It struck her as unfair that a man should
possess such enviably long black lashes, but then she mused
that Jake must have been at the head of the line when God
was dishing out extraordinary good looks…not to mention
sheer animal magnetism.

Caitlin sucked in a less than steady breath when the
scent of his cologne forged another assault on her belea-
guered senses. In answer to his question, she responded, 'I
thought I was.' Shrugging, she put her carton of food aside
and touched a paper napkin delicately to her lips. 'I only
had a sandwich at lunchtime…it wasn't very nice either.'

'You must have known this wasn't going to be easy. Still
sure you want to go through with it?' Jake challenged. 'You
need more than just talent in this game, Caitlin. You need
equal measures of grit and stamina too.'

'I can summon up plenty of grit and stamina when I need
it. Just try me.'

A flash of defiance lit up her defensive green eyes and
Jake chuckled softly. She'd freed her lustrous long hair from
its ponytail and now it flowed down her back like shining
black silk. Examining it more closely, he detected flashes
of mahogany within the darker strands. His fingers were
itching to touch it and he closed his hands into fists to stop
himself from reaching out to do just that.

'It's obviously going to take me a little while to learn all
the new songs,' she breathed, 'but I'll take a copy of the music
and lyrics home with me and practise them on my guitar.'

Jake had almost forgotten that Caitlin was a guitarist as

well. How good he didn't yet know, but judging by her vocal talent he guessed it wouldn't be far behind.

'Good move,' he commented, 'but the first thing you're going to have to do is to hand in your notice at the shop. There's no way you can have a full-time job there outside of singing with the band. In just three weeks' time we'll be on the road and you'll have to kiss this sleepy little village goodbye.'

The words sounded so *final* that Caitlin couldn't help shivering. But she immediately reminded herself that the most amazing opportunity had come her way, and she should take it with open arms and think herself blessed. No one got anywhere in life without taking risks. God knew she should have absorbed that fact by now, with all the New Age reading she'd done since working for Lia.

She'd lived in the village for most of her life, having moved from London with her family when she was just a toddler. When her parents had decided to join her brother Phil and his wife in California three years ago Caitlin had opted to stay put. She wasn't ready to leave the country, she'd argued. There was still a lot to experience living in the UK.

But most of all she'd stayed because she'd needed time to forge her own identity—the chance to bring her own dreams into fruition, not just tag along on someone else's. *She'd even needed to make colossal mistakes, like her relationship with Sean.* None of those things would have been possible surrounded by her well-meaning but highly controlling family.

She swallowed hard.

'So...does that mean you're offering me a full-time position with the band?' she asked.

Her stomach churned as she waited for Jake's reply.

'Looks that way doesn't it?' He smiled. Then, agile as a cat, he leapt to his feet and crossed the stage to join Rick and the others.

CHAPTER THREE

'WE'RE ALL GOING back to the Pilgrim's Inn for a few drinks—want to join us?'

Mike Casey stood waiting as Caitlin shrugged into her raincoat. Everyone else was outside. Steve and Keith were loading the van with the equipment and Jake and Rick were deep in discussion. Rick had extended the same invitation to her earlier, and Caitlin had told him she'd think about it. But the very idea of going into that particular pub again, after what had happened between her and Sean on her last visit, made her feel faintly ill.

Sean had been so bad that night—out of his head on a cocktail of drink and drugs—and she'd feared the worst. She had been right to. The cruel words and jibes that he'd taunted her with had just got worse and worse as the evening progressed. . *The sharpest knife couldn't have cut her more deeply.* Add to that the humiliation of his verbal attack being witnessed by a pub full of people before the landlord threw him out—well, it had been enough to make her want to give the place a wide berth for ever.

Lifting her gaze to Mike's, she said, 'It's kind of you to ask me, but I think I'll have to say no. It's already quite late.'

Stealing a quick glance at her watch, she saw that it was ten-thirty-five, and they'd been rehearsing since three o'clock that afternoon. Her throat was parched and her body ached from the sheer effort that Jake had demanded. The man apparently had endless reserves of energy that made

Caitlin feel as if she was the slowest runner on the track in comparison. No. She'd much prefer to go home, shower, get into her pyjamas and put her feet up with a glass of wine and a bowl of crisps at her elbow.

'You call ten-thirty in the evening *late*? We're talking Saturday night, here. Don't tell me the whole village goes to bed early?' Mike's dark eyebrows flew up to the tips of his tousled fringe. 'You must have led a sheltered life, if that's normal for you.'

At his disbelieving grin, Caitlin conceded a shy smile. 'You must think I'm pretty boring, right? No way could I ever claim to be a typical rock chick, that's for sure. But I realise my early nights will have to come to an end when the band goes on the road.'

'You two ready?' Rick appeared at the door, his hazel eyes appraising Caitlin and Mike with interest. 'I have to lock up. Caitlin? Jake would like a word.'

What now? ow? Caitlin groaned inwardly at the prospect.

Jake hadn't lied when he'd said he would go easy with her on the first night but that after that she'd have to roll with punches like everyone else. He'd been harder on her than on any of the guys in the band. Maybe that was because they already knew what was required and she didn't? But somehow Caitlin didn't think that was the only reason Jake had been yelling at her all night.

Maybe he didn't like her. Maybe he was already regretting taking her on due to her lack of experience. She could speculate until night turned into day but she'd be none the wiser until they had a conversation.

Wearing his familiar black leather jacket over a sweatshirt and jeans, Jake was leaning against his Jeep. He straightened as Caitlin walked towards him, and even at the distance that separated them she sensed an undeniable magnetic charge that put her on her guard. It had started to rain, and the sound of the other band members' voices floated on the air as they huddled round the big white transit van they transported their equipment in.

As Jake continued to hold her gaze Caitlin sensed something register low in her belly—*a combination of fear, apprehension and irrefutable sexual attraction.* She didn't know whether to smile or run.

A fierce gust of wind just then almost tore her open raincoat from her shoulders, revealing her curvaceous figure in perhaps more detail than she wanted him to see. She felt alternately hot and cold all over as her boots crunched across the gravel.

'Rick said you wanted to speak to me?' She was slightly breathless as she presented herself, her long black hair lashing across her face in the wind and rain.

Straight away Jake noticed Caitlin shiver in her insubstantial raincoat. *He knew a way to warm her up.* Another place, another time, he might have given into such an urge. God knew Caitlin Ryan had been testing all his powers of self-control from the very first moment he'd set eyes on her.

'So, are you going to join us for a drink or what?' he asked tersely.

'That's what you wanted to talk to me about?'

Catching the ends of her raincoat belt, she twisted it tightly round her waist. In vain she tried to shove her long hair out of her eyes and noticed her hands were trembling. *What was it about this man that could unravel her so easily?*

'I already told Mike that I wasn't coming. I'm going home to get an early night.' she said. 'Don't worry I'll make sure I'm here at three o'clock on the dot for rehearsals tomorrow.'

'I want you to come for a drink.'

The pupils of Jake's eyes had turned unsettlingly dark… so dark that there was just the palest blue circle ringed round them.

'It's a good opportunity for us to get to know each other. Tomorrow's Sunday. You can have a lie-in.'

Caitlin could hardly argue with his reasoning, even if her

heart *was* fluttering madly at the very idea of spending the rest of the evening in the company of the charismatic band manager. But there was also the not exactly small matter of her showing up at the Pilgrim's Inn. There was always a small influx of visitors from outside the village, but generally customers were mostly a local crowd, and there were bound to be people there who remembered how Sean had humiliated her.

'I—I'd rather not come, if you don't mind.'

'The invitation was an order, not a choice. You're going to have to get used to late nights if you're going to sing with this band. Get in the car. You can ride with me and Rick'

So that was how Caitlin found herself squeezed into a worn red velvet corner seat in the pub, with Rick on one side and Jake on the other, as the band members stood round the cosy fire in the iron grate, hogging the heat and nursing their pints of beer.

From the jukebox Sting's voice boomed out: something about not standing so close… *Caitlin could easily have echoed the sentiment.* Rick had hung her raincoat over the back of a chair but she wasn't bereft of warmth—not when Jake's hard-muscled thigh was pressed against hers. A full-on radiator couldn't have made her hotter. Every time he shifted even slightly the renewed contact made Caitlin's heart miss a beat.

'So tell me, Cait. What music do you like to listen to?'

Rick had been shortening her name ever since they'd arrived at the pub and she tried not to flinch, because her ex, Sean, had always called her that. Her gaze anxiously swept the room. There were several groups of young people seated around the tables, clearly enjoying themselves. Thankfully nobody had paid her any particular attention. Behind the bar two barmaids were busily serving customers, and one of them, a voluptuous blonde named Tina Stevens, was wearing a neckline so low that if she wasn't careful she'd be arrested for indecency.

Bringing her attention back to Rick, Caitlin answered. 'Oh, I have such a wide taste you wouldn't believe it. If I had to sum it up I'd say I love music with a good beat and great songs with good lyrics. How about you? What do you enjoy listening to?'

Shrugging, Rick took a sip of his beer then put it carefully back down on the cork beer mat. 'My taste is very similar to yours, honey. It's clear that you and I have a lot in common, a *hell* of a lot in common, in fact.'

'That's the beer talking,' Jake observed wryly.

The gravelled intonation of his deep voice made all the hairs stand up at the back of Caitlin's neck. *Was it her imagination or had his thigh moved even closer to hers?*

'He's just trying to get into your good books.'

'That's unfair. A man like me doesn't have to *try* to get into any woman's good books. They naturally gravitate towards me. I'm gifted like that. Talking of which…'

Suddenly getting to his feet, Rick carefully eased his way round the table so as not to dislodge their drinks. Caitlin saw that his avid glance was focused determinedly on a smiling Tina Stevens behind the bar, who at that very moment was leaning dangerously across the counter in her figure-hugging red top, chatting to yet another appreciative male customer.

'Excuse me, guys, but I can see a maiden's honour is at stake if I don't go and rescue her…' Rick headed purposefully towards the bar.

· Breathing out a relieved sigh, Caitlin was glad to have a little more room to manoeuvre, but she was still dizzy at the thought of having to deal with Jake on her own. As discreetly as she was able, she moved her leg away from the hot press of his jean-clad thigh.

'She'll have him for breakfast,' he said, and grinned.

The shock of suddenly meeting his steamy blue glance at such close quarters trapped Caitlin's breath somewhere between her throat and her mouth. She found herself a little too intimately aware of the faint shadow of beard across his top lip and jaw, his long straight nose and the sexy indentation in his sculpted chin. Most of all she was aware of the provocative message his hypnotic blue gaze seemed to be conveying to her. It was indisputably sexual. And it made every muscle in her body tighten and clench.

The whole room diminished down to just that look.

'He looks like he can take care of himself,' she murmured, hardly aware of moving her lips.

'So…' Taking a leisurely sip of his beer and studying her at the same time, Jake asked casually, 'Why no boyfriend?'

Hypnotised by the long fingers that curled round his glass, Caitlin found herself envying it his touch, wondering what it would be like to feel those same long fingers intimately touching *her*. The very notion made her *burn*, and she took a hurried sip of her dry white wine, deliberately focusing her gaze on the drink instead of him.

'I didn't know it was compulsory.'

'Did I imply it was?'

She didn't answer. Thinking about Sean and how she had let him come *that* close to wrecking her life was not something she wanted to revisit…certainly not in casual conversation.

The flash of pain he witnessed in Caitlin's eyes just then took Jake by surprise. As defensive as she undoubtedly was, she hadn't been quick enough to hide it. There were also faint lines of hurt round her mouth that betrayed her. *Clearly she had let someone get too close and got herself burned in the process.*

Even though he'd experienced a similar painful scenario in a relationship, something inside him said he should be careful not to let empathy lower his defences. Relationships by their nature were always going to be challenging, no matter what the situation. But Jake wasn't such a bastard that he couldn't find it in him to be concerned.

'So, what happened?'

'What do you mean?'

'You got hurt by a man,' he said thoughtfully. 'Who was he?'

'Do you mind if we don't talk about this?'

Jake's question was definitely too close for comfort. Taking another sip of wine, she felt her cheeks burn as she sensed the alcohol take effect.

'We're going to be spending a lot of time together over the next few weeks—the next few months, even. Things are bound to come out. Why not tell me now and get it over with?'

Inadvertently glancing down at her purple T-shirt, at the scooped neckline that revealed a tantalising glimpse of her cleavage, Jake felt the muscles in the pit of his belly clench. He shifted in his seat.

'That might be the case, but my personal life is not up for discussion. Please don't press me on this.'

There was a tremulous hitch in her voice that made Jake feel like the most insensitive oaf on earth. On impulse, he reached across and covered her hand with his own—even if he *did* risk going up in flames at the contact.

'I'm sorry…' he murmured.

Caitlin didn't know whether he meant he was sorry for putting pressure on her or whether he was sorry for what he guessed might have happened in her relationship. *Either way, she didn't welcome his sympathy.* It was easier to deal with his irritation. At least it stopped her feeling sorry for herself. In any case, she'd done enough wallowing in despair to last a lifetime.

But it was impossible not to stare down at the strong, capable hand covering hers. As she did so, she examined the unique silver and jet ring that he wore. It comprised two black stones in a figure of eight setting and didn't detract from his masculinity one iota… In fact it *enhanced* it. She found herself strangely reluctant to extricate herself.

Speaking her thoughts out loud, she commented, 'That's a beautiful ring.'

'Yes, it is. It was a gift.'

He probably should have got rid of the thing, come to think of it, because it certainly wasn't for sentimental reasons that he still wore it. But Jake wasn't about to tell Caitlin that the jewellery had been given to him by his ex-wife Jodie a year and a day after they were married and six months before they divorced.

It suddenly occurred to him to wonder if she'd read the sordid little story of their break-up in the newspapers at the time. But, as she hadn't even indicated that she knew who he was when they'd first met, Jake took refuge in the thought that perhaps the scandal had somehow passed her by.

Withdrawing his hand abruptly from hers, he glanced across the now slowly emptying pub at Rick, who was still engaged in conversation with the buxom Tina Stevens. There was no sign of the blonde's previous admirer, Jake saw.

Turning back to Caitlin, he asked, 'Have you had enough?' His glance fell on her barely drunk glass of wine.

'Is that a hint you want to leave?'

'I think I should take you home. You look done in.'

'You don't need to take me. I'm quite capable—'

'Why don't you just put your coat on?'

Outside the wind was fierce as Caitlin walked along the deserted pavement with Jake. He walked with eyes front, one hand jammed into the back pocket of his jeans, his handsome profile ominously unsmiling as his dark hair blew across his face.

'How far do you live from here?' he asked, 'We can take my car if you're tired. I've barely drunk anything at all.'

'I'm only ten minutes up the road and I prefer to walk. But I don't expect you to walk with me.'

Caitlin couldn't help feeling tense. It was near impossible to guess what he was thinking or feeling. The man was a law unto himself. And the tension between them hadn't eased one iota. If anything it was *worse*.

'So, how do you feel about the way things are going?'

Taking her by surprise, Jake turned his head to examine her as they walked. It took a few seconds for her to get her thoughts together.

'You mean the rehearsals? I think they're going well. I mean, I know I've still got a lot to learn, but as well as learning the songs when I'm with the band I'm working on them at home whenever I get the time.'

She tucked her flying hair behind her ear and tried to relax, but it was hard when her companion's enigmatic expression hardly revealed what he might be feeling.

He sighed. 'You're doing just fine, Caitlin. I have no doubt that you're the perfect singer for Blue Sky. You're got a great voice, you're beautiful and sexy…you're the whole package. But even great talent can't make it work on its own. Blue Sky isn't some five-minute wonder, like some of these manufactured bands that litter the charts. A lot of those bands are the product of slick marketing, purely designed to make money. They're not about real, dedicated musicians who get together because they're passionate about music. I told you it wasn't going to be easy. If anything, it's going to get harder. There's still a lot of work ahead before we start touring, and then the pressure really will be on. I suppose I just want to know whether your commitment is total, or whether you wouldn't prefer staying here in the village, working in your little book store? Don't get me wrong—I can see how that must have its appeal for a girl like you.'

'What do you mean, a girl like me?' Already bristling at what she perceived as Jake's patronising tone, Caitlin glared at him in the lamplight. 'You don't even *know* me.'

Raising a dark eyebrow, he smiled. 'I know you like to pretend you're tougher than you look, that you can handle anything I throw at you, but—'

'Stop right there!' Her hackles were really up now. '*Pretend* I'm tough? Do you think I'm such a wilting flower I'll break at the first sign of pressure? For your information, I survived two years of hell with a man who was a drug addict and alcoholic who took me for every penny I had. I even had to sell my piano, and it was my dearest possession. As well as that I lost my home, my car and my dignity. I lost it all just to pay for his drug habit. Yes, I was a fool—but one day I woke up and found the strength to tell him enough was enough. Then I picked up the broken pieces of what was left of my life and started over. I've survived hardship and pain and I'm all the stronger for it—so don't you dare tell me I *pretend* I'm tough!'

She paused to take a breath.

'As for wanting to be in the band—singing *is* and always was my greatest passion and I'll do whatever I can to make it my career. I sing because I'm compelled to—not because I want to be famous or have my picture in the papers. All I want to do…all I've *ever* wanted to do…is sing. So when you ask me if my commitment is total, my answer is categorically *yes*!'

By the time she'd finished her impassioned speech Caitlin found herself on the brink of tears. She'd blurted out all the things she'd never meant to reveal—things about her past that she really would have preferred to have kept hidden…especially from a man like Jake Sorenson, who probably thought she was an idiot for falling for a loser like Sean Gates.

But Sean hadn't always been a loser. Once upon a time he had been the sweetest man in the world, and Caitlin had believed that she loved him…

'Hey…' Reaching out his hand, Jake gently stroked the tips of his fingers down her cheek. 'I wasn't casting aspersions on your character. I'm sorry if it came out that way.'

The surprisingly feather-light touch made something clench deep inside her. Recognising it as a hungry need to be held, she immediately stiffened.

'I'm sorry, too.'

Shaking her head, she automatically moved away in a bid to resurrect her defences. But as she started walking again Jake caught up to her, grabbing her arm to make her stop. This time his hold was deliberately firm...*possessive*, almost.

'Don't run away from me. I only want to help you.'

As his intense gaze shot arrows of living blue flame into hers she caught her breath.

'Help me...*how*?'

Bending his head, Jake delivered his answer with a hard, hot kiss that was nothing less than volcanic.

As his lips moved rapaciously over hers, even though she was shocked to her core, Caitlin found herself kissing him back as if her very life depended on it. She even drove her hands through his hair to anchor him to her.

Instinct was like a wild river that had burst its banks and it was near impossible to think about anything above the untamed ferocious beat of her heart...except perhaps to realise that the man kisses were as good as he looked and even *better* than the most erotic fantasy she could imagine...

The delicious sensation of his velvet-textured lips against hers and the warm glide of his tongue in her mouth stirred feelings inside her that she'd never before experienced so wantonly or intensely. *It was during those explosive few moments that Caitlin knew the barriers of safety she'd erected so painstakingly round her heart had come under serious threat...*

Even as she had the realisation Jake brought the kiss to a reluctant end, examining her with a gaze that was more than a little stunned but still very much aroused.

In a low voice he murmured, 'Don't be ashamed because you told me your story. The music business is littered with casualties like your ex-boyfriend. I don't believe that they're bad people. Serious addiction is an illness, not a weakness. Don't shut me out because you've revealed something you wished you hadn't, Caitlin.'

She inhaled sharply and withdrew her hands from his hair. It had started to rain again, and droplets of moisture were settling in quick succession on the silken dark strands that she'd so hungrily slid her fingers into, sparkling there like morning dew.

He sounded so kind and concerned—as if he intimately understood every lash of hurt she had ever suffered and sincerely empathised. Everything about him was almost unbearably seductive, and it made Caitlin ache to lean into him, to perhaps invite another kiss and even ask him to come in for a cup of coffee… But she quickly came to her senses when it hit her just what she was contemplating—and the likely consequences of such a reckless act. *Hadn't she endured enough pain without inviting more?*

She shook her arm free.

'To shut you out I'd first have to let you in, Jake, and I'm not going to do that. Not even if you promised me the earth.'

'Now that it's come to it I don't want to let you go' Lia asserted.

Finishing stirring the mug of coffee she'd made, she brought it over to the small wrought-iron table where the girls sat for lunch. There wasn't a lot of room in the basement, where all the stock was kept, but Lia had had a worktop and sink put in, as well as installing a fridge and a microwave oven, so that the girls could have some hot food from time to time.

Lost in thought, Caitlin was jolted back to the present as the petite blonde pulled out the chair opposite and sat down.

'Sorry, what did you say?'

'I said I don't want to let you go.' Lia breathed out a heavy sigh as she curled her hands round the steaming mug of coffee, her pretty brown eyes not bothering to try and hide her emotion.

Caitlin was genuinely touched. The girls had been friends for a long time now, seeing each other through good times and bad, and it was going to be as much a wrench for Caitlin to relinquish her job as it was for Lia to lose her. She'd always considered the esoteric bookshop to be the best place in the world to work in. Not only was she surrounded by books that had the potential to heal and uplift, but many like-minded people came into the store—and the fact that she worked with her best friend was a blessing.

But for the past week and a half Blue Sky had become more than just a wonderful opportunity to realise a long-held dream. It had become *personal*. Not only had Caitlin grown to respect and admire her fellow musicians, she was also starting to really care about them too. They worked so hard, were passionate about their music, talented and dedicated to their craft, and when Marcie Wallace had walked out they'd been understandably devastated. Caitlin wanted to help put things right…she wanted to help them realise *their* dreams too.

'It's not going to be easy for either of us,' she agreed now, sliding her hand across Lia's. 'But I'm not leaving for good. I might not be working in the shop any more, but that doesn't mean I won't be around. I'll still live here in the village, and when I come home after touring we'll see each other every day because I'll come in and chat and have coffee with you.'

'I know all that.' Lia freed her hand and drove her fingers anxiously through her short blonde hair. 'But if you want to know the truth I've been worrying myself sick about you.'

'Why?' Caitlin was astonished.

'Well…going off with a bunch of strangers to God only knows where. How do you know you can trust these people?'

'Lia, I've got to know them. They're not strangers any more. They're professional musicians. Jake Sorenson, their manager, is—'

'Jake is who I wanted to talk to you about.' The blonde drew a deep breath in. 'Didn't you recognise who he was when you first saw him? Don't you remember there was a "kiss and tell" scandal about him in the papers a few years ago? His wife left him for one of the biggest rock musicians in the world then spilled the beans about their marriage in an article in the papers.'

Lia's words started to ring a bell. As memory presented a helpful picture of the artist her friend had referred to Caitlin stared at the other girl in shock.

'I remember. She left him for Mel Justice...the lead singer with the band Heart and Soul. I didn't realise the record producer she was married to, was Jake.'

'Well, it was. And the picture she painted of her life with him wasn't exactly flattering. Did you know she was a model? Not high-profile, but a familiar face in the magazines just the same. The main reason for the exposé was that Jake had promised to make her a star and he didn't. Apparently she wanted to give up modelling to become a singer. But when they got married and he didn't come up with the goods she had an affair with Mel Justice and eventually divorced Jake to be with him.'

'Then she sold her story to the newspaper,' Caitlin said quietly.

It jolted her to realise that he'd been married. She hadn't read the story, but just before Lia had nudged her memory about what had happened she'd been about to comment that Jake Sorenson was a true professional—a man who elicited respect and admiration from his peers—and that she felt very fortunate to have him as a mentor. *But even as the thought occurred accompanying it was the stirring memory of last night when Jake had kissed her...*

'Anyway, what has any of what you've just said got to do with what *I'm* doing, Lia? Why are you digging up old news about Jake Sorenson?'

'Why? Because I want you to know what you're getting yourself into that's why.'

Lifting her mug of coffee to her lips, her friend agitatedly put it down again without taking so much as a sip.

'As your best friend, I can't help feeling responsible. The people in the business you're getting into are open to all kinds of temptations and bad behaviour. They certainly don't seem to exhibit much loyalty towards each other. I'd hate for you to be associated with the band and have it all backfire on you if the press decide to dig up that kiss and tell story and speculate over if you'll do the same, should anything go wrong.'

'But I'm not having a personal relationship with Jake, am I? I'm only singing with the band he's managing. Plus, I wouldn't dream of selling my story to the press even if I had one! I'm twenty-six, remember? Not some gullible teenager. I can absolutely take care of myself.'

But Caitlin's heart still raced. Nothing Lia had said before had remotely indicated what her friend really felt about her decision to join the band. Up until now she'd been so positive…so encouraging. *'Follow your passion,'* she'd said. *'Don't let anything get in your way.'* Now Caitlin didn't know what to think.

It wasn't any of her business what had or hadn't happened in Jake's marriage. In fact it explained why he sometimes seemed a little aloof. As well as destroying any trust you'd once had for a person, to have your spouse sell their story about your marriage to the papers must have been truly demoralising. But at the end of the day Jake's personal life was nothing remotely to do with her.

'Okay, so if it's true that you can take care of yourself then what about Sean?' Lia's brown eyes sparkled.

Caitlin could hardly believe what she was hearing.

'That was below the belt, Lia,' she murmured. 'Okay, so I've made some wrong turns in my life. Haven't you? Hasn't everyone? It doesn't mean that everything I do is doomed to failure or disaster, does it?'

'I shouldn't have said that. About Sean, I mean.' Lia sniffed. 'I'm sorry, Caitlin. I should know better, considering the business I'm in, shouldn't I? It's just that sometimes it's hard to put wisdom into practice when it comes to someone you care about. You know what men can be like.

They've got a one-track mind when it comes to women like you, and I mean that as a compliment. You're beautiful and talented, with a sweet and trusting nature. They're bound to try and take advantage and here you are—going off into the wide blue yonder with five of them!'

'Well, you've got to try and stop worrying, Lia. I'm going to be just fine. I'm doing what I want to do, right? Nobody is forcing me. If I can trust that everything will be okay, then why can't you?'

Abruptly rising to her feet, Caitlin carried her empty mug over to the sink. Then she rinsed it out and turned it upside down on the drainer.

'I'd better get back upstairs and relieve Nicky so that she can have her lunch. Today's my last day at the shop, so let's not spoil it by having an argument.'

'I'm sorry. I'm just feeling a bit on edge because you're going. Don't be mad at me?' Lia pleaded as she got to her feet.

'Don't be silly!' Grinning, Caitlin fondly ruffled her hair. 'How on earth could I be mad at you for caring? Since that particular commodity has been sadly lacking in my life for quite some time, I can assure you I'm open to all the TLC I can get!'

But even as she laughed off her friend's concern Caitlin couldn't help dwelling on what she'd said about Jake. The revelation about Jake's former marriage perturbed her. She didn't often read the celebrity gossip that littered the newspapers and social media, and right now she was glad that she didn't. Whatever had happened between Jake and his ex-wife, it must have been painful for both of them, she reasoned. She should just focus on singing with the band and not concern herself with how Blue Sky's manager might or might not conduct himself in private.

CHAPTER FOUR

AT THE END of an emotionally fraught day, Caitlin sank back into a hot steamy bath and exhaled a heartfelt sigh. Flickering candles cast dancing shadows on the walls of the small, once shabby bathroom she'd sought to transform with some pink paint, pale blue curtains and accessories. She was genuinely pleased with what she'd achieved.

Closing her eyes, she breathed in the exotic perfume that filled the air from the scented candles and her favourite aromatic bath oil. Trailing her fingers idly in the water, she let her thoughts whirl. Electing to leave her job, she hadn't exactly burnt her bridges, she reflected, because Lia had promised she could have a job with her any day. But it was still a scary thought to realise that she was giving up something relatively stable and secure for something that was its direct antithesis.

Splashing a handful of water across her shoulders, Caitlin opened her eyes and absently watched the droplets roll down her warm, scented skin. Frowning, she thought about the afternoon's rehearsals and how Jake had regularly berated her for lack of concentration—not to mention for pretty much everything else. He'd yelled at her so often that the rest of the crew had cast each other quizzical glances, as if to ask, *what's going on?*

Was he behaving like that because he regretted kissing her? She hadn't *asked* him to kiss her! Her concentration might well not have been what it should, but despite the rights or wrongs of that inflammatory kiss how did the man *expect* her to react when she'd just left the job that she'd been devoted to for the past five years? It just wasn't that easy to detach herself from a person or a place she cared about.

At least Rick and the others had been more understanding. They had even brought along a bottle of champagne to celebrate her 'release', although Jake had declined to join them in their impromptu toast during the break. Instead, he'd collected his leather jacket and gone out for a while… 'To get some fresh air,' he'd tersely explained.

'Blast you, Jake Sorenson! I'm doing my best here. Give me a break, can't you?'

Grabbing the innocent plastic yellow duck bobbing about on the water, she flung it down in temper. It made a very sad little splash. Not nearly enough impact to vent the anger that was bubbling up inside her.

Then, as if on cue, the doorbell rang.

Caitlin cursed out loud, determined to ignore it. But when it rang for a second and then a third time her resolve crumbled and she hauled herself out of the bath, grabbed the blue terry robe off the peg behind the door and struggled into it, littering the air with vague mutterings of irritation as she did so…

Stomping through the living room, then down the cold linoleum-covered stairs, she wondered who could be so inconsiderate and foolhardy enough to disrupt one of her favourite pastimes.

'Jake.'

All the strength seemed to drain from her limbs as she came face to face with her unexpected visitor. His lean, athletic frame was clothed entirely in black, and his long legs and broad shoulders were outlined by the filtered orange glow of a nearby street lamp. No other man had the power to disturb her as much. Jake had a presence that scrambled her thoughts into a muddled tangle and almost made it hard to breathe. All compelling lean angles and shadows, his gorgeous cheekbones were almost impossibly perfect.

Meeting his bold gaze, she asked, 'What is it? Is something wrong?'

'Can I come in?'

Because the request had caught her off guard, Caitlin found herself nodding. Then she stepped back into the dimly lit hallway, with its unfortunate flocked gold wallpaper and worn red carpet, to let him enter. The damp hair that she'd screwed up so carelessly into an improvised knot hung loose and heavy behind her head and several long ebony strands had worked free to glance against her cheek. Beneath her robe her body was still slick with moisture because she hadn't had time to dry herself. And she was stark naked beneath that robe...

It was a fact that did little to add to her confidence. Not when Jake edged past her with an enigmatic little smile that made all the strength ooze out of her limbs like sherbet through a straw.

'Up the stairs,' she instructed weakly as he turned and waited while she closed the front door.

Glancing briefly up the narrow staircase that led to her flat, he said, 'You go first.'

Caitlin had been afraid he might say that. With her face burning she squeezed past him, inadvertently inhaling the heady scents of cedarwood and leather and the fresh smell of the outdoors that clung to him as her body brushed briefly against his. It was like coming into contact with a power supply, she thought as she began to ascend the stairs. There wasn't a cell in her body that hadn't felt the effect.

Every step she took in her slim bare feet with their scarlet-painted toenails was pure *agony* because she was acutely aware of Jake, just inches behind her. The belt round her waist had been fastened so tightly he couldn't fail to be apprised of her shape beneath the perfectly innocent terry robe, and Caitlin squirmed inwardly all the way up into her living room.

'Come in,' she invited.

His heart thudding, because his senses were still infused with the memory of their kiss the other night, Jake trained his gaze on his surroundings in a bid to divert his aroused recollection.

He immediately registered what had once been an ornate Victorian fireplace that was now home to a small electric heater that surely wasn't big enough to heat the whole room. There was a large pink ceramic vase with palm fronds in it just to the side of the hearth, and a large squashy red sofa with multi-coloured cushions arranged against the wall. Above it was a large gold-framed print of *Flaming June* by Frederic Leighton. The vivid orange of the lady's dress was clinging like a sunburst to her pale reposing figure.

Jake absorbed all of this in just a few short seconds, but inevitably his gaze was helplessly drawn back to Caitlin. In her charming state of *dishabille*, how could it not be? What *was* that scent she was wearing?

With her face scrubbed clean of make-up, her silky black hair escaping all attempts at confinement, and wearing nothing but a plain terry robe, to Jake she was temptation personified. If she had the power to make him hot when she was dressed in tight jeans and a T-shirt it was nothing compared to the effect she was having on him in her present get-up. He just prayed that her pretty green eyes wouldn't stray far south of his stomach, because right then he was fighting a losing battle to keep his lustful stirrings to himself.

So much for his promise to maintain a professional distance. He'd already broken that vow by stealing that incendiary kiss the other night. One taste of pure, unadulterated heaven had ensured that sooner or later he would be back for more. He'd already had to make himself scarce once this afternoon, because two hours of Caitlin up on the stage wiggling her hips as she sang, her breasts bouncing ever so slightly in her hot pink T-shirt, had almost made him crazy with want. Professing a need for some fresh air had just been a handy euphemism for what he really needed…a cold shower so icy it would freeze an ordinary mortal into a cryogenic trance.

When Jake didn't immediately speak, Caitlin nervously wiped her hands down her robe and motioned vaguely towards the sofa. 'Why don't you sit down? I just need to go and dress. I was having a bath when you rang the bell.'

'Don't get dressed on my account,' her visitor drawled, making no discernible move to sit down.

Her face flamed red.

'I'm still wet,' she gulped, immediately wishing she could take back her innocently meant remark, because Jake's glance was all but stripping her naked. Want, need and lust swirled between them. 'I mean I need…'

Caitlin's hand trembled as she saw Jake's eyes grow tellingly dark. Now his glance was focused on her mouth, on the soft, plump lower lip that her tongue had just innocently dampened.

'What are we going to do, Caitlin?' he asked softly, his gravelly voice reeling her in with its disturbing undisguised intonation of heat and sex.

'Do about what?'

'About *us*. Don't pretend you don't know what I mean. For God's sake, the kiss we shared the other night when I walked you home was no innocent kiss goodnight. I got the distinct impression that you enjoyed it as much as I did. Was I wrong?'

'Look, I really need to go and put some clothes on. If you wait here I'll make us some coffee once I'm dressed and then we can talk.'

Jake smiled. She was gazing at him as though hypnotised. As she studied him her bewitching emerald eyes were dazzled—*glazed*, almost. Whatever she felt about him, she couldn't deny there was a combustible attraction between them. And he couldn't think of another woman who had the ability to send his pulse sky-rocketing and his libido raging with just a simple glance.

It wasn't just her beauty that drew him to her. There was a refreshing innocence about Caitlin. Having met so many women whose hunger for fame and success made them employ any means possible to get what they wanted—*his ex-wife being a case in point*—he found Caitlin was like a breath of fresh air. Jake had never wanted a woman more in his life…wanted her with an ache that was the sweetest agony from the moment he woke up in the morning to when he lay down to sleep at night.

'Good. Because it won't go away,' he continued. 'Sooner or later we're going to have to deal with it.'

Caitlin's already pink cheeks flushed even pinker. Then she turned and fled into the bedroom to get dressed.

Sighing, Jake dropped down onto the squashy red sofa, picked up a cushion, then angrily jettisoned it onto the floor. *Just what the hell did he think he was doing?* He'd called in on her because he'd wanted to apologise for being so uncompromising at rehearsals, but as soon as he'd set eyes on her in that innocent terry robe of hers he'd known immediately that she wasn't wearing anything underneath it. Somehow his rigidly imposed self-control had gone out of the window and all he'd been able to think about was how soon he could get her into bed.

He wanted to bury himself so deep inside her he'd assuage every ache he'd ever had…*hers* too. Yes, he'd had the odd one-night stand since Jodie had done the dirty on him—how else could he satisfy a healthy libido—but nothing could have prepared him for a hunger so primal, so insatiable, that it threatened to consume him body and soul if it wasn't satisfied.

Dragging his fingers through his hair, Jake slowly shook his head. To add to his frustration Caitlin's provocative scent lingered in the room, tormenting him. Where was she, for goodness' sake? How long did it take to throw some clothes on? *Longer than it would take him to tear them off that was for sure...*

Restless, he got to his feet, his long legs taking him to the other side of the room and back again as he paced the floor. The living room was ridiculously small—almost oppressively so. A few family photos sat on the mantelpiece, along with a small glass jar full of assorted coloured crystals.

Jake was far too distracted to examine the photographs more closely, so he turned away to survey the rest of the room. A large pine bookcase dominated an entire wall, and there wasn't a shelf on it that wasn't crammed to bursting point with books. He barely stole a glance at the titles he was so keyed up, but he couldn't fail to notice that most of the literature dwelt on self-development or philosophy.

Had Caitlin been interested in those subjects before or *after* her catastrophic relationship with the drug addict? Jake was curious. Clearly she must have been driven to seek out some sort of guidance after such an ordeal. Somehow he felt chastened. Living with a drug addict and alcoholic would certainly be no picnic. He himself had had friends and associates who'd been drawn down a similar destructive route. He'd told Caitlin that the music business was full of such casualties.

But she'd confessed to him that she'd lost everything, including her home. That must surely be the reason why she was living in this *rabbit hutch*. Jake would go stir crazy, living in such a confined space. Being the grateful owner of spacious homes in London, New York and LA—which were admittedly empty most of the time, due to his peripatetic lifestyle—he doubted he would manage even half as well if he had to live the way Caitlin did. Even his room at the quaint Pilgrim's Inn was three times the size of this one.

Without realising it, his hands had curled into fists down by his sides.

He'd remarked to her that addiction was a disease, not

a weakness, but by God he'd like just ten minutes with the jerk who'd ripped her off so badly that she was reduced to living in two shabby rented rooms.

'What would you like to drink? Tea or coffee?'

Caitlin's voice took Jake by surprise. Turning round, he avidly noted her long shapely legs, which were encased in soft worn denim, and the pretty pink top she'd donned, which was fastened at the front with little pearl buttons. In her apparent haste to get dressed the top two buttons had been left undone, inadvertently revealing the creamy cleft between her breasts, and the arresting sight made him catch his breath.

But she might not have left the buttons undone deliberately—she hardly needed to resort to feminine wiles to get his attention. All the woman had to do was glance at him with those bewitching emerald eyes and Jake was all hers.

'Neither,' he answered. 'Why don't you just come and sit down so we can talk?'

Caitlin acquiesced, her brows puckering when she noticed that one of her multi-coloured cushions was lying on the floor. Inside her chest, her heart was galloping at what felt like a worrying breakneck speed.

When Jake had asserted that sooner or later they would have to 'deal with it', had he been saying that it was inevitable that they had an affair? Because if he had then he hadn't reckoned with her iron will. It didn't matter how attracted she was to the man, she wasn't the type to jump thoughtlessly into bed with him. Sean was the only man she'd ever been intimate with, and to be honest it hadn't been anything to write home about even when she'd foolishly imagined herself in love with him.

Being a singer and a member of Blue Sky was far more important than having a hot little affair with the band's manager, she told herself.

'I was rough on you today.' Still standing in the centre

of the room, Jake rubbed a hand round his beard-darkened jaw. 'I feel like I owe you an apology.'

'Why?'

'Because I pushed you too hard.' He flinched as though genuinely regretting it.

'You don't have to apologise. I know I've still got a long way to go and I need all the help and guidance I can get. Rick says that you're the best, and so do the others. I'm hungry to learn, Jake. You shouldn't lose any sleep over the fact that you had to yell at me a few times.'

Gritting his teeth, he silently cursed the ache in his groin that refused to be tamped. *It wasn't the fact that he'd lost his temper a few times that he was losing sleep over.* She was sitting on her sofa, looking about as tempting as Eve in the Garden of Eden, and her soothing velvet voice rolled over him like honey. She might not know it but she was seducing him as thoroughly as if she sat there naked, beckoning him to come to her.

'Are you always this reasonable?' He quirked an eyebrow.

Although he'd apologised, he was still spoiling for an argument—*anything* to defuse the sexually charged tension between them.

'No.' An amused smile played at the corners of her mouth. 'Sean used to accuse me of being unreasonable all the time.'

'Sean?'

'My ex-boyfriend.'

'The drug addict.' Jake hadn't meant to sound cruel, but the fact was he wasn't in the mood to be magnanimous. A stab of jealousy had sliced through his insides at Caitlin's reference to the man she'd previously been in a relationship with.

Suddenly rising to her feet, she let her fingers toy restlessly with the little pearl buttons on her blouse. The gesture inevitably drew his gaze.

'Amongst other things he was a painter and decorator by trade. Not that he was in work very often…For obvious reasons.' Her expression was briefly pained. 'But, like you said, just because he was an addict, it didn't mean he was a bad person. He was easily led by some unsavoury friends, that was the trouble.'

Caitlin dipped her head and Jake found himself automatically taking a step towards her.

'So, you were "unreasonable" because you tried to warn him off those so-called friends?'

'Yes… That and because I didn't give him money as often as he liked to buy his drugs. I was struggling to keep the roof over our heads as it was. I had a lovely flat that I'd bought with a legacy my grandmother had left me and I was eventually forced to sell it because of Sean. He was in so much debt due to his drug habit.'

'And where is he now?' he asked. *A million miles away, he hoped.* Outer Mongolia wouldn't be far enough.

'When we broke up he said he was going to London. His brother lives there and he was going to stay with him to try and straighten himself out. I hope for his sake he was able to. But, that said, I'm just so glad he's out of my life. Being with him had me fearing for my sanity. I hardly knew who I was any more. Sometimes I can't believe what a fool I was to trust him and believe that he would change. One thing's for sure…I'll never give my trust so easily to a man again.'

Her emerald eyes glistened briefly and Jake swallowed hard. He hated the idea that she wasted even a *second* of her time thinking about her ex and what he had put her through.

'Anyway, I don't know why I'm standing here telling you all this,' she finished.

'I asked you to. What about your family? Were they supportive when they found out what was going on?'

'My parents and my brother are in America. He moved out there first and they followed. They've started up a business out there. Anyway…'

With a shrug Caitlin briefly met his eyes and then looked quickly away again.

'I didn't want them to worry about me so I didn't tell them. I made my bed and I had to lie in it. They gave me the chance of going with them when they left but I opted not to take it. Besides, they always taught me it was important to stand on my own two feet, and I wasn't going to go running to them the moment I was in trouble. I wanted to prove to myself and to them that I could turn my life around and be proud of myself.'

'Whilst that's commendable, I thought families were supposed to help each other out when one of them was in trouble?'

'Do yours? Help you when you're in trouble I mean?'

Jake hadn't expected her to turn the question on him. For a dizzying moment he found himself awash in a sea of feelings that he usually tried to submerge...feelings of pain, confusion and a sickening sense of being abandoned by life.

His mouth drying, he answered, 'No... They don't. They *can't*. I don't know who they are. I was raised in a children's home.'

Caitlin's bewitching green eyes immediately softened. 'Oh, Jake...I'm so sorry.'

The suggestion of concerned sympathy in her voice was like a gun pointed straight at his heart. He immediately sought to deflect it.

'Don't be. I learned very quickly not to depend on anyone else for either my happiness or my wellbeing. I survived the experience—that's all you need to know. That's all *anyone* needs to know.'

Twisting her hands together, she took a few moments before commenting, 'You've done more than just survive, Jake. You've made an amazing success of your life.'

'Is that how it looks to you?' The question was painfully ironic.

'Anyway, regarding my own family, we're...let's just say we respect our differences. They have their life and I have mine.'

'You mean you haven't told them that you've joined the band?'

'I will tell them…eventually. But, just not right now.'

Jake shrugged. 'It's your call.'

'You said that you learned not to depend on anyone else to make you happy. What about romantic relationships, Jake? Have you had maybe one or two that haven't worked out?'

'Who *hasn't*?'

A reticent smile suggested that discussing his own experiences was the last thing he wanted to do. It wasn't hard to understand why he should feel that way. Nobody welcomed talking about the things that had hurt them. Yet Caitlin couldn't help wanting to know more. *Despite her vow never to easily trust another man, the idea of perhaps trusting Jake was strangely compelling.* After all, he knew what it was like to have been badly hurt by someone and wouldn't knowingly inflict similar hurt on someone else…would he?

Drawing in a deep breath for courage, she asked the question she'd been longing to hear the answer to since talking to Lia.

'My friend Lia—the manager of the shop where I worked—she told me that she once read in the papers that you'd been married.'

As Caitlin had expected, Jake's guard slammed down like a portcullis. 'Then why ask if I've had any relationships that haven't worked out? It must be obvious that my marriage didn't, if your friend read about it.'

He let loose an irritated sigh, but Caitlin detected weariness in the sound, as if he was well and truly sick of the subject.

'Presumably she also told you that my wife left me and then sold a sordid little tale to the press?'

She flushed, feeling uncomfortably guilty. 'Yes…she did.'

'Then that should tell you it was hardly a match made in heaven. My ex was a manipulative little liar…what else do you want to know?'

'Please don't be so defensive. I was hoping you might tell me your side of the story. I never read any details myself. To be honest, I didn't even recognise you when we first met. I don't often read the newspapers, and neither do I use social media very much. I honestly won't breathe a word of this conversation to anyone…not even to my friend.'

'I take it I have your word on that?' Jake's blue eyes were momentarily fierce.

With her heart thudding, Caitlin nodded. 'Of course.'

'Her name was Jodie and she was a model who wanted to become a pop singer. I had no idea of her ambition at the time. Anyway, we met at a party and had a few dates. She was pretty and engaging enough to capture my attention, and on a weekend break to Rome I foolishly asked her to marry me.'

He shook his head in mocking disbelief.

'Practically as soon as we were married she started to put pressure on me to help her get a record deal…all the while telling me I was the best thing that had ever happened to her and that she was madly in love with me, of course. You'd think I would have known better.'

He gave a harsh self-deprecating laugh before continuing.

'She couldn't sing, and when she realised I wasn't going to help further her career she started an affair with Mel Justice—the lead guitarist of the bestselling rock band on the planet. I was travelling in South America on business when she moved in with him and on my return she told me she was filing for divorce. Then, when the case came to court, she cited mental cruelty because I'd allegedly promised to help make her a star and I hadn't…'

The way Jake shook his head told Caitlin everything she needed to know about how he'd felt about that.

'In the story she portrayed me as some kind of Svengali who'd preyed on her naïvety and led me astray. If it hadn't been so painful and hadn't ruined my reputation it would have been funny. Anyway, with the help of a high-profile

American lawyer, courtesy of her new boyfriend, she got her divorce and was awarded a ridiculous sum of money from me for so-called damages. Then she married her lover and became Mrs Justice.'

Jake's telling of the painful events was succinct and to the point. But to have had his reputation sullied by Jodie's lies and for her to have sold her story to the newspapers because she hadn't got what she wanted out of him must have seriously shattered his belief in relationships. Sighing, Caitlin tucked some drifting strands of hair behind her ear.

Relieved to have done with his story, Jake moved across to the sofa to join her. Breathing out on a sigh, he gently touched his knuckles to the side of her cheek. *As soon as he'd done it he knew he was lost.*

Even though he'd kissed her, touching Caitlin was still a revelation. Her skin had the texture of the purest silk. An erotic image of her lying naked in his bed, her slender limbs tangled in black satin sheets, her eyes dark with desire and her skin flushed pink with arousal, slipped easily into his mind to taunt him even more. He wanted to touch her everywhere. He wouldn't rush. He'd take his time and savour every inch of her beautiful body, every flavour. Was she uninhibitedly vocal? Or would she whimper gently when he brought her to climax?

'Anyway, I think I've said enough. Thanks for telling me about Sean. I hope it hasn't upset you too much?' It didn't surprise him when his voice sounded less than steady.

'It hasn't. I'm fine.' Caitlin willed herself to move, to put herself out of reach of his seductive touch and wrest her gaze from the haunting blue eyes that made her feel so restless and hungry.

She burned for him. Could Jake see that? Could he tell? If she was going to make her dream come true she couldn't afford to let him know just how much she desired him. Becoming intimately involved with Jake Sorenson would be a disaster personally *and* professionally. Somehow she had to play it cool…for *both* their sakes. They were both recovering from seriously hurtful relationships and, if nothing else, they should exercise some common sense.

'I'm just very tired.' Faking a yawn, Caitlin surprised herself by following it up with a genuine one.

Jake immediately got to his feet. Planting his hands either side of his straight lean hips, he nodded. 'I almost forgot how late it was.'

He should be glad of the excuse to leave. *He didn't dare risk staying for much longer because being with Caitlin was putting an impossible strain on him to stick to his vow to leave well alone.*

'I know we haven't discussed the situation we've got but that will have to wait. At the end of the day, the band is the first priority. I'll see you tomorrow at rehearsals. Three o'clock, usual place.'

'I'll be there.' Caitlin pushed to her feet.

'Good. I'll see myself out. Don't come down.'

Following him onto the landing, Caitlin felt every muscle in her body tense as she stared at his back, at the soft leather jacket that accommodated his broad shoulders to perfection, at his long, hard-muscled legs and taut, lean behind. A wave of heat rolled over her and almost made her lose her balance. She'd never ogled a man in her life before, but there was something about Jake Sorenson that made her behave out of character…something wild and untamed.

She'd stared down into a yawning abyss of darkness many times during those two hellish years with Sean, and had lost count of the times she'd prayed for her life to be 'normal'. But, in truth, she'd always known that she could never be content with a conventional nine-to-five existence. She needed more than that…*much* more. That was why she'd shown up for the audition with Blue Sky. That was why she was willing to kiss goodbye to the sleepy little village that had been her home and that was why she wanted to take her chances with Jake and the others…

'Jake?'

Coming to a standstill at the bottom of the stairs, he glanced up at her. As she stared back into his fathomless blue eyes Caitlin mused that it was like falling into the sky.

'Thanks for dropping by and for…for our little chat.'

'No problem.'

Conveying that he was in a hurry, Jake abruptly opened the door and slammed it shut behind him.

CHAPTER FIVE

THE BLAST OF a car horn sounding right outside her front door made Caitlin jump. In the throes of getting ready for her evening out, she glanced at the clock on the mantel and saw that it was later than she'd thought.

Softly cursing, she yanked her hairbrush roughly through her sable hair, then quickly painted her lips with the new plum shade of lipstick she'd bought. Her hand was a little unsteady as she applied it and, to make matters even worse, she decided that the colour was a little too dramatic for her liking. But she was just going to have to grin and bear it. She was already feeling tense at the distinct possibility of being chastised yet again for lateness. That would make it the third time this week and it might just be the straw that broke the camel's back as far as Jake was concerned.

Hurriedly snatching her leather jacket off the couch and pulling it on, she grabbed her purse, shoved it into a pocket and flew down the steep, narrow staircase as if the hounds of hell themselves were after her. Her breath hitched as she hurried towards the ominous-looking black Jeep, its engine running.

Jake leaned across and pushed open the passenger door. 'Hi,' he greeted her.

His expression didn't give much away, and it couldn't help but increase the overall sense of trepidation that Caitlin was feeling. They were going to see a band tonight and would be spending a large amount of time together...*alone*.

She didn't doubt the experience was going to be a real test for them both.

'Hi.' There were three seats in the front of the vehicle and she automatically sat next to the window and slammed the door shut.

'I want you next to me.'

'What?'

The slow burning heat from Jake's gaze almost scorched Caitlin where she sat. He didn't embellish the comment. He didn't *have* to. They both knew only too well why he wanted her to sit closer to him. *Could day resist following night?* She'd have loved to have had a handy reason with which to refuse him, but her mind was worryingly bereft of anything helpful as his arresting blue eyes entrapped hers.

With thumping heart she murmured, 'Feeling lonely, are we?' Then, before he could reply, she somehow found herself sitting in the luxuriously upholstered leather seat next to his.

His lips lifted in a grin.

'Not any more.'

'Well, I'm glad that I've made you happy.' Her dark hair brushed against her reddened cheekbone as she bent to buckle her seatbelt. 'For *once*.'

Chuckling, Jake put the car into gear and steered it smoothly away from the kerb. It should have reassured her that he seemed to be in a particularly good mood tonight, but it didn't make things any easier. *Not when she was already gripped by the familiar disturbing waves of disorientation and desire that seemed to be inevitable whenever they were together.* And all day that combustible kiss they'd shared when he'd walked her home from the pub had played over and over in her mind.

Their attraction for each other had been growing stronger and stronger. It only needed the tiniest spark to turn it into a conflagration. It was made even more acute now, by the intimate space they shared in the car.

Caitlin couldn't help stealing a covetous glance at Jake

as he drove. True to form, he was clothed in his habitual black, with no apparent concessions to dressing up for their night out—although he didn't need to wear fancy clothes to draw a woman's eye. *Not when he exuded charisma simply by breathing.* Add to that, he had the intriguing persona of a man who'd been around musicians for most of his life and had seen it all…group bust-ups, wrecked hotel rooms, drink, drugs, groupies and corrupt management…and had lived to tell the tale. Jake had been there, done that, and worn the T-shirt.

Sighing, Caitlin smoothed her hand down over her jeans and couldn't help wondering what people would see in her when she finally took to the stage to sing. Would they quickly categorise her as just another starstruck wannabe? A wide-eyed innocent without much experience of anything at all? *If they did, then they couldn't be more wrong.* How could they know the narrow escape she'd had from the kind of destructive relationship that most mothers of daughters had nightmares about? Consequently, she was far from ignorant about the pitfalls that awaited girls who were too trusting, who kidded themselves that they could 'fix' a partner's problems simply by loving them enough. *Caitlin had found to her cost that that was one of the biggest lies believed by women.*

Jake must have sensed her shudder and he turned his head in surprise. 'Are you okay?'

'Yes, I'm fine.'

Obviously deciding not to pander to any sense of insecurity she might be feeling, he drawled, 'I trust your clothes aren't going to turn into rags if I don't get you home by midnight?'

He was, of course, referring to her habit of turning in early if she could. Caitlin's cheeks seared pink with embarrassment. Early nights free from anxiety had been denied her in the days when she'd waited up for Sean, praying he hadn't got himself into more trouble. If she'd had a pound for every prayer she'd uttered in those two harsh, unhappy years she'd be a rich woman.

When he hadn't come home when expected Caitlin had hoped the police hadn't got him in a cell somewhere, or that some drug dealer he owed money to hadn't beaten him up, or worse. When he'd lied to her yet again, let her down or stolen money from her, she'd prayed hard for the strength to cope—still foolishly believing that she could somehow rescue him from the dark road he'd been intent on travelling down. But when he'd started to bully her, threaten her and finally *hit* her, she'd dug deep for the strength to end the relationship before it ended *her*.

The bottom line was she wasn't about to apologise to Jake for something that had been an important part of her emotional recovery, no matter how much he scorned her early nights.

'There's about as much likelihood of that as you turning into Prince Charming any time soon,' she muttered.

To her astonishment, she actually detected a smile on Jake's lips. It was only slight, and a less sensitive person might have missed it, but she was so intimately attuned to the man's every unconscious gesture and nuance she couldn't help but be aware of it. It did funny things to her insides that 'almost' smile of his, not to mention other sensitive areas of her body...

Pursing her lips, she stared determinedly ahead of her as a sudden fierce shower of rain sheeted the windscreen's glass, temporarily obliterating the view until Jake switched on the wipers.

'And there was I, hoping we'd get a clear night with a romantic moon and starlight,' he quipped.

'Is that really what you were hoping for?'

Lifting a shoulder, he smiled again, this time more freely. 'Why? You don't think I have it in me to be romantic?'

The remark immediately threw her.

'How would I know? I don't know you well enough.'

'Then it's clearly time for me to do something about that, don't you think?'

He didn't turn his head to look at her. The provocative words were simply left hanging in the air between them, like a small but lethal incendiary device.

Urgently feeling the need to change the conversation to something far less dangerous, Caitlin asked, 'So, who's the band we're going to see tonight? You didn't tell me.'

'They're called Ace of Hearts. The lead singer is Nikki Drake and I'd really like you to see her. She isn't what you might call the best singer in the world, but what she lacks in vocal range she more than makes up for in her performance. It's electrifying. She lives and breathes the band and it shows.'

'And you're hoping that I might pick up a few tips?'

The rain ceased as suddenly as it had started, and as the wipers squeaked redundantly across the screen Jake's brief azure glance at Caitlin was like a heat-seeking missile that went straight to her womb.

'Sure,' he answered.

Jake was amazed that he'd even got the word out. Whenever he caught sight of Caitlin's bewitching face—whether by design or by accident—he was all but struck dumb. Ever since he'd kissed her he'd been filled with an insatiable desire to know her intimately. As far as he was concerned, not having to share her company with anyone else tonight was like being given the keys to heaven.

For a man that prided himself on always being in control of situations, his feelings for this woman were unravelling him. If he didn't act soon to counteract the danger then the walls he'd built around his heart, brick by brick, would come crashing down and render him helpless. Whilst he would do everything in his power not to let that happen, there was no reason why he shouldn't take Caitlin to bed to help get her out of his system…*was there?*

'Do you know her well? Nikki Drake, I mean?' she probed.

Hearing the curiosity in her voice, Jake smiled. He smiled because he detected the unspoken question that she *really* wanted to ask, which was *How well do you know her?* Although he'd never been remotely attracted to Nikki, he couldn't help but experience a certain male satisfaction at the idea that Caitlin might be a little jealous.

'I know her well enough. But then, I know a lot of people in my business,' he drawled.

Not for the first time Caitlin realised that Jake was a man of few words. But, whatever he said, there was always a wealth of meaning behind it that often required some serious detective work. Then again, perhaps she should just go with the flow and not worry too much about what he meant. Jake was Jake: enigmatic, taciturn, not giving an inch. She'd better get used to it if she was going to make a half decent job of working with him.

But what she wouldn't give for him to one day speak about *her* in the same admiring way that he spoke about Nikki Drake... She was feeling ridiculously jealous of the woman when she hadn't even seen her or heard her sing yet.

'Then I can't wait to see her,' she remarked, hoping that the amiable smile she gave would convince him that she meant it.

There wasn't a single gaze in the room that wasn't trained on the sexy strutting singer onstage. A small shapely blonde, her blue eyes heavily outlined with thick black liner, her generous mouth painted with bold red lipstick, Nikki Drake held the mike as if she owned it and commanded the small raised stage with every sexy thrust of her hips, every husky note that she sang.

Her slender body was encased in tight black satin and a wide scarlet belt was cinched tightly round her impossibly tiny waist. Her creamy breasts were clearly enhanced by the loving support of a daring uplift bra *Sex on legs,* as her friend Lia might say.

The performance was riveting. While the music throbbed around them Caitlin experienced an adrenaline rush like nothing she'd ever experienced before at a live concert. Was this how Jake wanted her to look? Commanding, sexy, wearing tight, hard-to-breathe-in clothing specifically designed to highlight every curve, every undulation? Unashamedly putting everything she had on show?

Her throat was dry from the combined heat of wall-to-wall people crammed into a space not much bigger than a living room. Taking a hasty sip of her rum and Coke, with the ice in the glass already melted to slivers, Caitlin almost jumped out of her skin when Jake moved up behind her. Her senses reeled with shock when his lean, hard body was all of a sudden on intimate terms with her back, his denim-clad thighs carelessly brushing the backs of hers as his warm, bourbon-laced breath drifted tantalisingly over her hair. Caitlin went rigid.

'What do you think?' he asked, and the husky timbre of his voice did seriously X-rated things to her body, draining her limbs of all their strength in the process.

'About—about what?' She could barely squeeze the words past her throat.

'About Nikki and the band of course. What did you think I meant?'

Jake's amused smile was almost tangible. She didn't need to see it to know that he was taking great pleasure in teasing her. She was suddenly grateful for the dim lighting and the intimate proximity of the other bodies around her, because she didn't want him to see that her face was burning.

'She's very good. They're all very talented. I'm really enjoying the music,' she told him.

'Without a doubt you're a better singer,' Jake responded. 'All we have to do now is find the right image for you.'

'As long as you don't expect me to pour myself into tight black satin. I'll definitely draw the line at *that*.'

To bolster her flagging courage, Caitlin tipped up her glass and drained the entire contents of the drink that remained. Her head swam a little as the alcohol hit home, but it was as nothing compared to the dizziness she was already experiencing with Jake getting closer by the second.

'I think we should go for something more classy. *Sexy...* but classy.'

His hand drifted over her hip to settle on her waist, his fingers deliberately sliding across the thin silk of the white camisole she wore beneath her jacket. Caitlin almost stopped breathing.

When she lifted her hand, ostensibly to move his away, his fingers caught hers and trapped them possessively. The words she'd started to form were suddenly obliterated as she closed her mouth, shut her eyes and sensed Jake press even closer. A tremulous shudder went through her as he brushed her hair aside and planted a devastatingly erotic kiss on the sensitive juncture between her shoulder and neck.

The unexpected caress went straight to her core and almost made her whimper with pleasure. *It was as though he had branded her.* Beneath the flimsy fabric of her strapless bra her nipples turned rigid and achy and her legs turned seriously weak. Thank God for the music and the crowd, because if they'd been alone right then Caitlin was certain her defences against such a passionate assault on her senses would have been zero.

Desperately needing to regain her composure, she straightened and turned round to face Jake. But the message his compelling blue eyes were conveying drove every coherent thought in her head straight out again.

'Don't. Please don't.'

Even as she softly uttered the words she thought they didn't make sense. *She* made no sense. Half plea, half whisper, they were carried away by the hypnotic beat of the music, by the laughter of the couple standing next to them, a young man with his arms firmly round his pretty Titian-haired girlfriend as they swayed together to the music.

'Please don't what?' Jake caught her hand and unhesitatingly drew her in tight to his chest.

Such eyes he had, Caitlin thought feverishly…piercing blue-grey, like mist swirling over a storm-ravaged sea…

Holding Caitlin against him was the most exquisite pleasure bordering on pain that Jake had ever experienced. Her soft yet slender curves fitted his embrace as though she'd been made for just that purpose.

The sound of the throbbing music, the approving cheers of the audience, the chink of glasses from the bar and the soporific scent of incense that hung over them like a heady cloud—they all faded away, leaving Jake with nothing but his overwhelming need for the woman in front of him.

His desire to make Caitlin his own in the most primal way a man and a woman could consummate their lust was testing him to the very limit. Already he was hurtling close to the edge of that self-imposed control. He knew he shouldn't want her so much. Professionally, it had disaster written all over it, and personally he wasn't ready to trust a woman. After what Jodie had done trust didn't come easily. Both those reasons should make him stay well clear.

With a supreme test of will, Jake slid his hands up to Caitlin's shoulders, where he briefly let them linger. Then he gently but firmly moved her away. Her eyes instantly registered surprise and confusion and Jake cursed himself for torturing them both.

'I don't want to hurt you,' he murmured.

Caitlin bit her lip and inclined her head in a brief nod. Then she turned back to watch the band, crossing her arms over her chest as if to protect herself. Her beautiful hair cascaded down her back like the most luxurious black silk and Jake ached with every fibre of his being to reach out and touch it. He had been captivated by women before, but not like this—*never* like this.

What he needed right now was another drink. He'd have to be careful not to exceed the limit, because he was driving, and even another drink would be no consolation for his present sexual frustration. Sensibly, he decided against it. Instead, he stayed put to watch the band and decide which elements of the performance he could point out to Caitlin that might help her when the time came for her to make her debut with Blue Sky.

'Hey, that was good. Where did you learn to play guitar like that?'

Mike Casey sat cross-legged on the living room floor, barefooted and tousled-haired, his guitar resting easily against his thighs. His brown eyes regarded Caitlin in admiration. She'd just given him a personal rendition of a well-known singer's most iconic track, with all its attendant complicated chord changes and a few innovative ones of her own. He wondered if Jake or Rick had heard her play yet, because Caitlin didn't just play a 'little', as she'd modestly confessed at her audition. The woman knew her way round a guitar as if the instrument were a natural extension of her own graceful hands.

Setting down her guitar to take a sip from the soft drink Mike had given her, she answered, 'I had lessons when I was younger. I pestered my mum for them until she got sick of me asking and conceded. She really wanted me to learn the piano, so I made a compromise and agreed to learn that too.' She grinned. 'After a while I stopped having the lessons and basically taught myself.'

She shrugged, not wanting to make a big deal about her ability. Her reasons for learning to play both instruments had always been purely self-motivated. The plain truth of the matter was that her music and her books had kept her sane whenever life had threatened to get a little less dependable and reliable—like when her parents had announced they were leaving the country to join her brother Phil in America.

Phil was the 'blue-eyed boy' who, in their eyes, could do no wrong. An old familiar twinge of resentment surfaced but Caitlin quickly squashed it. At the time her sense of abandonment had been acute and music had been her only solace—an anchor in a world where nothing had made sense any more. She'd often wondered if that was why she had hooked up with someone like Sean. He'd entered her life when she'd been feeling especially low and he'd charmed her with his boyish smile, amusing jokes and the sense that he was a bit of rebel. She, poor fool, had lapped up his attention as though she'd been marooned on a desert island for years without seeing a single soul.

Mike was thoughtful. There was a real buzz of excitement in the pit of his belly when he thought about Caitlin and what she could potentially bring to the table for the band. Not only had they found themselves an amazing singer, but he'd discovered another musician he could harmonise with as well. There was no doubt in his mind that they could be a great team. The girl was worth her weight in gold.

'What you did just now was more than "good", Caitlin. You really know how to play.'

'Thanks.' Her smile was shy, but appreciative. After last night's humiliating little encounter with Jake as they were watching the band she definitely welcomed a boost to her morale this morning.

God, she'd made such a fool of herself. Her heart thudded and slowed at the memory. It had been a bad mistake to let him see how much she wanted him. *Not that she'd had much choice in the matter, when her body had seemed to have an agenda all of its own...*

But then afterwards, when he had dropped her home to her flat after a near silent car journey filled with the most electrifying tension, Jake had confused her yet again when he'd insisted on accompanying her to her door and waiting until she'd got safely inside. There had been no sign of his earlier rejection at the concert.

The man was a genuine enigma and no mistake. Yet Caitlin understood why he had to put the band first. He wouldn't jeopardise Blue Sky's chances by having a meaningless fling with their new lead singer. *Not that any association with Jake, however brief, could ever be meaningless...*

'Have you had the chance to learn the two new songs I gave you?' Mike asked, his glance flicking interestedly over the pretty white gypsy-style blouse she was wearing with faded blue jeans.

'After I got home from the gig I was up most of last night working on them,' Caitlin told him, suppressing a yawn. She carefully withdrew a folded sheet of paper from her jeans pocket. 'Do you want to give them a try?'

'Sure. That would be great.' Picking up his guitar again, Mike started to tune it.

The unexpected sound of a ring on the doorbell interrupted him and he broke off to spring nimbly to his feet. During his absence Caitlin took the opportunity to lean back against the edge of the pink velour couch behind her, stretch out her legs and idly finger her guitar strings. As much as she wanted and needed to learn the songs, it had probably not been the most sensible thing to do to stay up long into the early hours trying to master them. *What she wouldn't give for a long lie-down...*

Her eyes drifting closed, she was just wondering how on earth she was going to get through the rest of the day when the sense that she had company alerted her. She looked up to find Jake staring down at her. He had a disconcerting glint in his eye that made Caitlin shiver helplessly, and she hastily sat up to drape her arm protectively across her guitar. *What had she done wrong now?*

'Hi.' It wasn't easy to sound casual when all she could think about was what had happened between them at the gig. But straight away Jake was all business.

'You're giving rehearsals a miss this afternoon. We're going out,' he declared.

Dazedly, she answered, 'We are?'

Mike had come back into the room behind him and her gaze swung from his to Mike's and back again.

'Not Mike,' Jake qualified firmly. 'Just you and me. I'm taking you shopping.'

'But I don't want to go shopping.' Caitlin didn't even pause to wonder what for. All she knew was that she was in no fit condition to trudge round some overheated shopping mall—with or *without* Jake.

'This has got to be a first. A woman who doesn't like shopping? Where have you been all my life?' Mike joked.

But Jake didn't look remotely amused. His handsome countenance was as implacable as usual. In his black leather coat and blue jeans, his square jaw fashionably unshaven, he looked as if he was in no mood to entertain an argument, no matter how convincing or passionate. Caitlin tensed.

'Get your coat,' he ordered.

'But Mike and I were just—'

'I'm not interested. I just want you to get your coat and be quick about it. I don't want this to take any longer than it has to.'

He had a nerve! It was at Jake's suggestion the previous night that Caitlin had come round to Mike's to get some guitar practice in.

'You can't just walk in here and tell me what to do.' She defiantly stayed where she was, even though her heart was beating like a jackhammer. Blue Sky's lead guitarist was staring down at his feet as if they were suddenly the most interesting sight in the world. *No moral support there, she thought irritably.*

'I thought I'd just done exactly that.' Lifting a mocking eyebrow, Jake was unimpressed. 'Now, if you want to continue to be a member of this band, I'd seriously consider doing what you're told and being quick about it. We're driving to London, and at this rate we won't get there before one o'clock. That hardly gives us enough time.'

'Enough time for *what*?'

Clearly mad at him, Caitlin finally got to her feet, gripping her precious guitar by its neck as if it was Jake's neck she'd like to throttle. Her pretty face was flushed with emotion, her bewitching emerald eyes spitting fire, and in that instant Jake experienced a longing for her so deep that it hurt.

He knew he was only being short-tempered because he was furious with himself for wanting her so badly. Tough. Life could be unfair like that. If there had been the remotest possibility that they could find another singer even half as good as Caitlin, then he would seriously have considered letting her go. The band and Rick would undoubtedly give him hell but, damn it, if it was a choice between confronting their rage and losing his sanity then he knew which one he'd plump for.

The sheets on his bed had been a crumpled mess when he'd woken this morning. If he'd slept two hours he'd be surprised. It had been a hell of a long time since any woman had got Jake in such a stew—not since Jodie, and that had been six years ago. But even at the height of his attraction to Jodie it had never been like this. This mindless, helpless, heated longing that he felt for Caitlin was driving him slowly crazy.

If she had been any other woman but Blue Sky's new lead singer he wouldn't have hesitated in succumbing to his carnal desires. But Caitlin Ryan was strictly off-limits. *Hadn't he said so to himself when he'd first heard her sing?*

'Jake?' When he didn't immediately reply, but levelled his compelling blue gaze straight at her in warning, Caitlin had to suppress the worrying impulse to leave, to put herself out of the line of fire. Why was he so furious with her? What had she done to make him so disagreeable?

'You need some clothes,' he explained grudgingly. 'Working clothes. The band plays its first date in London next week and we need to kit you out. I've arranged to meet a stylist I've worked with for years…someone I trust who will help guide you. Her name is Ronnie. Rick has had to drive up north on business, so today's a good opportunity to sort things out. Now, go and get your coat…*please.*'

Driving a weary hand through his tousled mane, Jake looked as if his patience was being sorely tested. In the meantime, Caitlin's mind was racing. *He was taking her to buy clothes?* That would mean she'd have to parade herself in front of him, not to mention this stylist, whilst getting hot and bothered, trying on garments in cramped changing rooms and no doubt feeling woefully inadequate when something didn't look right or didn't fit.

Was it really necessary that he go with her? And did she really need a professional stylist to help her choose the right clothes? Couldn't Jake simply trust her own judgement as far as dressing herself went?

One look into that arrogant male visage and she had her answer. She could stand there and argue until they got old and Jake would still insist on going with her.

'I hate and detest shopping,' she said, before turning on her heel and grabbing her coat off the back of the pink velour armchair. 'And if you think for one second that I'm pouring myself into some horrible skin-tight catsuit for the sake of this band then you've got another think coming!'

And with that she shouldered angrily past Jake out into the hallway—but not before suffering the added indignity of hearing the two men she'd left behind chuckling between them in some ancient patronising ritual of amused male bonding.

CHAPTER SIX

JAKE COULDN'T REMEMBER the last time he'd had so much fun. Nor could he remember his inflamed libido being put under such torturous conditions in an even longer time. An obliging assistant—a skinny little redhead, with pansy-blue eyes and freckles—had thoughtfully supplied him with a comfy chair while Ronnie, the dependable stylist, selected several items of clothing from the rails and at regular intervals handed them to Caitlin to try on.

As she disappeared in and out of the changing room, trying on various different outfits, her expression veered alternately from plain put upon to seriously contemplating doing him some damage. The funny thing was, even when she was scowling at him, Caitlin was prettier and sexier than any other woman he could think of. So, although their little shopping trip had a serious purpose, it was also providing Jake with some royal entertainment.

'You didn't tell me this would be one of the easiest assignments you've ever given me, Jake. This girl is an absolute dream to dress!' The fashionable and gamine stylist curved her scarlet-painted lips with pleasure as she dropped down beside Jake. 'I mean, I've dressed some of the best female recording artists in the world, and all I can tell you is if she sings as good as she looks…'

'She does,' he assured her laconically. Then, with a sigh, he added, 'Whether you're a record producer or the manager of a band, singers like Caitlin come along once in a lifetime…*if* you're lucky.'

'Then one thing's for sure, my friend,' Ronnie said, knowingly patting his knee. 'The rest of the music industry will be quaking in their boots—because without a doubt this amazing find of yours is definitely going to put you back in the game…with bells on!'

And on that note, as if on cue, with an impatient swish of the changing room curtain Caitlin suddenly appeared before them wearing red faux leather jeans cut low on the hip and a sheer white chiffon blouse that had a lacy frill edging the cuffs. And, because the diaphanous blouse revealed so much more than it concealed, Jake was treated to the captivating sight of her luscious breasts crammed into a flimsy white lace bra that appeared barely equipped to contain them. He also saw that she had a deeply sexy belly button that put him in mind of a harem and long, hot desert nights…

With her arms akimbo, she glanced first at Ronnie, then at him, and her bewitching green eyes clearly proclaimed her disdain.

'I hope you're both satisfied. In my opinion, I look utterly ridiculous in this outfit.' Flicking back her shining dark hair in a huff, Caitlin flushed, her apple cheeks growing even pinker.

When Ronnie would have gone across to reassure her, Jake immediately rose to his feet to take charge.

'Let *me*,' he told her meaningfully, lowering his voice.

He made his way over to his new protégée.

'Believe me, you look anything *but* ridiculous.'

A heated injection of pure carnal pleasure pulsed through him as he came face to face with Caitlin's arrestingly beautiful gaze. His blood had been simmering since she had got into the car with him outside Mike's place and, as entertaining and necessary as it was, this little fashion parade wasn't helping.

Everything about the woman was driving him wild…her scent, her beautiful emerald eyes, that gorgeous long black hair of hers, and even the endearing little habit she had of chewing down on her lower lip when she was feeling over-whelmed or anxious. *As for her figure… Ever since he had seen it he'd been thanking God he was born a man.* It was a shame they were in one of his stylist's favourite fashion houses or he might have demonstrated his appreciation a little more graphically.

'Well, I'm not going on stage looking like this. I haven't become a singer for people to ogle me. If you like the outfit so much, why don't *you* wear it and be done with it!'

Caitlin stepped towards Jake as if she'd like to wipe the smile right off his face with a slap. Towering over her, he immediately closed the gap between them and made him-self slowly breathe out.

'Calm down. You're getting all hot and bothered for noth-ing.'

Hot and bothered didn't begin to describe how Jake was feeling. God knew he was making a supreme effort to cor-ral his aroused feelings, but it was damn near impossible with Caitlin huffing and pink-cheeked in front of him, her luscious breasts rising and falling with every breath that she took.

'Ronnie and I just wanted you to try a few different looks. It doesn't mean you have to go with anything that doesn't feel right. Ultimately it's your decision.'

Jake's reassurance effectively took the wind out of Cait-lin's sails. She hadn't meant to be deliberately obstructive, but appearing in revealing clothing in front of *anyone,* let alone Jake, wasn't something that came remotely easy to her. It wasn't anyone's fault that she was so insecure about her body, but she *was*. She'd often been teased as a child for being 'chubby', and even though she knew rationally that she was in good shape now she guessed that the hurt of being picked on and singled out because of her appearance had never quite left her.

But maybe this was her chance to overcome her insecu-rities and act differently for once. In any case, the least she could do was have a sense of humour about the proceedings. The fact was, she was a singer in a rock band and people would expect her to look the part...even to look *sexy*.

Cringing at the thought, she suddenly found herself unable to meet Jake's glance directly. He was so arresting, from the top of his tousled dark hair and the haunting chiselled perfection of his face to the tips of his feet in his stylish worn leather boots. In his long leather coat, with tight jeans and a midnight-blue shirt opened casually at the neck, he wore his clothes as if he didn't give a damn...which made it all the more challenging for Caitlin, knowing she regularly had to face him.

'I don't like wearing this kind of revealing clothing. I'm just not comfortable dressing to show off my body,' she admitted quietly. And because she was feeling vulnerable, every cell vibrating with the tension of being so intimately scrutinised, she folded her arms across her chest, only too aware that Jake's heated blue gaze kept dipping helplessly to that area.

'Why?' Nonplussed, he shook his head. 'Tell me what's going on in your head that makes you feel embarrassed about revealing such a God-given asset? Because that's what it is, Caitlin.'

His glance momentarily flicked towards the elegant and manicured Ronnie, who sat waiting patiently for him to finish before coming over to join them and give her opinion.

'It's not easy to explain,' Caitlin answered.

Jake turned back to her to give her his full attention. Taking up where he'd left off, he remarked, 'You're beautiful, Caitlin. If I gave you a bin liner to wear you'd still look stunning. Why don't you just enjoy being young, having the freedom to dress a little outrageously?'

'It's all right for a man to come out with that, isn't it?' Furiously twining her hair behind her ear, Caitlin glared. 'Women don't leave men just because they get older. Even nowadays, when you'd think we would have got a little bit more enlightened, older men are labelled "interesting" or "experienced" while the complete reverse is applied to women.'

An amused smile twitched at the corners of Jake's lips.

Caitlin paused. Maybe she was overreacting. After all, surely he had a point—she should take advantage of being young and free and go wild. Still, his sentiment had struck a nerve. Was Jake the kind of man who would leave a woman just because she was getting older or had put on weight? The music industry was hardly known for nurturing healthy relationships, was it? Not when everything seemed to be dominated by image these days.

The pop charts were littered with pretty young things with average talent and attractive bodies who had their five minutes of fame and then disappeared. But, as far as relationships went, it didn't mean that she couldn't fantasise about one day finding a man who wanted to stay with her come what may. It was just a shame that Jake Sorenson clearly *wasn't* and never could be that man. He might be attracted to her because he admired the 'packaging', but that was all it was: a passing meaningless attraction that would no doubt blow itself out as soon as he'd taken her to bed... *if she let him.*

The thought made her heart slam against her ribs.

'Don't paint all us men with the same brush.' Reaching out his hand, Jake gently loosed the glossy strand of hair that Caitlin had tucked behind her ear and watched it glance against her cheek as it fell silkily down to her shoulder. 'I sincerely hope I'm not as shallow as you seem to think I am. When you get past the physical attraction, I'm quite aware there's got to be something deeper and more compelling to keep both parties in a relationship interested. If I found a woman I wanted to spend the rest of my life with I'd never let her go…no matter what happened.'

Jake's arresting blue eyes were regarding her so intently that Caitlin felt the imprint of his gaze resonate deep inside her. Along with the heartfelt words he'd expressed, his intensely examining glance shook and unravelled her. It made her body burn and her heart race. It stirred a longing in her for things that she knew could never be.

'This is the last outfit Ronnie gave me to try on. I think I'll go and get changed now. I suddenly feel quite cold.'

Despite the intimacy that Jake had woven round them, the harsh cold reality of the situation suddenly doused the heat that had all but drowned her just a moment ago. *Caitlin was beginning to care too much for Jake and that was dangerous.*

Turning away, she rubbed briskly at the chilled flesh on her arms in the diaphanous blouse, and was taken aback when he moved swiftly behind her and turned her firmly back round to face him.

'That first outfit you tried on…the purple velvet top and the long black skirt with the chain belt? That looked great. Shall we go with that for starters?'

A muscle flexed in the side of his lean jaw. The outfit he'd described was one of her favourites, too. *It seemed that they agreed on something after all.*

'Okay.'

'And, by the way, we're not going straight home after this. We're going back to Ronnie's place for a while, then I'm taking you to a club. We'll eat dinner there and enjoy some entertainment.'

He was taking her to a club? What was that all about?

'Why didn't you mention this before? What kind of club?'

Jake's expression remained as inscrutable as ever, yet he definitely had a twinkle in his eye. Caitlin frowned. *What on earth was the man up to?*

'I wanted it to be a surprise,' he drawled. 'Hopefully an enjoyable one.'

'I've hardly got the right clothes with me to go out for the evening…especially to a club. Can't we leave it for another night?'

Ignoring her hopeful plea, he clenched his jaw and firmly shook his head.

'Sorry, but you're not going to wriggle out of this one. Trust me. Tonight will be just what you need. As for not having the right clothes—why don't you pick out one of the outfits you were looking at to wear? You can get ready at Ronnie's.'

'Those outfits are ludicrously expensive, Jake! I can't afford—'

'I'm footing the bill. You can have anything you like—and I mean anything. Think of it as a gift.'

More than a little overwhelmed by his unexpected generosity, she was almost lost for words. 'Well...I mean, that's very kind of you, but just what kind of place is this club you're taking me to?'

He smiled one of his maddening sexy smiles that could stop a woman in her tracks in less than a heartbeat and said, 'It's classy...very classy. That's all you need to know.'

'Let me help you to choose something. Jake has told me where you'll be going and I know the perfect outfit. We'll also need to accessorise you with shoes and jewellery to complete the look.'

The fragrant Ronnie was suddenly at her side and, whilst Caitlin had plenty of reservations about being kitted out for an evening out with Jake somewhere 'classy', she sensed that any more attempts at wriggling out of the night's events would be a waste of energy.

In the sumptuous mirrored enclave of the exclusive members-only jazz club, frequented not just by aficionados but by many well-known celebrities from the worlds of music and film, Jake sat opposite Caitlin at a beautifully laid dining table and thanked the gods for giving him a legitimate excuse simply to sit and gaze at her.

Ronnie had helped select the perfect outfit for her tonight. The powers of the 'little black dress' should never be underestimated, she'd told him knowledgeably, and she'd been right. The slinky little number she'd come up with had taken his breath away when he'd seen Caitlin wearing it. It had a daringly low-cut neckline that immediately drew the eye to her sensational cleavage, and the fitted black satin clung to her body in all the right places. The voluptuous curves that she contrived to keep hidden from the world were tonight displayed in all their glory.

Add to that some sexy red lipstick and the sultry, alluring perfume that Jake had chosen especially for her—*he'd slipped out to purchase it as Caitlin had got dressed*—and he doubted there was a single male in the vicinity who would ever forget seeing her.

He sucked in some air and breathed it out again slowly. An unexpected need to protect her had crept into his blood and he couldn't help now and again surveying the other diners in case they looked a little *too* interested in her. He knew it was crazy when very soon Caitlin would be appearing with the band and from then on would be in the public domain. But in light of his protective feelings and undeniable need to keep her to himself, how was he going to handle it? he wondered. *It was a dilemma that had never affected him before...*

The manager of the venue—an immaculately dressed Frenchman called Dion, who famously took great pride in entertaining an elite clientele—had expressed delight at seeing Jake. It had been a long time since the two men had met. The last occasion had been just before his ex had written that dreadful exposé about him. After that Jake had retreated to lick his wounds and kept a deliberately low profile. Even so, the Frenchman had recognised Jake straight away.

'It's so nice to see you back in public again, Mr Sorenson,' he'd told him. 'It's been too long.' Then he'd turned to Caitlin and commented, 'Many beautiful women come to this establishment, but *you ma chère...*you take my breath away!'

In truth, Jake had almost been readying himself for a small stampede when he'd walked in with Caitlin on his

arm. He'd honestly sensed the moment when the other stylishly attired patrons seated at the tables had drawn in a collective awed breath. They might be surprised at seeing him
out in public again, but he doubted their interest was solely
in him. The woman by his side was the main reason they
glanced their way, and Jake would be a liar if he didn't admit
to feeling both pride and pleasure at the realisation. After
all, he was only human.

Although the club featured predominantly jazz, and there
was a smoky-sounding sax playing in the background, tonight was Burlesque night,—and that was what he'd brought
Caitlin to see.

'This is some place,' she commented shyly.

'And you've just elevated it to a whole other class,' he
said, and smiled.

Delicately sipping her Margarita, she added, 'I feel so
guilty drinking this when you're just drinking soda and
lime.'

'There's no need. I'm quite happy being teetotal tonight.
Especially when I have a very precious cargo to drive home,'
he teased.

Jake supposed it was inevitable that the compliment
would make her cheeks turn pink, but he loved to see her
blush. It reminded him that she was still relatively innocent...*quite a rarity in his world.*

'I've heard of Burlesque, but I don't know very much
about it. Isn't it some kind of variety show?' she enquired.

Even before he told her the answer Jake sensed the muscles in his belly clench hard in anticipation of her reaction.

'It can be that. But Burlesque is really an art form...it's
about celebrating the beauty of the female form.'

'Oh...? You mean it involves things like striptease?'

'It's much more than women simply taking their clothes
off. Sometimes all a girl might remove are her gloves. But
it's the way they do it that makes it an art form. Plus the costumes the girls wear and the way they move is part of the

spectacle. I just want you to sit back and enjoy it…to feel proud of being a woman.'

'Is that why you brought me here? To show me how women can be confident about displaying their bodies when they perform? So I won't be self-conscious when I perform with the band?'

'Yes. You're already going to command the stage with that incredible voice of yours, but I don't want any doubts about your body to hold you back. I want you to enjoy every second you're on that stage when you perform.'

To his surprise, Caitlin downed what was left of her cocktail with a flourish, licked her lips and declared, 'In that case I think I'd like another drink…a little Dutch courage wouldn't go amiss. Do you mind?'

'Are you serious?' Leaning over to her, Jake tenderly stroked the pad of his thumb down over her cheek and said huskily, 'Baby, do you have *any* idea how dangerously alluring you are in that dress? If you asked me to get you the moon I'd do my damnedest to get it for you.'

'Oh, I wouldn't expect you to go *that* far,' she said, and grinned.

His lips twitching in amusement and delight, because Caitlin was clearly starting to enjoy herself, Jake signalled for a waitress to take his order just as the sultry sax in the background came to a sudden halt, the lights dimmed and all eyes turned expectantly towards the stage…

The show was spectacular. Caitlin was swept away by the sumptuous display of dance and movement from the predominantly 'Rubenesque' women who took to the stage in their stunning costumes and exaggerated make-up. At no point did she feel remotely embarrassed or self-conscious at all the comely flesh on display. For perhaps the very first time she felt proud to be a woman and unashamed of her own voluptuous curves.

Jake had been right. It had been a good idea to bring her to a Burlesque night. *But her companion hadn't reserved all his attention for the show.* More than once throughout the evening she'd caught him looking at her as though mesmerised, despite having a bevy of stunning women on the stage in front of them.

That brooding glance of his had made Caitlin feel more than a little aroused. In fact it had made her long for him to take her somewhere private so that she could demonstrate exactly just how excited he made her feel... And Jake wasn't the only one who was enjoying the view. Dressed in the flawless single-breasted Armani suit that unbeknownst to her he'd brought with him to change into for their visit to the club, with his incredible blue eyes glinting like diamonds and his chiselled jaw dusted with late-night shadow, he looked expensive and assured, and he exuded the kind of charisma usually attributed to A-list movie stars.

Caitlin wanted to pinch herself to make sure she wasn't dreaming that he was solely hers for the evening. Who would have guessed that a man who famously adopted a 'don't give a damn' attitude about what he was wearing could wear a tux with such effortless panache?

Later that night, as Jake turned the Jeep onto the motorway to head home, he wondered wryly if Caitlin had any idea what a test it was for him to concentrate on his driving when she was snuggled in the seat next to him wearing that alluring black dress. The 'LBD', as Ronnie had called it, had put him in a state of highly charged sexual tension for the whole evening, and he knew it wasn't going to dissipate easily.

By the time they'd reached the village and Jake had pulled up outside Caitlin's flat he was honestly glad of the opportunity to get a breath of fresh air to help him think straight. But first he had to wake her and help her to the door, because she'd fallen asleep as soon as they'd got into the car. It was inevitable she would be a little drowsy.

'Hey, sleepyhead, we're home.'

Curling his hand round her slim upper arm, Jake shook

her gently. The second she opened her big green eyes the tension that already gripped him mercilessly doubled.

'Have I been asleep? I must have been, because that journey went in a blink.'

Shaking her head, Caitlin undid her seatbelt and sat up. Her lustrous dark hair spilled down over her shoulders and the air was suddenly provocatively imbued with the sultry scent Jake had bought her. *What had he been trying to do? Make her even more irresistible than she was already?*

'Well, we're home now, and you need to get straight to bed,' he stated, almost groaning out loud at his ill thought out choice of words—because that was *exactly* where he'd like to go with her. 'Give me your key. I'll open the door for you,' he added.

The cold night air hit him as soon as he stepped out of the car and proved to be just the tonic he needed to cool his blood. Quickly inserting Caitlin's key into the lock, he opened the door onto the hallway and waited for her to step over the threshold in front of him. As soon as she did Jake's blood was stirred all over again when she turned back towards him. She'd draped her jacket over her shoulders and now tugged the sides more closely over her chest, but not before he had a glimpse of her delectable cleavage. *For both their sakes he should say goodnight and leave her.* His usually dependable sense of control was rapidly deserting him.

But his decision was immediately compromised when Caitlin narrowed the gap between them and said softly, 'Thanks for a really wonderful evening, Jake, and also for the lovely clothes and everything. You made me feel like a princess, and no one's ever done that for me before.'

'It wasn't difficult, Caitlin. In my eyes you *are* a princess.'

It was then that Jake thought, *To hell with self-control* and pulled her into his arms. He kissed her with a hunger he could no longer deny, and the desire that was always just a breath away whenever they were together flared beyond control. But when Caitlin carefully freed her lips and he saw the longing in her eyes—*the kind of longing that went way beyond a desire simply to make love*—the immensity of what he was contemplating and the possible consequences hit him like a brick dropped from a great height.

With his heart thundering, Jake moved out of their embrace. 'I think it's time we said goodnight, don't you? It's been a long day for both of us and we're just a couple of days away from the band's first live performance. We need to get some rest to make sure we're fit for what's to come.'

'I know you're right, but—'

Even before Caitlin had finished what she was saying Jake was out through the door and walking towards the car.

Two days of intense rehearsal followed Caitlin's magical night out with Jake. And, although she'd had a wonderful time, she couldn't forget how quickly he'd distanced himself from her after he'd dropped her home—even though just before he'd left, his lips had passionately claimed hers as if he really meant it. Now he was acting as if the kiss had never even happened. It was easy to sense that his focus was back on the band and what lay ahead of them, but Caitlin couldn't help feeling he was somehow abandoning her.

A couple of evenings later Jake surprised them all by giving them a day off. They'd had two more gruelling days of rehearsal and they more than welcomed the unexpected opportunity for a bit of 'R&R'. But, although Caitlin appreciated being able to rest and have a day to herself, she started to fret about the upcoming live shows. The new-found confidence she'd experienced after seeing the Burlesque seemed to be rapidly diminishing.

Having the day off hadn't helped. All it had done was to make her worry even more. That was why she found herself making her way to the Pilgrim's Inn that night, hopefully to see Jake and express her concerns. Just a few dedicated patrons occupied the cosily lit lounge bar and Caitlin was grateful, because it had taken every ounce of courage she could muster to make this eleventh hour trip to speak with Jake.

As far as Blue Sky's enigmatic manager was concerned his new lead singer would be having an early night and dreaming about what a resounding success she was going to be when she debuted with the band—because tomorrow was the big day: the day when Blue Sky introduced their new female vocalist to the world…or at least to the audience at the famous rock café in London where they were playing.

But Caitlin wasn't just apprehensive about what lay ahead, she was plain *petrified*—so petrified that she was suddenly having some serious doubts.

I'm sorry but I've made a terrible mistake. She heard the words go round and round in her head and imagined the confusion and then anger in Jake's eyes when she said them.

She sighed. *She didn't really want to quit.* All she was looking for was a little reassurance. If Jake couldn't give it to her, after all his years of experience in working with singers and musicians, she didn't have a prayer.

Tina Stevens was busy polishing the bar, her jaw working overtime as she chewed on some gum, her long red nails clicking against the varnished wood as she ran a duster over the already shiny surface of the counter. The brown eyes that were heavily outlined with kohl gave Caitlin a cool once-over as she approached, but she continued to polish as though her life depended on it.

'Excuse me, I—'

'What can I get you, love? Are you on your own or are you meeting somebody?'

There was a distinct note of disapproval in the blonde's voice, as if she believed that women who came into bars on their own somehow spelt trouble.

For a disconcerting moment Caitlin wondered if Tina had been working that night when Sean had turned particularly nasty. But, unable to remember very much other than the soul-destroying humiliation of being insulted by her boyfriend in public, she opted not to dwell on it. *Goodness knew she had enough on her mind without fretting about the past.* All she wanted—all she needed—was for Jake to tell her that everything would be all right, that she wasn't about to suffer another humiliation tomorrow night when she sang.

'I'm not meeting anybody.' Pushing her rain-dampened fringe out of her eyes, she squared her shoulders in her long charcoal-coloured raincoat. 'I wondered if I could have a word with Jake Sorenson? He's staying here, isn't he?'

Immediately Tina stopped polishing, and her expression was far from convivial. As the two women faced each other the record that was playing on the juke box suddenly changed and a song that Caitlin remembered from her childhood replaced it. *It was her mother's favourite song.*

An avid music fan, Terry Ryan had played the tune to death when Caitlin was little. She would enfold her little daughter in her arms and dance round the room with her, crooning gently against her cheek as she softly sang the words, whilst Phil—Caitlin's older brother—who was disdainful of anything remotely 'girly' would groan in mockery.

'Typical boy!' her mother would say, and laugh, instantly forgiving him as though it was his birthright.

Memories... Caitlin suddenly found herself pole-axed by them. Treacherously, her eyes filled with tears. What was *wrong* with her?

She was missing her family—that was what was wrong. Here she was, on the eve of what could be one of the most important nights of her life, and where were her parents and brother? On the other side of the world! They were completely oblivious to the fact that Caitlin had resigned from her job, never mind joined a rock band as their lead singer!

She had never felt as alone or as afraid as she did right then. She was twenty-six years old, about to embark on the biggest challenge she could imagine, with nothing but her dreams, her wits and her talent to help see her through.

'You must be Cait...the singer.'

As if it had suddenly dawned on her who Caitlin was, Tina stopped chewing her gum and crossed her arms in front of her chest. The sudden movement jiggled her ample breasts in the red V-necked angora sweater she wore. Well... *nearly* wore.

'It's Caitlin.' The correction of her name was automatic. She remembered that Rick had been using the shortened version of it since he'd met her, and that he apparently had a real soft spot for the buxom Miss Stevens.

'Yeah...right. All set for tomorrow, then?' the other girl asked.

Not really.

'I hope so. Could I see Jake?' Caitlin's lip quivered a little as she made an attempt at a friendly smile.

'Room Three. Turn left at the top of the stairs.'

'Thanks.'

'Nice talking to you.'

Could have fooled me, Caitlin thought.

Making her way up the thickly carpeted staircase, with its faded floral tread, she focused her gaze on the landing at the top, on the ponderous oak sideboard with its gaudy Victorian lamp and the sepia-toned photographs of the village that were displayed on the wall behind it.

The dark old-fashioned surroundings seemed incongruous when she thought of Jake. She wondered why he hadn't rented a house in the village, like the other band members had. But then it occurred to her that maybe Rick had something to do with his decision to stay at the Pilgrim's Inn. Perhaps the voluptuous Tina Stevens had an equally arresting friend he wanted to introduce to Jake, for instance?

Disliking that particular train of thought, Caitlin arrived at the top of the stairs and glanced anxiously round her. Two doors faced each other across the landing. Before she could talk herself out of it she rapped briskly on number three. She immediately registered the sound of male voices coming from the room and realised that Jake and Rick must be in conference about the concert tomorrow.

She didn't know whether to stay put or turn around and leave. But the decision was made for her when the door suddenly opened and Rick appeared. Untypically, when his usual mode of dress was more extrovert, he was wearing a pair of ordinary faded Levi's and a plain white T-shirt.

He gave Caitlin his trademark roguish smile when he saw that it was her. 'Hello, gorgeous. Come to join the party?'

His candid gaze moved over her figure in her buttoned-up raincoat—possibly the most unsexy item of clothing she possessed. But Caitlin didn't give the thought much attention.

'No. I mean, I just came to see Jake…if I could?'

Her mouth suddenly drying, she stared across the top of Rick's hard-muscled shoulder and found the man she was looking for. His long-legged form was lounging in an over-stuffed green and gold striped armchair and his glance met hers, a knowing smile curving his lips. *He looked as if he'd been expecting her visit.*

Her feverish thoughts went into overdrive. He'd given them all the day off and advised them to get an early night in preparation for the following day, but he clearly didn't apply the advice to himself. Did the man *ever* get an early night in his business? Caitlin somehow doubted it.

'If I've come at a bad time—' she started, suddenly embarrassed. Had any of his other artists ever sought him out the night before a debut concert to seek his reassurance she wondered? Would her sudden attack of nerves disturb him and make him doubt his decision to hire her as Marcie's replacement?

He must have intuited that she was on the point of changing her mind about talking to him because he said suddenly, 'Stay right where you are.'

The words were uttered like a command from on high and Caitlin immediately froze. Rick sighed and moved away as Jake took a couple of leisurely strides towards her. As he drew near she saw that his hard, lean jaw was dark with late-night shadow and his slightly cool stare put her on her guard. That less than friendly glance hardly invited a frank admission about her doubts and feelings concerning the gig tomorrow, she thought anxiously.

'I thought you might come to see me tonight,' he drawled.

'Did you?' Caitlin heard the strength in her voice desert her.

'Yes, I did' He turned round to find Rick. 'Give us a few minutes, will you? Come to think of it, we'll probably need a little longer than that. Go and have a drink with Tina.'

Looking doubtful, his colleague shrugged. 'I'd really like to oblige, Jake, but whether Miss Cold-as-Ice down there will even serve me is another matter. We've had a bit of a falling out.'

'You brought it on yourself, Rick. Sort it out.'

'Sure. You're the boss.'

Clearly unhappy, Rick didn't say another word. But he still found a smile for Caitlin as he passed her. Then he left the room, shutting the door firmly behind him. She shivered. She suddenly didn't feel at all easy about finding herself alone with Jake.

'Can I get you a drink?' The charismatic manager strolled across to another ponderous Victorian sideboard and, opening a door, extracted a bottle of Bourbon along with two glasses.

'No. Not for me, thanks.'

When Caitlin declined his offer without further ado he poured himself a conservative amount of alcohol into a shot glass and advanced slowly towards her. Not for a second did he take his glance off her. His blue eyes glinted dangerously, just like a shaft of sunlight catching the burnished blade of a sword. She couldn't help tensing. *The charming man in the Armani tux who had taken her to the Burlesque had apparently disappeared.*

Tipping back his glass, Jake swallowed down the drink

before saying, 'So…care to tell me why you've come to see me tonight, Caitlin? It certainly isn't to make small talk, is it? What's on your mind? In my experience there's only *one* reason a woman comes to a man's hotel room late at night.'

As if to illustrate what he meant, he flicked his intense gaze over her as if he'd like to strip every stitch from her body and devour her, and then take his slow, sweet time doing it all over again.

Caitlin tried desperately to calm the rioting sensations he was stirring inside her.

'Well, that's not the reason I came to see you, Jake… as hard as that might be for your ego to take. My visit is a purely practical one.'

'Is it?' His expression doubtful, he put his glass down on a nearby side table and turned back to give her a deliberately lazy smile. 'You break my heart, Caitlin Ryan…but I think you know that, don't you?'

'What do you mean?'

Her mind was in a complete spin, and if she hadn't backed herself up against the door just then there was a distinct danger that she might simply have crumpled to the floor. Her legs were trembling so hard they hardly seemed to have the strength to keep her upright.

'What you do to me with those slow, hot looks of yours is nothing less than criminal.'

His voice a low, grating rasp, Jake yanked her away from the door and pulled her roughly into his arms.

CHAPTER SEVEN

CRIMINAL... CAITLIN COULD have used the same adjective to describe Jake's kiss. The way he took her mouth was near savage, and it almost knocked her off of her feet. This was no inept fumbling, no tentative exploration, but a devastating passionate assault on the senses.

With a hungry groan that seemed to emanate from the depths of his soul, he swept his tongue over the warm recesses of her surprised mouth as one firm hand possessively anchored itself in the long thick strands of her hair to render the contact between them even more intimate.

As his tongue thrust deeper, harder, mimicking the ultimate sexual coupling between a man and a woman, Caitlin swallowed her breath, tasting him, her senses intoxicated by the dark sultry flavours of bourbon and avaricious heat. She gripped onto the sensuous silk of his shirt with all the strength and tenacity of someone hanging from a precipice by their fingertips...as if she dangled into empty space and could fall at any moment.

But from the instant Jake had captured her mouth there had been no thought to deny him. Not when everything in her clamoured wildly for more of the same. Only a frigid woman could not want what Jake was giving her right now, and Caitlin was anything but that. She was a living, breathing, loving human being, and it was too long since she'd been held and desired—too long since she'd been loved like a woman longed to be loved by a man.

Oh God...how did I survive without this? she thought.

All she knew was that her legs suddenly didn't have a hope of holding her up for very much longer. Not when the equivalent of a hundred volts of pure unadulterated pleasure was pulsating through her as though she were plugged in to her own personal ecstasy machine.

Almost mindlessly driving her hips against Jake's, she heard herself moaning urgent little sounds of want and need—sounds that were as alien to her as this wild, savage joy that was pouring through her veins. Sean had never taken her anywhere *near* close to the kind of heights Jake was taking her to now. Never before had passion come at her like a wild, untamed river, bursting its banks, sweeping everything that stood in its way to exciting unchartered shores that left her dazed and trembling.

Hungrily she acquiesced as he alternately nipped and grazed at her mouth, every now and then her tongue meeting and dancing with his, her breasts burning into the hard granite wall of his chest. She was certain of one thing and one thing only...that she never wanted this sweet, irresistible agony to end.

Unbelievably, Jake turned up the heat. Now their invisible passion dial hovered somewhere between boiling and the point of no return. As he rocked his hips deep into hers the solid ridge of his button fly was testimony to his driving, hungry need, and when he suddenly broke contact to look down at her Caitlin glanced back at him in surprise.

It was a shock to witness the depth and strength of desire contained in that blistering gaze. His pupils were almost totally black, ringed with just the slimmest band of devastating blue. From his lips his breath issued hard and fast, and there was a thin sheen of sweat on his ridged brow.

'I don't want our first time to be up against a door. You've got to tell me what you want, baby.'

As he finished speaking he reached behind him and shot

the bolt, enveloping her in a dizzying cloak of heat and his disturbing, sensuous male essence.

'Do you want to stay with me tonight? We can go to bed now and finish what we started. I can keep you up all night and give you pleasure like you've never dreamed. Is that what you want?'

With deft fingers Jake freed the top three buttons on her coat and jerked the material aside to cup her breast through the thin material of her T-shirt. Her nipple, already rigid and tingling with need, pressed helplessly, wantonly into his palm.

Why did he have to stop and ask what she wanted? Caitlin thought. Why couldn't he just carry on the way they were going and take what she was so ready to give him?

She was shocked at the desperation of her wild thoughts. What he was doing—his long fingers now circling the nipple of her other breast, alternately nipping and squeezing—was making her womb throb with an almost unholy ache. If he took her right now she'd welcome the possession and count herself blessed. *That was how much she wanted him.* She was hungry to feel his sex deep inside her, to complete the electrifying bond that had been slowly and devastatingly drawing them together since the very first moment they had met.

But this was crazy—and not just crazy, but completely and utterly reckless. Jake must surely know that? He was the one who'd sternly advised Caitlin against 'fraternising' with the band out of hours, and as he was their manager he had to include himself in that warning. The potential pitfalls of turning a working relationship into a personal one could only spell disaster.

And, anyway, it was wrong to assume that Jake even *wanted* a personal relationship with her. A hot and fast seduction in a hotel room didn't usually pave the way to something deeper and more meaningful, did it? Was sex all that he wanted from her? If it was, then it was nothing less than an insult—because she was sure he could get that from any woman.

Realising how close she had come to throwing away something precious—namely her self-respect—Caitlin flung Jake's hand away and straightened her T-shirt. As she did so her heartbeat accelerated so hard she was momentarily dizzy. Seeing the spasm of confusion in his eyes, she sensed tension of another kind radiating from his body.

'What's wrong?' he ground out.

'I'm not going to sleep with you, Jake.'

'Sleeping isn't exactly what I had in mind.'

His words made her flinch. Her body hadn't stopped aching for him, and her mouth throbbed and burned from his unbelievably passionate kisses, but the idea that he would bed her simply just to 'scratch an itch' hurt her deeply. Having already had the soul-destroying experience of being used by a man, she wasn't about to set herself up to play the same old destructive tape again…

'All right, then, let me put it this way.' Impatiently she pushed back a drifting strand of hair from the side of her face to unwaveringly meet his gaze. 'I'm not going to have sex with you. I won't jeopardise my relationship with the band and neither will I be used by you because I happen to be "convenient". And, contrary to what you might believe, I didn't come here tonight because I had something personal in mind. All I wanted was a little reassurance because I was nervous about the performance tomorrow.'

Jake cursed softly beneath his breath. His disturbing blue eyes raked over her features, pinning her to the spot. It was clear to Caitlin that he was immersed in a deep inner tussle between utilising his common sense and trying to curtail his desire. Like her, he was still reeling from the throes of the incendiary passion they'd ignited. There was a thin film of sweat on his brow and it was evident he was still turned on. With the fulfilment of his desire evidently thwarted, now he was frustrated and angry as well as aroused.

'Is that what you think? That I'd take advantage and use you just because I wanted sex?' A muscle flexed warningly in the side of his exquisitely carved cheekbone. 'If you think that then I seriously underestimated you, Caitlin. You've listened to all the less than flattering stories about me, bought them as fact, and condemned me even though I told you the truth about what happened between me and my ex. Don't you remember that it was *my* reputation that got dragged through the mud because of the lies she wrote in that blasted article? *Not* hers?'

Caitlin hardly knew what to say. Was she guilty of judging Jake without trial? Without even giving him the chance to prove his character? After all, it wasn't just him that had suddenly found himself driven by the libidinous desires of the body. She was in exactly the same position!

Sighing, he agitatedly drove through his fingers through his already mussed hair.

'Anyway, perhaps you'd better just leave before my "questionable" character contaminates you even more. You'd better get home and get some rest. You know what's ahead of you tomorrow and I want you to be at your best.'

Her heart almost thudded to a stop. Tomorrow *would* be a big day…perhaps the most important one of her life so far. It was a shame that she'd spoiled things by coming over to Jake's and starting something she couldn't finish.

'I'm sorry that I—that I…'

'Don't beat yourself up about it. You're going to be just fine, Caitlin. That's what you want to know, isn't it? All you have to do is concentrate on the songs, the music. Blue Sky is a great band and they'll be helping you every step of the way. It's not going to be as hard as you imagine. Trust me. You've got a great voice and you're a stunning-looking girl. In terms of fulfilling the criteria for success in this business, you've got it all. You can't fail.'

If Jake had meant to reassure her he'd done it in a strangely reticent way. Caitlin still felt ill at ease. Plus she could easily sense the anger that simmered beneath his thin veneer of civility.

'I was going to say that I was sorry for—' Blushing, she was unable to complete the sentence when he was all but eating her up with his eyes.

'Turning me on?'

'I think I should go.'

'As much as it pains me to agree with you, you're probably right. Though that doesn't mean I wish you weren't.'

His words taunted her as Caitlin turned and fumbled with the bolt on the door. Then she fled from the room with a breathless 'goodnight' before she could change her mind.

Right then it was tempting for Jake to search for solace in the bottle of bourbon he had opened, but he couldn't fool himself that it would help. He'd been through enough heartache in his life already to think that it would.

His ex's wasn't the only betrayal he had endured. His mother had given him up for adoption when she'd found herself pregnant at just sixteen, and the home where she had placed Jake hadn't been able to find him adoptive parents due to his having a heart murmur. He had been in and out of hospital from birth up until he was eight years old for regular check-ups, by which time he had become quite used to being a bit of a loner. As he'd grown up and become stronger physically the heart murmur had corrected itself and he had resigned himself to living in the children's home until he reached sixteen.

Jake hadn't viewed it as a negative thing because by necessity it had taught him to be self-reliant. *The only friends he had depended on had been his books.* He had developed an insatiable curiosity about the world and had genuinely enjoyed reading and studying. Having done well in his exams, he'd managed to get himself a place at college, and then he'd found himself at university, studying cultural anthropology.

It was during that time that he had also developed an abiding interest in music. Jake's time at college and university had been his saving grace—along with a couple of genuinely caring and interested tutors who had encouraged him to go for his dreams and never to give them up.

Now, he stalked across the thickly carpeted floor and threw open the window onto the night. He was definitely in need of some fresh air. A fierce gust of wind hit him straight in the face, startling him, but it didn't remotely leech any of the heat from his body. *He knew himself to be too far gone for that.*

Even though Caitlin had left, he still burned from their passionate embrace. It was as though every nerve in his body throbbed with electricity and tension. Taking a cold shower was the obvious answer to try and ease his discomfort—but, frankly, it would be like putting a plaster on a third-degree burn. No…Jake would just have to wait it out. At least that or wait for some degree of common sense to return.

Caitlin Ryan had turned his whole world upside down. Here they were, at the start of the band's tour, and he had fallen like a ton of bricks for their new lead singer. He wouldn't go so far as to fool himself that he was in love with her—more *in lust*—but he was aware that one or two quick hot tumbles in bed were never going to be enough to satisfy the bone-deep yearning he had developed for her. Not for one moment had he meant for such a thing to happen, but somehow, in some way, Caitlin had got into Jake's blood and there wasn't much he could do about it.

How in hell was he supposed to keep a clear head and do all the things he normally had to do to help support and motivate the band? Get them out on the road with all guns blazing? Just seeing her every night for the next six weeks up on stage was going to be the sweetest torture. He already had to feel sorry for Rick and the others, because his mood sure as hell wasn't going to improve if he couldn't touch Caitlin in the way he ached to touch her. He'd either end up having to take religious vows or quit managing the band. Either way, his libido was definitely going to come under some serious duress.

The first shock Caitlin had received on reaching London was the discovery that she was going to be put up in Jake's flat in Chelsea for the two nights they were there. It had turned out that the rest of the band all had homes in the capital, including Rick. But Jake had quickly vetoed his friend's suggestion that Caitlin stay with him.

It had been too late for her to protest at the arrangement and organise an alternative, so she'd kept her doubts to herself and agreed. The most important thing was the coming performance, and she absolutely had to make a good impression...for *all* their sakes. But when they'd arrived at the fairly compact popular West London venue, Caitlin had found herself having to change into her stage gear in the ladies' room, because by the time they'd rehearsed, done a sound-check and had a meeting with the venue manager there had been no time to go back to Jake's place and get ready.

Frowning into one of the less than pristine mirrors, she had applied her make-up with a thumping heart and trembling hand, inadvertently spilling the contents of her make-up bag into the porcelain sink when she'd yanked out a tissue too hard to pat her lipstick dry with.

Now she stood in the wings with the rest of the band, feeling a bit like a little girl playing dress-up in her mother's best clothes, only partially tuning in to Rick's animated pep talk as he paced up and down in front of them, like an army sergeant pumping up his platoon for battle. In front of the small raised stage the crowd had swelled and the anticipation that crackled in the air was not dissimilar to the lightning strike before a torrential downpour.

There was a rumour going round that many of Blue Sky's fans who had supported them from the beginning with Marcie had turned up to support the band's return, in spite of their disappointment that she had walked out. Naturally Caitlin fretted that she would never pass muster.

Rick had told her that her style was quite different from Marcie's but that that was a *good* thing. Her strong vocal suited the band's music perfectly. *Like a match made in heaven,* he had assured her with a smile. But, while she welcomed the compliment, and was glad that the relative intimacy of the venue was perhaps not as intimidating as a much larger one might have been, her stomach was sick with nerves at the thought of being put through the ultimate baptism of fire for a new singer.

And where was Jake? He had been with them up until about half an hour ago, when he'd murmured something about 'last-minute arrangements' then disappeared. Caitlin found that now, when it came to the crunch, she needed his assurance more than ever.

'Is everyone okay?'

And suddenly he was there, his grin lighting up the dim little space to the side of the stage like a beacon shining in the dark, his misty blue eyes immediately seeking her out as though it was implicitly understood that she was the one who needed his assurance the most.

'You look terrific,' he told her.

Even as he spoke, Jake was thinking that she looked much better than that. *She looked nothing less than drop-dead gorgeous.* The purple velvet top she had selected on their shopping trip clung to her body in all the right places and her long black skirt skimmed the flat plane of her stomach and the soft swell of her hips as though it had been exclusively designed for her shape and her shape alone. Inevitably, his blood headed immediately south. Even if Caitlin couldn't sing a note, the men in the crowd were going to give her a lot of rope and that was a fact. It heartened him to know that they were all going to be pleasantly surprised.

'Trust me. You haven't got a thing to worry about. Just go out there and sing like you do in rehearsals, but even better.

If you get nervous, then just focus on me…I'll be out front as soon as you get onstage.'

'Okay. I'll do that… I can do that.' Caitlin managed to summon up a smile from only God knew where.

Eager to add his own brand of reassurance, Rick ran his hands up and down the sides of her slim arms and planted a sound kiss on her cheek. 'Just for luck, beautiful…not that you're going to need it.'

She barely opened her eyes during the first few bars of the opening number. It was much easier to simply shut out the sight of the crowd so that she could sing. She had been taken aback by the vociferous welcome they'd received from the fans when they walked onto the stage, somehow not expecting it to be quite as effusive as it had been. They didn't know her yet, and Caitlin had a lot to prove…

However, she was quickly swept away by the music and the need to sing, and as the wall of sound crashed over her she patted her thigh in time with the beat and started to enjoy herself. She was sure that performing in front of an audience must be an even bigger adrenaline rush than shooting rapids, and nothing had ever felt so right or so perfect.

That was when she finally opened her eyes. *That was when she saw Jake…*

He was clapping along with the rest of the crowd, watchful and silently assessing, his features so handsome and compelling that several women in the audience furtively glanced his way whether they were with someone or not. Releasing a long breath, Caitlin gave him a brief smile, then turned her attention back to the avid sea of faces in front of her.

Many people were capturing her and the band with their mobile phone cameras. She could almost feel the tangible sense of surprise in the air, the pleasure—and beneath the cool black satin of her long flowing skirt her legs couldn't help trembling. Steve Bridges gave her an extra drumroll to indicate his approval, and to her left Mike Casey muttered low, for her ears only, 'You're going to have them eating out of your hands, Cait.'

And she *did*. By the time they'd finished the final number of the night the crowd was with her all the way, cheering and clapping and stamping their feet for more. As baptisms of fire went, Caitlin couldn't have wished for a more favourable flame.

Backstage, she ran the gauntlet of well-wishers, road crew and fans alike, arriving in the small room the band had been allocated to more back-slapping, applause and champagne...courtesy of Jake. She barely registered the burst of bubbles on her tongue because everything felt so surreal. However, she *did* register the satisfying feel of Jake's strong arm wound possessively round her waist.

If anybody speculated on the 'extra-special' attention she was getting, no one dared voice it—least of all Rick, who was watching them with a stern 'headmaster' scowl as he bellowed to no one in particular that he needed another beer and *fast*.

Outside, as the venue emptied and the road crew loaded the van with Blue Sky's equipment—'Tank' and Dave, stalwarts of the industry, who had worked with Jake many times before—Rick pulled Caitlin aside as she was about to step up and get into Jake's familiar black car.

Jake had given her his keys and told her he wouldn't be long. He was still inside, checking arrangements for the following night when they would play their second and final London gig. There would be an even bigger crowd the next night, he'd told her, because the press would have got wind of her performance via the comments posted on social media sites and would come to check it out.

As Caitlin stood waiting to hear what Rick had to say, right on cue it started to rain.

'Is something the matter?' she asked warily.

'I don't know. You tell me.'

'Now you're being cryptic.' She started to smile, but straight away saw Rick wasn't in the mood to be placated.

'Is something going on between you and Jake?' he demanded.

Her stomach plummeted to her boots.

'And don't tell me you don't know what I mean.'

His hazel eyes were accusing and his shaggy blond hair was beginning to wave even more in the rain. Tugging up the collar of her raincoat, Caitlin shuddered.

It had been an amazing night. She had not only overcome her trepidation at singing in public, she had really begun to live her dream. She was bursting to talk to Lia and tell her all about it. Up until just a moment ago she'd wanted to shout out her news to the whole world. *I did it! I really am a singer in a bona fide rock band!* But now, as she gazed anxiously back at Rick, she felt as though someone had got a pin and deliberately popped her balloon.

'There's nothing going on between me and Jake other than him looking out for me and helping me settle in…with the band, I mean.'

'We can't afford another screw-up after the Marcie debacle. If you end up walking out on everyone because you got too involved with Jake then it will have serious implications for the band. I don't think they deserve that after all their hard work…do you?'

'No. Of course I don't.'

Caitlin knew what Rick was saying was only right, and she had no intention of letting anyone down. Just because Jake had put his arm round her when she'd come off stage and bought champagne to celebrate it didn't mean that the man was any more trustworthy than Sean. She had already intuited that f she had a physical relationship with him then her heart would seriously be at risk—because any woman with an ounce of common sense could easily see that he wasn't the type of man to commit to anything more meaningful. And Caitlin wasn't the type of woman to be intimate with a man and then forget it…as if were no more important than a trip to the hairdresser…

She lifted her chin. 'Don't worry, Rick. I promise you that the band comes first. Besides, I'm not looking to get personally involved with anyone.'

Liar. Nobody wanted to be alone for ever. And she wasn't the only girl in the world who hoped to find love again after the heartache of a failed relationship.

'Then we understand each other?' Rick reached out his hand to wipe away a raindrop glistening on her cheek.

'Understand what, exactly?' a deep male voice intoned.

CHAPTER EIGHT

JAKE HAD WALKED up behind them. Straight away you could have cut the tension with a knife. Caitlin found herself wishing she hadn't agreed to stay the night at his flat. If it was going to make things this awkward between the two men, then she'd see if she could locate a cheap hotel for herself.

When neither she nor Rick rushed to answer his question, the glance he gave them was searing.

'I said, *understand what*, exactly? We'll stand here all night in the rain if we have to, until I get an answer.'

Rick hefted a sigh. 'Okay, Jake, if you really want to know then I'll tell you. I was warning Cait about getting personally involved with you. Just a few weeks ago Marcie walked out, leaving us high and dry. By great good fortune and the gods of rock and roll we found Caitlin. The last thing we need is to screw up the band's chances because she might get hurt by you and end up leaving the band.'

'I won't leave the band—I told you!'

Exasperated and embarrassed, Caitlin wanted to shake Rick. Did he really think she was so naïve that she'd risk the fantastic opportunity she'd been given to sing with the band in favour of a fleeting romance with Jake? As far as she was concerned she was in Blue Sky for the long haul, whatever happened.

Jake also looked exasperated. 'If there's anything personal between me and Caitlin then that's where it stays… between the *two* of us. We're both agreed that the welfare of the band comes first. I've been in this business long enough to know where my priorities lie. Now, it's been a long night, and Caitlin ought to get some rest if she's going to give another good performance tomorrow.'

'Under the circumstances, perhaps she'd better stay at my place instead?' His jaw clenched, Rick defied the taller man to give him an argument.

But Jake wasn't having any of it.

'I've given you my decision, and as far as I'm concerned it doesn't need debating.' With a ferocious scowl he grabbed the car keys out of Caitlin's hand and shouldered past her.

She stared at the other man. 'Why did you have to go and say that?'

'Because somebody has to look out for you, sweetheart. Jake is my best buddy, as well as my boss, but the truth is he doesn't have the best track record where women are concerned. Apart from with his ex—a relationship which probably scarred him for life—he doesn't go in for long relationships. I'm sure you know what I mean? And you're not like any of the other girls he's been with. You're sensitive, for a start. If you get too involved with him and he dumps you, you won't be able to take it on the chin and simply put it down to experience.'

'And what about you, Rick? Have *you* got a better track record? Anyway, contrary to opinion, I'm quite capable of taking care of myself. This is like a dream come true for me, to sing with this band, and I don't intend to mess it up, believe me.'

Behind them Jake started up the car's engine. Glancing round, Caitlin found his unsettling blue gaze blazing back at her through the windscreen.

She turned back to Rick. 'I've got to go.'

Saying no more, she walked to the car and got in without a word. She was still fumbling with her seatbelt when the vehicle pulled away from the kerb with a loud squeal of rubber on Tarmac.

* * *

Jake made a final check on Caitlin where she slept in his bedroom...*in his bed*...and then quietly closed the door behind him. In the large and airy living room, with the blinds pulled down and the blond oak floor cool beneath his feet, he dropped down onto a futon-style armchair. Then he leaned back to stare broodingly up at the ceiling.

Rick had no right, warning Caitlin not to get involved with him. What the hell did his friend think he was doing? Had Jake ever interfered in Rick's many and varied 'relationships'? No—he'd stood back and watched the fall out so many times it wasn't funny. *But then Rick wasn't contemplating having a hot, steamy affair with the band's gorgeous new singer, was he?*

Jake was only too aware that if he went ahead and had an affair with Caitlin it would be an extremely foolish and risky thing to do, with perhaps irreparable consequences. If he had any respect for the guys in the band—*and he had that in spades*—he shouldn't even be considering it. But then he hadn't achieved the success he had enjoyed by *not* taking risks. He wasn't setting out to break Caitlin's heart, but if they did get involved for a while he'd make it clear that he was only responding to an undeniable physical attraction that he couldn't resist.

If she felt the same then there wouldn't be a problem. If she *didn't* then Jake would simply have to put the whole thing down to experience and do his best to turn away from her in that department. Although God knew it wouldn't be easy.

Maybe once upon a time he'd nurtured a secret hope that he'd find a girl, settle down and eventually raise a family, but that hope hadn't survived for long. *Jodie had seen to that.* He didn't know if he would ever trust another woman again.

Having had a mother who had abandoned him was bad enough. Discovering that his wife had been having an affair—and with someone who had such a high profile that the press would have a field-day—Jake hadn't had a prayer of protecting himself. Especially not when, in typically mercenary fashion, Jodie had concocted a vindictive story about their marriage and given the media carte blanche to say what the hell they liked about him. *He wasn't in a hurry to get burned a second time.*

Blowing out a breath, he let his jaded gaze take inventory of his surroundings. The fashionable and expensive apartment might be just a stone's throw from the King's Road in Chelsea, but its distinctly minimalist decor and general air of emptiness were testament to the fact that he was hardly ever there. Since leaving the children's home all those years ago he'd been regularly on the move—never staying in one place for any notable length of time.

Helplessly, he found his thoughts returning to Caitlin. If he was frank with her—made it clear that he was one of life's gypsies and wasn't looking for anything long-term or permanent—would she yield her body and a little of her time until the flames of desire they ignited together burned themselves out? And afterwards would they still be able to maintain a working relationship, see each other every day and have no regrets?

'You're a real prize, Jake Sorenson. You know that?'

Despising himself, because what he was prepared to offer her wasn't really very much at all, he pushed to his feet and paced the floor, restless and on edge because the woman he was crazy about was sleeping just a few feet away from him in the next room…in *his* bed…*alone.*

She had barely said a word to him when he'd brought her back to the flat. She had simply looked at him with those soulful green eyes of hers and made a polite comment that the flat was 'really beautiful', then walked round the living room examining every single print that decorated the walls as if fascinated.

They were mostly artistic photographic prints of well-known music artists Jake had worked with, along with one or two high-profile fashion models who had worked on video shoots. As Caitlin had studied them it had become eminently clear to him that not one of them could hold a candle to her.

He should have told her how beautiful she'd looked to-night, how great she'd done, that she'd made them all proud. But he had been too keyed up because he'd been fighting to keep the lid on his attraction. And Rick's warning had kept going round and round in his head like a mantra that was hard to shut out. So they'd had a cup of coffee, some brief conversation about nothing very much, and then he'd shown her into the bedroom.

It hadn't just been him and the band who had loved her performance tonight. The audience had loved her too. But, drawing on his extensive experience, Jake knew it wasn't all going to be plain sailing. Audiences were notoriously fickle until they really got to know a band, and they'd en-counter all sorts on this tour before it was finished. *There would be criticisms, too.* Jake just hoped that Caitlin could handle them.

But there was no doubt in his mind that, with her tal-ent and beauty, Blue Sky could win themselves a presti-gious recording contract. As long as they were consistently able to come up with the goods he had the contacts and the know-how to help make all their dreams come true. *Except maybe his own...*

Once again his thoughts turned to the beautiful girl asleep in his bed. She was a dark-haired enchantress, with a face and a body that could enslave *any* man, and Jake had un-doubtedly fallen under her spell. Cursing beneath his breath, he headed determinedly towards the bathroom and a long, cold, hopefully passion-killing shower.

The distinct sound of music playing disturbed him. For a few moments Jake just lay still, staring up at the ceiling. He was lying on the rarely used spare bed in the flat's guest room, but he'd phoned ahead to the caretaking agency he used for someone to come in and tidy the place and make up the beds with fresh sheets before they arrived.

Blinking away his disorientation as he properly came to, he realised that the radio was playing in the kitchen. *Caitlin*. She must be up and about. At the thought of the woman who had given him yet another sleepless night he groaned and propped himself up on his elbow. Then he dragged the fingers of his free hand through his tousled dark hair.

Glancing down at the distinctive bulge beneath the sheet, Jake released a long, slow breath. Jumping out of bed straight away wasn't an option when he was so heavily and obviously aroused. Better that he wait for a few minutes and concentrate his thoughts on something either mundane or unpleasant to help dispel the heat in his groin. But that was no easy task, with Caitlin beginning to join in the chorus of the song on the radio, her sexy tones making him tingle all over just as if she were lying next to him, crooning softly into his ear.

A few moments later she was knocking at his door. 'Jake, are you up yet? I've made you a cup of tea.'

Caitlin sounded so damn cheerful that he wanted to get up, drag her inside, throw her down on the bed and have his wicked way with her without further ado.

He released another heartfelt groan.

'That word doesn't get mentioned round here in the morning. I'm strictly a coffee man,' he grumbled, plumping up his pillow and jamming it behind his back.

'No problem. I can just as easily make you some coffee. How do you like it?'

'Hot, dark and sultry, with a little bit of sugar…just like my women.'

'I see you've recovered your sense of humour…'

'Apparently I have.'

Jake couldn't believe he was having this conversation through a closed door. He glared at the offending wood panel as if his gaze had the power to burn a hole through it.

From the other side Caitlin remarked brightly, 'By the way, thanks for giving up your bed to me. I hope you were comfortable too. Did you sleep all right?'

What a question!

He rubbed a hand round his beard-roughened jaw. Rocks on the desert floor couldn't have been more uncomfortable. He'd tossed and turned so much that he felt every single day of his thirty-six years this morning. *And little Miss Hole-in-her-Stocking wasn't helping, with her cheery wide-awake tone that conveyed she'd slept like a baby...*

'No, I didn't,' he growled.

There was no response.

For a few moments Jake thought his guest had returned to the kitchen. Then, to his surprise, the door opened and she walked into the bedroom. Wearing tight faded jeans, and a loose-fitting white T-shirt with clearly no bra underneath it, Caitlin fixed him with a tentative gaze. A soft flush suffused her cheeks when the corners of his mouth crooked upwards in a smile.

'Something wrong?' he asked huskily.

'You said that you didn't sleep?'

The way she said it let him know she was concerned, guilty, or both. It was too good an opportunity to waste and Jake wasn't a man who ever let a good opportunity sail by without grabbing onto it.

'Yeah...I might just stay put for a while longer and catch up a little.'

Caitlin couldn't take her eyes off Jake's heavenly chest. He was all lean, rippling muscle, rock-hard stomach and tanned flesh. With his sexy tousled hair and sleepy-eyed expression, the man was as handsome and seductive as a mythical warrior. And what did she think she was doing, daring to come into his room and stare at him as if she'd come to pay homage to one of the gods?

It was perhaps inevitable that he should pat the space

next to him in the luxurious bed and suggest, 'Why don't you come and join me?'

'I slept well. I don't need any more rest.'

'Did I mention rest?'

Caitlin swallowed hard. 'No, but…it doesn't look like there's a lot of room,' she said nervously.

Suddenly she was so aroused that it was impossible to pretend indifference. Jake was one sexy, charismatic specimen and she was only human. Could she help it if her neglected libido was nearing boiling point and needing resolution? Heat was already seeping up her thighs, between her legs, making her moist, while the sensitive tips of her nipples tingled painfully against her shirt.

'You underneath, me on top…how much room do we need?' Jake parried seductively, his blue eyes drowsy with desire. 'We can make it work.'

It was an outrageous suggestion and Caitlin didn't dare take him up on it…*did she?*

Glancing up at the faint morning light filtering through the slats of the rolled-down blinds, she was suddenly consumed by an avalanche of doubt. And not just doubt at her ability to get herself out of trouble when the situation demanded it, but at putting her common sense versus a desire so red-hot it was already burning her.

The sheer, unmitigated sensual tug of Jake sitting up in bed, with his chest bared and his eyes goading her towards something so deliciously sinful that it made her weak just thinking about it, was in the end too hard to resist.

With her heart thudding, she replied, 'I've never…I've never gone in for casual sex. I just wanted you to know that. Do you have some protection?'

He stared. 'I've got everything we need right here.'

Jake had known he'd finally lost his battle against temptation as soon as Caitlin had walked into the room. The longing to hold her in his arms and to know her intimately had finally overridden all sense of right and wrong.

He wasn't aiming to hurt either her or the band. He had too much respect for all of them for that. He was merely following an irresistible impulse that wouldn't be denied. That said, there would be nothing casual about sex between him and Caitlin. Even though she was gorgeous—the ultimate male fantasy come to life—Jake admired her for the courageous woman she was.

He sighed with pleasure. Beneath the thin protection of her virginal white shirt her aroused nipples were practically drilling a hole thought the material, and he knew that if he touched her at the apex between her delectable thighs she would be hot and ready for him straight away. The thought slowed and thickened the blood coursing through his veins. It was like being drip-fed with unadulterated honey. And he was so desperate for her, so hungry, that if she didn't soon join him he seriously thought he might explode.

Her hands were shaking as Caitlin undid the zipper on her jeans and stepped out of them. Then she nervously moved towards the edge of the bed, dressed in nothing but the T-shirt and white cotton panties. The scalding, hungry gaze that Jake pinned her with was so blatantly carnal she thought she would melt. No man had ever looked at her with such unfettered desire in his eyes before, with such wild, primitive heat.

Low-voiced, he murmured, 'Why don't you take off your shirt'

What's a girl to do? Caitlin thought wildly. Then simply did as he asked.

A carnal whirlpool had rolled over her, snatching her up in its maelstrom so completely that there was nothing she could do but give up struggling and let it carry her where it would.

Her movements were unknowingly sensual and provocative as she pulled her shirt over her head to remove it. Her full, perfectly rounded breasts with their dusky dark nipples jutted towards him and every delectable line and curve of her sexy body was revealed in all its glory. Her small, slender waist, the voluptuous swell of her hips and her smooth, shapely thighs all came under his hungry scrutiny as he gazed his fill.

When she finally removed the shirt and let it fall to the floor her flowing dark hair drifted silkily across her breasts and partially hid them from view.

'Shall I take these off too?' she asked shyly, indicating the white panties.

'No.' Jake reached towards her and pulled her firmly down onto the bed. 'That particular pleasure is going to be mine.'

With her hair spilling wildly across her face, Caitlin gulped down a shocked breath as he slid expert hands down over her hips and practically ripped off the flimsy underwear.

'Jake, I—' But whatever she'd intended saying next was cut off by the hot press of his mouth and the skilful invasion of his tongue seeking hers as his heavily aroused manhood pressed deeply into her soft belly.

Her senses were all but overwhelmed by his intoxicating heat and the erotic masculine scents of his body. One of his hands slid across her breast, rubbing and kneading the already inflamed nipple, nipping and squeezing until she gasped her pleasure into his mouth and bucked her hips against his. *It was clear they were singing from the same song-sheet.* His mouth closing over her nipple, Jake suckled hard and Caitlin whimpered her delight.

Lifting his head, he breathed, 'I've got to take care of something…'

Reaching across to a nearby chair, where he'd left his jeans, he delved into a pocket and withdrew a foil packet. He wasted no time in expertly tearing it open. Sheathed in the protection, Jake turned his attention back to Caitlin, kneeing her slim thighs apart to insert an explorative finger into her moist heat.

Even as she gasped, she knew she was more than ready for him, and was gratified when he positioned his sex and thrust assuredly inside her. Her thoughts utterly deserted her as she drowned in an ecstatic pleasure like no other she'd ever experienced. The sheer emotion she felt at the wonder of it caused her eyes to fill with tears. Then she cried out as Jake's mouth found the hollow between her neck and shoulder and bit her there.

His lips sought hers again and his kiss was deep and hard as he thrust into her mouth with his tongue even as his sex filled her and he felt her scalding satin heat engulf him. If he died right now he'd die happy. He'd never experienced pleasure or desire like it. Beneath him, Caitlin writhed and moaned, her breath released in hot little gasps that seared his skin, and when she raised her hips to welcome him even more deeply, and suddenly convulsed round him, she cried out for a second time and he saw that her beautiful emerald eyes were moist with tears. Her expression was stunned. She looked like a woman who had never experienced the full orgasmic impact of climax before.

The mere thought undid Jake. Within seconds he was thrusting even deeper, whispering against her ear how beautiful she was, how perfect. Then his own desire and need reached its crescendo and he was swept away on a cascade of a joy so fierce and so perfect that he had no words to describe it. In fact it stunned him to silence.

His blue eyes glittering with feeling, he manoeuvred himself carefully to lie down beside her and with his fingers gently traced the exquisite line of her jaw. 'Caitlin?'

'What?'

Jake was stroking her ear, securing a silken strand of long ebony hair behind it. Gazing back into the incandescent eyes that looked like bewitching green fire, he silently acknowledged that he'd never experienced such depth and strength of emotion lying with a woman before. He only knew that he had the sense of feeling strangely privileged.

'I think you're the most beautiful woman I've ever known.'

Even as his words lifted her spirits higher than they'd ever been lifted before, Caitlin was already missing the warm heavy press of his body. She wanted to tell him to come back, to love her again and never stop... Only the icy fronds of harsh reality swept through her like winter just then.

She thought, *But he doesn't love me, does he? All we enjoyed together just now was great sex.*

The fact that she'd never even got close to orgasm with Sean, and that more often than not she'd seen to her own needs after the event, would hardly register with Jake. Besides, a properly committed relationship wasn't what he was looking for, was it? They both knew that. When he stopped desiring her body Caitlin would just have to learn to concentrate all her energies on her singing and view him solely as Blue Sky's manager.

Could she do that? Could she cut off her emotions so easily when what had just taken place between her and Jake had been nothing less than earth-shattering? *Her whole world had been utterly changed forever.* Did he realise that just the merest touch from him was enough to set her on fire, to make her need him as much as she needed to breathe?

Glancing back into his steady blue gaze, she wondered how it was possible for a man to have such luxuriant long lashes and still be so incredibly masculine. Perhaps it was the hard, lean jaw, with that slight indentation in the chin, or was it the exquisitely shaped mouth with the slightly fuller lower lip? A mouth made for passion...for the erotic pleasures only shared by lovers.

Of course it went without saying that Jake must have had a few of those...perhaps more than Caitlin cared to know about. Right now the thought of even *one* was enough to make her heart jolt sickeningly.

'That's high praise, coming from a man like you,' she

answered, affecting a light, breezy tone to shield her true feelings from him.

He frowned. 'What do you mean, a man like me?'

'I just mean you must have known many beautiful women. I won't kid myself that I'm particularly special.'

Now his handsome visage looked perturbed. 'Hey. Why say that? Don't you know how much pleasure you've just given me? You mesmerise and intoxicate me, Caitlin. Sharing what we just shared was beyond wonderful.'

Caitlin couldn't help but smile—even as she came to a distressing conclusion about what she had to do for *both* their sakes.

'Thank you. I'm glad you think that. I thought so too. But now I think we should both come back down to earth, don't you?'

Lightly removing Jake's hand from where it lay across her stomach, she rolled over and leant down to pick up the clothes she'd discarded on the floor.

'Where do you think you're going?'

He sounded surprised, upset. Not immediately answering, Caitlin stepped into her panties, then got to her feet. She hurriedly pulled on her T-shirt and quickly got into her jeans, sensing him watching her broodingly.

'Are you going to tell me what's going on? Why the sudden urgency to get up when we can take our time? We can stay here all day if we want. There's no hurry.'

Combing back her hair with trembling fingers, she turned to face him.

'I suddenly came to my senses, that's all. Hopefully, now that we've got this out of our system, we can get back to normal and concentrate on work. I think we should both ensure that what happened between us won't happen again, Jake. From now on our relationship should be strictly about the band. Now that I'm clear about our priorities I'll go and get a quick shower and then make some coffee.' She started to move towards the door.

'Forget the damn coffee, woman!' Jake threw back the covers on the bed, to all intents and purposes coming after her. 'Come back here and get into bed.'

'Why?' Despite her resolution not to let herself down by crying, Caitlin knew her eyes were already filling with tears. 'So that I can be even more reckless and stupid than I've been already?'

When he didn't answer but instead shook his head, as if her outburst was totally incomprehensible, she flew out through the door without another word and headed determinedly for the bathroom.

CHAPTER NINE

I'M SORRY I didn't talk to you a bit more about how I felt. Silently rehearsing the words, Caitlin wished she'd said them out loud to Jake before he'd abruptly left the flat that morning to go God only knew where.

He'd barely acknowledged her when he got up, and when he'd emerged from the bathroom he'd simply told her he was going out for a while and slammed the door. His cold manner had made her want to curl up into a little ball and disappear. Even as he'd moved towards the door Caitlin had wanted to plead with him to stay.

It was evident that she'd soured things by getting out of bed and declaring that they should come back down to earth and concentrate on the band. Even though it was the sensible thing to do, the *right* thing, she knew it wouldn't make either of them happy. How could it, when the intensity of their lovemaking had clearly demonstrated how strong their attraction was? Would doing the right thing help them to deny it?

Weary with going over the same ground over and over again without resolution, she diverted her restless energy with undertaking a little light cleaning round the flat. Although it was obvious that the fashionably minimalist living quarters barely needed it, to Caitlin's mind it was better to do *something* rather than sit there twiddling her thumbs and worrying herself sick about what had happened.

She would never regret their lovemaking. How could she ever regret revelling in the joy of being a woman, in the power of her body to give and receive such mind-blowing pleasure as she had done with Jake? Their brief union had stirred feelings and emotions long buried, and she couldn't be angry about that. Not when her body still glowed and throbbed with the attention he'd given her.

And even if he hadn't been motivated by love, the truth was…Caitlin *had*. There was no longer any point in denying it.

Locating a vacuum cleaner and duster, she cleaned the flat to within an inch of its life. When all the surfaces gleamed to her satisfaction, and the living room sang with the scent of beeswax, she opened the windows to allow fresh air to circulate. Then she went into the kitchen to make herself some toast and coffee.

Her appetite taken care of, she retreated to the living room to browse a lone copy of a glossy music magazine. Her attention was immediately caught by an interesting little snippet ringed in red. It was all about Jake.

What's former music promoter and artist supremo Jake Sorenson up to these days? Rumour has it he's gone back to his roots and is managing a tight little foursome called Blue Sky. After the lead songstress Marcie Wallace recently walked out, a little bird told yours truly that the search is on for a dazzling new diva to replace her.

All we know is that she'll have to be pretty exceptional to meet Jake's well-known exacting standards. Remember that this is the man who made his fortune bringing world-class bands Soft Rain and The Butterfly Net to prominence, then dropped out into self-imposed obscurity for five years after a vindictive exposé by his ex, Jodie Parks.

Knowing Mr Sorenson's famed proclivity for discovering matchless talent, we'd seriously advise watching this space…

'"Dazzling diva"? Are they serious?'

Chewing anxiously on the inside of her cheek, Caitlin dropped the magazine onto the small mahogany table as though she'd suddenly been burnt. Because the idea of her being a diva in any shape or form was preposterous.

She leant back into the cream-coloured futon and gathered a cushion close to try and absorb the shock and disbelief that rolled through her. Yes, she'd made a good start with the band—she'd dipped her toe in the water and got her feet wet, and the enthusiastic reception from the audience last night had been more, *much* more than she'd hoped for. But could she come up with the goods night after night for the next three weeks without letting herself and the others down?

Her fingers tentatively stroked down the sensitive skin of her throat. She'd have to seriously think about taking better care of her voice, for one thing. That aside, her most pressing thought right now was Jake. Where on earth had he got to? Was he still mad at her for deserting him so abruptly this morning?

It stunned her to realise that she was in love with him. She hadn't been in the market for a relationship and hadn't intended to be for a very long time. But then she'd never dreamed fate would bring a man like Jake into her life. A man who one minute wanted her as much as he wanted to take his next breath and the next…

Her insides knotted anxiously, and because the feeling so unsettled her she jumped up and went in search of some window cleaner and a cloth and started to clean the windows.

'What the hell do you think you're doing?'

Caitlin nearly fell off the chair she was precariously balanced on. Even with its aid, the glass corners of the window frame were particularly tricky to get to. But it was hard to believe she'd been so absorbed that she'd somehow blotted out the sound of Jake's key in the door and had therefore been unprepared for his appearance.

She turned to observe him. 'What does it look like I'm doing?'

'You'd better get down from there before you break your neck!'

Before she could react Jake had moved across to her and caught her by the waist. Then he unceremoniously hoisted her off the chair. Caitlin felt her face flame red.

'Stop treating me like a child, will you? I'm perfectly capable of cleaning a few windows without supervision.'

'That might be the case, but who in hell asked you to clean the windows in the first place? I hire someone from a cleaning firm to do that. I hired *you* to sing in a band, not become my domestic.'

Jake glanced impatiently around him and Caitlin saw him register the spotless parquet floor, the plumped-up cushions on his easy chairs and futon, the shining glass on his framed prints. Aware that his hands still lingered at the sides of her waist, she wished her heart wouldn't beat quite so fast—because his touch was already making her feel weak.

'I can't help it' She shrugged, 'I always clean when I get tense. I can't stand inactivity…not having something to do.' Her teeth clamped down on her lip.

'I see.'

Beneath his impenetrable glare, she felt like a small child being told off by her parent.

Because she was nervous, she remarked thoughtlessly, 'By the way, I notice that you don't have many personal photos around?'

As soon as the words were out Caitlin wanted the floor to open up and swallow her.

Jake's expression was immediately dismayed. 'If by "personal photos" you mean of family, then you know very well that I don't have any.'

Her insides turned over. 'I…I'm so sorry I said that. I was just nervous. But personal photos could equally mean friends. Didn't you have any close pals when you were young?'

When he didn't immediately comment, she felt as if the hole she'd just dug herself had got even deeper.

'You mean at the children's home? Not really.'

His tone was chillingly matter-of-fact. Caitlin knew she should steer the conversation away from his heartbreaking childhood as quickly as possible, but care and concern for him made her not want to shy away from it.

'Do you mind if I ask how you came to grow up in a children's home, Jake?'

'My mother gave me up because she was just sixteen when she fell pregnant with me and in her wisdom decided to have me adopted. Only I *wasn't* adopted. I was hard to place because I was born with a heart murmur. The people at the children's home told me that most interested adoptive parents were wary of taking on a sick baby.' Shrugging, he shaped his lips into a sardonic smile. 'Not that I minded… it was their loss. As I grew older I realised what an asset it was to be left alone by people. I learned to enjoy my own company, to pursue my own interests without interference.'

Caitlin stared, trying hard to assimilate everything she'd heard. 'And what about the heart murmur? Do you still see a doctor or specialist?'

'No. I grew out of it. It got better all by itself. It hasn't been an issue since I was young. Anyway, are you going to tell me what's making you so tense, or do I have to guess?'

Suddenly impatient, he relieved her of the scrunched-up cleaning rag she was still holding onto and threw it onto the window ledge.

As Caitlin fought hard to marshal her thoughts, Jake sucked in a breath and let it out again slowly. 'I don't want you to worry about what happened between us.'

'I'm not. I mean, I was just…I was just…'

He held up his hand to indicate she should stop talking. His blue eyes glittered. 'Hear me out. I don't want you to worry about it because I don't regret a damn thing. And, contrary to what you might think, I'm not going to pretend it never happened.'

A warm rush climbed into her chest. The anxiety that had propelled her into her frenetic cleaning bout slowly subsided, leaving her with a sense of joy so acute she couldn't resist the smile that tugged at her lips.

He didn't regret it... That surely had to signify something, didn't it?

'However,' he continued, 'even though I won't pretend it never happened, I agree we can't risk a repeat performance. You were right when you said we should concentrate on the band.'

Caitlin's brief joy was quickly replaced by crushing disappointment. It was so intense that it was as though all the breath had been brutally sucked from her lungs.

'You think that's the best idea?' she murmured.

'It's not because I don't want us to be together again like we were this morning…'

Capturing her wrist, Jake firmly wove his fingers through her own. His misty blue eyes mesmerised her, and she saw that he was hungry for her again—and yet it was clear he was furious with himself. She suddenly realised that he didn't *want* to desire her so much, and was furious because she was hardly helping him to resist.

'You got into this because you wanted to realise a dream,' he went on. 'One day soon this band is going to be very successful…that is if we're all committed to the same goal. If you and I don't maintain a professional relationship then the whole thing could fall apart. I think that would be a great shame, don't you?'

She wasn't going to disagree. With a brief nod she dropped her gaze. To her surprise, Jake released her hand, slid his fingers beneath her jaw and lifted her chin.

'I've been to see Rick and I've arranged to stay over at his place tonight. You can stay here. Treat the place as if it was your own. I'll be over to pick you up at about six. We'll do a sound-check and run through the playlist. Tomorrow, when we go to Brighton, I've booked you into a separate hotel from the rest of us—a much nicer hotel, because you deserve a little luxury. All in all, I think the arrangement is for the best.'

Caitlin swallowed hard.

'Why? Don't you trust me, Jake? I'd much rather be in the same hotel as everyone else. Do you think that because we made love I'm going to make a nuisance of myself?'

Hurt cramping her throat, she pulled out of his grasp and strode across to the other side of the room. Folding her arms, she stared blankly up at a large photographic print of a beautiful redhead. The sight of it made her even sadder when she remembered that there weren't any more personal photos around because Jake had no family. It broke her heart to think that he'd grown up without someone to love him.

'Are you crazy?' he ground out. 'It's *me* I don't trust. It's like I told you before—I have a job to do and a little bit of distance wouldn't be a bad thing right now…at least when we're not working together.'

Everything he said made the utmost sense, but it didn't prevent Caitlin from feeling desperately disappointed. Hope was futile, she realised. She didn't have a right to hope for anything as far as Jake Sorenson was concerned. And thank goodness at least one of them was taking charge of the situation. Of *course* it was right that the band should come first.

Wasn't her passion for music and singing the reason she had auditioned in the first place? It certainly hadn't been because she was looking for another relationship. And she was sure she wasn't looking for some 'on-off' hot little liaison with Blue Sky's charismatic manager. The sooner she let Jake see that she wasn't going to waste her time crying over spilt milk, the better.

'It sounds like you've taken care of everything. Good. I

can't say I'm not glad about that. Rick was right when he said it would a bad idea, making things personal between us.'

'Leave Rick out of this' with a grim scowl Jake walked angrily towards her. 'What's between you and me is nobody's business but our own. You got that?'

What could Caitlin do beneath that frosty glare but acquiesce? Even if what he had just said contradicted everything he'd said previously. Their relationship *wasn't* just their own business—wasn't that the point? Blue Sky had a vested interest in her not having a personal relationship with their manager. They were probably concerned that Jake would break her heart and she would end up leaving the band...just as Marcie had.

Perhaps it really *was* for the best if Caitlin and Jake pretended that their passionate liaison hadn't happened after all. If Jake could be cool about it then she would just have to learn to do the same.

That night, having heard positive feedback about Blue Sky's performance the previous night, the music press turned out in force. Onstage, determinedly giving her all, Caitlin had had to contend with flashbulbs popping in her face at regular intervals and backstage afterwards it was even worse. A huge number of people had squeezed into a room not much bigger than a cloakroom. The atmosphere was hot, stuffy and claustrophobic, and the smell of alcohol mingled liberally with the accumulated heat of bodies pressing in too close. All she really wanted to do was to get back to Jake's flat and escape.

The sense of panic that gripped her had taken her by surprise, and she'd more or less clammed up when too many questions had been catapulted her way by over-zealous reporters who barely gave her even a second to answer them. If it hadn't been for Jake, dealing with their questions with cool professionalism, as well as Rick protecting her from the crush, Caitlin would have fled in a heartbeat—never mind that publicity *any* publicity…was meant to be good.

Mid-morning the next day found her sitting in the foyer of the old-fashioned seafront hotel in Brighton that Jake had booked the band into, delicately hiding a yawn behind her hand as Rick and Jake conversed with the desk clerk. The rest of the band members were out on the small square patio, chatting. Caitlin stifled another guilty yawn as she watched them.

'Are we keeping you awake, Cait?'

Taking her by surprise, Rick gave her shoulder an affectionate squeeze, then dropped down beside her on the padded seat, stirring the air around them with the musky scent of his cologne.

'I couldn't sleep last night.' Shrugging her shoulders in the faded denim jacket she wore over a blue maxi-dress, she attempted a smile.

'Excitement keeping you up, huh?'

Rick was grinning, and she saw her companion's astute hazel eyes were curious. 'Something like that,' Caitlin replied.

Let him think that, she decided. It was a lot less complicated than confessing that she'd been missing Jake. That her body had been aching for him all night.

She would swear that she'd tossed and turned from midnight to dawn because she needed him so much. No wonder she felt as if she could sleep for England this morning!

Jake had bunked down over at Rick's, and the Chelsea flat had been soulless and empty without him. Even last night's undoubted success and the ensuing interest from the press hadn't been able to console her.

Was it really so wrong that she should want Jake as badly as she did? Her gaze helplessly gravitated towards him as he leant casually back against the reception desk, his glance sweeping thoughtfully over her and Rick. Today, his long legs were encased in faded black denim, a leather belt with a buckle was slung low on his tight, lean hips and his leather jacket was folded casually across one arm. His expression made her heart turn over. She wondered if he'd had similar trouble getting to sleep last night.

As his searching glance deliberately sought hers Caitlin sensed the hot sizzle from the contact erupt in her belly like a flare.

'We've got a few things lined up for today, but perhaps you can catch up on some rest later on, before the gig tonight.'

With her face warmly glowing, Caitlin guiltily turned her attention back to Rick.

'Sounds good to me…what things?'

'You mean you don't know?'

'No, I don't.'

'Didn't Jake tell you about the photographs?'

'What photographs?'

'We're booked into a studio in a couple of hours.'

Jake was suddenly there in front of them.

'We're getting some promotional shots of the band.'

Caitlin refrained from commenting. She was wondering if a couple of hours would be enough to transform her sleepy-eyed expression into something half resembling awake. Aside from that, she *hated* having her photograph taken. Next to eating beetroot, it was right up there on the list of things that made her squirm.

'So be sure to wear something sexy,' Rick piped up with a grin. 'You're bound to give the current babes in the charts a run for their money!'

Caitlin immediately rounded on him with an affronted glare. 'The campaign for equal rights for women clearly just passed you by, didn't it? Why strive for intelligent observation when you can just go for the lowest common denominator?'

In his usual incorrigible fashion he returned, 'Because life is complicated enough, without trying to be clever. I'm a simple guy. Can I help it if I have an eye for beauty?'

'You've made your point, Rick.' Jake's blue eyes were icy as he flashed him a warning glare. 'Now, why don't you just leave it there?'

'Can I check into my hotel now?' Caitlin interjected quickly. 'If these photos are strictly necessary then I'd like to get a shower and make myself presentable before we go.'

Rising abruptly to her feet, she pulled the edges of her denim jacket more closely across her dress's scooped neckline. All the testosterone flying around was making her nervous.

'Sure—I'll take you. Let's go back to the car.' Jake handed Rick a bunch of key cards. 'You guys go and sort yourselves out. I'll make sure Caitlin is okay and catch up with you in about half an hour.'

Getting to his feet, Rick frowned. 'Gee, I wish taking care of our "best asset" was part of *my* job description. It can hardly seem like work, can it?' he quipped.

Almost imperceptibly Jake's shoulders stiffened. Feigning indifference to the undoubted tension between the two men, Caitlin started to walk away. But Jake caught hold of her elbow and led them across the shiny parquet floor towards the exit.

She shook off his hold. 'I'm quite capable of—'

'Not now, Caitlin.'

Without even sparing her a glance, he conveyed the fact that his temper was on a very short fuse. Only a fool would seek to ignite it, so she swallowed down her indignation and turned her attention to keeping pace with his long-legged stride.

Flipping off the top of a bottle of beer from the mini-bar in his room, Jake imbibed a generous draught of the ice-cold contents and then dropped back down onto the bed. Sounds of the city permeated the forest-green curtains he'd drawn to shut out the night, and inside the images on the television screen silently flickered.

He'd deliberately muted the sound, but for a moment or two his attention was caught by the intense expressions of two lovers bidding each other goodbye at a railway station. The corners of his mouth lifted in a smile and a warm feeling climbed steadily into his chest—but it wasn't just because of the touching scene. *The sight of the lovers had inevitably made him think of Caitlin.*

Her name alone had the power to convey feelings inside him that he scarcely knew what to do with. Watching her pose with the rest of the band that afternoon for photographs had been both heaven and hell. She'd worn fitted black jeans with a virginal white stretch top that had clung lovingly to her breasts, and at the photographer's behest had taken off her boots and socks to leave her feet sexily bare. With her river of ebony hair, sparkling green eyes and naturally beautiful smile, Jake's hadn't been the only jaw to hit the floor when she'd stood as instructed with the other band members to pose for the camera.

'Anyone need some ice to help them cool down?' Rick had quipped as they'd stood together, observing the proceedings, and the comment had made Jake feel far from friendly as he thought of his colleague fantasising about the woman who had so recently become his lover...the woman he was trying desperately hard not to want because protocol demanded he abstain.

Dismayed by the violence of his feelings, he'd taken a couple of steps back to compose himself as he'd wrestled with a near overwhelming urge to kidnap Caitlin after the shoot and take her back to his hotel room. That was when his imagination had gone into overdrive.

Groaning, he took another swig of beer and glared at the television as the thought of yet another cold shower made him want to grab the offending equipment and throw it out the window. *That would be a coup for the press*...the band manager at the centre of a scandal with his model ex-wife a few years ago drawing attention once again with a demonstration of typically 'rock star' behaviour in a hotel room.

Irritably dismissing the thought, Jake brought his attention back to Caitlin. She had yet again done them proud that night, her sexy, heaven-sent voice alternately whipping up the crowd or innocently seducing them, her vocals melding perfectly with the band's tight, rich sound. In just three short weeks she'd learned more, given more, and was shaping up into more of a professional than some people in the business he'd known for years. He might be biased, but Jake knew they were onto something good.

But if he didn't touch her again soon he would lose his mind. That was if he hadn't lost it already.

He stretched out his hand for the telephone next to the bed. He could at least talk to her, tell her... Tell her *what*, exactly? That he was going crazy just thinking about her? That he was desperate to hold her and demonstrate in no uncertain terms just how much he desired her?

He let the receiver clatter noisily back onto its rest. He couldn't do it. He wouldn't put Caitlin in such an untenable position. He'd just have to find some other way of working off all his nervous energy. *Was that the correct term for a raging libido these days?*

With a humourless smile, he drained the bottle of beer dry, then stood up and threw it into a nearby wastepaper bin. Then he reached for his jacket and slammed out through the door without even pausing to switch off the TV.

The jarring sound of a bell ringing right next to her ear had Caitlin burying her face into her lilac-coloured pillow in a bid to shut the noise out. *It must be someone's car alarm going off down the street—or a fire drill, perhaps.* Her mind played games with the sound, encouraging her to carry on sleeping. Someone would see to it soon, she thought vaguely.

Only all of a sudden she was wide awake and scrambling to sit up as it finally registered that it was the phone beside her bed that was ringing. Clamping the receiver to her ear, she impatiently pushed her hair away from her face and squinted at the glowing green digits blinking back at her from the alarm clock…

Two-thirty a.m.? What the…?

'Hello?'

'Caitlin. Were you asleep?'

Jake. At the sound of that gravelly bass voice her heartbeat accelerated like a rabbit being chased by a fox.

'What's the matter? Is anything wrong?'

Had something happened to him? Was he hurt? In trouble? Caitlin's fertile imagination went into overdrive.

'Nothing's wrong. I'm downstairs in the lobby. Can you come down?'

'It's half past two in the morning!'

'I'm quite aware of the time.'

God, it was so good to hear his voice.

'Why? I mean, why do you want me to come downstairs at this time of night?' Even as she asked the question she was swinging her legs out of bed and seeking out the jeans and warm red sweater she'd folded onto a chair.

'Because I want to see you.'

His tone immediately conveyed his impatience, making his statement sound more like an order than a request.

Caitlin frowned, 'You could see me in the morning after breakfast. I don't make much sense until I've had my cup of tea.'

'Damn it, Caitlin! Just put some clothes on and get down here, will you?'

Jake hung up on her, leaving her staring at the telephone as though it had suddenly sprouted a beak and a couple of wings.

Shaking herself out of the daze she was in, she hurried into the bathroom. Splashing her face with some cold water, she quickly brushed her teeth, then combed her dishevelled hair with her fingers. There was no time to even think about applying some make-up. At any rate, what did he expect? It was two-thirty in the morning, she was tired and dazed—and…if she admitted it…more hopeful than she had a right to be considering he'd kept her at a deliberate distance for the past two days.

Crossing her arms over her soft woollen sweater, she stepped warily out of the lift to find him waiting by the doors, his lean jaw dark with night-time shadow, his hair mussed and his piercing blue eyes preternaturally bright. Desire for him was like a flash flood, fierce and elemental, and it rendered her immediately weak.

'Jake…' His name on her lips was little more than a murmur.

'Come for a walk' he said, catching hold of her hand and urging her towards the rotating glass doors of the exit.

Mid-stride, Caitlin ground to a halt to stare at him. 'You want to go for a walk? Are you crazy? It's two-thirty in the morning.'

A muscle tensed visibly in his jaw and Caitlin allowed him to guide her outside. The wind cut through her like an icy blade and, catching her shiver, Jake immediately shrugged off his jacket and draped it around her shoulders.

Her eyes wide, she glanced up at him. 'What's all this about, Jake?'

'Come on—let's walk. It's too cold to stand around.'

They headed out towards the pier, Jake catching hold of her hand again as if it was the most natural thing in the world for him to do. The night sky was almost black, but there was still plenty of light. Aside from the stars and the curved sliver of moon that permeated the velvet blanket there was plenty of neon to light up the streets, and even the occasional car's headlamp as it flew past.

For most of the way Jake had stayed silent. Now he stopped, drawing Caitlin close against him before staring out to sea.

'You were amazing tonight.'

He turned back to survey her. Heat slid down her spine and radiated down into her pelvis. The unexpected compliment took her by surprise.

'Thanks…I really enjoyed myself. The band were great, weren't they? I particularly liked—'

Jake silenced her with a hard, hot kiss that made her stumble against him.

Her lips were like soft satin pillows that couldn't help but invite him to keep tasting them. But he didn't just want to kiss her. He wanted to do so much more… The very idea made him tighten. Then it made him hard.

Lifting his head, he examined the dazed expression she wore—the moist, softly opened mouth that he'd so spontaneously and heatedly ravished, and the shining green eyes that he defied any man not to lose his soul to.

'I'll go crazy if I can't make love to you soon,' he confessed.

'We can't. Remember, we agreed…?'

Emitting a curse, Jake stared at Caitlin and drove his hands through his already windblown hair in frustration.

'I know what we agreed. I know what we *should* do. But the truth is that when you were posing with the others today at the photo shoot I hated every single one of them for looking at you…for no doubt imagining what it would be like to make love to you… No one has a right to look at you like that but *me*.'

Nervously, Caitlin slid her tongue over her lips. 'What's the meaning of all this, Jake? What are you telling me?'

'I'm telling you that I want us to be lovers. I'm not saying I expect it to be forever but I want us to be together.'

'What you're saying is that if we get together you don't expect it to be a permanent arrangement?'

'Yes.'

The expression in his eyes looked haunted for a moment. 'The idea scares you?'

'I just don't trust that long-term commitment can ever really work. Look at the examples I've had.'

'You mean there's no chance you might be able to change that view? We've all been hurt, Jake…including me. After what Sean did to me it was never going to be easy to trust another man. If I can open my mind to the idea…can't you?'

He sighed. 'I'd like to tell you I could…but in all honesty I don't hold out much hope. I know myself too well.' He shook his head in frustration. 'Look, do things have to be so serious? Can't we just have some fun together?'

'I take it you're talking about sex? Is that how you see relationships, Jake as a chance to indulge in a little light-hearted sex with no commitment whatsoever?'

'No! You're taking everything the wrong way. Look, Caitlin, I'll respect you and take care of you for however long our relationship lasts…we'll enjoy whatever time we have together—that's all I meant. I only know that I want us to be up-front about things to everyone—not play cloak and dagger and pretend we aren't an item. After all, we're adults, aren't we?'

He seemed quite certain that their relationship couldn't last. Yes, his past had made him wary, and perhaps even *scornful* of any kind of commitment, but didn't he want to change that belief to something better? As much as she loved him, if Jake didn't have any faith that things could be different Caitlin wasn't going to settle. Her self-respect was paramount, and she wasn't about to risk losing it for even a second…not even for the man she loved.

'I'm sorry, Jake.' Pulling his jacket from her shoulders, she pushed it into his hands. 'If all you're offering me is some temporary little affair—some supposed "fun" until you grow tired of me and move on to somebody else—then I'm going to have to say no. You once asked me if I was sure I was committed to this band and I told you categorically *yes*. Right now that's all I'm interested in—the *band*. Now, if you'll excuse me, I really need to get back to my bed. If I don't get at least six hours' sleep then I won't be fit for anything tomorrow. Goodnight, Jake.'

Just before she turned and walked away Caitlin had the bittersweet satisfaction of seeing the bewilderment and hurt in Jake's eyes. But as she put more and more distance between them the pain she felt at knowing they would never be lovers again was so intense that she felt as if it drilled a hole right through her heart and out the other side.

Jake stayed where he was, staring out at the frigid sea for what seemed like an eternity. It was hard to take that Caitlin had turned him down. But then everything he'd wanted to say to her had somehow come out wrong.

His heart had leapt at her soft-voiced confession that she'd found it hard to trust another man after what her ex had done to her, and she'd given him a genuine opportunity to meet her halfway when she'd said that if she could open her mind to the idea of learning to trust again, why couldn't he? But he'd completely messed it up when he'd let fear take over instead. She'd been insulted that all he seemed to be offering her was a temporary affair.

Did she really believe that, given time, their association could become more permanent? Was she perhaps hoping for marriage?

He couldn't help it, but the idea of marriage made Jake's blood run cold when he recalled what Jodie had put him through. Caitlin was nothing like his mercenary ex-wife, but if she became well known, with all the temptations that fame would undoubtedly bring to a beautiful girl like her, wasn't it possible that *she* would be the one who grew tired of the relationship and wanted to move on to a better prospect? It would kill him to have to go through another bitter court battle if his new wife treated him in the same heartless way his ex had.

As he dug his now freezing hands into his jacket pockets and moved back down the pier Jake knew that as much as he cared for Caitlin, as much as he *desired* her and yearned

A RULE WORTH BREAKING

to protect her, he couldn't risk losing his heart to her and having to endure the consequent fall-out should things go wrong.

Because if that happened, this time he really would be a broken man.

CHAPTER TEN

PLANTING HIMSELF AT the back of the crowd that night, Jake sensed the familiar zig-zag of electricity shoot through him—as he always did before a band walked onto the stage…especially a band he was managing.

The day he stopped being excited about his work was the day he stopped living. He'd witnessed too many managers in the business become lazy or complacent when they got rich, content just to milk the financial rewards without actively contributing to a band's or a singer's success. Jake was scathing about such behaviour. For himself, music was its own reward—and if he could help a band attain success, then every sleepless night and grey hair was worth it.

Blue Sky was a week into their tour and the venue that night was a noisy and popular music pub on the Kent coast. The band were booked to play there from eight-thirty onwards. At Jake's suggestion they had made some last-minute alterations to the playlist, taking out a couple of the original tunes and replacing them with two slower numbers that Mike had written and that in Jake's opinion were outstandingly good. He was also showcasing Caitlin's skills as a vocalist.

On a more personal note, he loved to hear her sing those love songs—loved to hear the emotion in her voice that made all the hairs on the back of his neck stand up. Those performances sent shivers down his spine. *Not that he'd admit it to anyone—least of all to Rick, who seemed to be watching him like a hawk these days.* He couldn't exactly blame him. He was so sure that if Caitlin and Jake got together the result would be the break-up of the band.

Folding his arms across his chest, he released a frustrated sigh. He hated being in such a bind. But what the hell was he supposed to do? *Ignore* the feelings he had for her? The woman had got so deep into his blood that if he didn't get his daily fix of her he felt as if someone had died. If Jake hadn't know better he'd have sworn he was in—

Whoa. He reined in the thought with an accompanying sense of genuine panic.

'Good crowd tonight.'

Suddenly Rick appeared beside him, depositing a dark pint of real ale into Jake's hands with relish. Taking a deep draught of his own drink, he exhaled with pleasure, wiping the froth from his top lip with a grin.

'I've been told by the barman that this stuff is like nectar. It certainly beats that pint of warm dishwater masquerading as alcohol that I had last night.'

'I'll take your word for it.' Warily, Jake raised his glass to sample some of the dark brew for himself. As it slid down his throat the bitter taste of hops lingered unpleasantly in his mouth, confirming what he already knew to be true… he was no real ale aficionado. Give him a bourbon and Coke any day.

'So, how do you think things are going?' Rick asked, turning briefly to flash an irrepressible grin at a shapely blonde who'd walked by.

'So far so good,' Jake answered, his glance instinctively guarded. 'The band sounds great, and Caitlin's singing just gets better and better. We're going to be getting more great reviews…it's a given.'

'Man, I bless the day she walked into that musty old church hall and her voice blew us away. The gods were smiling on us that day, that's for sure.'

'I agree.'

'Hey, Jake, I hope you didn't take my advice about not getting involved with Cait too personally. I mean, we've been friends for a long time. We've never let a woman come between us before.'

'It was sound advice,' Jake replied soberly.

'Not that I blame you for being attracted to her. She sure is one beautiful woman, isn't she?'

Taking another reluctant sip of his beer, Jake remarked, 'You won't get an argument from me.'

The lights suddenly dimmed, and amid the tangible air of expectation that rippled round the audience the band walked onto the stage.

Jake's excitement was heightened along with everyone else's, but the smile on his face quickly turned into a frown when he saw what Caitlin was wearing. In place of the long skirts and silky tops she'd been favouring since they'd started the tour she was dressed in black bootcut jeans that hugged her hips like a second skin and a stretchy little white top that emphasised her eye-catching chest.

The males in the crowd weren't slow in demonstrating their appreciation. Jake did his best to try and shut out some of the more ribald comments. But with her flowing black hair, smiling green eyes and long legs, Caitlin was doing serious things to his blood pressure. He knew it was crazy, but he hated the mere idea that every red-blooded man in the room was fantasising about her. And underneath the hot, swift stab of jealousy that assailed him Jake felt a growing admiration for her daring. It seemed that Little Miss Hole-in-Her-Stocking was finally coming out of her shell.

Registering the looks of delight on the faces of the other band members as well as the crowd's, Caitlin launched into a mesmerising rendition of an iconic blues number and Jake silently acknowledged that her talent was astounding. As he watched her hips sway sexily to the music, her little white top riding up almost to waist level, he didn't think he'd ever felt so aroused or more hungry for a woman in his life.

* * *

Caitlin was quickly learning that after the almighty adrenaline rush of a live performance it was easy to crash down to the absolute depths shortly after. Now, alone in yet another hotel room—albeit a very luxurious one—with her room service supper left untouched on a tray, she sat in her pyjamas and robe with her head in her hands, feeling lonely and depressed.

An attack of the blues was the last thing she needed. But, as well as missing Jake's touch, the truth was that she was missing Lia—missing the easy camaraderie they shared. She also missed the buzz of working with her in the bookshop. Caitlin wasn't ungrateful for the privileged position she found herself in—actually living her dream of being a singer—but she'd be lying if she said she didn't miss the people and the place that she thought of as home.

Sighing, she reached for a magazine that was lying on the coffee table and decided to take it to bed with her. She was heading towards the prettily covered divan when there was a soft knock on the door. She opened it to Jake.

'Hi,' he greeted her. 'Can we talk?'

With her heart skipping a beat, she automatically stepped aside to let him enter. Her whole world immediately narrowed down to the force of his presence, her senses registering sensation overload with just one whiff of that sexy cologne he wore and one scorching glance from those extraordinary blue eyes of his.

Jake was a big part of the reason that Caitlin had crashed so low after tonight's performance. She still didn't really know where she stood with him, and the situation was making her as jumpy as if she was walking barefoot on tin tacks. One minute he was scowling at her and the next he was eating her up with his eyes. No wonder her nerves were stretched tight to the point of snapping.

Tonight he'd been very cool again, addressing her only when he had to, while in contrast Rick and the guys in the band had been elated with her performance and hadn't hesitated to show it. She was seriously perturbed that Jake seemed intent on giving her the cold shoulder. Had he decided that she was right about keeping their relationship a purely business one?

'You didn't eat your supper.' He glanced at the untouched tray of food balanced on the coffee table..

'I wasn't very hungry.'

'You have to eat to keep your strength up. Performing night after night can really take it out of you.'

'Thanks for your concern.' Making no attempt to couch the sarcasm in her tone, Caitlin raked her fingers through her recently washed hair, then caught the belt on her robe and wound it round her hand.

'Your performance tonight was wonderful. Anyone would think you'd been doing this for years. The others can't sing your praises enough.'

'And you?'

She barely managed to get the words past the ache in her throat. She ached to touch him, to drive that too serious expression from his haunting eyes and make him smile.

'If I started to tell you what I really think about you I wouldn't get back to my room tonight.'

His voice was huskily low, and every word he uttered sent inflammatory arrows of desire scudding crazily all over her body. Grabbing for a lifeline, Caitlin's gaze found and settled on the bottle of mineral water she'd ordered with her meal.

'Would you like a drink? It's only water, but—'

'I don't want a drink. I know I'm breaking all the rules here, but the truth is, Caitlin, I just can't stay away.'

His glance never leaving her face, he shrugged off his leather jacket and threw it onto a chair. Her mouth went dry at the sight of the hard, lean biceps that defined his upper arms in his black short-sleeved T-shirt. Startled, she focused on the dimple right in the centre of his chin—as usual his firm jaw was fashionably unshaven—but the dark shadow of beard didn't detract one jot from his heartbreakingly good looks. If anything, it simply added to the 'bad boy' persona he seemed to project without even trying.

'Well, you should,' she snapped. Turning on her heel, she unscrewed the top of the bottle of mineral water and took a swig. When she'd finished she turned back again and said, 'Because I don't want you here.'

Not commenting, Jake strolled across to the light switch and dimmed the overhead lights to a softly seductive glow.

Barely aware of what she was doing, Caitlin placed the water bottle back down on the tray. 'What are you doing?'

'I want you to come over here.'

'No.' But even as she answered in the negative she moved slowly towards him, as if she didn't have a will of her own...

When she was almost there she stopped and stared at him with desperation in her eyes. Jake opened his arms. In less than a second she'd closed the space between them to bury her face in the warm, musky scent of his T-shirt, registering the strong, steady throb of his heartbeat beneath the steely hardness of his chest. His hands fisted into her hair and he pressed her even closer against his body. Her heart was racing harder than it had ever raced before.

'Jake? Jake, I—' Raising her head, Caitlin stared into his smouldering gaze, want and need clawing at her as she registered the pure raw desire in his eyes.

Planting his palms either side of her face, he slanted his mouth hotly across hers to steal a hungry kiss that left them both stunned. With a groan she invited another kiss, her tongue intimately dancing with his, savouring the seductive flavours of bourbon and coffee and the hot, drugging sensuality that was uniquely *Jake*. Her hands slid down his back and lifted his T-shirt eagerly to trace the hard ridge of his spine with her fingertips. She was weak with wanting him, and when he backed up against the wall and deftly turned her in his arms, so that she took over his position, she allowed him to do it without so much as a murmur of protest.

'You know what I want to do?'

Her eyes widened in shock as well as anticipation as he expertly relieved her of her robe, then started to undo the buttons on her pyjama top.

'What?' Caitlin's voice was a barely-there bedroom rasp, because what Jake was already doing to her with his strong, sure touch and his drugging, sexy voice was nothing less than X-rated.

So much for years of trying to convince herself that her sex drive was low! Right now she didn't know how she wasn't just ripping his clothes off and taking what she wanted without hesitation. With a soft whimper, she briefly closed her eyes as he divested her of her top and feasted his hungry glance on her bared caramel-tipped breasts.

'I want to take you right here…and I want it to be hot and slow and deep…until we both go out of our minds with the pleasure.'

Even as Caitlin's heart beat wildly in her chest Jake lowered his head to claim her breast, drawing it deeply into his mouth. Bucking against him, she drove her fingers into the silky strands of his hair, crying out as ravenous need spiralled from her breast to her womb. He suckled and laved, teasing her rigid nipple with his tongue, then took her deep into his mouth again, his unshaven jaw sliding roughly cross her more tender skin, abrading her, marking her with his brand, leaving the trail of his scent all over her. Then he applied the same treatment to her other breast.

She was still quivering when Jake released her throbbing wet nipple and moved back up her body, with the wickedest smile she had ever seen. His pupils darkened to black as he settled his hands on the waist of her pyjama bottoms. With a firm tug, the silky fall of material shimmied down to her ankles. Her cheeks flushing heatedly, Caitlin watched him retrieve the protection he'd brought from his back pocket.

Her gaze immediately gravitated to his belt. He opened it to let his trousers slide down over his thighs and reveal his boxers. He loosened them, then ripped open the foil packet that contained the protection. He sheathed himself and Caitlin released a long, slow breath. Sliding her slender arms round Jake's neck, she pressed her body ardently against his. Immediately his hands moved to settle on the silky curve of her bottom, skimming her flesh and then pressing and kneading it until she was weak with want—until she thought she might die if he didn't take her soon.

Then he ravished her mouth again, before trailing hot damp kisses across her cheeks, her forehead, her eyelids, his clever hands stroking her body well past the point of no return, moving deftly to cup her in her most feminine place. Caitlin couldn't help but whimper his name, her lips pressing into the juncture between his neck and shoulder, kissing the warm masculine flesh with growing desire, taking lascivious little nips with her teeth...

Her body was primed to accept him. She knew she could no more prevent this act from reaching its logical conclusion than deny herself breath. Jake might be wary of commitment and find it hard to trust, but right then she impatiently pushed the thought aside—because she was greedy for his loving and would take anything she could get...*rightly or wrongly*. She would enjoy this time with him and revel in it. Revel in the fact that she was a sensual, desirable woman and that Jake was the only man in the world she wanted as her lover.

'Open your mouth,' he instructed, gravel-voiced and when she did he kissed her hard, sliding his hand beneath her bottom and raising her hips to the level of his. As her long, slender legs easily straddled him he plunged inside her with one sure, firm thrust, sending her world spinning off into another galaxy.

'Oh, Jake!'

Caitlin held on tight as he filled her again and again, each thrust more sure, more urgent, deeper than she could imagine, stealing kisses from her lips, her throat, her earlobe, until she thought she might die from the sheer dizzying pleasure of it.

'This is what I've been fantasising about doing all day,' he breathed against her neck, and at the same moment her world really did spin off its axis.

Jake quickly followed her. At the moment of climax he bucked hard against her, raggedly saying her name, the muscles in his toned hard body quivering like ropes of steel in the aftermath.

As his head fell forward onto her chest Caitlin drove her fingers through his tousled dark hair and had to bite her lip hard to stop herself from confessing that she loved him. *More than that, she wanted to marry him and one day have his children.*

Her certainty was so all-consuming that she thought surely Jake must sense it. But fear that all she would achieve by making such a confession might be to scare him away forever stopped her telling him. Jake had been a gypsy all his life, Rick had said, and probably always would be. What made her dare to hope for even a second that *she* could change his mind about that and help him see that they could still enjoy the pleasures of home and family?

'All right, everybody, time out. Cait? I'd like a word.'

Vaulting nimbly onto the small raised stage, Rick couldn't hide his exasperation as yet again Caitlin failed to come in at the right time on the intro.

Flushing a mortified pink, she turned round to shrug an apology to the rest of the band. To give them credit, they unanimously agreed that everyone was entitled to an off day now and then, and discreetly left the stage to her and Rick.

'What's going on with you this morning?' Rick didn't shy away from expressing his irritation. 'Didn't you get much sleep last night?'

She sighed. Sensing her cheeks burning at the accuracy

of Rick's innocent statement, she frantically thought of what she could say in answer.

To her surprise and delight Jake had spent the night. He had only returned to his room just as the sun came up—and then only reluctantly. Consequently neither of them had had much sleep...not when there had been far more exhilarating pleasures to occupy them. Caitlin knew she must have the dazed look of someone who'd burnt the candle at both ends. Her body still ached from Jake's passionate attentions and her concentration was all but shot to pieces.

Arriving for rehearsals at the intimate jazz club where they were appearing this evening, Rick had announced that Jake wouldn't be joining them until later and that until then he would be looking after things.

'I never sleep well in a strange bed,' she mumbled.

Rick's hazel eyes narrowed. 'You sure that's the reason?'

Agitatedly spearing her fingers through her hair, Caitlin sensed them tremble. Then she winced as she accidentally yanked out the silver hoop in her earlobe.

'What other reason would there be?'

'I don't know, babe...you tell me.'

She felt besieged—not to mention guilty...*guilty as hell.* Why couldn't Jake be around when she needed him? He would have taken charge of the situation in a second. She wasn't happy about lying to Rick about their relationship. With all her heart she wished they could be totally up-front about it, just as Jake had said he wanted to be.

'I don't know what you're getting at, Rick. I told you it would take me a while to get used to the change of lifestyle. It's hardly a crime that I'm feeling tired, is it?'

'No, it isn't.' Sighing heavily, Rick moved behind Caitlin and started kneading her shoulders. 'You're too tense. That's the trouble. Relax, can't you? Drop those shoulders. C'mon...listen to Uncle Rick.'

As jumpy as she was, she had to admit that what Rick was doing felt good...fantastically good. Right now her spine might have been made of concrete, she was so on edge, and anything to alleviate the tension had to be a step in the right direction. If she could only grab a couple of hours' sleep before the gig tonight she would be back on track again.

Dropping her head, she groaned as Rick's fingers applied some deeper pressure at a particularly tender spot between her shoulderblades. 'You're good at this, aren't you?' she murmured. 'You could have a whole new career, you know.'

'I must confess I've been told that before.'

Caitlin heard the smile in his voice.

'By one or two very grateful ladies who've succumbed to the pleasures of these hands.'

'You're quite the Casanova, aren't you?'

'Yes, well…if the cap fits.'

Her masseur halted his ministrations to drop a brief teasing kiss at the side of her neck… Unfortunately at the very same moment that Jake walked into the room.

The band's charismatic manager stopped dead in his tracks.

'Is this how you rehearse the band, Rick? Because if it is then we've got a serious problem on our hands…wouldn't you say?'

CHAPTER ELEVEN

WITHOUT REALISING IT Jake had clenched his hands into fists down by his sides. As he fought to corral his steadily growing temper his blazing blue eyes burned back at them both, his gut swirling with jealousy. *What the hell did Caitlin think she was playing at, allowing his best friend to fool around with her like that?*

Pink-cheeked and embarrassed, she stepped towards the edge of the stage. He wasn't surprised she was defensive.

'We *were* rehearsing, Jake. I just had a couple of problems Rick was helping me with.'

'Oh?' Jake's lip curled scathingly. 'Since when did I employ Rick as the group's masseur? Clearly I missed that.'

'For goodness' sake—the girl is tired! Tired and tense… I was just helping her iron out some of the kinks so that we could get on. The guys have gone outside for a break. I think I'll go call them back in.'

'No. Stay right where you are.'

His boot heels ringing ominously on the wooden floor, Jake strode towards the stage.

'We don't do anything else until I get to the bottom of this.'

With a horrible sinking feeling in the pit of her stomach, Caitlin jammed her hands into her jeans pockets and took a deep breath in. Was he jealous? Was that why he was so angry?

Her heart beat double-time, because she couldn't help noticing how gorgeous he looked. Dressed in fitted black jeans, a maroon shirt and a dark pin-striped suit jacket that flowed over his lean hard body as if it was tailor-made, he resembled one of those seriously unapproachable Italian models that featured in glossy magazines. His dark tousled hair and glittering blue eyes gave him a dangerous sexy edge and ensured there was nowhere else she'd rather look than at him.

'What are you talking about, Jake?' Rick jumped off the stage to confront the other man. 'You'd better explain.'

'I'm talking about you kissing her!' Jake glared at his friend.

Rick was bemused. 'I was just fooling around. You know me…I never could resist a pretty face.'

'That's a poor excuse for fondling my—'

'Go on… Your *what,* Jake?'

He'd been about to say my woman.

The realisation hit him hard—like a brick dropped on his head from a great height. As statements of ownership went, he couldn't have put it much more clearly. Here he was, standing head to head with his best friend and long-time associate, the pair of them like a couple of prize-fighters about to go into the ring. Jake cursed under his breath. He couldn't keep a lid on his temper, could he? He'd just had to let it out. Now he'd blown the whole situation wide open.

Rick's hazel eyes narrowed. 'You're sleeping with her, aren't you?'

Caitlin bristled indignantly. She most definitely didn't appreciate being discussed as if she wasn't there…as if she was some inconsequential possession rather than a human being. But as Jake glanced up and his heated glance locked onto hers it was as though he'd reached out and touched her. For a few debilitating seconds, her head swam.

'You just couldn't keep your hands off her, could you?' Rick's tone was scathing.

'Isn't that supposed to be *my* line?'

'Don't get cute with me, Jake! Just answer the damn question.'

With a terse shrug, the other man folded his arms. 'Yes. Caitlin and I are having a relationship. But don't start jumping to conclusions. It doesn't mean it's going to impact negatively on the band.'

'Is that right? Then how come we're at loggerheads? Answer me that. How long have we worked together? It's been a long time, Jake. In all that time we've barely had an angry word—and that's something in this business. Damn shame it has to happen now…and all because of a woman!'

'And just what's *that* supposed to mean?' Stooping down to climb off the stage, Caitlin dusted her hands and wiped them shakily on her jeans. 'In case you hadn't noticed I'm a person—just like you are. What is it with you and women, Rick? You like us well enough when it suits you, but something tells me you're deeply suspicious of our motives. Just to reassure you—I have no hidden agenda, and neither have I any intention of leaving the band. That being the case, you have no reason to doubt me. When I give my word, I keep it.'

'Right now, honey, it's not *your* word that I'm concerned about.'

'Okay, Rick… If you want to discuss this any further then you'd better meet me back at the hotel when we're finished here. I'm not prepared to stand around and lock horns with you when we're already eating into valuable rehearsal time. The band has a performance to give tonight and that's priority number one.'

With a brief glance down at his watch, Jake turned his attention to Caitlin.

'I want you to pull out all the stops tonight,' he told her. 'I didn't tell you before, because I didn't want to make you nervous, but there's going to be an A&R man from one of the big labels watching the show tonight. I can't make any promises, but if you and the band impress him enough there's a real possibility of getting a record deal. Kenny Swan knows that I don't back losers, and his interest has been snared by footage of you and the guys on social media over the past few nights. I'm counting on you—so don't let me down.'

Dumbly, Caitlin nodded. The possibility of the band gaining a recording contract so soon into their tour was nothing short of amazing. Yet right at that moment it paled into insignificance next to her unquenchable longing to be in Jake's arms.

She was relieved that he'd openly admitted to Rick that they were intimate, and she wanted the chance to show him that what they felt for each other could indeed flourish into something meaningful and lasting if they trusted their feelings and gave it a chance. At least now there would be no need to hide the fact that they wanted to be together, and she could really put her heart and soul into her singing.

Jake smiled. 'Work hard and I'll see you both later. I have a couple of important calls to make.'

'Jake?'

Suddenly finding her voice again, Caitlin stopped him in his tracks as he strode towards the back of the venue. Her anxious glance encompassed a scowling Rick as he leant back against the edge of the stage.

'I don't want you and Rick to fall out over this. My commitment is first and foremost to the band. I know you know that, but I just wanted to reiterate it.'

Jake's expression was as implacable as ever. 'I'm glad to hear it. Just concentrate on giving your best performance tonight and we might all come out on top.'

And with that he walked away.

He had the worst headache in living memory. The pain was so intense it had sent him hurrying down the narrow streets at half past five in the afternoon in search of a chemist.

Holding the packet of painkillers just a few minutes later, Jake ripped out two white tablets from the foil strip and swallowed them down with a warm can of cola. Grimacing, he threw the barely touched drink into a nearby wastebin and, biting his lip against the merciless throb in his temple, returned to his hotel.

Bolting his room door, he drew the curtains shut tight to blot out what was left of the daylight, then threw himself down on the bed and stared contemptuously up at the ceiling. *One thing was certain...he couldn't go on like this.* He only suffered migraines this bad when he was pushed into a corner, and his head was letting him know that right now he was probably jammed into the tightest corner he'd ever encountered.

There was no question that he wanted Caitlin. The situation between them wouldn't have developed if he hadn't. The electricity they generated between them could turn on the Christmas lights in Oxford Street without a power socket in sight. But lust was one thing and—dared he say it?—*love* was something else entirely.

He caught his breath, mulling the thought over.

Was love what he felt for Caitlin? If it was, then where did he go from here? In most people's books love meant commitment...the one thing he had always shied away from.

Jake was pretty sure now that what he'd felt for Jodie definitely *hadn't* been love. His decision to marry the woman had been crazy and it had cost him dearly. The truth was he had never committed himself properly to her. Wasn't that why he'd taken every opportunity to distance himself by travelling so often? She'd probably sensed his reticence at being with her long before she'd had her affair.

But what if the desire to escape reared its head again when he was with Caitlin? *He couldn't bear the thought that he might break her heart.* After the hell her ex had put her through she deserved someone who wouldn't cut and run. Someone who would support her journey as a singer. Someone who would be there when she needed them. Someone she could count on to stay around for more than just a few short weeks or months… In fact *someone the complete antithesis of himself.*

And now, to make matters worse, he had Rick on his case. When all was said and done his friend had every right to be furious with him. Jake had broken his own unwritten code about fraternising with band members and he'd potentially put the band at risk because of his fascination for Caitlin.

He would endeavour to put things right as soon as Kenny Swan from Lightning Records had seen the band perform tonight. If the man gave them a recording contract then hopefully it would help Jake decide what he needed to do, and maybe then—*and it was a big maybe*—he would finally be able to have some peace.

'You can come? Lia, that's fantastic!'

Dropping down onto the bed, with its prettily embroidered quilt, Caitlin clamped her mobile firmly against her ear. To hear that her best friend was at last able to get away and come and hear her sing was the best news she'd had all day…next to the chance of Blue Sky getting a record deal, of course. But ever since that uncomfortable exchange between Jake, Rick and her at rehearsals that morning she hadn't been able to help worrying about what might happen next.

Rick's mood hadn't improved since Jake had left him in charge, and Caitlin feared for their friendship. *Was she to blame for their falling out?* If she was, then she would do her utmost to put things right. But in less than a couple of sentences Lia's cheery voice had managed to dispel her worry and doubt and replace it with a sudden rush of optimism and hope.

If Caitlin gave a good performance tonight—the *best* performance she'd ever given—the band might get that record deal, Jake and Rick's friendship might return to its previous status, and Jake might start to see that he and Caitlin had a future together outside of the band.

'I might be a little late if the traffic is bad,' Lia was saying, 'but I'll definitely be there. I've booked a room at that bed and breakfast you're staying at, like you suggested, so we'll be able to have a good old natter when we get back from the club. I'm so excited I can't wait! Hey—and you know what else?'

'What?'

Holding her hand out in front of her, Caitlin frowned at her chipped purple nail polish, wondering if she'd have time to repaint her nails before the gig tonight. It had to be right. Everything had to be right or it would be *her* fault if things went wrong. She was suspicious like that, and she wasn't taking any chances.

'I took a peek at your horoscope today,' her friend continued. 'Do you know what it said?'

'Go on.' There wasn't a muscle in Caitlin's body that didn't clench tight.

Lia took a deep breath in. 'Well, Saturn is meeting Venus today, and I'm sure you know that Venus is the planet of love and money? The timing is perfect. Saturn meets Venus beneath the auspices of the Mars/Jupiter rendezvous, so if you long for something in the money or romance stakes today's probably the time to ask for it. What do you think of that?'

Caitlin couldn't help but concentrate on the romance aspect. What would it take for Jake to see that she was serious about him? That she wanted to spend the rest of her life with him? That she'd go anywhere at any time with him and wouldn't regret a thing just so long as they could be together?

'Well, I've just been paid, so I'm okay for cash. As for romance, I…' She fell silent.

'Has something been going on?'

'What do you mean?' Leaning back against the plump pillows stacked against the padded headboard, Caitlin nervously wound a silken strand of burnished dark hair round her finger.

'Are you having an affair with someone in the band? Wait

a minute… I bet it's with the manager, Jake Sorenson.' Lia sounded emphatic. 'It's *him*, isn't it?'

'Next you'll be telling me that you're psychic.'

Smiling grimly at her own bad joke, Caitlin deliberately stalled for time. She had the beginnings of a headache and prayed that her friend wouldn't start giving her a lecture on the wisdom—or *lack* of it—in pursuing a relationship with Jake. Besides, it was far too late for her to start taking advice on *that* particular subject.

'That's not good news. It may or may not be deserved, but the man has a certain reputation after that scandal with his ex. Are you looking for trouble, or what? You're in a vulnerable situation as it is, and now you've gone and done possibly the worst thing you could do by getting involved with him! Oh, Cait…how *could* you?'

Shutting her eyes briefly tight, Caitlin slackened her hold on the phone, thought of Jake and the damage he could do to her heart with just a smile, and mused silently, *How could I not?*

'I've been looking for you.'

Jake.

At the sound of that familiar low-pitched voice Caitlin almost broke out in a sweat. Hanging her coat more securely on the old-fashioned peg in the dressing room, from which the garment had just slipped for the third time, she turned slowly round to face him. Her gaze made electrically charged contact with his.

'I popped out for some fresh air, but I've been here for about half of an hour,' she told him.

With its gilded French-style furnishings, including a sumptuous gold couch, a chaise-longue, two matching armchairs and a chic glass-topped coffee table, the room that had been designated for the band was full of old-style glamour, making it quirkily appealing and atmospheric. The walls were covered in photographs and posters of the bands and

musicians who had played there over the years—some extremely well known—and Caitlin had already spent several minutes studying them and marvelling at how fate had
brought her there to perform.

But her attention was no longer on the room. Jake's brooding presence was already making her feel feverish with need,
and she didn't think she could be any more intimately aware
of him if she tried.

'Rick's just gone to the bar to get you a drink.'

'Thanks.' She agitatedly twisted the silver bangle she was
wearing, then pushed her fingers through her hair. 'It's far
too hot in here…don't you think?'

He was smiling that roguish smile of his that could scram-
ble her brain in a second and turn her limbs to damp strands
of spaghetti.

'It's always hot when we're in a room together, Caitlin…
Don't tell me you've never noticed?'

'Yes. Well…'

'By the way, you look sensational tonight.'

Jake's glance couldn't help but avidly home in on Caitlin's
figure. She was dressed from top to toe in black—bootcut
jeans that clung lovingly to her slender thighs and a slim-
fitting shirt cut high on the waist that dipped just low enough
to give him a tantalising glimpse of her delectable cleavage.

Just thinking about the taste of that satin-smooth flesh
when he kissed her, he had to suppress the compelling urge
to lock the door behind them and keep her captive. He hoped
that Kenny Swan would appreciate the supreme sacrifice he
was making in letting Caitlin go out there to sing tonight.

'I really hope there are no hard feelings between you
and Rick.'

Jake shrugged. 'Rick and I will sort things out. We always do.'

A moment later he had shortened the distance between
them. Reaching out, he laid his palm over her cheek. Soft
as a newly opened petal, it beckoned him to touch again. As

if anticipating the event, her plump lower lip quivered and the sight inevitably made his blood slow and thicken. Now he wanted to taste her, to plunder, to *brand*...

But he was swiftly denied the pleasure when Caitlin caught hold of his hand and lifted it firmly away.

'I need to talk to you, Jake.'

'After the gig tonight. We'll have a proper conversation then.'

'No. I need to tell you something now. I've got a friend coming back with me tonight. A friend from home.'

Disappointment, heavy and crushing, cramped his chest. 'Male or female?' he quipped jealously, straight away knowing that as a matter of principle he disliked the person already. *It didn't matter about the decision he ultimately had to make for both their sakes.* Right then, Jake wanted the dark-haired beauty in front of him exclusively for himself.

'It's Lia.' She shrugged a shoulder. 'The owner of the shop where I worked.'

'I remember...the one who had to have some wisdom teeth removed?'

Smiling wryly, Jake lifted a strand of Caitlin's hair and stared down at it, transfixed. Her green eyes widened.

'Jake? Is everything all right?'

Even as she asked the question dread coiled in the pit of her stomach. Somehow she knew that everything *wasn't* all right. There was something he wasn't telling her...something she was certain would cause her untold hurt...something she didn't want to know until she absolutely *had* to—because right then all she wanted to do was keep this man in her company until the last possible second...

'Stop worrying. Everything's fine.'

Jake had just bent his head to kiss her when Rick pushed opened the door and strode in. Depositing the tray of drinks he carried down onto the coffee table, his hazel eyes locked accusingly onto them both.

'Still taking care of business, Jake?' he commented sarcastically.

Even before Jake stepped out of their embrace Caitlin sensed his anger and irritation. Once again she put the blame for helping to create animosity between the two men squarely on her own shoulders.

'Don't blame Jake.' Lifting her chin, she unwaveringly met Rick's glance. 'It's my fault. I was the one who—'

'Save it, sweetheart.' His smile was resigned, but not unkind. 'You wouldn't be the first woman to become infatuated with Jake, and if I'm not mistaken you won't be the last.'

'I'd stop right there if I were you.' The cold glare that Jake directed at his colleague glittered like the sparkle of ice in a glacier.

'Why?' Rick demanded. 'Because you don't want her to hear the truth?'

'What truth?' Caitlin's mouth had already gone dry as sand.

'Jake doesn't have a particularly good track record with women. In this business not many men do...the temptations are often too great to resist. But, to be fair...' His glance focused even more intently on Jake. 'He *was* burned badly by his ex, and after that he swore never to commit to another woman again. I'd be very surprised if that view had changed. In any case, whatever he's told you, I wouldn't take it too seriously, Cait.'

The tension that rebounded between them deepened. In the pit of her stomach Caitlin felt sick, cold dread. Was he telling the truth? Was Jake intending to end their relationship before it had even really got started? Had she been painfully naïve in thinking that their passionate lovemaking really mattered to him? Jake had already made it clear that he wasn't offering her anything more meaningful.

What an idiot she was! When was she going to learn that some men were in the business of *taking*, not giving? Every time her ex Sean had told her that things would be different, that he would change, that they had a bright future together, she had believed him. Yes, she had even believed him when she'd bailed him out with the last five hundred pounds in her savings account, because he'd sworn to pay it back with interest. *Of course he never had.*

This wouldn't be the first time she'd been deceived by a man. But then, maybe *she* had done some of the deceiving. Hadn't she deceived herself when she'd believed that, given time and the chance to really get to know her, Jake might want to take their relationship more seriously? Her heart ached with renewed hurt when she realised finally that it wasn't true…could *never* be true.

'It's all right, Jake.' Even though her eyes had filled with tears, Caitlin faced him with an unflinching stare. 'Whatever you might think, I'm not as naïve as you imagine. We slept together, we made love…but deep down I never thought you intended to take things further. Don't worry. I'm not going to make a scene. And, despite what *you* might think, Rick, I'm not going to go to pieces because it's over between Jake and me. We'll still have a professional relationship…a good one, I hope. And now that that's clear I think I'll go and find the others and check in with them.'

She made a move to turn away.

'No—not like this, Caitlin.'

Jake scraped a frustrated hand through his hair. He was furious with Rick for putting him in such an untenable position. But he was also furious with himself—because now it looked as if he'd deliberately used Caitlin. *Nothing could be further from the truth.* He was crazy about her. Thinking of her practically consumed his every waking moment. What he felt for her was like nothing he'd ever experienced before, and the power of it took his breath away. And if he had trouble telling her that, then it was surely down to an inherent lack of trust that anything good could ever last?

Never in his life had he experienced feeling safe. Even as a small boy in the children's home he'd known that when he fell he fell alone. There would be no loving parent to pick him up and reassure him that everything would be all right.

Jake swallowed hard. Caitlin's beautiful emerald eyes were glistening with tears and in those few heartrending seconds he had never felt lower.

'I never meant to hurt you,' he breathed, lifting his hand to dry the moisture that tracked down her cheek.

She immediately backed away. 'Forget it.' Not giving him even the merest glance, instead she looked at Rick and enquired, 'Are the boys in the bar?' He nodded. 'Then I'll go and join them.'

She headed towards the door—but not before she heard him say to Jake, 'Just as well I'm around to pick up the pieces.'

CHAPTER TWELVE

JAKE COULDN'T BELIEVE that Caitlin had accepted a lift back to her guesthouse from Kenny Swan. The man was a smooth-talking Lothario, old enough to be her father. What on earth had possessed her? He had been all over her like a cheap suit, and if it hadn't been for the fact that Rick had pleaded with Jake not to make a fuss, because at the end of the gig Swan had offered them a lucrative contract, Jake would have put him straight about a few things.

As far as he was concerned a deal wasn't a deal until all the 'i's had been dotted and the 't's crossed, and he wasn't agreeing to a damn thing until he examined the details for himself...*preferably* under a microscope. He hadn't spent fifteen years working in the industry for nothing.

But right then, even though Blue Sky's good fortune should have been uppermost in his mind, it wasn't. *Caitlin* was. He could have strangled Rick for forcing the issue between them out into the open like that, without any regard for their feelings. No wonder Caitlin was mad at Jake. She had every right to be. And now he was suffering all kinds of agony, wondering if Kenny Swan had taken her straight back to her guesthouse or whether he had persuaded her to go home with him to his penthouse in Mayfair.

As far as pretty women went, rumour had it that the man had very few scruples. And it was little consolation to Jake to recall that Caitlin's friend Lia had been with her. He'd in-tuited that the blonde could easily take care of herself, and

Kenny wouldn't have hesitated to drop her off at the guest-house and then continue on to London with Caitlin, should she agree to the arrangement.

But even as he had the thought Jake knew that she *wouldn't*. She would never abandon her friend...she was far too loyal for that.

If only Jake hadn't been waylaid by the rest of the band, wanting to discuss the record deal, at the same time that Caitlin had been ensnared by Kenny at the bar, he would have persuaded her to go outside with him and get some fresh air. By the time he'd been able to return his attention to them Jake had seen that they were gone. He'd dashed outside, only to see the tail-end of Kenny's gleaming sedan with its tinted windows disappearing into the night—no doubt with Caitlin seated snugly beside him while her little blonde girlfriend sat in the back.

'I thought you could probably use this.' Rick placed a steam-ing cup of black coffee on the bar and pulled up a stool next to Jake.

The venue was slowly emptying of late-night revellers who'd watched the band and were clearly reluctant to go home. Behind the two men bar staff were methodically clear-ing tables and stacking chairs. A mournful-sounding love song was playing softly in the background, and Jake couldn't help but feel despondent. The relentless longing for Caitlin that had taken up residence in his heart didn't abate, and he knew it was serious. The mere idea that she might walk away and find somebody else was simply not to be tolerated. *It dawned on him then that he'd move heaven and earth just to be with her...*

'Thanks.'

'I scrounged it off a pretty barmaid...charmed her with my good looks and irresistible wit.'

'Now, there's a surprise,' Jake commented drolly.

The two men fell silent for a while.

As if disturbed by the gloomy expression that flitted across his friend's features, Rick remarked consolingly, 'Kenny's probably just dropped her off at the guesthouse. Cait's a clever girl. If he tries anything she'll soon put him straight.'

'You think? But I could hardly blame her if she *did* go home with him, could I?' Jake stared grimly down into his coffee.

'You really care about her, don't you?'

There was a tone of genuine surprise in the other man's voice.

'Is that so hard to believe?'

'I'm sorry, buddy. I just—'

Jake sighed. 'What I felt for Jodie all those years ago wasn't love, Rick. I was just tired of being alone and I kidded myself she was important to me in the ridiculous hope that my feelings might grow fonder. Needless to say, when I realised she only wanted me for what she could get, they *didn't*. As things turned out…I'm glad about that. I'd rather she took my money and everything I possessed than broke my heart. That's a pain I couldn't get over so easily.' Grimacing, he shook his head. 'But what I feel for Caitlin is… Well, it's like nothing I've ever experienced before. I already know she's got the power to break my heart.'

'Sounds to me like it's love, Jake.'

He didn't dispute the fact. For a few heartfelt moments he let the thought settle.

'Look, I know I should put the band first, but to tell you the truth I've been thinking about resigning as manager and asking you to take over. I was thinking I should get out while the going's good and limit any disappointment and ill feeling it might cause. Things are really starting to take off for Blue Sky, and you know exactly what to do to maximise their potential and take them right to the top. They trust you, Rick. You'll all be just fine without me.'

'Why would you want to resign, Jake? Is it because you're afraid of hurting Cait?'

'She deserves this chance just as much as the others do. What she *doesn't* deserve is for me to screw it up because I've become personally involved with her. I don't know if I'm capable of maintaining the necessary professional detachment any more. I feel like a house of cards that's been knocked down. It's not like me to lose my head over a woman. But since falling for Caitlin I can't eat, I can't sleep, and my concentration feels like it's been blown apart by a scatter gun. At this rate I'm not going to be much use to anyone—let alone myself.'

With a rueful grin, Jake raised his coffee to his lips.

It was Rick's turn to sigh. 'Trust me, resigning isn't the answer. Cait wouldn't want that, and nor would the guys. And *nor*, for that matter, would I. If you want her then go after her, man! What are you sitting here for? If she *has* gone back to Kenny's—'

'I thought you said that wasn't likely?'

Jake's cup clattered against the saucer and hot black coffee sloshed messily over the side. He was suddenly seized by the most terrible doubt. *Would* Caitlin have been persuaded by Kenny to go home with him? What if she had agreed in order to teach Jake a lesson?

'Hey, slow down. Of course it's not.' Rick said. 'Look, I'm sorry if I haven't been as supportive as I could have been. I guess I'm just very protective of the band. I'll just have to accept the fact that you and Cait are an item now. Having got to know her a little, and knowing you like I do, I'm sure you won't let your relationship damage the band in any way. To tell you the truth, I'm glad you've finally found someone you really care about. In my opinion, you couldn't have found anyone better than Caitlin. She's pretty special. If you really want to check that she's okay why don't you drive over to the guesthouse and see if you can talk to her?' he exhorted.

Moved by his friend's support, and clutching at a ray of hope he perhaps had no right to cling to, Jake glanced down at his watch.

'It's two in the morning, Rick. I booked her into a guest-house because she said she didn't want to stay in another soulless swanky hotel, and the place is run by a landlady who's about as friendly as Attila the Hun. When I booked the place that reassured me. She keeps strict hours and she likes her guests to be back before midnight. The prospect of banging on her door at this hour of the night just so that I can tell Caitlin I—'

'Love her?'

The grin hijacking his friend's face was wide. Jake scowled. Then he drove his hands agitatedly through his hair.

'Is that what you call this perpetual longing and needing and climbing the walls when I can't be with her?'

The other man nodded knowingly.

Inside Jake's chest his heartbeat stumbled at the realisation that he'd allowed Caitlin to believe that his attraction to her was purely physical. *He'd been seriously kidding himself.* Now he knew that he'd put her happiness and wellbeing way above his own. That was why he'd told Rick he was willing to resign as the group's manager.

He blew out a long, slow breath. 'Then I guess you're right. But if she thinks that means us moving in together into some detached mock-Georgian in the suburbs then we're likely to have our first real fight. I couldn't do it. That's why I've never settled anywhere. I'm a born gypsy. I get too restless to stay in one place for long...you know that.'

'Yeah, and I also know that you haven't even asked the lady what she wants yet. First you need to tell her that you love her. Caitlin's a great girl, Jake. She's as passionate as you are and she loves the band. She loves singing. Do you think she would have auditioned if she'd wanted to settle for some safe little existence in the suburbs? I hardly think so.'

Glancing back at Rick, he felt the ray of hope that had surfaced earlier suddenly grow much brighter.

'Hey, if you ever get tired of being on the road I could see you winding up as some sort of relationship counsellor.'

'You think so?'

'No, I don't.' To Rick's consternation, Jake lightly punched him on the shoulder and laughed. 'Not in a million years.'

'That aside, what are you going to do about Cait? Are you going to try and see her tonight?'

'No... Not tonight. It's been a tough few days and she needs her rest. I'll just have to trust she went back to the guesthouse with Lia and go and see her in the morning. In the meantime...' He reached into his back pocket to retrieve his mobile, 'I'll send her a text...just to check.'

'Sounds like a plan. Now that's settled, how about a *real* drink?'

Signalling to one of the barmaids, Rick gave her one of his incorrigible smiles and looked hopeful.

Having ordered a latte and a blueberry muffin, Caitlin stared out through the café window at the frigid purple and grey sky that definitely heralded rain. It didn't particularly disturb her. She couldn't feel much gloomier than she did already.

The impersonal little text she'd received last night from Jake had hardly been reassuring.

Hope you enjoyed last night's gig and got back to the guesthouse OK. I'll catch up with you in the morning.

He hadn't even included an 'x' to denote a kiss.

But then she knew she had played her part when she'd stupidly accepted a lift from Kenny Swan without even telling him. She'd done it because Jake had been busy talking to the rest of the band and she had felt inexplicably jealous. *Ignored.* She knew it was ridiculous, because he *was* the group's manager, but right then she hadn't wanted to share him with anyone. Even Lia's reassuring presence hadn't consoled her.

The news about the recording contract was wonderful, but her pleasure was sadly tainted by the hurtful realisation that the man she loved didn't love her back.

'Cheer up, love, it may never happen.' The handsome young assistant who had taken her order returned with her coffee and cake.

'What did you say?' She glanced up at him, not comprehending.

'You looked sad…I was just trying to cheer you up. Anyway, enjoy your coffee.' With a cheeky wink and a tuneless whistle, he returned behind the counter.

Discovering that she'd suddenly lost all desire for cake, and after taking just a few sips of her coffee, Caitlin scraped back her chair, left the money for her bill on the table and hurriedly left. *How could she possibly eat when all she could think about was Jake?*

'Where have you been?'

He was waiting outside the guesthouse when she returned and the expression on his face was as implacable as ever. Steeling herself against the blast of icy wind that suddenly hit her, Caitlin shoved her long hair out of her eyes and stared.

'It's nice to see you, too,' she murmured..

'I was worried about you. I even got your landlady to check your room—which was no easy feat, I can tell you. She told me that your bed was made but she couldn't tell whether you'd slept in it or not.' Stepping towards her, he frowned. 'What's going on, Caitlin?'

'Nothing… I just went for a cup of coffee, that's all.'

'So you *did* sleep in your bed last night?'

'Of course I did.'

'Why didn't you reply to my message asking if you were Okay?'

'It was two o'clock in the morning when you sent it— that's why. I was tired and I fell back to sleep. Wait a min- ute…where did you think I'd slept if it wasn't in my bed at the guesthouse?'

'You were eager enough to go off with Kenny.'

'The man offered us a lift, and because you seemed busy talking to Rick and the others I accepted. I was tired, Jake. I'm still a novice at this game and I expend a lot of energy trying to get it right.'

'You're doing just fine, Caitlin. In fact you never cease to amaze me with how dedicated you are in giving a great performance. Last night you were flawless. You knocked it out of the park!'

'Thanks.'

Her smile was guarded and a flash of pain squeezed at Jake's heart. *Had he pushed her too hard?* He'd hate to think she wasn't deriving any pleasure from singing with the band any more.

Making a concerned examination of her features, he no- ticed for the first time that she was unusually pale, and be- neath her lovely green eyes he could see bruising shadows.

'We should talk,' he said quietly.

'Not right now. I need to go inside and pack and say good- bye to my friend. She'll be wondering where I am. I didn't wake her to let her know I was going out.'

She moved towards the steps that led up to the house's front door. Jake stared in disbelief. Then he came to his senses and caught hold of her arm.

'Are you trying to hide something from me, Caitlin?'

'What do you mean?'

'Tell me the truth. *Did* you stay at Kenny's place last night?' He was unable to hold back his fury at the thought.

Her green eyes flashed.

'I already told you that I didn't. The man is a snake. I

know he wants to sign us, but if the agreement means he has some unspoken right to make suggestive remarks to me whenever he gets the chance then you can find another singer—and I don't say that lightly. I love this band, and I want it to do well. But I've played the part of sacrificial lamb before, and I'm damn sure I'm not going to play it again. Not for anybody!'

'Did he insult you? Hurt you?' Jake's voice was a gravelly undertone.

He could hardly believe that he'd put Caitlin in such a vulnerable position. When he saw Kenny Swan again he'd have to be physically restrained from connecting his fist to his jaw…contract or no contract. And he was pretty sure the rest of the crew would feel the same.

'Of course he didn't. Apart from making me cringe at some of the comments he made about his sexual prowess and inviting me to join him in his hot tub he didn't try anything. Anyway, Lia was with me,' she answered. 'Plus, like I told you before, I'm tougher than I look. Lucky for me I wear any bruises I acquire on the *inside*.'

The idea that he might be responsible for some of those invisible bruises affected Jake more deeply than he could say.

'I'm sorry. But you should never have agreed to let him drive you home. You should have come to get me and I would have taken you and Lia back to the guesthouse straight away. Now, why don't you go and say goodbye to Lia, then come back to my hotel with me?'

Caitlin couldn't easily hide the resentment that flashed through her. She pulled her arm free and rubbed it.

'What would be the point, Jake? If you want to talk about our relationship then there's really not much to discuss, is there? Why prolong the agony? We had an affair…a meaningless affair. It happens all the time—especially in this business. You of all people should know that.'

'Meaningless? Is that what you think this is?'

Jake hated hearing her talk like that...as if he made a habit of sleeping with different women just because he could. He'd never been a saint, but neither was he promiscuous—despite what the gossip columns might have suggested over the years.

For the first time since he'd acknowledged his feelings about Caitlin to himself Jake was forced to consider that perhaps she didn't feel as intensely as he did. The thought was so unpalatable that it hit him with all the force of an express train travelling at full speed. Suddenly being uncertain of his ground shook him badly.

'Like I said, you've made your feelings about me pretty clear.' She sighed. 'It was me that clouded things with my stupid hopes and dreams. You'd think I would have learned after Sean, wouldn't you? Anyway, the band is the most important thing...not whatever's going on between you and me. At least we're agreed on that.'

Twisting her hands together, Caitlin managed a tremulous smile just before she turned away.

If I can just hold it together until he goes, she thought, then I might...just might...get through this with my pride and dignity intact. And I might stop him from ever finding out that he's the only man who has my heart and always will...

'You're wrong, you know.'

Still with her back to Jake, Caitlin released a weary sigh. 'Wrong about what?'

'The band *isn't* the most important thing to me.'

She froze. Then she slowly turned round to find him wearing a smile that was uninhibitedly warm and sexy, and it drove every single thought out of her head. His twinkling glance fused to hers and she couldn't have looked away even if she'd wanted to. As her body was suffused with unexpected heat even the icy wind swirling round them seemed suddenly to grow less frigid.

Her mouth drying, she asked, 'It isn't?'

'No, it isn't. *You* are, Caitlin. You're the most important thing in my life. I'm not proud of the way I've handled things between us, but to say I've never felt like this before would be the understatement of the century. An earthquake couldn't have shaken me up more.'

'I wondered where you'd got to, Cait. Now I see what's delayed you.'

The front door opened to reveal the diminutive Lia, dressed in pink sweatshirt and jeans, her brown eyes alighting on Jake as if she'd inadvertently stumbled upon the devil incarnate.

'What's *he* doing here? Unless he's come to talk to you about work then I think you should tell him to go. He'll only upset you, and you've had enough grief from him already to last you a lifetime.'

'Hang on a minute, Lia, I—'

Caitlin was cut short when the blonde hurried down the steps and pushed her aside to plant herself in front of Jake. With her hands on her hips, she proceeded to tell him exactly how she felt.

'She broke her heart over you last night, Jake Sorenson. She cried like the rain. I've never seen her cry like that since she was with Sean—and he took her for a ride too, making promises he never intended to keep. I *told* her you'd break her heart. Well, I hope you're feeling proud of yourself. And then, if your own conduct wasn't bad enough, you go and leave her in the clutches of that middle-aged Lothario, reeking of enough cologne to sink a battleship! Thank heaven I was with her last night or God only knows what might have happened. If you and he are an example of the kind of people in the music industry then Caitlin would be better off singing at our local pub on a Saturday night. At least she'd be safe.'

Shock jack-knifed roughly through Jake at the thought that he hadn't protected Caitlin when he should have, and regret that he'd caused her even a moment's pain. He could see how the situation must appear to Lia, and he'd be the first to admit it didn't look good. It was a crying shame that his reputation preceded him, because no matter how he behaved he was damned—in the blonde's eyes at least And Kenny Swan's conduct didn't exactly create the best of impressions either.

He fixed the girl with a steely glare.

'Please don't slot me into the same category as Kenny Swan. At least spare me *that* particular insult. I assure you that Blue Sky won't be dealing with him again. More to the point, I'll ensure that Caitlin deals with someone else at the record company. There are plenty of genuinely good people who work there. As for the rest—I think that's between Caitlin and me...don't you?'

'Caitlin?' Her brown eyes glinting like a protective mama bear's, Lia folded her arms and looked round at her friend for confirmation.

Caitlin nodded. 'I'd like to have a few minutes alone with Jake. I think it's needed.'

'Just as long as you don't let him persuade you to do anything you don't want to do. You've got free will, remember? You got over Sean and you can get over *him* too.'

With a warning glance at a bemused Jake, Lia sprinted back up the stairs and went inside the house.

'Does she always behave like an aggrieved matador about to pick a fight with a bull?' he asked dryly.

Caitlin's smile was tentative. 'For some reason she's very protective of me.'

'I'm glad.'

Although in future Jake wanted to be the one doing all the protecting. He knew that now—knew it without a single doubt. The thought was exhilarating...like a hang glider hitting a warm air thermal. All he had to do now was convince her that he was in earnest.

'Will you come back with me to the hotel for a while? I'd really like to say what I have to say to you in private.'

Smoothing her hand down the front of her raincoat, Caitlin sucked in a steadying breath.

'I have something I want to say to you too, Jake. But I'm not waiting until we get back to your hotel. It's better said out here, in the open. You've told me that I'm important to you, but the truth is…the truth is I don't know if I can be enough for you.'

She swallowed hard, her cheeks glowing a little with embarrassment.

'What about the next pretty girl who becomes infatuated with you? You like your lifestyle just the way it is. You don't want to commit yourself to one person and I don't want anything less.'

There…she'd finally said it. She'd put her cards on the table and the consequences be damned.

'Is that what you think? That you're not enough for me?'

To Caitlin's consternation, he laughed out loud.

'I don't know if I could handle you if you were any more woman than you are already, but I'd willingly die trying! What's all this talk about not being enough? Caitlin, you're my fantasy come to life—my most heartfelt dream come true. Why would I be remotely interested in any other woman? It's true that there will always be pretty women in this business, but that doesn't mean I'll be remotely interested. Why would I if I have you? In any case, most of my time and energy goes into my work, and that's the way I've wanted it…up until now, that is.'

With a meaningful pause Jake allowed his gorgeous blue eyes to reflect a promise that Caitlin hardly dared believe.

He continued. 'And now I'm planning on using some of that time and energy in keeping you one very happy and contented woman, Caitlin Ryan…for the rest of your life.'

'What are you telling me, Jake?' She still wasn't convinced of the startling equation her fevered brain had helplessly arrived at.

'Is it really so hard to comprehend?' He smiled, 'I'm asking you to marry me.'

'You're serious?'

Her breath caught on a gasp. She was giddy and light-headed at the same time, just as if she'd been spinning on a carousel.

'I'm perfectly serious.'

Jake purposefully covered the short distance between them and took hold of Caitlin's hands in earnest.

'Don't you get it? I love you and I want you to be my wife. I think you already know what a nomadic life this is, being on the road with a band…it's never going to be a conventional lifestyle. I'd be lying to you if I said it would be.'

'That's a relief, because that wouldn't suit me at all. I'm a bona fide rock chick now, remember? I have my reputation to consider.' Caitlin's smile was uninhibitedly warm. 'Home will always be wherever we are together, Jake. There's a big wide world out there and I want to see some of it. If you're willing, you could show me, couldn't you?'

'I can't think of anything I'd like more.'

Suddenly impatient, Jake pulled her into his arms and planted a hot, hungry kiss on her mouth. He heard the soft helpless moan she breathed as he gently withdrew. Drawing the pad of his thumb down over her cheek, he was deeply satisfied to see the mutual desire and longing that her pretty green eyes reflected back at him.

'But I don't want you to think that I'm not open to compromise regarding a more permanent home,' he told her. 'Eventually I'd like us to have children…buy a place in the country, maybe? A place where they'll have plenty of space to play and grow up.'

Caitlin couldn't help but be moved by his heartfelt declaration. To hear Jake say that he wanted them to have children, that he was more than willing to embrace the prospect and ensure that his own children did not have a lonely childhood bereft of family or siblings like he had done… Well, it was *beyond* wonderful.

She sighed. 'I love you, Jake…I love you with all my

heart. There's no one I'd want to be the father of my children but you. Do you really want to marry me?'

'Right now I can't think of anything I want more than for you to be my wife. Except perhaps to have you naked in my bed.'

'And us being married—it won't cramp your famous rock and roll lifestyle?'

Jake grimaced. 'The so-called rock and roll lifestyle isn't all it's cracked up to be. For one, it's bloody lonely out on the road for weeks at a time, and after a while one hotel room looks much the same as another…whether it's in Islington or Istanbul. I'm never going to be a conventional nine-to-five husband, Caitlin, but I'll always be there for you when you need me. That's a promise.'

'Then I suppose my answer to such a sincere and heartfelt proposal has to be yes.'

'Yes, what?'

Lia put her head impatiently round the door, her chin jutted warningly towards Jake.

Grinning, Caitlin told her. 'Jake has just asked me to marry him.'

Lia's face was a picture. Tussling between giving them both a lecture and fighting the urge to smile, because of the way Jake's twinkling blue eyes were all but devouring her friend, she concluded that it would be a crime against passion for the two of them *not* to get married.

'Oh. I suppose that's all right, then.'

Jake's eyebrows flew up. 'You mean we have your permission?'

'You know very well that Caitlin doesn't need my permission.' With an irritated huff, Lia stepped out to survey them properly. 'But when you care about people you naturally want what's best for them.'

'I agree.' Glancing towards her, he said clearly, 'I love your friend, Lia. And, if you'd be so kind as to leave us alone together for a while, I won't hesitate to demonstrate the fact.'

The neatly painted front door of the guesthouse closed behind Lia with an obliging click.

As Jake's mouth descended avariciously on Caitlin's lips a profound sense of coming home rolled over her. The sensation was so powerful and so warm that she knew to the depths of her soul that there was no more room for doubt or mistrust. She was no longer a displaced person, aching for someone to love who would unreservedly love her back.

She'd grown in confidence since joining Blue Sky, and wherever her journey as a singer took her everything would be all right—because Jake would be there with her, loving her and rooting for her all the way…her husband, her manager, her friend—and, one day, the beloved father of her children.

Long seconds later Jake broke off their kiss to gaze deeply into Caitlin's eyes. 'There's just one small snag,' he said seriously.

'Oh? What's that?'

'You *do* know that we're probably going to have to contend with Rick singing a solo at the wedding?'

'Is there any way we can divert him?'

'We can always ask Tina, the barmaid at the Pilgrim's Inn, if she'd help us out.'

'Do you think that she would?'

'How could she *resist?*'

They were still laughing as they ascended the guesthouse steps, intent on sharing a celebratory drink with Lia.

* * * * *

THE MAN SHE
CAN'T FORGET

MAGGIE COX

CHAPTER ONE

IT HAD SEEMED like a good idea at the time. If only Lara had remembered her brother Sean's sage advice to 'expect the unexpected', then she might have thought twice about agreeing to stay at their parents' home while they took a much needed restorative break in the south of France.

But then Sean wasn't there any more to remind her of that particular little pearl....

And, in truth, she would never have dreamt of refusing her mum and dad's request to house-sit for them when they were still reeling from the tragedy that had hit them all six months ago. *Their son, Sean, Lara's brother, was dead.* He had contracted malaria whilst undertaking the charity work that he loved in Africa and had not recovered from it. It hardly seemed real that such a thing was possible in the twenty-first century, but sadly it was.

Having already been back in the family home for a week now, Lara still expected him to walk through the door with a cheery, 'Put the kettle on, sis, I could murder a cup of tea!' just like he had done when they were teenagers.

Time seemed intent on playing tricks on her these

days. One minute it passed like a slow and choking mudslide, threatening to cut off her ability to breathe, and the next... The next it seemed to vanish completely, leaving her feeling that she was stuck in a desolate and unhappy dream that she couldn't wake up from.

Whilst she loved her work, she was glad that the college term had come to an end. Her duties and responsibilities in the library had been particularly arduous this past month, what with so many students wanting help with research to take home with them. But now that that frenetic time was over she had no choice but to fully embrace her grief and process the soul-deep pain that she felt at losing Sean.

But, truthfully, she didn't relish the prospect of the endless summer days stretching ahead of her as she normally would have done. With nothing to lighten her mood but the daily walks she would go on with Barney, her parents' devoted Border Terrier, Lara had been dreading the time to be spent alone at her parents' house.

She could have arranged to go on holiday herself when they returned from France, but she hadn't had the heart for it. A couple of friends had asked her to join them on a trip to Italy but she'd declined. How could she possibly be good company when she was still grieving so badly for Sean?

Now, in the middle of her second week's stay at the family home, Lara was sitting at the sturdy oak kitchen table, making a half-hearted attempt at eating a bowl of unappetising breakfast cereal, when the doorbell rang. Such a lyrical bell-like sound shouldn't pierce her to the very core, but it did. In fact it made her flinch. She seemed to be afraid of everything these days. But Sean being taken from them so suddenly like that had made her fear that nothing good would ever happen to her or her family again.

Rousing himself from the relaxed position he'd assumed, lying across her feet, Barney shot up and started barking and wagging his tail—just as though he was anticipating a welcome friend or visitor. Lara's nerves were jangled even more. It was eight-thirty in the morning…. Who on earth would be calling at this time?

'For goodness' sake,' she muttered beneath her breath, 'it's probably just the postman.'

Forcing herself to relax, she moved down the hardwood hallway in her bare feet, Barney eagerly following her. The day was already promising to be particularly warm, and the sun that shone through the door's decorated Victorian glass panes lit up the interior with the glare of a powerful spotlight.

Lifting her hand to shield her gaze, she squinted at the tall shadow behind the glass. Even though she didn't have a clue who it was she knew it wasn't the postman. Whoever it was, his straight, ominous stance suggested someone official. Lara's stomach executed a nervous cartwheel. *Please, God, not more bad news.*

She opened the door warily. 'Good morning.'

On the other side of the door stood a man with eyes so heartbreakingly blue that the sight of them made her catch her breath. Waves of disconcerting shock flooded her. Staring at the carved, high-cheekboned visage, with its cut-glass jaw and arresting dimple, Lara thought she was dreaming. To be confronted by the man that she'd thought never to see again, and so early in the morning, she found she was both lost for words and stunned right down to her marrow.

He was dressed in an exquisitely tailored dark suit with a dulled gold pinstripe, and the clearly custom-made clothing showed off her visitor's athletic, broad-shouldered physique to perfection. He had always looked classy, even when he was a student. Some people were just born with that exclusive air about them and this man was one of them.

As the sexy, expensive cologne he wore wafted tantalisingly beneath her nose she wanted to pinch herself, just to make sure she wasn't dreaming.

Her visitor proffered a tentative smile and she immediately sensed his uneasiness, as though for a disconcerting moment he wasn't sure what the appropriate greeting was.

'I was wondering if I might have a word with Mr or Mrs Bradley?' he asked. 'I'm a— I *was* a friend of theirs. I'm sorry I'm calling so early in the morning, but I've just got back from New York and I wanted to pay my respects to the family for their loss.'

Lara stared hard, her legs threatening to buckle beneath her. She was suddenly aware that Gabriel Devenish, her brother's best friend at university, hadn't recognised her.

Her initial reaction was to feel blessedly relieved, but that was quickly followed by a churning in her guts that made her fear she might faint.

The memory of Gabriel had haunted her for years.

He and Sean had studied for the same degree together. But while the big-hearted Sean had elected to go into charity work after graduating, Gabriel had followed in his rich uncle's footsteps and gone into the more lucrative and some might say cut-throat world of high finance.

Her brother had once told her that he'd heard on the grapevine that his friend had made an absolute fortune since moving to New York, but he'd said it in a way that had implied he almost felt sorry for him.

In any case, from the very first moment that Lara had set eyes on Gabriel, on a blistering-hot summer's day thirteen years ago, when she'd been just sixteen, she had developed the most massive crush on him. She might have been four years younger, and still at school, but that hadn't tempered her feelings. And a foolish impulse that she had lived to regret had once driven her to confess them to him.

Her memory was transported back to that night when Sean had thrown an impromptu party for some friends at the house when their parents were away.

Seeking to bolster her courage, because Gabriel had been there, Lara had drunk a little too much wine and had consequently embarrassed herself. Dancing with him a few hours later when the party was in full swing, delighted by his flirtatious comments and what she'd imagined was an invitational smile, she'd reciprocated by shyly telling him how much she liked him…that she liked him a *lot*, in fact. Then, shutting her eyes, she had moved her face up to his for a kiss.

She still remembered the look of shock on his face and the sensation of hurt that had flooded her when he'd firmly but carefully moved her away, telling her that she was his friend's little sister and that she'd read him wrong…he'd only been teasing her.

Lara practically remembered what he'd said to her word for word. He'd added, *'I'm sure there are plenty of boys your own age who would love to go out with you, Lara, but I'm a little too old for you, I fear. Anyway,*

*I have my sights set on that tall, slim blonde standing
over there. She's one of my tutors and has made no secret of the fact that she likes me.'*

Even the false sense of courage that the alcohol had
given her hadn't been able to protect Lara from being
devastated by Gabriel's rejection.... Yes, devastated,
and *humiliated*, too. Over and over again she'd speculated on the reasons why he'd spurned her. Had it really been just because she was younger than him and
because she was Sean's 'little sister'? If you cared for
a person—*really* cared—then what did it signify that
there was a bit of an age difference?

Lara had been left with the conclusion that, apart
from the bond of friendship that was between them
because she was his best friend's sister, Gabriel didn't
care for her at all. Even back then he'd set his sights on
much more potentially lucrative opportunities—a prime
example being the slim blonde tutor from his university.

Ever since that painful incident at the party Lara's
relationships with men had never seemed to progress
much beyond friendship, even when she'd wished that
they would. The trouble was she no longer trusted herself to read the correct signals as far as the opposite sex
were concerned. Also, in spite of Gabriel's rejection,
she realised that she still harboured impossibly romantic feelings towards her brother's friend. Had she turned
him into a bit of a fantasy figure over the years? A fantasy that no other man could possibly hope to live up to?

He had definitely been a hard man to forget....

Lara's throat was uncomfortably dry, but looking
back at him now, she somehow managed to speak.

'It's Gabriel, isn't it? Gabriel Devenish? You were
my brother's best friend when he was at university. I'm

sorry but my parents aren't here at the moment. They've gone away to the south of France for a break.'

Behind Lara, hating to be ignored, Barney started barking again. Glad of the momentary distraction in order to gather herself mentally, she instantly dropped down to her haunches to stroke his rough wheaten-coloured coat affectionately.

'Hush, Barney, you don't have to make such a fuss.'

'You're Lara? Sean's little sister?'

Lifting her gaze, she fell into Gabriel's mesmerising crystal-blue stare like a diver plunging straight into the sunlit Mediterranean.

With her heart slamming against her ribs, she nodded slowly. 'That's right. Though not so little any more, I'm afraid.'

Rising to her full height again—five feet seven of slim limbs and womanly curves in light blue denims and a fitted white shirt—she was nothing like the plump, awkward teenager she'd been when she was sixteen. It was no surprise that Gabriel hadn't recognised her.

'Well, I'll be…'

He seemed to be genuinely shocked. Lara even detected a faint flush of heat in his chiselled countenance.

'You *have* grown up. Look…'

Tunnelling his long fingers through his thick chestnut hair, he inadvertently drew her attention to his strong, indomitable brow—a brow that was etched with two deeply hewn furrows. It didn't suggest he utilised that devastating smile of his very often these days. Whatever road life had taken him down it hadn't all been plain sailing, she thought. He might be rich, but no matter how much money a person had it didn't protect them from the slings and arrows that life aimed at everyone along the way... No one got off scot-free.

'I only learned of Sean's death yesterday,' Gabriel confessed. 'I saw an article in the newspaper about charity workers that had died of malaria and his name was mentioned. The piece said that he'd recently won a prestigious award for his work. I was stunned to hear that he'd died. I feel bad that I never kept in touch with him after we left university.'

'You took different paths.' Lara shrugged, her smile unsure.

She'd hate Gabriel to think she was criticising him, even though she'd never understood why he'd chosen to go into a profession that, in her view, was about taking rather than giving—a profession that was the polar opposite of Sean's.

'But it's good of you to call round to pay your respects. Mum and Dad will be touched when I tell them. I'm sure you must know they were very fond of you. Anyway, you're probably busy, so I won't keep you.'

Lara fervently willed him to take the cue she'd offered and leave. There was no way she wanted him to think that she was especially pleased to see him again. She was no longer the foolish sixteen-year-old whose crush on him had probably painfully embarrassed him.

But Gabriel sighed and stayed where he was. 'Look...I don't mean to be presumptuous, but is there any chance of a cup of tea? I promise not to take up too much of your time.'

As much as she wished she could come up with a convincing excuse that she was indeed busy, Lara had glimpsed an unexpected look of vulnerability in his eyes and she didn't have the heart to refuse him.

'Why don't you come in?' she invited. 'I was just about to have one myself.'

Feeling relieved, Gabriel followed Lara down the hallway towards what he remembered was a spacious and homely kitchen. As he walked slowly behind the brunette his astonishment that the sometimes shy and bookish teenager had blossomed into such a beauty made him stare at her shapely hourglass figure in wonder.

What her curvaceous body did for a simple pair of jeans and plain white shirt should be committed to art or poetry, he mused. Even though he wasn't remotely artistic or poetic himself, it certainly didn't mean he didn't appreciate the more aesthetically pleasing things in life—which was why he'd selected a New York apartment that had a stunning view of the Metropolitan Museum of Art.

Every now and then, when he found the time, he'd visit to remind himself that money wasn't the only thing in life worth appreciating. Yes, it gave a person a lot more options if he had it, but it didn't buy happiness. God knew he'd learned that to his cost over the years.... The contemplation of beauty and art 'soothed the troubled soul', as one wise guide at the museum had put it to him once, and although he would never dream of sharing such a view with any of his colleagues, Gabriel had agreed. That was why he admired the artists who created it.

But his admiration of Lara's beauty was set aside as he entered the kitchen. It was indeed as homely as he remembered. And the old-fashioned stand-alone fixtures and fittings, including the 1930s pillarbox-red

AGA, straight away transported him right back to when he and Sean had been young.

He recalled with fondness the countless delicious meals Peggy Bradley had made for them—in particular during that seemingly 'endless' summer when he and Sean, in between revising for their exams, had laughed and joked together, listened to the music of their favourite bands, mercilessly teased Lara and generally enjoyed being young and free of care, not burdened with responsibility as so many of the adults that they'd known had seemed to be. It had been easy to fantasise then that that those halcyon days would last for ever....

Gabriel's senses were suddenly awash in a sea of poignant and heartfelt memory. As if to compound his feelings, he saw that the cream dresser was full of engaging family pictures, and taking pride of place was an eye-catching photograph of Sean as he must have looked before he died. His mischievous brown eyes were full of laughter and his wide smile highlighted the chipped front tooth that Gabriel had accidentally broken when he'd too zealously bowled a cricket ball in the garden for him to bat. He had been the closest friend that Gabriel had ever had, and even though he hadn't kept in touch with him it cut him to the quick to think that he was no longer here....

'Everything looks just the same,' he remarked huskily, reaching his hand up to loosen the shirt collar that suddenly felt constricting.

'Mum and Dad aren't great lovers of change. They're old-fashioned like that.' Lara smiled fondly. 'Not to mention sentimental. They've become even more so since losing Sean.' Her smile vanished and, clearly needing a moment, she turned towards the sink to fill the kettle.

'It must have been a terrible shock to you all to receive the news that he'd died,' Gabriel murmured sympathetically.

'It was. One minute we were talking to him on Skype, hearing all about the events of his day, and the next…' Sadly shaking her head, Lara turned off the tap that had been gushing water into the kettle then moved across to the generous granite worktop to plug it into a socket to boil. 'How do you like your tea?' she asked, tucking some of her glossy dark hair behind her ear as she turned back.

'Don't you remember?' Gabriel teased, recalling with pleasure the numerous cups of tea an eager-to-please young Lara had made him whenever he'd stayed over or visited Sean. 'I used to tell you that, next to your mum, you made the best cup of tea in the world.'

'You did, didn't you?' Her generous mouth curved with pleasure. 'Okay, then, I'll see if I can remember how you like it. Don't tell me—just let me have a go. Pull up a chair and make yourself comfortable.'

He didn't need to be asked twice. This house was the only place he'd ever known that really felt like home, with everything that that word represented.

Jaded and tired from the demands and rigours of inhabiting the soulless world of high finance for what had probably been too many years to stay wholly sane, Gabriel had a secret yearning for some simplicity and comfort in his life. He was frankly weary of the kind of comfort epitomised by the opulent living of a lot of bankers in New York, although he himself had embraced it, thinking it was his 'due' for working so hard and making others as rich as he was.

He hadn't fully explored the realisation, but he was longing for the kind of comfort that might be attained by being amongst people who were authentic, with no hidden agendas and the ability simply to be themselves. In short, people who were naturally *good* rather than unscrupulously self-seeking.

And even as he had the thought his mind went straight away to Lara's parents. They had welcomed him into their home without any judgement or expectation when their son had befriended him, and had even expressed their sadness that he'd been raised by a wealthy but often absent uncle who more often than not had left him in the care of a hired nanny. They were appalled that Gabriel had never known the joys of growing up in a 'real' family as Sean had.

'Would you like some toast and marmalade with your cuppa?'

'Sorry...what did you say?' Blinking up into the melting chocolate-brown eyes of the lovely brunette who was suddenly standing in front of him, for a surreal moment Gabriel honestly forgot who or where he was because she was so enchanting.

Her brow puckering, Lara seemed taken aback that he hadn't heard her the first time. *Perhaps she didn't know how mesmerising she was?* He shrugged. He doubted it. He hadn't met a beautiful woman yet who wasn't intimately aware of her own appeal. Beauty was a very desirable cachet in the avaricious world that he inhabited—not to mention an *asset*. In his opinion every attractive woman who aimed for the top in his profession had no compunction in using such an advantage to the max.

'I just asked if you'd like some toast and marmalade with your tea....'

'Just tea will do thanks. Then, if you've got the time, I'd like you to sit down and talk to me. We've got quite a bit of catching up to do. It's been years since we've seen each other, Lara, and as well as talking about Sean I'd like to hear what you've been doing with yourself.'

'Okay.' She chewed down on her lip, as if taken aback by the invitation. 'But didn't you say you'd just flown back from New York? Don't you need to at least relax and unwind for a little while after your flight?'

Gabriel couldn't help but smile. It seemed that the once self-conscious and unsure teenager had inherited some of her mother's endearing natural ability to think of others' needs first. It wasn't something he often came across in his world—if *ever*—and he had to admit it was appealing. But he could just imagine the response of his more cynical male colleagues should they meet Lara and be exposed to her kind disposition for very long. They'd wonder if she was 'for real'.

'I assure you that right now I don't need to do anything else other than be here with you, Lara.'

If ever a man's statement had sounded more seductive and appealing then Lara hadn't heard one. And the huskily low-pitched velvet cadence of Gabriel's deeply arresting voice couldn't help but render the words even more provocative. Her insides felt as though they'd suddenly been heated by a fiercely burning erotic flame. Could it be that her teenage fascination for this man hadn't died with his rejection of her at that party, but instead had been quietly simmering inside all these years?

The realisation was akin to standing on a crumbling cliff edge and frantically trying to maintain her balance. It had been thirteen long years since she'd seen this man. She knew nothing about his life now, or what had transpired in the years since they'd last met, and she was pretty certain that if he had any interest in her at all at this moment it was only because of his past association with her family.

For all Lara knew, the man could be happily married to a stunningly perfect model wife in New York—the kind epitomised by the glossy magazines—with a brood of pretty blue-eyed offspring to boot. Her stomach helplessly churned at the thought.

'All right, then. I'll make us some tea and then we'll catch up. Just don't expect any tales of adventure or excitement. I live a very quiet and ordinary life that's probably miles away from how you live yours.'

Giving him a faintly wry smile, she moved back across the kitchen to the granite worktop and hurriedly arranged the teapot and matching china cups and saucers on a tray. But her hands were visibly trembling as she poured hot water onto the tea leaves, and her heart was pounding as though it would never be at ease or calm again....

They moved into the living room to drink their tea, and Lara opened the generous-sized patio doors that led out onto the garden so that they might enjoy the sunshine. She also didn't want to miss the opportunity of hearing the birds sing. That was one of the reasons why early morning had always been her favourite time of the day.

'You've made it just how I like it,' her handsome visitor announced, taking a sip of his tea as he lowered his long-limbed frame down into one of the comfortable Chesterfield armchairs. 'You've got a good memory.'

'Thanks.'

Suddenly self-conscious, Lara sat down in the chair opposite him and stirred her own tea. She'd never been able to drink the beverage without at least one sugar. *She'd bet that Gabriel never touched the stuff.* Even though he'd acquired a couple of lines on his forehead over the years, his lean, toned physique radiated the vim and vigour of a seasoned athlete rather than someone who spent his days immersed in making eye-popping deals on Wall Street.

The thought prompted a question. 'You said you'd just come back from New York? Is this a flying visit or are you going to stay for a while?'

A definitely guarded expression stole into his mesmerising blue eyes and his lean jaw clenched a little. Leaning forward, he placed his cup and saucer down onto the walnut coffee table arranged between them.

'I'm not sure. Right now I've no idea how long I'll stay. I've come back to deal with some legalities regarding my uncle's estate, to tell you the truth. He died a few weeks ago and I'm his sole beneficiary.'

'Oh, Gabriel, I'm so sorry...about your uncle dying, I mean. Did you come back for the funeral?'

'I did. Anyway, I have a meeting with his solicitor tomorrow.'

He shook his head, as though the matter pained rather than gratified him. But then why should he be pleased by the fact that his only family member had died? Lara reasoned. Even if he had bequeathed him everything he owned? If the scant details that she knew about Gabriel's upbringing by his uncle were right, then surely he would have preferred to have the man's love and affection, not to mention caring support, when he was a boy, rather than be left all his worldly goods when he died? Did he even *need* them when he was purported to be so wealthy in his own right?

'Did you see your uncle much over the years after you left to go to New York?'

'No, I didn't. We weren't close. He adopted me when my mother—his sister—decided she wasn't cut out to be a mother after all…that she wanted her freedom above all else. At least he was decent enough to do that, I suppose.'

'What about your father?' Lara frowned. 'What happened to him?'

In answer Gabriel's brow creased in a formidable scowl. 'Your guess is as good as mine. My mother put him down as "unknown" on my birth certificate.'

'How sad.' The comment was out before she could check it.

'Why? I grew up in an impressive home in a very desirable area and I wanted for nothing. What's sad about that?'

'It's sad that you never knew your real father, or had a relationship with him, and it's sad that you weren't close to the uncle who adopted you—that's all I meant.'

'Well, don't give it another thought. In the circles I move in I'm considered to be a great success, and everything I've achieved I've accomplished on my own. I wasn't held back by the fact that I wasn't close to my family or they to me. End of story.'

But Lara guessed that was *far* from the end. She was pretty certain that anyone who'd been abandoned by their mother as a child must have a river of pain and anger flowing through them that couldn't help but affect their sense of self-esteem and self-worth. But she sensed, too, that now wasn't the time to try and press Gabriel into telling her more. He'd come to pay his respects to the family for Sean, not to be grilled by his friend's sister about his less than idyllic upbringing.

'Anyway, I'd like to hear about what you've been up to since we last met.' Deftly, he changed the subject. 'What do you do for a living? If I remember rightly, you were either going to be a vet or a politician. We had some passionate discussions, you, me and Sean, about setting the world to rights, didn't we?'

His comment made Lara burn with embarrassment as she remembered their often heated and animated discussions. Especially when she recalled that her views had always been the most passionate and vehement. But when you were sixteen you thought you knew everything. You could even fool yourself into believing that a more experienced older man could seriously fall for you, when, in truth, he was only flirting with you because he could....

'Well, I didn't become a vet *or* a politician,' she said. 'Being responsible for setting the world to rights was too tall an order, so I became a librarian instead.'

'Well, well, well...a librarian?' Gabriel's expression was wry. 'I know you loved books, but I always thought you were far too passionate to squirrel yourself away in some dusty hall, lending them out to the great unwashed public!'

'In case you hadn't noticed, we're not living in the Dickensian era.'

Lara couldn't help but bristle at his mocking tone, but at the same time she couldn't help registering the disturbing fact that he'd called her 'passionate'. Had he always thought that about her? The thought made her heart race even as she reminded herself that he'd once painfully rejected her.

'Amongst other things, I issue books in a state-of-the-art college library with every bit of modern technology you can imagine at my disposal. If you think I chose a "safe" option in becoming a librarian, instead of a vet or a politician, then I can assure you that dealing every day with the demands of diverse and sometimes tricky students is no walk in the park.'

'But you love it?' Lifting a dark eyebrow, Gabriel smiled. 'I'm glad that you found a career you enjoy, Lara. And, just for the record, I still think you're passionate. I'm sure you would be whatever you decided to do in life. You can't help your nature.'

CHAPTER TWO

'AND WHAT ABOUT YOU, GABRIEL?' Lara asked, feeling suddenly hot again, because she seemed to be the focus of attention and she would much prefer to learn more about him. 'What line of work are you in these days? Are you still involved in finance?'

The smile Gabriel returned was faintly rueful. 'Yes, I am.'

'What exactly do you do? I mean, do you have a job title?'

In answer he rose to his feet, and it was clear to Lara that her questions were unsettling him.

'I'm a CRO on Wall Street—and, before you ask, that stands for Chief Risk Officer. I deal with analysing risk-and-reward formulas in financial businesses and banks.'

'Oh.' She raised her shoulders in a shrug, feeling none the wiser with the explanation. 'It sounds complicated.'

'Does it?' A visible muscle flinched at the side of his carved cheekbone. 'At any rate, I'd advise you not to lose any sleep trying to figure it out.'

'Meaning you don't think I'm intelligent enough to understand?'

'You always did take umbrage when you thought I

was being mocking, didn't you? Perhaps you should try not to take things so personally.'

As Lara mulled over the comment, to try and ascertain exactly what he meant, Gabriel moved across to where she sat, leaned down and gathered her hands in his. Then he silently pulled her to her feet.

There wasn't an adequate description for the huge wave of both panic and pleasure that suddenly engulfed her…except maybe abject disbelief that it was happening. Over the years, she had fantasised many times about what it might be like if Gabriel ever touched her or held her close as if he meant it, and while her heart sang to have him near she couldn't help but remember the time when he'd so purposefully moved her away from him and told her he could never be for her. But even that agonising memory couldn't stop her from thinking that being close to him like this felt so—so *right*.

Then she realised that his brilliant blue gaze was examining her with a searching intensity that couldn't help but make her apprehensive.

'Tell me about Sean,' he commanded quietly, his tone almost reverent, as though even uttering his friend's name out loud distressed him.

Relieved that it wasn't anything she'd inadvertently done or said that had made him study her so intently, Lara took a nervous swallow. It still upset her terribly to talk about Sean and remember afresh that he had died. The thought was akin to sharpened cold steel being plunged into her heart.

'What do you want to know?'

Gabriel didn't release her and she found she was in no hurry to be free. His hands were large and warm and they made her feel strangely secure, made her ache for the kind of loving, sensual protection that only a man like him could provide. She was suddenly aware of a small vein throbbing in his forehead.

'Why—*how* did he contract malaria?' he enquired huskily. 'Don't volunteers have to have some kind of protection before going out into these godforsaken places?'

'Of course they do.' Lara was taken aback by the underlying rage she heard in his voice…touched that he still felt so strongly about Sean after all these years.

She was angry, too, that the brother she'd loved so dearly had been ripped from her so suddenly and without warning, and the wounds of that loss were so great she feared they might never heal. Yet she wouldn't run away from grief, no matter how hard it hurt. She'd made a vow to face it head-on and not wound her heart further by denying how she felt. Something told her that it would be disrespectful to Sean if she did. But still, she utterly sympathised with Gabriel's confusion and pain.

'He had all the necessary jabs and medical examinations before he went over there,' she said softly, 'but malaria is caused by a mosquito bite from an infected mosquito, as I'm sure you probably know. Shortly after his death, a tear in the netting over his bed was discovered. Unfortunately the charity was always short of the money to be able to replace the old ones when they were no longer any good.'

'So he was given a faulty mosquito net?' His tone disparaging, Gabriel abruptly dropped Lara's hands and stepped away.

Feeling both bereft of his touch and chilled by the

memory of how Sean had died, she crossed her arms over her cotton shirt and nodded sadly. 'It seems so.'

As if he didn't know what to do with his rage to contain it, he strode over to the other side of the room to stare blindly out at the sunlit garden. Suddenly he spun round again to face her. 'How could Sean have been such an idiot?' he asked angrily.

'What?' The brutal question had the same effect on Lara as if Gabriel had slapped her hard across the face.

'I mean, why didn't he think of the consequences of being so careless about his own welfare? Probably because he'd never dream of putting himself first—and that was the problem. Why else would he accept a faulty net and risk being bitten? Even if he hadn't realised it wasn't intact. He should have checked. But he was always too busy thinking about others, wasn't he? No wonder he went into charity work. What a waste *that* turned out to be.'

His blue eyes glittered with fury and then, seconds later, looked utterly *desolate*.

'He was a genius at maths and science. He could have gone into any investment bank or financial concern and gone straight to the top. If it was so important to him to support worthy causes he could have done so from the safety of his office, using as much of his money as he wanted, without putting himself in the eye of the damn storm! It's a dog-eat-dog world out there—a world where it's every man for himself—and if you don't make yourself number one then you're dead in the water.'

As Gabriel angrily scraped his fingers through his hair it was clear that it was near impossible for him to contain his growing frustration.

'God knows I told him that enough times. You'd think he would have had the common sense to take it on board.'

Taking a deep breath in, Lara slowly breathed out again. Her anxious heartbeat started to ease and return to a calmer rhythm. Gabriel hadn't been being cruel when he'd asked how Sean could have been such an idiot—he was merely angry and frustrated at the sense-less waste of his friend's life. As they *all* were.

'My brother was a good man—as I'm sure you know, Gabriel. And he was happy doing the work he'd cho-sen, helping others less fortunate than he was. It simply wasn't in his nature to put himself first. I don't know about you, but that's the way I want to remember him. Happy and fulfilled and enjoying his life. I know that if he were still here he'd want you to be happy and ful-filled and enjoying your life, too. *Are* you?'

Her question hung suspended in the air like the sword of Damocles. Gabriel was staring at her as though trans-fixed, but then he rubbed his hand round his jaw in a bid to stir himself from the seeming trance he'd fallen into and shrugged.

'In my view, being happy is given too much credence in this world. A far better goal is to aim to be success-ful. If you're successful then that's fulfilling. That at least gives you choices in life. Anyway…'

Moving back to his chair, he lifted his cup of tea to his lips and took a long draught. Then he put the cup and saucer back down and gave Lara a haunting smile that was part regret, part anguish.

'I'm sorry if I upset you with my rant about Sean. But he was a good friend to me—probably the best friend I've ever had. I only wish I'd realised it sooner. I should have stayed in touch with him—but it's too late now, isn't it? It's an absolute crime and a travesty that he was taken from us so soon. Please convey my heartfelt condolences to your parents, won't you? I'm sorry they aren't here for me to speak to personally. At any rate, I think it's probably about time I went.'

The thought that he was leaving and that she might never see him again hit Lara like a thunderbolt.

Before she was sufficiently recovered from the shock to think it through properly, she blurted out, 'Must you go? If you stay for a while we can have lunch together. You can even come for a walk with me and Barney first, if you like? A walk is the perfect remedy to blow the cobwebs away and clear your head. We've got woods at the back of the house, remember? I wish you'd seen them when the primroses were out in the spring—they were a picture.'

It was at that very moment that Gabriel knew he couldn't walk away from this woman as easily as he wanted to—as easily as he *should* walk away. Because he knew if he stayed he would only hurt her. The savage hunger and need that he had buried inside for so long—and from time to time had sought to assuage with pretty bodies who only saw him as a 'golden ticket' to the lavish and expensive lifestyle they craved—would only end up consuming the innocent Lara and filling her with the most bitter regret for issuing that invitation to stay a while.

But Gabriel knew already that he couldn't resist accepting it. And who could blame him for seeking sanctuary in her fresh and innocent company for a little while longer?

'All right, then. I'll stay…at least for lunch and a walk with Barney.'

'That's great. But you *do* realise I have an ulterior motive for asking?'

She smiled, and for the first time Gabriel noticed the two engaging and rather sexy dimples in her cheeks. But her words suddenly made him stiffen. He wasn't ready for his illusions about her—if illusions were what they were—to be shattered so soon.

'What motive would that be?' he asked warily.

She lifted her slender shoulders, then dropped them again. 'It's just that I've been a bit lonely here on my own, surrounded by memories of my brother. It would be nice to have some company for a change to help take my mind off things…. That's all I meant.'

Feeling ridiculously pleased at the admission, Gabriel relaxed. 'Then far be it from me to deny you the one thing I can give you today. Shall we go for that walk now? The sun is shining and it's a beautiful day. It would be a shame to waste it staying indoors.'

'I agree.' Lifting her long dark hair off her shoulders and dropping it down again behind her back, Lara moved gracefully across to the door. 'I'll just go and get my walking boots on—the terrain in the woods is quite rough and uneven in places. Will you be okay walking in those?' Her glance was doubtful as she surveyed the ebony Italian loafers that he wore. 'They look pretty chic and expensive.'

'I would have brought something more suitable to change into if I'd known you were going to entice me into the woods with you,' he remarked drolly, and his lips split into a grin when she blushed vividly.

'Don't kid yourself I'd even dream of such a thing. For one thing, I wouldn't know how.'

Beneath his immaculate white shirt Gabriel's heart started to pound disturbingly. More than that, a profoundly arousing heat invaded his blood.

'Now, there's a challenge if ever I heard one...' he commented huskily.

'I didn't mean it as a challenge. I was only— Oh, never mind. I'll go and get my boots on.'

Clearly flustered, Lara hurriedly left the room, and straight away Gabriel missed her presence and longed for her to return.

He was being introduced to a completely different world from the one he was used to inhabiting—a world that he realised he'd been missing for far too long.

Walking through the woods with the beauty he had once known as 'Sean's little sister' by his side was delightful. She laughed often and unselfconsciously—a huskily engaging sound that made all the hairs stand up on the back of his neck. And every now and then a waft of the delightful perfume she wore, which smelled like a bouquet of wild flowers, deluged Gabriel's senses and hit him in the gut. Coupled with the earthy, resinous scents that abounded in the woods, it made for a sensual experience bar none—a million miles away from the tense, charged atmosphere of Wall Street that was his usual daily experience.

'I'm going to take Barney's lead off now. This is his favourite neck of the woods. We know it well and I like to let him have a run.'

Gifting Gabriel with another sunny smile, Lara stooped to free the excited terrier from his leash and he bounded away through the thicket of dense undergrowth and trees like a whippet, joyously barking.

'He's not the brightest chicken in the coop,' she commented affectionately. 'He's a natural hunter, but the trouble is he announces his arrival so that his prey can get away before he reaches it!'

Shaking her head in amusement, she laughed again, and Gabriel couldn't help but smile with pleasure. Driven by sheer instinct—for once letting his heart rule his head—he found himself drawing closer and reaching for her hand. The hotly fierce tingle that shot through his body when he touched her was like being glanced by lightning and almost made him stumble. The startled look Lara gave him in return indicated that she'd felt the electrifying sensation, too.

'I'd forgotten how funny you are,' he confessed. 'And that you have the most beautiful eyes. They glisten like jewels when you laugh.' It didn't come naturally to him to compliment a woman and mean it, but he meant this particular one with every fibre of his being.

'Thank you.'

Carefully she disengaged her hand from his, and the becoming flush on Lara's cheeks told Gabriel that he'd been right about her being disturbed by the shock of electricity that had arced between them.

'You're blushing,' he teased.

'If I am it's because I'm not used to receiving such effusive compliments.'

'Not even from the man in your life?'

He experienced no remorse whatsoever for shamelessly fishing. But Lara's expression looked troubled now, and the light in her eyes dimmed a little.

'There isn't a man in my life—at least not at the moment.'

Gabriel couldn't deny he was relieved to hear it, although he wasn't ready to explore *why* right then.

'You mean to say that there potentially *might* be someone? Someone you perhaps have your eye on?'

'No. I don't mean that at all.' She didn't bother to try and disguise her annoyance that he should quiz her on the subject.

'What about you?' she asked, turning the tables. 'Is there anyone significant in *your* life? For all I know you might even be married by now.'

'I'm not—married, I mean. And neither am I in a serious relationship. I'm married to my work, Lara. I know that sounds extremely dull and boring but it's true. However, that's not to say I lack the company of a pretty woman when I want it.'

'You mean you like to play the field? I suppose that's why there's no one serious in your life, then.'

She sighed. But whether that sigh signified disapproval or disappointment Gabriel couldn't guess.

Staring at the dense shroud of trees and bushes that her lively pet terrier had disappeared into, she suddenly called out, 'Barney! Here, boy! Come on back, now.'

When the dog didn't immediately appear, Lara turned her gaze back to Gabriel.

'I worry when he suddenly goes quiet,' she admitted, 'I'd better go and see where he's got to. He might have got stuck down a rabbit hole or something. It's happened before. Why don't you wait here for me? You've already got your posh shoes all muddy, and the ground on the other side of those trees and bushes is invariably quite boggy. Hopefully I won't be too long.'

'I don't give a damn about my shoes, and I haven't left my jacket back at the house and rolled up my shirt-sleeves for nothing. I'm not concerned about getting dirty. I'll come and help you find the dog.'

'His name's Barney!'

Again Lara looked affronted, and again Gabriel couldn't resist goading her.

'Who's he named after? One of your ex-boyfriends?'

'He's my parents' dog, not mine, you ninny.'

'You always used to call me that. You might be surprised to know I found it quite endearing.'

'Now, that I *don't* believe. My perception was that it irritated you. I was the pesky sixteen-year-old sister of your friend, remember? You didn't take me at all seriously. You put up with me out of politeness to Sean and my parents, I'm sure.'

'That's not true.' Gabriel frowned, perturbed that Lara had believed that.

'Come on, then.' As if intuiting his disturbance, she gave him a cheery smile. 'Let's go and find Barney.'

As he squelched through the dense and muddied undergrowth in his thousand-dollar Italian loafers, with the damp leaves of bushes and thickets brushing against his immaculate white shirt, occasionally stumbling when he lost his balance, Gabriel had to smile at the ludicrous image he must present. His colleagues on Wall Street would have a field day if they could see him.

Strangely enough, that made him smile even more. In truth, he wasn't predisposed to be glum or morose. He honestly thought that he had the best of it. How could he *not* when he was following behind the long-legged beauty in tight jeans in front of him?

Lara was negotiating the uneven muddy trail through

the woods like a latter-day female Indiana Jones, hardly pausing for breath and calling out 'Barney!' every now and then with renewed gusto. Gabriel knew himself to be a fit man who welcomed a challenge—be it mental or physical—but his companion's agility and stamina had to be seen to be believed.

Suddenly coming to a halt, and with frustration and apprehension in her voice, Lara shouted, '*Barney!* This isn't funny. What do you think you're playing at, you naughty boy?'

'Sounds like you're expecting him to reply.'

'Ha-ha, very funny...*not.*'

This time Gabriel was treated to an irritated glare which, thankfully, he didn't take seriously—not when he guessed that Lara would be utterly distraught if they couldn't find the dog. It made him want to make more of a concerted effort to help her.

'Barney!' he yelled, striding towards an even denser section of the woods that they hadn't yet explored, at that point not giving a fig that his shoes were now more or less ruined by the rough, muddy terrain.

Was that a glimpse of a dark sandy-coloured coat he'd just spied through the trees? He squinted searchingly. Gabriel would bet his bottom dollar that it was.

'Barney! Here, boy!' he called again, moving more deeply into the shrouded area in front of him.

He hadn't gone very far when he saw the terrier's wriggling rear-end pointed upwards towards the sheltering canopy of leaves. The dog was furiously digging in the earth as though intent on finding treasure.

'I've found him!' he called out to Lara, spinning round only to find her hurrying towards him. Her white shirt was splattered with mud, as his was, her long dark hair was engagingly dishevelled, and her pretty face was visibly flushed pink with the heat of her exertions.

'Thank God!' she exclaimed as she flew past Gabriel to reach her adored family pet, dropping down onto her knees on the rough woodland floor.

She didn't seem to care that she might potentially hurt herself or ruin her clothes.

'Barney, you're a very naughty boy,' she scolded fondly, lifting the animal away from his enthusiastic digging and hugging him to her chest, uncaring that the terrier had made her white shirt even muddier.

Crazy as it was, Gabriel couldn't help but *envy* the small hound. He wouldn't mind his once spotless tailored shirt getting even dirtier if Lara held him to her fulsome breasts like that.

'He was probably digging for rabbits.' She grinned up at him, her dark eyes shining. 'He can't help himself.' Turning back to the dog, she crooned, 'You're a natural-born hunter, aren't you, baby?'

Then, before Gabriel could take command of his besieged senses and help her, she gracefully rose to her feet and slipped the leash back on the terrier's collar.

'I don't know about you, but I'm suddenly starving. Let's get back and I'll fix us some lunch.'

Starving didn't come close to describing Gabriel's appetite right then—and it wasn't food that he hungered for. His best friend's little sister was seriously challenging his libido and winning. Of all the things he might have envisaged happening on this trip to the UK, it wasn't that.

Just what the hell he was going to do about it he didn't rightly know. But to seriously consider bedding the shapely brunette and risk sullying his once good relationship with her and her family almost didn't bear thinking about.

'I want you to take off that shirt when we get home,' Lara instructed as she airily swept past him with Barney.

'What?'

Coming to a sudden halt, she turned to flourish at him a cheeky grin that would've shamed a mischievous schoolgirl.

'Don't worry—it's not because I have designs on your body or anything. You're quite safe. I was just going to put it in the washing machine. You can borrow one of my dad's shirts in the meantime. He's about the same build and height as you, although of course not quite as—not quite as…'

As her big brown eyes swept over him, and she clearly struggled to finish the sentence, Gabriel once again couldn't resist being provocative.

'Fit?' he suggested, smiling.

'You know that saying? It should be "Vanity, thy name is *Man*—not Woman".'

Crossing his arms over his shirtfront, Gabriel mockingly raised an eyebrow. 'That quote is from Hamlet, and it's, "*Frailty*, thy name is woman"—*not* vanity. Just thought you'd like to know that for future reference.'

His pretty companion tossed her head and spun away, striding through the undergrowth again with Barney yapping happily beside her—but not before Gabriel saw her look daggers at him, as if she'd like to abandon him in the middle of those dank, dark woods and leave him there.

Lara honestly didn't know where she was finding the courage to deal with the disturbingly charismatic presence that was Gabriel. And neither had she fully dealt with the shock of him turning up out of the blue like that at her parents' door.

As time had gone on, her day had grown more challenging. When they'd been chatting in the living room earlier and Gabriel had drawn her up from her chair to ask about Sean she'd really believed she might faint from the sheer dizzying pleasure of the contact—not to mention the mesmerisingly intense glance he'd given her. His brilliant blue eyes had stared back into hers as though wanting to see into her very soul…as though even that wouldn't be enough for him to find what he was searching for.

She'd seen so many things in that seemingly endless glance to take her breath away, but rage and hunger— for what, she didn't know—had been predominant.

The second time he'd touched her, catching hold of her hand in the woods and smiling down at her, as though her company genuinely gave him pleasure, the sizzling jolt of electricity Lara had experienced when he put his hand round hers had left her feeling dizzy and confused. Such an extreme reaction to a simple friendly touch didn't bode well for her peace of mind when the time came for her to say goodbye to Gabriel again. And this time she didn't doubt his departure would be for good.

He would go back to his high-octane life on Wall Street and she would return to her much more simple and ordinary routine as a college librarian. Except that would be no consolation for watching her brother's one-time charismatic best friend walk out of her life for a second time….

On their return from the woods they stood in the

porch at the back of the house as Lara schooled Barney to wait while she and Gabriel removed their muddy footwear. Seeing that her companion's black loafers were liberally weighed down and caked in once-oozing but now dried sludge, she let out a groan.

'Oh, why, oh, why did they have to be *suede*?' she asked, sincerely regretful that because of her Gabriel had ruined what was an undoubtedly expensive pair of shoes.

She could just imagine Sean shaking his head and saying, *Not one of your best ideas, sis—taking Gabe on a woodland walk when he was wearing classy Italian loafers. What on earth were you thinking?*

It took her aback to remember that he'd always referred to his friend as Gabe, not Gabriel. Lara had never been bold enough to do the same. Aside from that, Sean would have been right to wonder what she was thinking about. The trouble was her wonderful brother hadn't realised that Lara never *had* been able to think clearly round Gabriel.

'I should have lent you my dad's walking boots,' she reflected ruefully.

'What size is he?'

'He's a nine.'

Grimacing as he stood up in the generous-sized utility room that his impressive physique had made appear suddenly small, Gabriel emitted a playful sigh. 'Wouldn't have been any good, I'm afraid. I'm a size twelve.'

Having removed her own boots, Lara rose to join him. 'In any case, I think your lovely shoes are completely ruined. Were they very expensive?' She flushed as she privately wondered how she could possibly find the money to replace them if they'd been even half as expensive as she guessed they had. God knew a college librarian didn't earn a fortune....

'If I told you, you'd probably read me the riot act for being so vain and wasteful. Forget about it. The damn shoes don't matter. Anyway, I've got a spare pair in the car.'

'You've got a spare pair in the car? Why didn't you tell me?'

His arresting gaze made him look to be carefully considering the question. 'I didn't think about it. Besides, it's no big deal. Now, if you'll go and get me that shirt you promised, I'll get out of this one and give it to you to put in the washing machine.'

He was already starting to unbutton the stained shirt as he spoke, and Lara suddenly panicked at the thought of seeing him standing there bare-chested.

'Okay...won't be a tick,' she murmured, hurriedly turning towards the door that led out into the hall.

Her senses were already bombarded by Gabriel's presence alone—how was she supposed to handle being presented with the arresting beauty of his naked male chest and act as though she were unaffected?

CHAPTER THREE

FOR A MAN WHO LIKED to be in command of situations, Gabriel found himself to be uncharacteristically all at sea in his old friend's home with Lara. Being in that house again, and recalling some of the happiest memories he had ever known, made him yearn to replicate the feelings they evoked—the predominant one being a sense of belonging.

He hadn't experienced that reassuring sense of being welcomed, being regarded without judgement or conditions being attached, since he'd left the UK all those years ago. God knew, the pressurised career he'd chosen wasn't likely to engender anything *close* to that feeling amongst the single-minded and driven individuals he worked with. The phrase about them probably selling their own grandmothers if it made a profit often sprang to Gabriel's mind.

From time to time it alarmed him to realise he was becoming equally mercenary, and he wasn't proud of the fact. But in truth, like all addictions, it was hellishly hard to give up—and making money was definitely his drug of choice. Yet it was strange that he wasn't exactly overjoyed at being bequeathed his uncle's substantial residence, plus all his possessions and a generous monetary legacy.

All attending the man's funeral had done for Gabriel was to remind him of the sense of abandonment and excoriating pain he'd lived with since he was a child and his mother had left, leaving him with a man who—although related to him by blood—had been as distant as the Milky Way and even *less* accessible.

And now, as well as the unwanted complication of having to deal with his uncle's legacy, there was the totally unexpected dilemma of *Lara.* Just knowing that she was in the homely kitchen right now, preparing their lunch, shouldn't give him the inordinate amount of pleasure that it did, but along with an undeniable sense of contentment that *was* how it made him feel. That in itself was unusual, because he hadn't met a woman yet he trusted enough to relax with—except perhaps Peggy Bradley, Lara's mother.

Occupying Lara's father's comfortable wing-backed chair in the living room, Gabriel knew his eyelids were drifting closed, but made no attempt to check their descent. Outside, the beneficent sun was shining and its soporific rays beamed in on him through the opened patio doors and inevitably made him feel sleepy.

On the scented summer air a distant melody floated by, teasing at the memory of a small gathering Sean had once spontaneously thrown at the house…. Lara in a long magenta-and-green dress, dancing for all she was worth, throwing her arms wide as if to embrace all that the world had to offer and drawing his eye more than once because she looked so pretty and so free….

'Gabriel? Sorry to wake you, but lunch is ready. I thought we'd sit out in the garden and eat?'

Hearing the velvet-toned voice of the woman he'd been thinking about, and unsure whether he was still in the throes of his dream or not, Gabriel opened his eyes. His startled gaze was straight away captured by the heart-shaped face that had once been so familiar to him.

Now the innocent young girl that he remembered from his youth had turned into a woman who made him catch his breath and made his blood turn molten simply by looking at her. Devoid of any artifice or make-up, her skin was as fresh and clear as the petals of the creamiest rose, and her lips… Her lush lips were the shape and kind that would draw any man's attention and make him long to know what they would feel like beneath his own if he were lucky enough to kiss them.

Straightening in the chair, he murmured, 'I was dreaming about you….' Playing for time in order to marshal his thoughts, he let a helpless smile tug at the edges of his mouth. 'Yes, I was dreaming about you at a party Sean had once. You were just sixteen and you were dancing like some ethereal wild child to a Jimi Hendrix track. You looked so free and pretty. I remember thinking you would have fitted right into the era of peace and love in the sixties.'

Lara's dark brows furrowed as though the reference displeased her. Clearly that particular recollection from the past didn't fill her with the same wistful pleasure as it did Gabriel.

'Sixteen was a horrible age for me. I was always so self-conscious and shy, and I sometimes said stupid things I didn't mean and came to regret. I said something *very* stupid that night at the party.'

'Did you? Well, you should put it behind you and forget about it. For goodness' sake that was *years* ago, sweetheart, and if my recollections are right I seem to remember that there was plenty of alcohol doing the rounds that night—no doubt that was partly to blame. Besides, we can all say stupid things sometimes. If you can't be stupid when you're sixteen, then when *can* you? Anyway, I was actually quite envious of you that night.'

'Were you? Why?'

'Because you looked so carefree. To me you represented a freedom that I longed for—the kind of freedom that no amount of money could buy me.'

Now it was *his* turn to feel self-conscious and awkward. Gabriel had never revealed anything quite so personal about how he felt to anyone before. Like many young men, the programming that he'd absorbed from an early age had taught him that expressing emotion was akin to revealing a weakness, and right then he kicked it strongly into touch.

Pushing out of his chair, he moved across the room to glance out at the sunlit garden again. Immediately he noticed that the wrought iron picnic table with its matching green umbrella was laid for lunch. It was just the diversion he needed. Too much introspection was liable to make him irritable. He was already regretting being quite so frank with Lara.

'Were you saying something about us eating outside?'

'Yes. Lunch is ready. Why don't you go and make yourself comfortable and I'll bring it out?'

Lara couldn't get Gabriel's remarks about how she had looked at Sean's party out of her mind. At no point had he given any indication that he remembered spurning her—first when she had lifted her face up to his for a kiss and then by tactlessly suggesting there must be boys her own age who were interested in her and telling her he had his sights set on the slim blonde who was his tutor.

He hadn't even taken the bait when Lara had mentioned that she'd said something stupid that night that she regretted. Had her flirtation with him been so insignificant to him that he didn't even remember it? The fact that he'd said he'd been dreaming about her with what sounded like genuine admiration seemed too unreal for words. But, however seductive it sounded, Lara would remain on her guard. She wouldn't let the immature behaviour of her past rule her present by repeating it.

But she also couldn't forget Gabriel's stark and heartfelt admission that her dancing that day had represented a freedom that he longed for—a freedom that 'no amount of money' had been able to buy for him. Had he been feeling trapped in some way?

She couldn't suppress the longing that infused her that one day he might reveal more of his innermost feelings to her—at least as a friend. It was easy to glean the fact that he was troubled. In the short time they'd spent together since his turning up at the door she'd begun to intuit that Sean's death wasn't the only grief that haunted him.

He didn't talk much during lunch, except to remark on how good the chicken salad she'd prepared was. Lara didn't mind. It was a glorious day and the warmth from the sun had helped ease any tension she might have felt because she was sitting opposite the man who had mesmerised her when she was just sixteen. The truth was he *still* mesmerised her. She'd fantasised about Gabriel so many times over the years—had even entertained the foolish hope that one day he might come back into her life, see the woman she'd become, and be enthralled by her.

But, seeing him again now, she knew that was just a pipedream. He was even more out of Lara's league than he had been all those years ago.

However, as they sat in the garden together she realised that the past association Gabriel had enjoyed with her and her family had definitely engendered an unspoken agreement between them that they could at least let their guards down enough around each other for a while and relax. They didn't need to present some awkward or uneasy façade that would prevent honest communication.

Reaching for the bottle of wine that she'd opened and stood in an ice bucket on the table, she poured some crisp white Chardonnay into their glasses and, raising hers in a toast, smiled. 'To old friends.'

A fleeting shadow passed across Gabriel's brilliant blue irises. His broad shoulders visibly tensed. Then he, too, raised his glass.

'To Sean, who once told me that the best bottle of wine was the one you shared with a trusted friend, whether it was vintage or a common or garden bottle of plonk.'

The expression on his sculpted, handsome face was indisputably wry, but it was tinged with a sadness and regret he couldn't hide.

'Your brother was far too generous. I wish I'd exhibited more of that quality towards him when I had the chance. But I was too set on carving my own path to properly consider him. I certainly wasn't around dur-

ing the times he might have needed an ally or someone
to confide in. Some "trusted friend" I turned out to be.'

'You're too hard on yourself, Gabriel.'

Not for a second could Lara deny the impulse that
suddenly arose in her to touch him. God knew it was
a big risk for her to give in to it, but she ached to give
him some comfort. It was hard seeing him so down
on himself like this…. Sean would have hated it, too.

Gently, she laid her hand over his. He stared down
at it as though hypnotised. Then he shook his head.

'The fact is I'm not hard enough. I'm constantly creating strategies and contingency plans so that I don't
have to face myself and confront the truth about who
I've become…a man I'm hardly proud of.'

'But you've already told me what a success people
think you are, Gabriel. You should be proud of what
you've achieved.'

'So you think I've made a success of my life, do
you?'

The pain Lara saw reflected in his gaze made her
draw in a helplessly tight breath.

'What I think isn't as important as how you feel,
Gabriel. You must have worked hard to get where you
are, and you did it without help from either family or
friends. That shows the kind of strength and determination that most people would love to have.'

'Does it?'

Shockingly, Gabriel seized her hand, as though he
meant to make her his prisoner, and the intense, hungry
glare he swept over her face made her heart thump hard.

'You're too damn generous for your own good, Lara.
Let me put you straight about the kind of man I am, in
case you're harbouring the belief that I'm somehow bet-

ter. I'm *not*. I don't consider others. I'm a taker—not a giver, like you and your family. In the kind of world I inhabit the weak fall by the wayside and are quickly forgotten. I've had to learn to be tough. On the road to achieving what I want I've learned not to let anything or anyone stand in my way. If I come back into your life again I'm guaranteed to hurt you and make you rue the day you met me.'

Her mouth drying, Lara couldn't hold back the hot press of tears that surged into her eyes. His words had been like knives and her need to self-protect immediately kicked in.

'You're talking as if I'm nurturing some kind of hope that we might get together. Don't worry about that, Gabriel. I'm not.'

She sniffed and wrenched her arm free.

'New York has changed you, Gabriel—and not for the better. You used to be quite friendly and amusing. But it sounds like the path that you've chosen has corrupted you instead of made you happy. That worries me. And, just so that you know, I'm *not* looking for a man to be in my life. And I assure you that if I was I'm afraid it wouldn't be *you*.'

'Is that right?'

In a flash Gabriel was on his feet and yanking her up towards him, moving his hands down to her slim waist to hold her fast and pulling her against the iron wall of his chest. There was no time for Lara to think or even to feel alarmed. But her heartbeat went wild when his hand cupped the back of her head and forcefully directed her face up towards his.

Then the world as she knew it disappeared as though it was nothing but a hazy dream. Her eyelids shut tight as he crushed her lips beneath his, his hot silken tongue mercilessly invading and plundering the satin interior of her mouth in a kiss that seemed to be driven by passionate hunger and fury combined.

The frightening demand she sensed left Lara reeling. But it also stirred long-dormant feelings in her body, making them want to rise up and meet that furious hunger. Along with that shocking realisation there were other disturbing feelings and sensations that hit her. The foremost was how seductively delicious Gabriel tasted and how he exuded the most provocative scent— almost a primeval scent—that wasn't just down to the expensive cologne he wore. And the sheer strength of the man's hard, honed body against hers made her blood pound in her veins just as if he were some hungry lone wolf, intent on carrying her off to his lair to savour at his leisure.

But hers wasn't the only heart that was hammering. And when Gabriel suddenly and without warning let her go, cursing vehemently beneath his breath, Lara stumbled. Her legs felt as weak as strands of damp linguine.

Retrieving her balance as quickly as she could, she stood on her father's immaculately mown lawn and tentatively touched her fingertips to her lips. They were already slightly swollen and still throbbed from Gabriel's savagely hungry kiss. The man himself had already distanced himself and stood shaking his dark head in what looked to be disgust. When his gaze lifted to meet hers she had never seen an expression more nakedly stark.

'I'm sorry if I hurt you. Despite what I said, it was never my intention to do that,' he intoned huskily. 'But it's better you know now what I'm really like than find out later. At least now you have the chance to shut the door on me and vow never to see me again.'

Wiping the back of her hand over her tear-moistened eyes, Lara unflinchingly met his tortured gaze. It was then that she made a silent vow not to abandon him as his mother and uncle had done. Her friends might not have understood her decision if they'd been privy to his little speech about being 'a taker not a giver', but then none of them had known the Gabriel of old, and nor did they know how it felt to set your eyes on a man and believe that he might—*just might*—be your destiny.

Despite her private feelings about that, Lara was still determined not to let Gabriel have the upper hand. Even if she couldn't deny the powerful chemistry between them, she certainly wasn't about to let him use her and then discard her as if he wouldn't give her so much as a second thought. She didn't want to be one of the 'weak' that fell by the wayside.

'You probably didn't mean to hurt me, Gabriel, but the truth is you did. Perhaps you need to leave and reflect on that for a while?'

His glance was more than a little bemused. 'Do I take it that you'd be willing to see me again despite what just happened?'

'I would. But you won't behave like you have every right to kiss me like that again, Gabriel. Because I won't let you.'

Folding her arms across the fresh pink linen shirt that she'd donned after their walk as if she meant business, Lara sighed.

'I sense that you only did what you did out of sheer frustration at not knowing what to do with your feelings. Feelings that must have been building up inside you since you heard about your uncle and then about Sean. I can totally understand that. Grief can make even the most stable of people go a little crazy sometimes. It can make them act in ways they normally wouldn't.'

'So you think I kissed you purely because I didn't know what to do with my grief and went a little crazy?'

Sensing her face flooding with heat, she twined a long strand of rich brown hair round her fingers and unwaveringly met his gaze. 'Yes…yes, I do.'

'Then clearly you've learned nothing about men and their base desires, have you?' He raised a sardonic dark eyebrow.

Shocked more by his remark than by his rapacious kiss, Lara wanted the ground to open up and swallow her. Clearly Gabriel still thought of her as Sean's innocent little sister after all—a woman who had probably been sheltered from the world by kind but undoubtedly misguided parents and was consequently too naïve for words.

Gathering every ounce of determination and resolve she could muster, she refused to let his mockery get to her. Naïve or not, she still didn't believe Gabriel was displaying his true nature. Her intuition told her that presenting himself as cruel and uncaring was just a ruse. It wasn't the truth. She'd put money on it.

'I may not have a lot of experience with men, Gabriel, and I know it's been a long time since we last met, but I'm not as naïve as you seem to think I am. I'm quite aware of what goes on in the world, and of the— of the *desires* that people have. And, in spite of what you said, I don't believe that it's in your nature to take what you want just because you can. You've probably built a wall around your feelings for a long time, and it's only natural that those feelings should spill over since coming back home and being forced to face the losses in your life.'

She paused to take in a deep, steadying breath.

'I may not be as worldly-wise as you, but neither am I insensitive to the fact that you must be hurting.'

Even as she said the words Lara wondered how she'd dared express them when she saw Gabriel's lip curl disparagingly. He was rubbing his hand over the borrowed cobalt-coloured shirt that belonged to her father—a colour that brought out the intense glittering blue of his stunning eyes—and for a few heart-pounding moments she honestly thought he was about to walk away. To walk out of her life for ever.

'I hate to shatter another illusion, sweetheart, but I didn't kiss you because I was hurting.' Again Gabriel raised a rueful dark eyebrow. 'At least not in the way that you believe. I kissed you out of pure *lust*. If you find that shocking, then look in the mirror. The little girl that I once knew has grown up into a very beautiful and desirable woman. A very *sexy* woman. There's not a man in the world who would blame me for wanting you in my bed.'

'If you expect me to be flattered by that comment then I—'

He strode towards her again but Lara didn't flinch. Gabriel could taunt her all he liked, but she would stand her ground and refuse to believe him to be doing anything other than play-acting—seeking to divert her from the truth of what he was really feeling by making her think that he was a cold, heartless playboy with no remaining vestige of the friendly, teasing youth she'd known as a young girl.

'I don't expect you to be flattered, angel.'

Lifting his hand, he stroked his palm down over her cheek. The gesture both warmed and froze her at the same time. One thing she couldn't deny was the realisation that there had always been something unpredictable about his nature. Something *dangerous*, even.

Sean had once commented that women swarmed round Gabriel like bees round a honeypot because as well as having good looks he exuded a 'bad-boy' image they all seemed to find irresistible. Lara didn't doubt that was true, but she had never been frightened of him. She might be naïve, but she didn't think he would ever deliberately hurt her or cause her pain. Strangely, even his savage kiss hadn't changed her mind about that.

He sucked in a deep breath and the warmth of his ensuing sigh feathered over her cheek. It had the same startling effect as if she'd imbibed a shot of the most intoxicating brandy. The dizziness and weakness that flooded her made her wonder if her legs would ever hold her safely upright again.

'Rather than be flattered…for *both* our sakes…I'd prefer you to just tell me to go to hell and warn me never to darken your doorstep again.'

The exquisite carved male lips in front of her twisted, almost as if he wished she would put an end to his inner agony by readily acceding to his wish to tell him to go to hell. But Lara couldn't and *wouldn't* do it.

'No, Gabriel. I won't ever tell you that—not unless you deliberately cause me harm. Call me weak, or even stupid, but my brother would turn in his grave if I turned you away. My parents wouldn't be too pleased with me, either. I think our emotions have been heightened today because of what we've both been through….

losing people that we love. So let's put this upset aside for a while and finish our lunch, shall we? I've got some fresh fruit salad and cream for dessert.'

Feigning that she was unperturbed by what had just transpired between them, she lightly lifted Gabriel's hand off of her cheek and walked back to the table. But her heart was thudding like crazy as she pulled out her chair and turned back towards him. He was standing stock-still, staring at her as if he couldn't begin to fathom where she was coming from.

'No, Lara. I won't stay. Thanks for the lunch, but I think I'll pass on dessert.' He shrugged. 'In spite of what just happened I want you to know that I wish you a happy future—I really do. The *best*. I've no doubt you'll break a few male hearts along the way…that is, if you haven't done so already.'

Just as Gabriel finished speaking, Barney shot out through the patio doors like a bullet from a pistol. Fresh from the nap he'd been having after their woodland walk, he made a direct beeline for Gabriel, jumping up at him and yapping wildly with excitement as if he was his new best friend.

Lara could have kissed the terrier because, taken by surprise and with his defences down, Gabriel immediately dropped down to his haunches and appeared to gladly make a fuss of the animal. The action was just what was needed to defuse the tension between them.

'I think he likes you.' She smiled. 'I don't think he's going to easily let you go, Gabriel.'

'And how about *you*, Lara? Are you going to easily let me go?'

Even across the expanse of lawn that was between them the diamond glitter of his eyes seemed to burn a hole right through the centre of her soul, and it shook Lara. Licking lips that were suddenly achingly dry, she smoothed a tremulous hand down the front of her jeans and made herself hold his gaze unwaveringly.

'Probably not. I'm a bit like a terrier, too, when it comes to my friends. It takes a lot to shake me loose. By the time you go back to New York you'll probably be heartily sick of the sight of me.'

'You think?'

Lifting a joyful Barney into his arms, Gabriel rose to his full height again. The maddeningly enigmatic smile on his face made her limbs feel as insubstantial as cotton wool.

'Let's have that dessert now, shall we?' she suggested, aiming for a matter-of-fact tone and fearing she'd completely missed the mark. 'It seems a shame to let it go to waste.'

'Temptation personified—that's what you are, Lara Bradley,' Gabriel drawled huskily.

'I'd probably make a good saleswoman, then, wouldn't I?'

Hugging a now much calmer Barney to his impressively broad chest, he smiled. 'Sweetheart, you could sell me any damn thing you wanted and I wouldn't be able to resist. See how much power you have over me?'

If only he knew it wasn't *power* over him that she craved, Lara mused achingly, but something much deeper and more lasting.

CHAPTER FOUR

WHEN THE TIME HAD COME for him to bid Lara good-bye that day, his policy to keep them keen by not always being readily available—as was his habit with women—had made Gabriel strive to keep his tone and manner as non-committal and cool as possible. But all it had taken was one more lingering glance into Lara's big brown eyes to make him realise this was the *one* woman he wouldn't be able to employ his usual 'laissez-faire' technique with.

That incendiary kiss he had stolen from her might have left her thinking what a merciless bastard he was, but it hadn't been planned. He'd never known a hunger and a need for a woman like it, and in the midst of his surprising need to confess how driven he'd become in his bid for success his desire for her had reached fever pitch.

Add to that the fact that he had been mad at himself, mad at the world, and mad at the cards that fate had dealt him and it had been a recipe for fireworks. Now Gabriel couldn't get the taste of her or the memory of her soft and shapely contours out of his mind.

Realising he didn't want to leave before spending some proper time with Lara, he'd decided he would

just let things unfold naturally between them instead
of sabotaging his chances by being overly demanding
and dictatorial. With that in mind, he had suggested that
after his meeting with his uncle's solicitor the next day
he pick her up and take her with him to see the house
he'd been bequeathed, show her around. Somehow the
thought of visiting his old home with her by his side
was altogether more appealing than if he confronted
the bittersweet memories it would undoubtedly evoke
on his own. After the visit he would take her back to
her parents' house so that she could walk Barney, and
then in the evening he would take her out to dinner.

After hearing her gladly acquiesce to both those suggestions, Gabriel had left Lara to drive back to his hotel
in Park Lane with his spirits raised even when by rights
they shouldn't be—because not only had he lost Sean
but he still had to face the ghosts of his past back at the
manor house he'd grown up in.

That aside, he'd begun to sense that he and Lara
had some 'unfinished business' between them. Why
else would they have this chemistry after not even setting eyes on each other for years? Gabriel knew that
he wouldn't be returning to New York any time soon
without discovering the reasons for it.

'Do you mind if I ask you how your meeting with the
solicitor went?'

In the sleek black luxury saloon car that Gabriel had
hired for the duration of his stay Lara's tone was cau-
tiously measured, as if she was unsure of what kind
of response she would get from him. Gabriel couldn't
blame her for being wary after what had happened yesterday. But right then, despite being secretly thrilled

that she was sitting beside him, smelling as fragrant as a rose and looking breathtakingly lovely in her strapless pink summer dress, a more disturbing topic was dominating his thoughts.

That morning he had discovered that there was a surprising codicil to his uncle's will. How it would impact on his life should he go along with it had presented him with a dilemma he'd never anticipated. It seemed there was yet another complication for him to confront and deal with. Dear God! Was he *never* to be free of the demoralising legacy of his past?

Swallowing hard, he deftly steered the car off the main road and onto a thoroughfare that he knew led out into the countryside. It was an all too familiar route— one that he had travelled many times as a boy and rarely with any pleasure.

After travelling for a while in silence, Gabriel finally turned briefly towards Lara and answered her question.

'The meeting went as well as expected, I suppose, if not entirely to my satisfaction. Anyway, you'll see the house in a few minutes and we can go in and have a look round. I'd like to check a few things over and you can come with me. Then we'll have a cup of coffee. I'm expecting my uncle's housekeeper to meet us. She still maintains the place for me and sees to its upkeep.'

'It must be very reassuring for you to have somebody you know taking care of it.'

Seeing they were approaching the long fir-tree-lined drive that led up to the house, Gabriel grimaced.

'I don't exactly *know* her. Her name is Janet Mullan and I only met her when I came over for my uncle's funeral. She's nice enough, I suppose. A cheerful sort. God knows she would have to be to have put up with my taciturn uncle for so long. He wasn't the greatest conversationalist, that's for sure.'

Beside him, Lara emitted a soft-voiced sigh. 'You've never told me what his name was…your uncle, I mean.'

The question made his stomach clench. He'd always made a point of not calling his uncle by his name, because dignifying the man with a personal address might have suggested that he'd mattered to him—which he expressly *hadn't*.

'He was called Richard Devenish—or, to give him his full title, *Sir* Richard Devenish.' He wasn't able to prevent the acerbic inflection that crept into his tone. Being the man's only kin—apart from his errant mother, of course—Gabriel might have inherited the title but it meant little or nothing to him. He would probably never even use it. If he did, it would always be a bittersweet reminder of where he had come from.

His pretty companion shifted in her seat, and he sensed her big brown eyes staring at him in what was likely disbelief.

'You mean to say that you come from landed gentry, Gabriel? I didn't know that.'

'Why should you? I've never advertised it.'

'Did Sean know?'

'I must have mentioned it to him once, because every now and again when we got drunk he'd give me a mock bow just to rile me. Neither of us took it seriously, though.'

'You sound as though it embarrasses you. To have a title, I mean. I don't understand.'

'No.' Staring out through the windscreen at the gracious and mellow redbrick manor that had materialised at the end of the drive, Gabriel felt his insides lurch painfully. 'And I don't suppose you ever will…not unless I tell you. Anyway, we're here.'

Parking the car on the gravel and turning off the ignition, he turned towards Lara to survey her. Once again a rush of pleasure and a need so acute pulsed through him. It was hard to think about doing anything else but making love to her. The sleek bared shoulders in the fetching summer dress she wore didn't exactly help divert the idea. The way the bodice hugged her curvaceous breasts made it hard to look anywhere else.

'By the way…' He smiled, consciously changing his previously gruff tone to a gentler one. 'Have I told you how pretty you look today? That dress is sensational on you.'

Lara's small pink tongue slipped out to moisten her lips and the colour in her cheeks went from a beguiling tinted rose to a deep cerise. The desire that was already gripping Gabriel with a vengeance veered towards the painful.

'No, you haven't,' she answered. Clearly perturbed by the compliment, she quickly moved her gaze to make an interested examination of the imposing building in front of them. 'What an amazing house. It makes my parents' place look doll-size in comparison.'

'Yes, but I know which one I prefer.'

Before she could comment Gabriel put his hand on the door handle and stepped out onto the gravel, then he stooped down to glance in at her. 'We should go in.'

Last night Lara had found it nigh on impossible to sleep. She'd lain awake long into the night, thinking about Gabriel and the fact that he was returning the next day. The shirt that he'd worn during their walk through the woods was draped over a hanger that she'd hooked on the back of the slipper chair by her bed. She'd washed and ironed it, but it still smelled indelibly of its owner, and every now and then Lara had reached out her hand to pull the material to her and sniff it, to remind herself of how compelling and sexy Gabriel's scent was.

She had also touched her fingertips to her lips as she'd recalled the devastatingly passionate kiss that he'd stolen. And every time she had done so it had been as though she lay close to a furnace. There wasn't a single inch of flesh on her body that didn't feel scorched by the man. Just the memory of his heated passion had the ability to arouse her more than she'd ever been aroused before.

Although the beautifully tailored white shirt that belonged to Gabriel was no guarantee that he would keep his promise and return, Lara had chosen to believe it was. Even a man as rich as Gabriel surely wouldn't want to lose an expensive shirt…would he?

She needn't have worried. Gabriel had indeed returned, as he had said he would. And if yesterday when he'd shown up unannounced at her parents' door had felt like a dream, then the surreal sense had definitely intensified today. Lara knew her brother's friend came from wealthy stock, but she'd had no idea that the house he'd grown up in was as grand and palatial as *this*. Certainly Sean had never mentioned it. Had her brother sought to protect the other man's privacy by keeping the information a secret? Lara wouldn't be surprised if he had. Sean had always been fiercely loyal to his friends. Especially Gabriel.

Janet Mullan, the housekeeper, was a diminutive and pretty woman of around sixty, with a wing of silver hair amid surprisingly dominant chestnut curls, and she did indeed turn out to be just as cheerful as Gabriel had said she was. Her twinkling blue eyes lit with pleasure when she greeted them at the impressive Georgian double doors, and she seemed genuinely pleased to see the manor house's handsome new owner.

Straight away she demonstrated her thoughtful nature. If there was anything she could do to help Gabriel or his guest feel more at home, she told him eagerly, anything at all, then he shouldn't hesitate to ask. Would they like some iced tea or a cold drink before they looked around? The news this morning had forecast a 'scorcher' of a day.

Glancing briefly at Lara, Gabriel saw that she was happy to agree with his decision and declined. However, he did request some coffee and biscuits for after they'd finished touring the house.

After he had requested the key to his late uncle's study, because he needed to look at some correspondence that had been left for him, it was clear to Lara that her companion was restless, and she had the sense that Gabriel didn't want to spend any more time at the house than he absolutely had to.

It was hard to understand when he was now master of this incredible property.

When Janet Mullan returned with the key he politely thanked her and, touching his hand to Lara's back, partly exposed by the fitted pink dress she'd impulsively decided to wear that morning, Gabriel led her towards the palatial winding staircase that led to the upper floors.

After looking round several elegant and beautiful rooms they arrived at the light and perfectly proportioned library. Lara had been wondering if Gabriel would show her the bedroom he'd occupied as a child, in the hope that it would give her a little more insight into the man he had become, but she guessed he would probably prefer to visit it on his own. However, as soon as they entered the library, Lara fell silent in wonder. She couldn't help it.

Before her were floor-to-ceiling shelves perfectly arranged with books of every size and volume. More avaricious and ambitious girls might dream of diamonds and sports cars, but she would feel blessed beyond measure should she ever have a room totally dedicated to her books, a room that she could read and relax in—even if it was only small. Gabriel's library was beyond her wildest dreams, but she honestly felt privileged to see it and to experience its gracious ambience, however briefly.

Catching what looked to be a rare pleased smile on his handsome face as he noted her pleasure, Lara found herself walking across the gleaming parquet floor to the generous Georgian windows. Glancing out, she saw that the beautifully furnished book-lined room looked out onto a stunning river frontage, with acres of lush meadow stretching further than the eye could see beyond it.

But she quickly set aside her pleasure at the view when she realised that Gabriel had grown increasingly quiet. Was he unhappy or upset about something? Lara wished she knew specifically what was troubling him. However, what she *did* know was that she could hardly take her eyes off of him. Even dressed in jeans and a navy blue T-shirt, with a casually open chambray shirt, the man didn't look remotely out of place against the impressive grandeur of his childhood home. Yes, Gabriel Devenish exuded class, whether he was conscious of it or not.

Yet the serious, almost solemn expression crossing his strongly delineated features didn't suggest he was remotely pleased at the fact that, as well as being a rich financier, he was now a seriously wealthy landowner, as well. In fact his preoccupied expression suggested he wished he were anywhere else in the world but here.

Just what was going through his mind? Was he remembering his uncle, perhaps? Yesterday he'd confessed that their relationship hadn't been a close one. For a boy whose mother had already abandoned him that must have been cruelly hard. Seeing his home again, was Gabriel perhaps regretting the now lost opportunity to make amends with his uncle and work towards repairing their estranged relationship? If only he would share some of his feelings with her.

'Gabriel?'

'What is it?'

Turning towards her, he pierced her with a troubled yet forceful stare, as though challenging her to say anything that displeased him. Lara didn't need to be a trained psychologist to sense that his composure was balanced on a precarious knife-edge. Now definitely wasn't the time to quiz him about his past.

'From what I've seen so far, this is probably my favourite room in the whole house,' she declared, endeavouring to convey an upbeat cheerful tone. 'How lucky were *you* to have had a personal library at your disposal growing up? If I had lived here I know this is where I would have spent most of my time.'

'Of course you would. That's why you became a librarian, isn't it? Because you love books?'

'I don't deny it.'

'Well, sweetheart…'

To her surprise Gabriel joined her at the window embrasure—but he was still looking troubled, and his compelling blue eyes had darkened like the precursor to a storm.

'Although you might think I was lucky to have a library and such a beautiful house at my disposal, it was anything *but* a pleasurable or happy experience. In fact most of the time the house felt more like a prison than a home to me. It wasn't until I went to university and met Sean, and then you and your parents, Lara, that I got a taste of how different my life could have been if I'd had a similarly happy family.'

Resisting the urge to touch him, even though she badly wanted to, Lara proffered a sympathetic smile instead. 'I'm sorry that you didn't experience a happy family life when you grew up—I really am. But I hope you know that my parents and Sean practically thought of you as family. Mum and Dad were equally as pleased for you when you graduated as they were for Sean.'

'And what about you, Lara?'

Gabriel startled her by reaching out to coil some burnished strands of her silken dark hair round his fingers.

'Did *you* regard me as practically family, too?'

Even though her heart slammed hard against her ribs, and her mouth dried uncomfortably, she bravely met his searing intense gaze without glancing away. It was clear that her answer was important to him and it behoved her to tell him the truth, come what may.

'No, Gabriel. I can honestly say that I never thought of you as family.'

There was a definite hitch of surprise at one corner

of his sublimely carved mouth but he maintained his steady, searching glance.

'Well, well…' His voice lowered meaningfully, and then he freed the strands of hair he'd captured and slid his warm hand beneath her jaw instead. Tipping up her chin to trap her gaze, he said, 'I have to commend you on your honesty, Lara. So, if not family then what *did* you think of me as?'

A sudden attack of nerves seized her. Running her hand down over her dress, Lara sensed it tremble. Gabriel's nearness and the seductive warmth that emanated from his body made it hard to think straight, never mind string a sentence together.

'I don't mean that I didn't regard you highly. Of course I did. You were my brother's best friend and I—and I thought a lot of you.'

'And how do you think of me now?'

She supposed the question was inevitable, but it didn't make it any easier to answer. 'I'm—I'm still fond of you.'

'Fond?' His fingers gripped her chin a little tighter. His blue eyes had never looked stormier. 'That's got to be the most insipid expression of feeling I've ever heard and I can't say that I like it.'

Lara shivered. Inside her strapless dress her nipples had tightened almost unbearably against her bra. They were like molten steel buds and they stung as though burned by a flame as she helplessly watched Gabriel's mouth descend towards hers.

An instinctive need for self-preservation, along with the need to maintain a modicum of equilibrium before she found herself irretrievably lost, swept over her and she found herself halting his lips' descent by laying her hand flat against his chest to stop him. It felt like an impenetrable iron wall, and even as Lara halted him her body clamoured feverishly for his touch.

'We shouldn't— We shouldn't be doing this, Gabriel,' she breathed.

'Says who?' One corner of his devilishly teasing mouth twisted wryly and he caught the hand that was attempting to stop him and lightly threw it away. Then he crushed her against him without the slightest remorse. 'If it's what we both want, then who's to say we should stop?'

Again Lara made a last-ditch attempt to utilise common sense. But Gabriel's desire had lit hers like a flame to touch paper and being sensible was the last—the *very* last—thing her inflamed body wanted to do.

His hard, honed physique felt incredible, pressed up close to hers, and it was clear he was aroused. But somehow she managed to tell him shakily, 'What I want is to be your friend, Gabriel…a *good* friend—not one of the "pretty ladies" with whom you spend the night when you want some company. Our friendship means a lot to me. I wouldn't want sex to cheapen it.'

He immediately dropped his hands down by his sides, looking stricken. Then he looked furious. 'So you would feel cheap if you slept with me, would you? I can't say that does a hell of a lot for my ego. But perhaps in the fairy-tale world that you inhabit, Lara, you were hoping for some kind of knight in shining armour to bed you?'

Gabriel swallowed hard, and his fierce expression was disparaging.

'Well, that's *never* going to be a role I can play, sweetheart, and if all you want is a friend then I suggest you look elsewhere. It's not as if you don't know my history and what a lousy friend I was to your brother. Why would you think I'd behave any differently towards you?'

It was inexplicable why she was so prone to make him angry, but rather than try to understand it right then Lara preferred to try and get to the root of why he was so furious. In spite of his rejection all those years ago, she honestly didn't think it was because he disliked her.

'My statement about sex cheapening our relationship came out all wrong, Gabriel....' She chewed her lip in frustration. 'I didn't mean that the act would make me *feel* cheap—it's just that it would be a shame to reduce the quality of the long-held regard we have for each other just because we succumb to a desire that might be quickly forgotten and...' Her face flamed red as she said the next words. 'And regretted.'

His answering frown was formidable. 'So you think I'd be such a lousy lover you'd immediately regret it?'

Lara could hardly believe how adept she was at saying the wrong thing sometimes. Briefly glancing out of the window and wishing for some kind of mystical inspiration, she couldn't help sighing. 'I don't think that at all. You—you seem determined to misunderstand me.'

Folding his arms across his chest, Gabriel gave her another long, examining look. The sun streaming in through the window behind him made his chestnut hair glisten like copper and she found herself transfixed by the sight.

'Then tell me this,' he said soberly. 'Do you believe there's something wrong with succumbing to desire? Do you think you'll be somehow punished for giving in to it?'

'I'm not some kind of nun who's taken holy orders, Gabriel.' Feeling uncomfortably foolish, Lara flushed.

'Excuse the pun, but thank God for that,' he commented drolly, making her immediately feel weak again when his mouth curved into one of his devastating smiles.

'Is there anywhere else in the house you'd like to show me?' she said quickly, moving across to the door and impulsively taking the opportunity to put some distance between them in a bid to try and calm her wildly beating heart.

With a wry shake of his head he replied, 'That could easily be misconstrued as a leading question, sweetheart, and to save your very charming pretty blushes I'll keep the answer for later. Right now I need to go to my uncle's study and look over some papers. Think you can make your way back downstairs, find Mrs Mullan and ask her to make that coffee for us? Hopefully I won't be too long.'

'Of course.' Feeling glad of the temporary reprieve, in order to get her thoughts together, Lara was happy to agree. But then a thought occurred. *What if the correspondence his uncle had left for him upset or distressed him?* What kind of mood would he be in when he returned downstairs? And would she be able to handle it adequately and give him the support that he might need?

CHAPTER FIVE

APPROACHING THE REGENCY-STYLE oak desk in a room that was imbued with the familiar scent of Havana cigars, Gabriel stared down at the cream vellum envelope with his name on it that sat atop the green baize blotter and unconsciously clenched his fists. Recognising the imposing inked script with the letter 'G' curled with an exaggerated flourish as his uncle's hand immediately made him shudder.

He'd been instructed by his uncle's solicitor that a letter would be waiting for him back at the house and had been asked to read and digest its contents as soon as possible in order to help make up his mind about the unexpected demand in the codicil.

Having already had that document meticulously outlined to him by the solicitor, Gabriel was in no mood to read what would in all likelihood be another disagreeable demand. He'd quickly learned that inheriting the manor was not going to be the straightforward formality that he wanted it to be. But at the end of the day he was an astute businessman as well as a banker, and it just wasn't in him to relinquish the desire to add to his already considerable fortune if the opportunity presented itself, no matter how testing the task would be.

Having seen the house and its extensive grounds again, he was already certain that he would put it on the market and sell it as quickly as he could before returning to New York. He certainly didn't want to take up residence here for six months in order to decide what he was going to do with the place, as the codicil stipulated he would have to if he wanted to inherit.

Had his uncle seriously thought that he would? He was sick and tired of being tied to the unhappy childhood memories that dogged his adult life. The sooner he was rid of the house the better. At any rate, Gabriel knew he could hire the best damn lawyer in the business to help him get round that particular complication. And he personally knew of at least two property developers who would all but rip off his arm to get their hands on the place as soon as they got wind that he was selling it.

He didn't feel an ounce of loyalty either to his uncle or to his forebears when it came to making a profit from the sale. After all, what had his esteemed so-called family done for him?

Feeling impatient, because he'd much rather be spending time with Lara, Gabriel tore open the envelope, unfolded the enclosed letter and hurriedly scanned it.

His heart was thumping hard in shocked disbelief before he even got to the end of the first paragraph.

Dear Gabriel
If you are reading this letter then it must be be-
cause I am no longer here. Knowing that must
be the case, it behoves me to finally tell you the
truth about your mother, Angela. She did not wil-
fully abandon you, as I once told you. That is the

first important thing for you to know. The second is the tragic fact that my beloved sister took her own life.

She had a serious depressive illness that there was no known cure for, and shortly after you were born it became apparent that she was unable to take care of you by herself. She herself needed round-the-clock care and supervision because her illness drove her sometimes to harm herself and her pregnancy exacerbated the tendency.

I lived in fear that she would harm you, too, Gabriel, although with hindsight I should have known that she adored you and would have protected you from harm with her life.

It was a wretched disease that she endured, and I told you that she abandoned you because she begged me to do so should anything happen to her. She was convinced it would be better if you believed that rather than knew that she was sick. She feared that you would get it into your mind that you might have inherited the affliction and that it would stop you from having the successful and happy future that she envisaged for you.

As for your father—I honestly don't know who he was, Gabriel, because Angela would never say. She did tell me once that she loved him, and that he was good to her, but also that he was married. When she knew that she was carrying you she broke off all contact with the man, and I stopped asking her about him because I could see that it distressed her.

I have not been as good an adoptive father to you as I should have been, Gabriel. I know that now and I deeply regret it. But my own father was an austere and uncommunicative man who never displayed much emotion and I suppose I must have picked up the traits. Consequently I fooled myself into thinking that if I provided every material asset you would need to help you get on in life that would be enough. But the truth is because of my own emotional inadequacy I denied you the one thing that you perhaps needed the most—love and friendship.

I will never know if you can find it in your heart to forgive me for the tragic lie that I told you about your mother, Gabriel, but I hope that given time, if you do, then my beloved sister and I will rest in peace.

Look after the manor house for us, my boy, and fill it with your own dear children. One day the sadness and pain that has hurt us all beyond imagining will, I hope, be banished for good and be replaced with sunshine and laughter instead of heartache.

I did you another grave disservice, Gabriel. I once told you that money would buy you anything you wanted—even love. I was wrong. I hope you know that now and can find the woman of your dreams to make a life with. Home and family— that's where true happiness lies.
Sincerely
Your uncle, Richard Devenish

As he finished reading, Gabriel felt numb to his very core. The sensation was quickly replaced by a sense of rage and despair the magnitude of which he had never experienced before.

With his hands shaking he watched the neatly folded letter slip out of his loosened grip and drop back onto the green baize blotter. Leaning forward to rest his arms on the desk, he dropped his head into his hands and squeezed his eyes shut tight. So many feelings, thoughts and sensations rose up inside him at the same time that he felt he would drown beneath the crushing weight of them.

Opening his eyes, he murmured, 'Dear God—why hit me with this now, after all these years? It just doesn't make sense. It makes no sense whatsoever!'

Unable to stay still for a moment longer, Gabriel shot to his feet, heedlessly scraping the chair against the immaculate parquet floor. Vacating it, he furiously kicked at one of the legs and it crashed to the ground and lay on its back like a floundering whale. He had no inclination to set it right again.

It was hard to breathe suddenly, and the desire to escape both the house and the shocking truth of his tragic past was strong in him—too strong to be overcome or ignored. Snatching up his uncle's letter, he slammed out of the room and hurried downstairs.

'Gabriel, please don't drive so fast!' Genuinely frightened at the speed at which her companion was taking the narrow country roads, Lara felt her spine rigid with tension. But she was even more perturbed by the furious tight-lipped expression that hadn't left his face since he'd sought her out in the kitchen, where she'd been talking to the housekeeper, and unceremoniously declared that they were leaving right away.

'But what about your coffee and biscuits, Mr Devenish?' Janet Mullan had asked mournfully, clearly concerned that her new boss wouldn't be staying for refreshments after all.

Gabriel had looked even more irritated, and his tone had been surly. 'Don't stress about it. I'll be in touch again soon, to let you know what I'm doing. Just do your job and take care of the place in my absence. That's all you need be concerned about, Mrs Mullan.'

And with that he'd grabbed Lara's hand and urged her towards the door without pausing even once to explain why.

Lara had already guessed that he'd discovered something in his uncle's study that had disturbed him. He *must* have, she thought anxiously, because although he'd been a little quiet he'd seemed more or less okay before he'd gone in there.

'I'll get you home safely—you don't have to worry,' he said now.

His classic chiselled profile was as coolly perfect as one of Rodin's marble sculptures and he didn't even steal a momentary glance round at her.

Twisting her hands together in her lap, Lara sucked in a breath and answered, 'I'm not worrying so much about your driving, Gabriel, as about your state of mind.'

'What the hell do you mean by that?'

This time he did deign to glance at her, and his crystalline blue eyes were fierce.

'I mean I can see that you're upset, that's all. Why don't we stop somewhere and talk? It's not a good idea to drive when you're feeling distressed.'

'Why don't you let *me* be the judge of that? And do me a favour, Lara—please don't treat me like I'm one of your family's infamous waifs and strays that you can pet and nurse back to health. In case you hadn't noticed, I'm all grown up now and I can perfectly well take care of myself!'

Gabriel was indeed 'all grown up now', she thought privately, but that didn't mean he had the tools to try and heal whatever had distressed him on his own. He at least needed to talk things out with someone.

Turning her head to glance out of the window at the verdant country scenes that flashed by, she hoped that perhaps later, when he'd calmed down a bit, there might be a chance of reaching him and getting him to confide what had so disturbed him when he'd gone into his uncle's study. She could only pray that an opportunity would present itself.

Back at her parents' house, as soon as Lara opened the door Barney leapt up at her, barking an enthusiastic greeting, his short tail furiously wagging as if she'd been gone for *years* instead of a mere couple of hours. As was her habit, she dropped down to make a fuss of him, tickling him behind the ears, stroking his back and talking to him as though he understood every word she said—which she didn't doubt that he *did*.

'Hello, you little scamp. Have you missed me? I know you don't like being on your own for long, do you?'

The terrier emitted a short, sharp yap as if to agree.

Staring down at Lara's slim back and silkily smooth bared shoulders in that far too alluring summer dress she was wearing, Gabriel couldn't help fantasising about how easy it would be for him to unzip the garment and, using every seductive technique he had—and there were *many*—coax her into bed with him, rather than let her waste any more time and attention on the family's dog.

He realised he was becoming more and more reluctant to leave the brunette's side for even a minute. And after reading the hauntingly disturbing contents of his uncle's letter he was in no mood to be on his own. The only thing that could possibly help ease his soul-deep distress was Lara, preferably naked and lying beneath him.

As if suddenly remembering he was there, she rose to her feet, her lips curving in a tentative smile. 'What are your plans for the rest of the day? Are you in a hurry to leave? Only I was wondering if I could get you a cup of coffee, since we didn't have one back at the manor house.'

Her comment couldn't help but raise Gabriel's hopes. 'Are you angry with me because I didn't stay at the manor longer with you?'

Her expression softened. 'Of course I'm not angry. I was just concerned because I could see that you were upset.'

'Nearly everything to do with that damn house upsets me. But that's not your problem, Lara. I'll make it up to you when I take you out to dinner tonight. I'll book us a table at the Dorchester.'

'You have nothing to make up to me, Gabriel.'

'Yes, I do.'

'In any case, shall we have that coffee now?'

Rubbing his hand round the back of his neck, Gabriel grimaced. 'I need something a lot stronger than coffee. Have you got any brandy?'

Absently smoothing back the curtain of dark hair that framed her face, Lara frowned. 'But you're driving back to your hotel at some point, aren't you? I won't give you alcohol if you're intending to drive, Gabriel.'

'You really *are* a little Miss Goody Two-shoes, aren't you? I bet you never once sat on the naughty chair at primary school, did you?' he jibed, hating himself for sounding so disparaging when she was only displaying her natural concern for him.

But his ill-mannered retort didn't seem to faze her. As she lifted her chin he saw her glossy brown eyes were defiant.

'Call me what you will,' she said, 'but I won't collude with any plan that might potentially harm you or get you into trouble, Gabriel—however much you insist on having your way.'

Not releasing her perturbed gaze, he deliberately stepped towards her. 'What if I want or need some help?'

He'd knowingly pitched his voice low to engage her intimately, and Lara's sharp inhalation of breath immediately drew Gabriel's avid glance to her cleavage. He witnessed the provocative rise and fall of her luscious breasts in the fitted bodice of that sexy pink dress and, God help him, what was a healthy male supposed to do in such testing circumstances?

'What kind of help?'

A corner of his lips quirked in a teasing smile. 'I'm sure you must know the answer to that by now, Lara.'

'You have a worryingly one-track mind—you know that? Do you *really* think us being intimate is going to help resolve whatever upset you earlier? Something disturbed you when you went into your uncle's study—don't you think it might be more help if we discussed that?'

'No, I don't. I'm far more interested in what's going
to help me right now, sweetheart. Not in what happened
in the past. And, yes, I really *do* think it would help if
we were intimate. The last thing I want you to do is
worry about what happened earlier. That's *my* problem.
Can't you stop trying to be Lady Bountiful for a minute
and just be a woman for a change?'

Her pretty face was immediately stricken. It was obvious he'd touched a nerve, but although he regretted
that he might have hurt her it didn't stop him wanting
to seduce her. It might not ease any of the devastation
he'd felt on finally learning the truth about his mother,
and the lie about her abandoning him that his uncle
had colluded with, but fulfilling the intimate connection he craved with Lara would go a long way to help
satisfy the burning desire that had mercilessly seized
him since seeing her again.

It was a carnal hunger that made it almost impossible for him to think about anything else but being with
her in the most intimate way. Had the woman put some
kind of spell on him?

'That was uncalled for, Gabriel. I'm just as much a
woman as you are a man and you damn well know it.'

Hands planted firmly on her shapely hips, her dark
eyes glinting with fury, Lara had no compunction in
displaying her temper—and in truth right then those
fulsome breasts of hers, along with her rosily flushed
satin cheeks, ensured she was a sight for sore eyes.

Gabriel couldn't help concluding that Sean's 'little
sister' had turned into a woman who would stir lustful longings in a stone, let alone a healthy red-blooded
male. It was an honest-to-God mystery why she was
still single.

'And if your criteria for judging femininity means that a woman is only feminine if she agrees to have sex with a man when he tells her that he's "in need" then you're seriously deluded.'

'Of course I don't think that!' Now it was his turn to feel aggrieved. 'You make it sound like I'm some stranger off of the street, instead of someone who's known and regarded you since you were young. Is it so hard for you to believe that I'm attracted to you, Lara?'

Gabriel was finding it increasingly hard to tamp down his growing frustration at her reticence to be closer. Perhaps he should open up to her a little bit more? Let her know that he had just as much feeling and sensitivity as she had, even though he rarely displayed it? Could he risk revealing such a thing to her?

The thought instantly made him want to retreat in order to protect himself. What if Lara laughed at his confession and concluded it to be a cynical ruse he was using in order to persuade her into bed? What if opening up more personally to her turned out to be a colossal mistake he'd come to regret? He had never yet given a woman that kind of power over him and he didn't want to start now. If he couldn't seduce her with his usual prowess and the skill that was innate to him, then he shouldn't even waste his time trying.

Reaching out to push the door shut behind him, and unknowingly tantalising him with her alluring sun-kissed scent that reminded him of a garden full of honeysuckle, Lara sighed heavily.

'I don't want to argue with you, Gabriel, but I *am* going to make us some coffee. Then I really think we should sit down and talk.'

Frustratingly having to own to losing this particular

little battle, but reluctant to walk away, Gabriel ruefully shook his head. 'Okay, have it your way—at least just for now. Perhaps some coffee will help clear my head. God knows right at this moment it feels like a herd of buffalo are stampeding through it.'

'That's probably the jet lag. Unless you have some kind of cold or fever brewing? Let me see.'

Reaching up, Lara laid her hand against his forehead, as if to ascertain his temperature, and her silkily cool touch made Gabriel suck in a surprised and pleased breath. It renewed his hope that she would continue to play nurse should he stick around a bit longer.

'You feel a little warm, but I don't think it's anything to worry about. If you start to feel any worse I'll give you something to help take your temperature down.'

'It won't work.'

'Why?'

'Let's go and have that coffee and maybe I'll tell you.'

Finding a perfectly legitimate excuse to touch her, when it was becoming more and more difficult for him *not* to, Gabriel slid his hand beneath her elbow to lead her down the hallway and out into the kitchen.

CHAPTER SIX

IT WAS ONE OF THE hardest things Lara had ever had to do—to sit down opposite Gabriel at the kitchen table and try to pretend she was impervious to the naked longing in his eyes. It would be so easy to give him what he wanted, what *she* wanted, too. But then what would that achieve other than fulfilling their mutual need for sexual gratification?

She didn't doubt he could get that anywhere. After all, what woman in her right mind could look at the man and *not* imagine what it would be like to make love with him? Never mind get the chance to actually find out! He was pure erotic female fantasy come to life. But although the thought of her body entwined with Gabriel's was a dream she'd often fantasised over—one that she'd longed to make a reality—she wasn't about to diminish her fantasy with just one or two stolen experiences in bed with him and then have him walk away. Not when she yearned for so much more.

'Can I ask you why you wore that particular dress today?'

'What?' Startled by the question, Lara stared back into Gabriel's darkly captivating blue gaze and frantically wondered what to tell him.

The outfit wasn't her usual style—that was for certain. When it came to more 'dressy' items of clothing she usually erred on the side of caution—not too revealing and not too showy. But her friend Nicky had persuaded her that this dress looked 'hot' and would be perfect for when she found herself going on a special date with someone.

She supposed that when she'd known she was seeing Gabriel the following day, and that he would be taking her to visit his ancestral family home, she'd decided it *could* constitute as a sort of date. Now, in the cold light of day, having his heated gaze examine her as if he'd like to peel off everything she was wearing, preferably slowly and stitch by stitch, Lara wished she'd been more sensible.

'I knew it was going to be a hot day, that's why.' She shrugged her shoulders as though it was scarcely worth even commenting on.

'Well,' he drawled, leaning across the table to pin her with a tantalising gaze it was impossible to wriggle out of meeting. 'I'd like to commend you on your choice. It shows off your figure to perfection.'

'Gabriel?'

'Yes, Lara?'

'I think we need to change the subject and talk about what's been troubling you. Can we do that?'

The answering scowl on that handsome hard-jawed face was not dissimilar to that of a small boy denied a treat. Under different circumstances Lara might have found it amusing. But she was becoming very familiar with Gabriel's avoidance tactics, and right at that moment she would have been hard-pushed to raise even the smallest of smiles. Not when anxiety about him was gnawing away at her.

'I know you probably think I'm being a bit too pushy, but I'm concerned. If you don't at least share with me what's troubling you then who *will* you share it with?'

Lifting his mug of coffee to his lips, he took a sip, then returned it to the table. 'So you want to hear the whole sorry tale of my hopeless and hapless family, do you?'

Straight away Lara registered the pain in his voice that he'd obviously hoped to conceal with self-deprecating mockery. Her heart twisted as apprehension and fear about what he might be going to reveal invaded her. She nodded slowly.

'All right, then.' Even though he'd agreed, Gabriel looked far from easy and stared down at the floor. 'My uncle left me a letter revealing things about my mother that I never knew.'

The words were followed by a near deafening silence that told her his feelings must be in utter turmoil. Somewhere outside a bird sang. The lyrical sound pierced the air, adding a heartrending poignancy to the moment.

Wanting to encourage him to resume his story, and fearing he wouldn't because the prospect of revealing his family secrets and potentially making himself vulnerable was something he no doubt despised, she remarked quietly, 'You said she left when you were very young. You don't remember her?'

He lifted his head. 'No, I don't. In any case, it turns out that that was a lie.'

'I don't understand.'

Gabriel's carved mouth twisted bitterly. 'Oh, she left, all right.'

He stared at her, lost in some unhappy reverie that he was still trying to make sense of, she guessed.

'She killed herself.'

Lara could scarcely think straight above the sonorous thump of her heart. 'Oh, Gabriel, I'm so sorry.'

As his confession sank in she felt even more stunned and sorry. She couldn't begin to imagine what it must be like to hear that your mother had committed suicide. How did a child—a child who was now an adult—pick up the pieces of his life and live anywhere *near* normally again after learning such devastating news?

Gabriel shook his head as though bemused. 'My uncle told me that she left because she didn't think she was cut out to be a mother. That was the story she begged him to tell me so that I wouldn't try and find out the truth about her.'

'But why—why would she do such a thing?'

Shrugging his big shoulders, the gesture momentarily straining the soft blue chambray of his shirt, he grimaced. 'He said it was because she was suffering from a depressive condition that was incurable. She was afraid that if I knew the truth I might think I'd inherited it and it would ruin my life.' A harsh semblance of a laugh left him. 'She must have really been disturbed if she thought it was better that I believed she'd deserted me!'

Leaning forward, Lara studied Gabriel as if seeing him for the very first time. There was no hiding his distress. She had a heartrending glimpse of the small boy who'd grown up believing that his mother hadn't wanted him and had consequently abandoned him. With every fibre of her being she longed to go to him and draw him into her arms. But she sensed there was a lot more yet to this terribly sad story.

'It sounds as though she was just trying to protect you, Gabriel,' she remarked softly.

'Protect me? From what, exactly? Her love and devotion?' His tone was bitterly disparaging. 'I may not be parent material, but I'm damn sure mothers are supposed to love and care for their children—not just abandon them on some whim!'

Several thoughts jostled for position in Lara's mind just then, but the strongest was her musing that if his mother had been mentally ill, then it was surely no 'whim' that had driven her to insist that her son didn't know the truth about her condition. The poor woman must have really believed it would hurt him.

But she didn't share the thought with Gabriel right then. The clenched fists he'd laid on the table and the tortured look in his eyes told her it was best to stay silent and simply allow him to express how he felt without interrupting the flow of pain and anger that must be coursing through him. Better that he let it out than keep it all in. Afterwards, bit by bit, Lara would do her utmost to try and help him.

'My uncle said in his letter that she'd been a danger to herself but he honestly believed she never would have harmed me. Did he think that would be a consolation when I learned that she'd killed herself? Did he never consider the effect it might have had on me, growing up believing that she'd left because she didn't want me?'

'Oh, Gabriel…'

It was no good. It was impossible for Lara to remain sitting in her chair when his feelings were clearly tearing him apart and she ached to console him. But when she got up and dropped her arm gently round his shoulders she sensed them instantly stiffen.

'Didn't I tell you not to treat me like some waif or stray that needs your help?' he growled, catching hold of her hand and gripping it.

Staring back into the starkly haunted blue eyes, she felt an answering quiver that was part fear and part desire run down her spine.

'I don't regard you as some kind of waif or stray, can't you see that? You're not a stranger to me, Gabriel. I'm treating you like I would any dear friend who needed my comfort and support.'

'So it's back to us just being friends again, is it?'

Her action purely instinctive, Lara retrieved her hand to lay her palm against his smoothly shaven cheek. His skin felt like sensually roughened velvet. 'Everyone can use a friend, can't they?' she breathed.

She didn't plan for her voice to catch on the final two words but it did. Even as she saw the pupils in Gabriel's blue eyes darken and flare she suddenly knew that it wasn't just comfort she wanted to dispense. Right then she needed him as much as he needed her and it was impossible to deny it.

'No, Gabriel, not just friends.'

In less than a heartbeat his big firm hands pulled her down onto his lap and without preamble he drove them deep into her hair. Although his warm breath fanned her face like a spine-tingling summer breeze, it still made Lara shiver.

'I want you so much I think I'll die if I can't have you,' he declared.

His voice was low and deep, the unfettered emotion it expressed so raw that it almost took her breath away.

Lara would have crumpled at the declaration if he hadn't been cupping her face and anchoring her. But his lips were against hers, his hot tongue invading her mouth and devouring her, and a low, hungry groan emanated from his throat that she couldn't help but echo as she surrendered to the irresistible fire that he'd ignited.

If it were possible she would kiss him for ever, she thought wildly, yet even for ever couldn't possibly be *enough*. Her hands weren't idle as Gabriel's lips worked their honeyed and stirring magic. They splayed out over the hard chest encased in sensuous cotton and chambray, her fingers helplessly curling against him in a voracious need to know and feel every part of him, to have the insatiable memory imbued in her mind and heart for ever.

Leaving her hair, Gabriel's hands slid down over her shoulders onto her back. Lara sensed his fingers fumble impatiently with her zip. As if shaken awake from a dream, she suddenly became aware that things were fast getting out of control.

Not wanting their first intimate exploration of each other to take place mindlessly and perhaps awkwardly on a chair, she twisted her mouth away from his and said, 'No, Gabriel, not here.'

Straight away she registered the confusion and protestation in his eyes.

Administering a reassuring smile, she gently extricated herself, then stood up and reached down for his hand. 'We'll go upstairs to my room,' she added softly.

'You're sure?' he murmured.

She hadn't expected to hear doubt in his voice, but doubt was what she heard—and it made her want him all the more because he wanted to make sure.

'Yes, I am. It's what I want, too,' she answered firmly.

Lara needed to show Gabriel that she was equally as aroused and needy as he was. She wasn't going to bed with him purely because she wanted to console him. The man turned her on like no other man ever *could.*

Rising to his feet, he impelled her into his arms as if he couldn't bear to let her go for even an instant. For Lara, too, it was difficult to contemplate leaving that safe haven when the familiar scent of his cologne and the arresting heat from his body made her feel as if she was, albeit briefly, abandoning a vitally integral part of her.

Staring down into her eyes as if he would see into her very soul, Gabriel loosely circled her waist with his arm. 'Then let's go.' He smiled.

The gesture was indisputably possessive and it thrilled Lara right down to her innermost core. Knowing that Gabriel really wanted her made her feel beautiful. How could it not when she'd loved her brother's charismatic friend from the moment she'd laid eyes on him all those years ago? There was an undeniable sense of inevitability about them meeting up again like this—as if they were meant to find each other again. Did Gabriel feel that way, too?

The seductive scent of her perfume lingered in the air as Lara took Gabriel by the hand and led him into her bedroom. The room was awash with afternoon sunlight but she made no move to draw the blinds. The most seductive shiver ran down Gabriel's spine as, instead, she led him across to a queen-size bed that was draped with a purple silk coverlet.

Truth to tell, it would have been difficult for him to note much else in that room other than Lara herself.

His blood was infused with a longing to hold her close so profound that it was as though he were caught in the grip of a dangerous fever that was steadily growing hotter. All he could think of to help ease his pain was getting her naked and joining his body with hers. And if he was seeking shelter from the storms of life that had battered him, seeking it in the only way he sensed might provide some brief respite, then he made no apology for it.

At the foot of the bed Lara turned to face him. Her silken dark hair framed her lovely face like a picture. Lifting her hands, she positioned them either side of his waist. As her melting brown eyes examined him it was as though she were touching him in the most intimate way. Gabriel burned to take her. But through the fog of his desire he vowed to take things slowly, so that the experience would be pleasurable for her. It would surely be worth the sacrifice.

Trailing his fingertips softly and deliberately over her mouth, he said, 'Will you undress or do you want me to do it for you?'

With a soft catch in her voice, she returned, 'You decide.'

He couldn't have wished for a better answer. Bending his head, he gently touched his lips to hers. As he did so he tugged at the zip at the back of the sexy pink dress and slid it down with ease. Momentarily breaking off the kiss, he stepped back so that he could tug down the bodice. The satiny material shimmered silkily down over Lara's bewitching form to the floor. As she stepped out of the dress she put her hand in Gabriel's to steady herself and then kicked off the cork sandals that she wore.

She lifted her head to study him. The undisguised need he saw reflected in her eyes all but undid him. He responded by deftly encircling her chest to undo the catch on her bra. When her beautiful breasts were freed, he was gratified that she didn't immediately try to cover herself.

For long seconds Gabriel just stared at her, drinking in the arresting sight before him as though not quite believing his good fortune. Then he put his mouth to one tip-tilted breast and suckled hard. Just as an electrifying bolt of heat ricocheted through his body and went straight to his groin, hardening him, Lara released a soft-voiced moan of pleasure.

Glancing up at her, Gabriel smiled. Flattening his hand, he laid it against her breastbone and gently pushed. As she gracefully fell back onto the purple counterpane the full extent of her curvaceous figure was at last revealed to him in all its irresistible glory. The luscious breasts with their peaked nipples, her slim concave belly and shapely hips, the silky smooth legs that were even longer than he'd imagined, the toenails that were painted with a sassy fire-engine-red.

After his initial heated examination Gabriel's thoughts were suspended as the urgent need to make love to her instinctively drove him instead. Tearing off his shirt and T-shirt, he jettisoned the clothing onto the floor. Ridding himself of his shoes and socks, he undid his belt buckle and left the belt to fall loosely against his jeans. Then he joined Lara on the bed.

He couldn't have said who welcomed whom first. The only thing he registered was their mutually ravenous need to hold each other close and be intimate. The rest of their clothes were quickly dispensed with as they embraced, and the vow he'd made to take things slowly fell mockingly by the wayside as soon as touched her. Ravishing her mouth more deeply and hungrily than he'd ravished any other woman's before, Gabriel ran his hands down over her shapely body and explored her. She was hot silk and sensuous satin, and the devastating revelation about his mother that had torn him apart that day freed some of its imprisoning hold on him.

When Lara disengaged her lips from his to whisper his name, Gabriel heard the unspoken invitation he was longing to hear and sucked in a shaky breath. Moving to sit astride her, his smile drowsy with pleasure and acknowledgment, he bent his head to continue the drugging kiss that he'd quickly become addicted to. Even as his mouth took hers captive he felt her silken thighs come round his waist to enfold him.

A second invitation was hardly necessary. He helplessly took her there and then, pressing himself deep inside her with a hungry primal groan. Her heat was like a honeyed river and Gabriel knew he would willingly drown in it—not just once but over and over until he was spent—until every hurt and bitter sorrow that had ever plagued him was laid to rest for good.

Lara had feared the relinquishing of her virginity to Gabriel. Not because she didn't want to lose it, but because she'd been afraid that the initial discomfort would prevent her from giving herself as wholeheartedly as she wanted to. But his heated sensual possession had quickly banished her fears. The most intimate core of her womanhood had softened so naturally to accommodate him that any discomfort she experienced quickly disappeared as she surrendered to the tidal wave of passion that consumed her.

But Lara did briefly wonder if, when Gabriel entered her, he had noticed that her muscles were a little tight— perhaps tighter than women with a lot more experience than her? She should perhaps tell him that this was her first time, but she was still wary of trusting him too much in case he either didn't understand or couldn't believe that she would wait so long to be with a man. If she were to confess that she only felt she could be intimate with someone she loved, would it scare him away?

The thought was swiftly quashed by the sensation of wondrous bliss and excitement that gripped her as Gabriel moved rhythmically inside her and her hands clutched the iron-hard biceps in his bulging arms to hold on. During that incredible, passionate ride Lara soon learned that imagination was no substitute for the breathtaking reality that was making love with a man she had been crazy about for years. Not for one second did he fail to live up to her hopes and dreams about the experience—in fact, he *exceeded* them.

As the heat between them gathered force Gabriel glanced down at her, his blue eyes blazing with hunger and desire as if there was no other woman on earth for him but her. It was then that Lara had to bite back her heartfelt need to tell him how much she loved him— how much she had *always* loved him.

She determinedly quelled the impulse as he moved deeper inside her and she wound her arms round his neck to pull his head down to hers. Even as they hungrily kissed, the need in her that had been helplessly building towards fulfilment suddenly reached its peak. She found herself on a trip to the stars that took her breath away, that made her feel mindless and boneless, that made her shake and quiver and cry out all at once.

Her heart thumped so loudly that she would swear Gabriel must hear it.

As she slowly came back to herself he gave her a lazy, satisfied smile, lowered his head and whispered in her ear. 'You're so beautiful you take my breath away.'

The edges of her lips curved in an answering smile and he lifted himself and drove into her even more deeply. Once again Lara had to hold on tight to the iron-muscled biceps as they contracted and grew hard beneath her fingertips. Then he stilled and convulsed with a harsh-sounding groan that seemed to emanate from deep inside his soul.

The sound made Lara shiver. It was as though every hurt and betrayal he'd ever endured had culminated in that groan and was now released. Feeling the hot press of tears against her lids, she wove her fingers gently through his hair and held his head, secretly thrilling that he stayed inside her instead of immediately moving away. Knowing he was a man who didn't trust easily, she was pleased and gratified that he must trust her enough to do that.

As he laid his head between her breasts, his warm breath skimming gently over her skin, she registered his racing heartbeat and murmured, 'It's all right, Gabriel, just let it all out. I'm here for you.'

He didn't look up, just stayed where he was, his body still as a statue. But Lara knew she didn't imagine the brief shudder that went through him or the near silent sob that was quickly suppressed in case she should hear it.

CHAPTER SEVEN

GABRIEL HAD NO IDEA how long he'd been sleeping. All he knew was that it was like the most delicious dream he could ever imagine finding himself waking up next to a softly slumbering and naked Lara.

Raising himself up onto his elbow, he gently moved the silken strands of dark hair that caressed the side of her face. She was lying on her belly, her lovely face turned to the side. At some point during the afternoon she must have pulled the purple counterpane over them, but it had slid back down to her waist to leave her back and shoulders exposed. It was then that Gabriel saw the perfect facsimile of an ebony and sky blue butterfly, whose delicate wings spread out over the base of her spine. The woman constantly surprised him. Who would have thought that the once shy young girl he'd known all those years ago would have opted for a tattoo, albeit one that only a lover would see?

Shaking his head, Gabriel breathed out a bemused sigh. But it was quickly followed by a stinging flash of jealousy. The thought of Lara being naked with another man, even if it *was* in the past, made him feel almost physically ill.

Making love with her had been one of the most ec-

static and meaningful experiences of his life since he
had shared some of the hurtful secrets about his past
with her. That had made the experience truly intimate.
Never before had he shared such personal information
with a woman. Shuddering, he remembered how he
hadn't been able to hold back his grief when he'd climaxed—recalled too that Lara had gently advised him
to 'just let it all out' and told him that she was there
for him.

Then he remembered that he hadn't used protection.
It hadn't even crossed his mind. That was another first
and a not so acceptable one. Was Lara on the pill? Damn
it all, he should at least have thought to ask her. But he
had been so consumed by the fever of longing that she
aroused in him that rational thinking just hadn't been
on the agenda.

If she were to become pregnant after this, what
would he do? What would Lara *want* to do? Would
she agree to an abortion if he asked her? It was such
a shockingly disagreeable notion that a knifing pain
cramped his chest.

At that precise moment Lara stirred and opened her
eyes. Gabriel couldn't believe he'd forgotten for even
a moment how beautiful they were—dark-roast coffee
fanned by long, luxurious ebony lashes.

She was staring blankly up at him, as though caught
in a spell. Then her gaze fully registered his and she
asked softly, 'Are you all right? I mean, how are you
feeling?'

'I feel good,' Gabriel answered frankly. 'Better than
I've a right to, probably. I can't help feeling that I'm
very fortunate to have found you again, Lara. I guess
I must have done something right to please the gods.'

She dimpled. 'Maybe you're not all bad boy, then?'

'Is that how you see me? As a bad boy?'

'I think you have a little bit of that in you, but rather than detract from it, it just adds to your charisma.'

'Tell me more.' He grinned. 'I'm not averse to hearing about all the qualities that make me attractive to a woman.'

'What? And pander to your already inflated ego?'

Gabriel chuckled and realised how much he was enjoying just lazing in bed like this with Lara, in the middle of the afternoon, without feeling remotely guilty or having the need to get up and think about work.

'You don't have to do that to make me stay here with you, baby. Whatever you've got, I'm already addicted to it. That's why I'm still here.' Stroking his knuckles gently down her cheek, he smiled. 'You don't get rid of me that easily, either. I guess you're not the only one with a touch of the terrier in her.'

'Talking of which…' Lara sat bolt upright, grabbed the silk counterpane and pulled it up over her breasts. At the same time her cheeks flushed pink as though she was suddenly aware that she was naked. 'I've got to walk Barney. I can't believe I actually fell asleep in the middle of the day. I *never* do that—even if I'm exhausted.'

'This seems to be a day of firsts,' Gabriel observed smilingly.

'What do you mean?'

'It's not important.' Shrugging his shoulders, he levelled his gaze at her more seriously. 'However, what *is* important is the fact that I didn't use protection when we made love. That's a pretty major mistake, Lara, and whether you believe me or not it's one that I've never made before.'

Frowning, she told him, 'You don't have to worry, Gabriel. I'm on the pill. I should have mentioned it earlier, but we—I…' Her smile was a shade unsure. 'We got a bit carried away.'

Gabriel felt as if he'd been sucker-punched and didn't know why. Then he did. If Lara was taking the contraceptive pill then she must have the occasional lover. If she did, then it must have been quite a while since the last one, because she'd felt exquisitely tight when he'd entered her—as if having sex wasn't a regular occurrence for her. But the thought hardly reassured him. It made him feel disappointed, when in fact he should be grateful that at least one of them was taking the proper precautions.

Mentally gathering himself, he murmured, 'Thank God for that.'

Lara flushed and glanced away. Turning back to him, she asked, 'Do you know what the time is?'

He checked his watch. 'It's just gone four.'

'Four o'clock? You're joking?'

Amused, Gabriel drawled, 'Why the panic?'

'The panic is Barney must be desperate to answer the call of nature and I've got to go and have a shower.'

'That's an interesting dilemma. And there's one more thing you have to add to your list of things to do.'

'What's that?'

'You need to kiss me hello.'

Finally succumbing to the irresistible impulse that had been growing steadily stronger from the moment he'd opened his eyes and found Lara lying naked beside him, Gabriel put his hands onto her slim shoulders and pulled her against his chest. The silk cover slipped away from her breasts to expose them, and his senses were immediately aroused by the silken texture of her soft flesh and the peaked nipples pressing against him.

His blood thickened and slowed at the thought of seducing her again. Just as he was about to capture her lips in a drowsily sensual kiss that he hoped would be the precursor to so much more, right on cue the terrier downstairs made his presence known with a round of impatient barking.

'Oh, Lord. I'll have to go and see to him. I won't walk him—I'll just let him out the back. Sorry.'

With a sheepish glance, Lara wriggled out of his embrace and moved to the edge of the bed. Glancing down towards the floor, as though searching for something, she murmured an audible expletive beneath her breath and huffed out a sigh.

'What have you lost?' Gabriel enquired innocently, even as he reached behind her to pick up the bra and panties that had been partially hidden in the folds of the silk counterpane. He quickly slid them under her pillow.

'My underwear. But never mind.' Rising to her feet, she hurried across the room to grab a pair of jeans and a pink T-shirt from her wardrobe.

Transfixed by the wholly arresting sight of her bare bottom and long, slim legs, Gabriel found his gaze drawn to the exquisite butterfly tattooed at the base of her spine. Leaning back against the pillows, he drawled, 'I think this is the best wake-up call I've ever had. So what's the story behind the butterfly?'

Lara was in the midst of pulling up her jeans. She completed the task and turned round. The pink T-shirt she'd retrieved was held protectively over her breasts, as if it was still important to her to preserve her modesty even though she'd just presented an uncensored view of her delectable derrière to Gabriel.

'Sean sent me a picture of a butterfly just like it in his last letter home before he died. He told me it was extremely rare and that he felt privileged to have seen it.' With a nervous swallow she glanced briefly down at the floor. 'I suppose I had the tattoo done as a kind of homage to him. He often used to tease me that I "played safe" and didn't take enough risks in life. It makes me smile to imagine what he would have said if he'd seen it.'

'I think it's a work of art—and so are you, angel. You and the butterfly are an exquisite combination.'

'Thanks.'

The smile Lara gave him was so endearingly shy that it provoked Gabriel's carnal hunger even more. In fact he didn't know why he had even let her out of bed. Broodingly, he watched her hurriedly don the pink T-shirt she'd been holding against her. Braless, the garment was more revealing than she was probably aware. One thing was for sure: he wasn't about to complain about the fact.

'I'd better go and see to Barney. I won't be long.'

His mouth drying, Gabriel couldn't resist a final comment. 'So you're going commando, are you? What are you trying to do? Torment me? Do you know how close I am to hauling you back into bed?'

'If you do, then who's going to clean up the mess that Barney will undoubtedly leave on my parents' prized parquet floor? I can tell you now, Gabriel Devenish, it won't be me!'

In spite of his frustration Gabriel was still grinning at

the quick-fire remark, and devising lascivious ways he might repay her for it, long after Lara had left the room.

Gabriel's relief had been plain when she'd told him that she was on the pill and didn't have to worry. But as Lara stood at the back door that looked out onto the garden and watched Barney scamper across the lawn she knew he must assume she was a lot more experienced than she actually was.

What Gabriel didn't and couldn't know was that she took the contraceptive pill to help regulate her monthly periods and ease painful cramps. And, whilst Lara knew it wasn't a good idea to risk pregnancy when she wasn't even in a steady relationship, she couldn't help feeling regret that Gabriel probably would have hated it if he'd made her pregnant. After all, he didn't know how deep her feelings for him ran, or that she'd surrendered her virginity to him because he was the only man she'd ever loved and she loved him still. Trying to be realistic, she guessed that he probably wouldn't welcome anything that cramped his high-octane lifestyle—least of all a baby.

Determinedly brushing aside the moisture that surged into her eyes as she recalled how wonderful it had been to make love with him, she unconsciously held her hand over her heart. She still throbbed and tingled where he had touched her, where he had united his body with hers.

Although she'd naturally wanted to help give Gabriel the comfort that he'd needed after learning the devastating truth of how his mother had died, and how his uncle had lied to him to protect her, what Lara had said to him just prior to the event still held true. Their lovemaking had been something that she had wanted, too. Not just wanted but needed. Whatever happened now, or in the future, she would never regret it.

'Oh, what a tangled web we weave when first we practise to deceive....' The famous quote stole into her mind as she thought of the pain and distress the deception had visited on Gabriel—the pain and distress that would probably plague him for the rest of his life. Now he would quite likely sell the magnificent manor house he'd inherited because he would see it only as a lucrative investment he could cash in on and not as a family legacy he could be proud of. How could he when the wounds of his past were so great that no one would blame him for wanting to turn his back on the whole scenario? After he'd sold the place he would probably just return to New York and Lara would never see him again.

'No.'

It jolted her to realise she'd voiced the protest out loud. But already she was making a vow not to let such a bleak scenario occur if she could prevent it. Somehow there must be a way to get Gabriel to see the gift he would be turning his back on—the gift that might be the key to helping him heal the grievous wounds from his past and make him see that he didn't need to bear them for ever, that his future could be so much brighter if he would only give himself the chance to explore the possibility and not run away.

Lost in her heartfelt reverie, Lara sighed. Then Barney started to bark and she glanced down to see the terrier scampering past her, no doubt in search of his basket and a nap. It was then she remembered that Gabriel was waiting for her upstairs. She almost wanted to pinch herself to make sure she wasn't dreaming. It wasn't necessary. The stinging tips of her tender breasts where Gabriel had kissed and suckled them were an apt reminder that this was no dream but instead a heart-poundingly wonderful reality.

· Hugging herself, she headed out into the hall and quickly returned upstairs.

To her surprise, Gabriel wasn't in bed where she'd left him. Just as Lara sensed her stomach plunge at the thought that he'd slipped away whilst she'd been keeping an eye on the dog, the en-suite bathroom door opened and he stepped out, fully dressed and combing his fingers through his lightly tousled chestnut hair. His charismatic smile was both rueful and rakish at the same time.

Before she could ask what was going on he strode over to her and possessively wound his arms round her waist. Even though his embrace instantly rendered her weak with pleasure and desire, Lara suspected her secret hopes about how they might spend the rest of the afternoon weren't going to come to fruition.

'What's wrong? Why—why are you dressed?'

'I had a phone call from New York while you were downstairs. Sweetheart, I'm afraid I've got to go back.'

'You mean back to New York?'

Grimacing, Gabriel nodded. 'They've got a real crisis on their hands on the trading floor. They want me to go back and help sort it out.'

'But what about the legalities you said you needed to deal with here? I mean the ones concerning the house?'

'They're just going to have to wait. Right now my priority is getting back to New York. The sooner I leave, the sooner I'll be back.'

Lara stared into his captivating blue eyes and couldn't help offering up a silent relieved prayer that he intended to return. But she still didn't want him to go. 'So you *are* intending on coming back, then?'

Lowering his head, he captured her lips in a slow, seductive kiss that melted her and made her long for more. The touch of his mouth against hers was oh so drugging and sensual that she thought there couldn't be a woman alive who wouldn't surrender to the magic of it without the heartfelt hope that there would be more—much more—to follow.

'Of course I'm coming back. Do you honestly think I'd turn my back on the treasure that I've found?'

'You mean your family's manor?'

Gabriel tipped up her chin with his knuckle. 'No. That's not the treasure I mean at all, angel.'

As Lara stared back at him her heart skipped a beat.

'You make it very hard for me to leave when you look at me with those big brown eyes of yours like that, but nonetheless—' He abruptly dropped his hand and said briskly, 'I'd better be off. I've got to get back to my hotel and pack a bag. Can you give me your phone number?'

Retrieving his mobile from his jeans pocket, he looked at her expectantly.

'What do you want it for?'

'Do you really need to ask me that? So that I can let you know when I'm coming back, of course.'

'Oh.'

The number duly given, Lara gasped when once again Gabriel drew her into his arms.

'I know you've only been back a short time but it's going to feel strange not having you around,' she admitted.

'I feel the same, sweetheart.' Smiling ruefully, he cupped his hand to her cheek. 'Now I really do have to go.'

He moved across the room to the door and opened it. Then he pivoted, and the expression on his carved face was indisputably serious as he glanced back at her.

'I don't want you to be lonely but I hope you won't think of being with anyone else while I'm gone?'

Feeling her cheeks flame red, Lara couldn't help but be offended. Her telling him she was on the pill had made him naturally assume she was sexually active. The thought made her shiver with distaste, especially when she had always believed that the most precious thing you could give to the man you loved was your virginity. Yes, the idea was outdated and old-fashioned but Lara made no apology for it.

'Do you honestly think I would want to be with someone else after what we've just shared, Gabriel? I know we haven't committed to making our relationship serious or anything, but I'm not the kind of woman who operates like that. I'm loyal. How would you feel if I asked *you* the same question?'

His expression thoughtful, he answered soberly. 'You need have no worries on that score. Apart from the fact that I'll be too busy working, the only woman I'll be thinking about while I'm in New York is *you*, Lara.'

She released a soft breath of relief and followed it with a smile. 'That's all right, then. Have a safe journey and let me know that you've arrived safely, even if it's just a text.'

The corners of Gabriel's eyes crinkled with pleasure. 'Of course. It'll be nice to know that someone I care about is thinking of me while I'm away. That's another first.'

Feeling elated by his assertion that she was some-one he cared about, Lara felt the rest of his poignant comment squeeze her heart. How had he felt when he was little and knew there was no one there to look out for him and give him a cuddle when he got home from school? A hired nanny could never have replaced a lov-ing parent.

Right then he looked so endearing that Lara won-dered how she didn't run to him and beg him not to go. But she knew that she shouldn't reveal that she cared as much as she did in case it made him want to back off a little. That was the very *last* thing she wanted to happen.

'Well, here might be another first for you, Gabriel. I'm really going to miss you when you're gone.'

He gifted her with another devastating smile that she wouldn't easily forget.

'I'm going to miss you, too, baby.' Raising a rueful dark eyebrow he opened the door and went out.

The days following Gabriel's departure dragged by in-terminably. Lara's initial excited optimism and belief that he would return, and that when he did he might consider making their rekindled association more se-rious, started to evaporate distressingly.

Since he'd texted her that he'd arrived safely in New York her mobile had been worryingly silent. To add to her worry and concern, memories of that long-ago party from her youth, when Gabriel had rejected her in pref-erence for the tall slim blonde who had been his tutor, returned to haunt her painfully and made her fear that he wouldn't keep his promise if someone more attrac-tive came on the scene when he was back in New York.

When her parents returned from France Lara stayed

on for a further couple of days to satisfy herself that they were coping and to give them whatever support she could. But she also stayed on because her family home now seemed indelibly imbued with Gabriel's presence. She almost feared to leave it in case it signified shutting the door on the magical and heartfelt time they had spent together there—a repeat of which might never happen.

CHAPTER EIGHT

IT HAD NOT BEEN the best of days. How could it have been when they were still experiencing the aftermath of a serious crisis on the trading floor and heads were starting to roll as some key players were called into account?

Gabriel had nothing to fear on that score—his record was exemplary and so were his dealings—but he still felt a huge responsibility towards the shareholders he had guided and advised. Especially when some of the companies he'd recommended for investment had gone to the wall during the past few days due, amongst other things, to bad management. God knew he'd warned the CEOs of said companies enough times that good management was key and they shouldn't be in a hurry to let go those with a proven track record in order to replace them with the current 'flavour of the month'.

But most of all it was a bad day because he couldn't be with Lara. He'd been back in New York for over a week now and already the separation felt interminable. As he had expected, work had consumed him.

Back in his high-rise apartment later that evening, he threw himself down on his opulent silk-sheeted bed fully clothed and mused on whether he should ring her just to hear her voice and assure himself that he hadn't dreamt the blisteringly hot connection that they'd shared.

The situation had undoubtedly rocked his world. When he'd read about Sean's death, Gabriel never would have believed that going back to see his friend's parents to offer his condolences would result in him meeting Lara again and finding himself insanely attracted to her. She had been a pretty teenager, but nothing could have prepared him for the stunning woman she'd become.

He'd since asked himself if he should actually be feeling guilty because he'd taken a long-ago friendship to a whole other level just because the opportunity had presented itself. But he hadn't been able to resist. After reading the gut-wrenching letter his uncle had left him which had revealed the tragic truth about his mother, Gabriel had found himself craving the kind of comfort that only a woman could supply. A lovely woman like Lara, whose caring and selfless nature was like a price-less gem that was rare to find.

Checking his watch, he noted that it must be about four in the morning over in the UK. Would he risk waking her from sleep simply just to hear her voice? Of course he would. Hadn't she told him when he was leaving that she would miss him? Well, now was a good opportunity to find out how much.

Sitting up, he undid his tie, then shrugged off the suit jacket he wore and carelessly threw it onto a nearby chair. Then he kicked off his shoes, plumped up the satin pillows behind him and rang her mobile.

Even the realisation that she would be asleep couldn't stop him from feeling impatient when she didn't pick up straight away. Holding the phone close against his ear, with his other hand he dragged his fingers wearily through his hair, thinking that if he had even half a mind to be sensible he should probably get some sleep himself. He'd been working flat out in a charged and nervous atmosphere since the early hours of the morning and felt like death.

But he instantly jettisoned the thought when he heard Lara's sleepily husky voice at the other end of the line.

'Hello? Who is this? Have you any idea what time it is?'

Gabriel couldn't resist chuckling. 'Who else would be ringing you at this ungodly hour if it wasn't me, baby?'

'Gabriel?'

He told himself he heard pleasure in her voice, as well as surprise, but he couldn't know that for sure. What if Lara hadn't missed him even half as much as he had missed her? What if, despite her asking him if he really thought she would want to be with someone else after being with him, she had sought out the company of an ex-boyfriend to help alleviate her loneliness?

Biting back a savage curse at the mere thought, he schooled himself to breathe more slowly. A potential coronary wasn't something he wanted to add to his already considerable cache of woes.

'Yes, it's me.' Despite his anxieties, Gabriel thought of her shining dark eyes and pretty face and his lips shaped a smile. 'I should say I'm sorry for ringing you so early in the morning, but if I were to tell you that then it would be a lie. Were you asleep?'

'Not really. I was only dozing. I don't fall asleep very easily these days. I just can't seem to settle.'

'Are you still at your parents' house?'

'No, I'm not. I've returned to my flat. Mum and Dad

came back from holiday a couple of days after you left. By the way, they asked me to tell you that they'd like to see you sometime. They've got a couple of photos of you and Sean they'd like you to have as a keepsake.'

Gabriel's insides churned at the prospect of meeting Lara's parents again when he had so recently seduced their daughter. Would he be able to handle the guilt that was bound to surface when he was in their presence? Their good regard had once upon a time been very important to him. It still was.

'It would be good to see them again,' he said warily. 'And I wouldn't mind having the photos.'

'Good. I'll tell them. Anyway, it's good to hear your voice. The last time I had word from you was when you texted me to say that you'd arrived in New York. How are you?'

'Never mind how *I* am. What do you mean, you can't seem to settle? Is there something on your mind? Tell me, Lara, I'd like to know.'

Registering her quietly indrawn breath, not for the first time Gabriel wished he hadn't left her so abruptly when he'd got the call from his office in New York. But when he'd learned his presence was urgently required because of a crisis that could potentially escalate if he didn't return and help resolve it, it had been unthinkable that he would refuse—especially when his professional reputation had been built on finding solutions that would fox many of his peers.

'I've—I've just been missing Sean, that's all. It's at times like these—times when I'm a bit low and down in the dumps—that I'd ring and talk to him. No matter what the situation he'd always help put things into perspective and make me laugh.'

'It's perfectly understandable that you're missing him, sweetheart. His death isn't something you're going to get over or come to terms with overnight. All you can do is to give it time. Isn't that what they say?'

'Yes, and isn't it ironic how plausible and sensible that sounds when it isn't someone that's personally close to you who dies?'

Dry-mouthed, Gabriel honestly didn't know how to answer her. He'd lost the one person who was universally meant to be the closest to a child, yet he hadn't known his mother at all. Not even for a little while. How were you supposed to grieve for a relative stranger? Because that was what she had been. Yet since he had found out that she'd taken her own life a sense of bitter sorrow at the futility of it all had slowly and undeniably crept into his heart and taken up residence there. Not usually given to fantasising, he had found himself wishing for the power to turn back time so that he might remake the past and ensure a different and better future for both of them. Perhaps he was experiencing grief after all?

He heaved a sigh.

'Gabriel? I wasn't being dismissive of your advice. I know you're dealing with your own grief.'

'Is that what you call it?' Even though he'd briefly flirted with the fantasy of remaking the past, he couldn't prevent the scathing inflection in his tone. 'What the hell would I know about it? Aren't you supposed to have a relationship with someone before you can grieve for them?'

'Just because you didn't have a relationship with your mother doesn't mean that you don't wish that you had. Look, let's talk about something else, shall we? Late at night, or even in the early hours of the morning, isn't the best time to be dwelling on things that make us sad.'

For a moment, Lara's gentle voice somehow subdued the influx of pain that had threatened to submerge Gabriel.

'And I hate to think of you being sad when you're so far away and I can't be with you to help make you feel better.'

'I'm not sad, for goodness' sake. I'm *angry*. Furious that the people who were meant to take care of me were such liars that they would deceive their own flesh and blood and not even consider the horrendous legacy that would leave me with. You can't possibly know how that feels.'

Shaking his head, Gabriel fought hard to recover his equilibrium beneath another crushing wave of emotion. What the hell did he think he was doing? He'd been longing to make contact with Lara for days—the mere thought of talking to her had been the light at the end of the tunnel when he'd been so consumed by work that there wasn't even a spare moment to ring her—and here he was, wasting precious time talking about his hopeless family.

He swallowed hard.

'Forget I said that, will you? I think it's just fatigue talking. Up until now it's been a hell of a day. But I already feel better knowing that you're thinking about me.'

'I'm glad. I know it doesn't solve anything, but it helps to know that you have a friend you can reach out to, doesn't it? I know it does for me.'

Trying hard to ignore the fact that she'd referred to him yet again as a friend and not as her lover—

had his lovemaking been *that* forgettable?—Gabriel sighed again.

'Look, don't you have some holiday left? Why don't you come over to New York for a few days?' Even as the idea made his heart race and his blood pump hard he knew it was a brainwave he couldn't ignore. Why hadn't he thought about it earlier? It was, after all, the perfect solution. If he had to spend many more nights without seeing Lara and having her in his bed he'd honestly go crazy.

'I do have some holiday left, but don't you have to work, Gabriel? Isn't there some big financial crisis or other you have to deal with?'

'There is indeed.'

The charmingly innocent question made him smile. The world Lara inhabited was a million miles away from the feverish atmosphere on Wall Street, where dealings often had serious global financial implications that could make or break economies overnight. He was fiercely glad that she wasn't part of that world.

He was also relieved that she wasn't remotely like some of the clever but brittle women he regularly came into contact with in that arena—women who had seemingly forgotten what it meant to be soft and feminine, who preferred to concentrate their energies on rising to the top of the career ladder, making their fortune, and didn't care what they had to do in order to achieve it. Some men might find such barefaced single-mindedness admirable, but oddly enough Gabriel *didn't*.

'It won't be sorted overnight,' he explained. 'But we're making some good inroads. Anyway, let's not talk about that. I really need to see you, Lara. You have no idea *how* much.'

The other end of the line went ominously quiet and Gabriel tensed. Her rejection wasn't something he wanted to contemplate even briefly.

'Say the word and I'll arrange the flight,' he said quickly. 'I'm not saying I'll be able to spend as much time with you as I'd like when you get here—especially not during the day when I'm working—but you'll have my driver at your disposal to take you wherever you want to go, and you won't want for anything. If you want to buy clothes, perfume—*anything*, in fact—I'll foot the bill. It will be my pleasure. And as often as I can manage it we'll have the evenings together. The nights, too.'

Again, Gabriel's blood heated at the thought. He blessed the photographic recall that, even throughout his pressured working days, helped him easily access the memory of Lara's seductive scent and the satin texture of her flawless skin.

'Are you sure, Gabriel? I mean, my coming to see you won't interfere with your routine?'

'My God, do you know how painfully dull that makes me sound? I don't deny that my work is important, but even *I* refuse to make it the be-all and end-all. Especially not now, when I know that I'll be seeing you.'

'All right, then. You can go ahead and arrange a flight for me. When you have the details you can ring or send me a text to let me know. My mum said just yesterday that I ought to have a holiday before I go back to work.'

'She was right—and if my memory serves me correctly your mum usually *is*, sweetheart.'

Rubbing his hand round his stubbled jaw, Gabriel was elated that his powers of persuasion hadn't failed him. If all went to plan Lara would be joining him in just a couple of days' time and his photographic memory would no longer be necessary to remind him of her charms—not when the delicious reality of her presence would be so much more satisfying.

Even though she'd accepted it—because what else could she have done?—Lara had been heartbroken when Gabriel had abruptly left her to return to New York. At that point she really hadn't known whether she would ever see him again. All she'd seemed to see in that carved, handsome face of his when he had announced he had to return to work to help alleviate a crisis was a man who put his career way above personal relationships and matters of the heart. *No question.* What if he had even felt *relieved* when he'd had the call telling him he was needed urgently?

Yet even knowing that Gabriel was a supremely driven individual, whose priorities were vastly different from her own, Lara didn't give up hope that one day soon he would come to see that there were far more important things in life than money and the admiration of his peers.

The devastation of his mother taking her own life and his uncle betraying him might have caused him to believe that love and family could never be for him—not when his trust had been so cruelly tested—but Lara refused to relinquish the hope that if only she could reach him—*really* reach him—then she might help him see that it didn't mean that love and family should be denied him.

It had lifted her beyond belief when he'd rung her in the middle of the night and invited her over to New York and she hadn't hesitated to accept the invitation.

Could it be that he'd been reflecting on the possibility of enjoying a serious relationship with her? She prayed that was the case. She certainly wasn't going to pass up the chance of finding out.

When he'd asked her what had been unsettling her she hadn't been completely truthful. Of course she was still grieving for Sean, but she'd also been missing Gabriel—missing him so much, in fact, that she could scarcely think about anything else.

Sometimes the memory of their lovemaking seemed like the most delicious dream she had conjured up to help compensate for the loneliness she had endured all these years. And other times, because it meant so much to her, it fuelled her fears about what she would do if she never got the chance to be intimate with him again. Lara had already lost the brother she'd adored. To lose Gabriel would be an equally grievous blow.

Now, travelling in the back of the beautiful limousine Gabriel had sent to the airport to collect her and heading over to Fifth Avenue, where his apartment was situated, Lara stared up at the high-rise buildings piercing the faultless blue sky and couldn't help shivering. It was as though she'd been dropped into an alien habitat in some distant universe, such was the contrast to the much more unhurried environment she was used to.

'This is it, Miss Bradley. If you tell the concierge at the door that you've come to see Mr Devenish, then he'll take you up to his apartment.'

'Thank you.'

'It's my pleasure, Miss Bradley. If you just wait there for a moment I'll get your luggage.'

When he came round to open the car door for her, Lara accepted the immaculately presented chauffeur's hand and stepped out onto the sidewalk outside the building. Already the concierge was approaching, and as she thanked the driver again she was rewarded with a genuinely warm smile.

'I'm Barry, by the way, and Mr Devenish will give you the number to contact me on when you want to go anywhere. He's already given me instructions to take you wherever you want to go during your stay,' he told her. 'So I'll look forward to seeing you again sometime soon, Miss Bradley. Have a good day, now.'

'You, too.'

It hit Lara then just how diametrically opposite Gabriel's lifestyle was to her own. She had just about got over travelling business class on the plane out here, but was he *really* expecting her to tour the city in a limousine every time she went out?

As the ultra-polite concierge took charge of her conservatively small suitcase and led her to the elevator she was suddenly seized by an acute attack of nerves. What would it be like, seeing Gabriel again? Would he still want her as much as he'd wanted her back home? Compared to the beautiful and fashionable women he must see every day at work, would he start to see her as painfully ordinary and homely? She glanced down at the royal blue, fluted-sleeved tunic dress she was wearing that she'd thought so pretty in the store and winced.

'This is Mr Devenish's floor, Miss Bradley.'

The ascent up to the top floor had been so swift that she'd hardly realised they'd been moving. She'd been too lost in anguished reverie about Gabriel.

The concierge pressed the doorbell and with a brief, officious smile asked, 'Would you like me to wait with you until Mr Devenish comes to the door?'

'No, thank you. I'm sure he'll be here in a minute.'

With a brief nod of his head, he left her. They had arranged that Gabriel would take a couple of hours off from work to welcome her and acquaint her with her new surroundings, but time seemed to deaden and slow as Lara waited outside the door for him, and she couldn't help worrying that because he was so busy at work he'd forgotten about her.

But suddenly he was standing there, immaculately dressed as ever, and even more devastating than she remembered. His eyes locked on to hers immediately. They drank her in, ate her up and all but consumed her, body and soul.

Lara opened her mouth to speak but no words came out.

Looking slightly dazed, he said, 'My phone rang just before you knocked and I stupidly took the call. My God, I've been waiting so long for you. Too long.'

And then further dialogue was abandoned as he hungrily drew her into his arms, drove his hands through her hair and pressed her against him as if she was as vital to him as taking his next breath.

If that first kiss he had stolen from her back in England had been akin to being scorched by flame, this one was an inferno that burnt her down to her very core. In response, her lips couldn't help but cling ravenously to his, and her heart leapt with sheer delight at the seductive velvety texture of his lips and the sensation of his hard body enfolding her. Then she greedily welcomed his hot searching tongue, taking breathless little gasps of air as she struggled to assimilate the tide of longing and desire that rendered her almost too weak to stand.

Gabriel groaned as if he couldn't bear being bereft of

her kisses for even a moment. Defenceless and desperate for his deepening touch, Lara was scarcely aware that he had dragged in her case and pushed the door shut behind her, then manoeuvred her up against it. But when his hand hotly covered her breast through the thin cotton of her dress, and when he replaced it with his lips to nip at the already tender flesh of her aroused nipple, she whimpered as an arrow of molten heat shot directly into her womb.

Even as she moaned her pleasure Gabriel moved his hands urgently down her back and onto her behind. In answer, Lara eagerly drove her fingers through his hair to hold him more tightly against her. A second later, he freed himself to examine her. As she met the intense azure gaze that had instigated her love and devotion all those years ago when she was not much more than a girl, she silently reaffirmed the vow she'd made that she would love him for ever.

'This wasn't the way I wanted to welcome you, baby,' he said wryly. 'But what can I do when I confess I'm an addict for you?' He bent and kissed her, capturing her plump lower lip with his teeth then slowly releasing it as he drew away. 'And I might just die if I don't get my fix.'

In one fluidly effortless movement he suddenly lifted her up high against his chest. Still avidly kissing her, he strode across the honey-coloured wooden floor and headed towards a closed door at the end of it. When they reached the door he kicked it open and carried her across to the palatial black-silk-covered bed that dominated the room. He toed off his shoes and Lara followed suit. And when he drew back the covers and lowered her down onto the sensual silk sheets niceties were forgotten as they tore at each other's clothes and breathlessly dispensed with them.

Their hungry eyes met in mutual wonder just once before Gabriel covered Lara's trembling body with his. And as soon as their skin made contact conversation was rendered redundant. There was simply no need for preamble to the seduction they both longed for.

Gabriel nudged Lara's slim thighs apart with his knee and she immediately sensed her hips soften and then naturally relax. But as she held on tight to the bunched iron biceps in his arms she found herself momentarily tensing as he urgently pushed his hard silken shaft deep inside her. He stilled for a moment. She was more than ready for him, but strangely she felt the eagerly anticipated invasion even more acutely this second time round.

She saw a briefly questioning look in Gabriel's eyes. But the suggestion of uncertainty—if that was what it was—was quickly banished as he started to move deeply inside her, bending his dark head to devour her lips, then her breasts, his searching hands exploring her even as he seduced her.

Yearning to tell him that she loved him, Lara didn't know how she suppressed the impulse. *I'll tell him afterwards*, she vowed, gasping aloud in shock and then pleasure as he bit down on the delicate skin at the juncture of her neck and shoulder with the edges of his teeth.

She couldn't help revelling in the thought that he would be leaving his mark on her in more ways than one. But then she was gasping for a second time when the hot, pulsating need inside her peaked and flooded her with dizzying warmth and she found herself riding an exhilarating wave of pleasure that stole every thought from her head to replace it with unmitigated joy.

The profoundly exquisite experience was heightened when Gabriel suddenly tensed and cried out, spilling his liquid heat deep inside her. His sculpted, handsome face looked to be deeply stunned by the intense release. Lara couldn't help but feel gratified that she had been the one to give him such a gift.

Just before Lara's hot satin heat had enfolded him and he'd driven himself deep inside her Gabriel had shivered hard at the terrifying realisation of how much this woman had come to mean to him. He had been like a cat on a hot tin roof waiting for her to arrive. Not even the demands of the trading floor had been able to distract him from the thought of her for long, and never in his history had he let his guard down so completely around a woman so that she might easily breach it.

He didn't doubt there would be a serious price to pay. But after the stunning satisfaction of their urgent lovemaking he almost didn't care what that price would be.

'That was amazing,' he breathed, lying down beside her and gathering her against him.

Glancing up, Lara smiled warmly into his eyes. 'I'm glad I wasn't the only one who thought so.' Dropping down again, she pressed her face close to his. 'Gabriel...?'

She whispered his name close against his ear, her soft lips brushing the tender lobe and sending a flurry of goosebumps scudding across his flesh.

'What is it, baby?' He lifted his head to examine her. When he saw that her sultry dark eyes glimmered with tears he immediately tensed. 'What's wrong?'

'Nothing.' Her lips parted in the most engaging and

bewitching smile, and again he was caught off-guard by her incandescent beauty—so much so that his heart *hurt* just looking at her.

'I just want you to know that I'm so glad I waited,' she said gently.

'Waited? For what, sweetheart?'

'To make love with the only man I've ever loved and to give him my virginity.'

If she had struck him hard Gabriel couldn't have been more shocked. He ached for her, body and soul, but somehow right then he found himself immobilised by the confession.

Lara had been a *virgin* when they'd first made love? It didn't make sense. She'd been so willing and ready. Even as doubt settled in the pit of his stomach and seriously unnerved him he remembered that when he'd first taken her she had indeed been exquisitely tight—not at all like an experienced woman…a woman used to having lovers.

In the throes of his passion he had stupidly dismissed the fact. However, he'd thought about it again just now, when they'd made love again.

But what had him reeling even more was Lara's declaration that she loved him—that he was the *only* man she had ever loved. Gabriel honestly didn't know how he felt about that. Love was not something he had ever figured as coming into the equation.

Clearly there was a red-hot attraction between them, but not *love*…surely? Besides, what could a relationship with him bring her other than more grief and pain? She deserved a man who was utterly devoted to her happiness, a man who was whole in every respect of the word, not some embittered automaton that just went through the motions of life but didn't truly enjoy any-thing very much.

As the waves of shock and surprise and, yes, *fear* continued to eddy through him, Gabriel expelled a long breath in a bid to try and regain his equilibrium. Then he lifted himself away from the lovely woman at his side to lie back against the bank of satin pillows behind them. Glimpsing the confusion in her eyes as he moved away, he felt his heart drum hard as he tried to think what to say to reassure her.

Sitting up, Lara lightly shook her head and folded her arms over her breasts. As she turned to face him he saw the silken skein of long, dark hair that nestled against her collarbone and he longed to give in to the impulse to wind it round his fingers as he had done once before, when things between them had been far less compli-cated than they suddenly seemed to be.

'Did I—did I say something wrong, Gabriel? Some-thing you didn't like?' she enquired hesitantly.

'You told me that you were on the pill,' he replied, endeavouring to keep his voice steady. No easy feat when his whole world had just been tilted on its head once more.

'It's true. I am. But why should that disturb you? Was it because you thought I must have had other lov-ers before you?'

'Frankly, yes. I *did* think that.'

'But—but couldn't you tell when you— When we...' Her cheeks reddening, Lara stared at him as if his an-swer was hard to comprehend.

Emitting a heavy sigh, Gabriel sat up. 'I seem to recall I was driven by lust and desire at the time and wasn't exactly thinking straight. But tell me this, Lara.

If it's true that you were a virgin then why in God's name are you on the pill?'

She drew up her legs beneath the covers and folded her arms round them. 'I take the pill to help regulate my periods. A lot of women do.'

'And you've never slept with another man before me?'

'No.' Her dark eyes flashed. 'I haven't. I don't tell lies, Gabriel.'

'No. Of course you don't. How *could* you, coming from the family that you do?'

It was a back-handed compliment and he wasn't proud of it. Lara had flinched when he'd delivered it. But things between them seemed suddenly to have gained a momentum he hadn't envisaged, and his instinct was to perhaps put the brakes on a little in order to have some time to reflect.

She'd given her virginity to him and told him that she loved him. Whilst both acts were significant in their own way, and had definitely pleased him, did it mean that she was hoping they could make their relationship more permanent? Right at that moment Gabriel didn't see how such a thing could possibly be achieved. How could it when both their lives and their lifestyles were poles apart? As much as he wanted to be with Lara, he couldn't see her taking to life in New York. As beautiful and intelligent as she was, she was more hometown girl than ambitious career woman, and he didn't deny he liked it that she was that way.

Moving across to the edge of the bed as he wrestled with what to do, he reached down for the black silk boxers that, in his haste to make love to Lara, he'd thrown onto the floor. Hastily pulling them on, he turned back to survey her and saw her shiver.

Despising himself for not being able to summon up the words that might help ease her distress, he remarked, 'You should probably get dressed.' Jerking his head towards another door, he continued, 'You can get a shower, then come and join me in the living room. You should find everything you need. I'll use the bathroom down the hall. We don't have much time before I have to get back to work and I need to tell you a few things.'

CHAPTER NINE

WHAT THINGS DID HE need to tell her? Lara wondered. She was sure that whatever it was it couldn't possibly bring more distress than she felt already.

Her heart bled because Gabriel hadn't exhibited the slightest pleasure or even *concern* that she'd been a virgin when they'd first made love. In fact he had sounded quite angry about it. Neither had he looked remotely pleased when she'd confessed that she loved him.

Was he really as cold-hearted and uncaring as all that? What if she had made the most horrendous mistake in confessing her feelings to him? She surely hadn't forgotten that he'd rejected her advances once before, albeit a long time ago. But it chilled Lara's blood as she contemplated that perhaps Gabriel really *couldn't* commit to her, or allow himself to love her.

She knew there was a genuinely good man behind those ice-blue eyes, even if the evidence was far too rare, but he was like a wounded bear that snapped at anyone who exhibited concern or ventured too near and she knew the reason why. His fractured—and some might say, dysfunctional—past haunted him. That was why he found kindness and concern so difficult to deal with. Maybe that was also the reason he couldn't immediately accept that she loved him or that she'd given her virginity to *him* rather than another man?

With that unhappy conclusion dominating her thoughts she hastily showered and dressed in the luxurious Art Deco bathroom, reapplied the lipstick that she kept in the pocket of her dress and went in search of the living room to find him.

Promising herself that she would play it cool and not let him see that he had hurt her, nonetheless she felt her heart skip an anxious beat when she saw him again. Gabriel was relaxing on one of the sleek black couches in the light and airy living room with its arresting clear-glassed views of the New York skyline. He had changed into another stylish Italian suit.

The far from welcoming expression on his hard-jawed visage made her insides plunge.

Standing in the doorway, she anxiously smoothed her hand down over the blue tunic dress she'd admired and bought especially for her trip to see him and made a silent vow never to wear it again. In her mind it was jinxed. Moistening her lips, she gave him a greeting that was understandably cautious. From now on she wasn't going to presume anything.

'You said you had some things that you needed to tell me?'

'Why don't you come over here and sit down?' he invited.

Lara thought she spied the merest glimmer of a smile on his lips, but because she wasn't sure she didn't allow herself to believe it. As yet she had no idea what he was going to tell her and couldn't help but fear the worst.

'Did you find everything you needed?' he asked.

'In the bathroom, you mean?'

Gabriel nodded.

'Yes, I did.'

She walked towards him, twisting her hands nervously together in front of her, then stopped, feeling her body helplessly warming when she remembered what they'd been doing just a short while ago. Who could have believed that such heated passion could turn cold so quickly? Gabriel had poured ice water on her feelings when he'd so hastily left her alone in his bed. What if he'd come to the conclusion that she should leave? That he'd made a mistake in inviting her to New York?

Sick with apprehension, she asked, 'Is my suitcase still out in the hall?'

'I've put it in the guest bedroom for now. Later on, when I return from work, I'll take it into my room.'

Even as relief washed through her Lara couldn't help feeling it wasn't right he should have everything his way. 'There's no need.' Lifting her chin, she defied him to disagree with her.

Making her knees knock together, Gabriel rose to his impressive height and covered the space between them. Just bare inches away from her, the scent of his arresting, sexy cologne sent Lara's pulse nervously skittering. Her tender nipples still stung from his attentions in bed, and as she came face to face with him again they burned and tingled fiercely.

'I know I might not be able to give you what you want, Lara,' he said, gravel-voiced. 'But I haven't brought you to New York for us to sleep in separate rooms. I should have been more thoughtful, more caring when we were together just now, but what you told me robbed me of all ability to think straight. I've been reflecting on things and I want to make amends.'

'And how do you plan on doing that? By buying me things? By showing me a good time as is probably your style with the women in your life before you kiss them goodbye and move on to the next one?' Despite her vow not to let him see that he'd upset her, Lara couldn't suppress the scalding angry tears that burned at the backs of her lids. She impatiently wiped them away. 'To be honest, I'd rather go home.'

'No. I don't want that.' A perturbed muscle flinched in the side of his hollowed cheek. 'I want you to stay. Whatever you think of me.'

'Why should it always be about what *you* want, Gabriel? Don't you think that I have needs, too?'

About to turn away, Lara choked back a gasp when she suddenly found herself slammed against his chest and her lips taken prisoner by a hard, hot, almost punishing kiss. Her resolve to leave melted like ice cream beneath the burning rays of a Sahara sun.

As the kiss eased in intensity to become surprisingly tender, Gabriel lifted his head to study her.

'I want you to have what you want, Lara, I really do. But while you're with me I'm afraid I'm driven to be greedy. Perhaps I can't quite believe that you'd surrender your virginity to a man who's notoriously selfish, who puts himself above everyone else when it comes to getting the thing he wants and consequently doesn't consider feelings. But I'm too enamoured of you not to see it as the most unbelievable blessing that you're here, and I can't help but want to make the most of it.'

Reaching out, he cupped the side of her face and looked to be aiming for a smile, but he didn't quite manage it.

'Don't go. Please don't go.'

Lara caught her breath. It wasn't just the simmering desire she saw reflected in his eyes that took her aback, but the almost childlike need that told her he would be nothing less than devastated should she insist on leaving. It was then that she was poignantly reminded that he'd grown up bereft of his mother's love and care, and likely believed he didn't deserve similar consideration from any woman who came into his life.

Moistening lips that still throbbed from his ravenous kisses she carefully examined his carved features. 'I'm not going to leave, Gabriel.' She breathed out a gentle sigh. 'I wouldn't walk out on you when I've given you my word that I'll stay—at least until my holiday comes to an end.'

Seeing the relief that spread across his handsome features, Lara was pleased that he seemed to be reassured.

Recovering her good humour, she teased, 'Besides, do you really think I've come all the way out to New York not to see some of the sights while I'm here?'

'I'll make sure you get to see everything you want to, I swear. Just say the word and I'll arrange it.' His hands dropped to her shoulders. 'And, by the way, one of the things I needed to tell you was that we're going out tonight to a function. It's a corporate dinner at a restaurant not far from the Stock Exchange. I can't duck out of it, I'm afraid. I have to go and I want to take you as my escort.'

It was on the tip of Lara's tongue to say no. She would be so far out of her comfort zone in such elite company and in surroundings that were about as alien to her as the grand Regency house where Gabriel had grown up that it would be no joke. But then she saw the hint of steel in his eyes that told her it would be a waste of time even attempting to refuse, because one way or another he would persuade her differently.

He had never felt more possessive of a woman than when he walked into that stylish New York bar and restaurant with Lara. From the moment they'd arrived heads had turned—not just to greet him, because Gabriel knew everybody who was *anybody*, but to cast curious, admiring glances at his companion. And how could he blame them when Lara added a whole other level to the term 'drop-dead gorgeous'?

The little black dress that she'd insisted was the only suitable garment she'd brought with her to wear to a 'posh' dinner made Gabriel feel like the mythical Ares worshipping at the feet of Aphrodite. It didn't cling to her sublime curves but it couldn't help but pay homage to them whenever she moved. And the way that she wore her hair, in a very feminine loose topknot, with curling tendrils brushing the sides of her cheeks, and with her shoulders bare courtesy of the halterneck style of the dress, she looked utterly exquisite.

Gabriel's hand gripped Lara's a little tighter as they moved through the crowd milling around the bar. There were more greetings and back-slapping as people recognised him, and frankly for once he could have done without it.

When he sensed that his companion was drawing back, and guessed she was feeling overwhelmed, he deliberately pulled her near and his smile was reassuring. She wasn't used to this. The stylishly attired Wall Street patrons and the competitive atmosphere they created whenever they were together was a million light years away from the world Lara inhabited.

Although the air was drenched with the smell of alluring perfume and expensive cologne, the predominant scent was that of money. It was strange how the realisation didn't give Gabriel his usual sense of pleasure or the satisfaction that he'd grown to depend on.

Looking for an out, he caught the eye of the maître d' and asked him to show them into the private dining room where they were scheduled to eat.

The gathering had been set up in one of the most intimately sophisticated rooms of the restaurant which was frequently the chosen venue for the private meetings he had with his executive clientele. But tonight Gabriel's fellow guests would be some of the key players who had worked with him to help avert yet another serious financial crisis. After the tough few weeks they had endured, and the intense few days when it had been touch and go and Gabriel had been called in to join them, they would be in the mood to celebrate. Although by no means could anyone rest on their laurels yet.

The effusive greetings of his fellow diners over, Gabriel was relieved to be able to sit down next to Lara and look at the menu. It didn't escape his notice that her slender fingers shook slightly as she perused what was on offer, and neither did he miss her soft-voiced sigh. His broad-suited shoulder brushed against hers as he leant towards her and he caught the faint but arousing scent of her honeyed perfume. His stomach clenched hard with desire.

Lowering his voice he asked, 'How are you bearing up? I promise this won't go on for too long.'

His reward was a too brief glimpse of a smile.

'I'm all right. I think.'

Gabriel's own smile was more generous. 'I can't

say that *I* am. I'd much rather we were alone together than here at this dinner,' he confessed. 'And, trust me, I wouldn't be here at all if I had the choice.'

It was impossible to suppress the need and desire that crept into his tone. In truth, it was hard even to think straight when Lara was around.

'I'm bowled over by the fact that you're actually here,' he went on, 'and that you came all this way just to see me. By the way, this is a very good menu. "Bankers' fare", they call it. If you want a recommendation, can I suggest the filet mignon?'

Unable to resist, he let his avid gaze into her sultry brown eyes deliberately linger, quite aware that there was running speculation round the table about their relationship. After all, Lara was an unknown entity to them. A very beautiful and desirable unknown entity.

Before she could comment on his suggestion of cuisine, one of the top city bankers across the table—a man called Lars Jensen—leaned towards them and asked confidently, 'So, Lara—can I call you that?—I'm intrigued, as all my colleagues are. How did you meet Gabriel? He has a reputation of being a bit of a wizard here on Wall Street—a regular Croesus. Whatever he touches turns to gold. Did you perhaps have some business dealings with him in London? If you did, lucky you.'

The suited young man seated opposite her, with his fashionable, close-cut fair hair and too-inquisitive green eyes, had honed in on Lara like a missile poised to attack. Having no idea how much or how little Gabriel wanted her to reveal, she made her quietly voiced response carefully measured.

'I know nothing about the financial world and, no,

we didn't meet in London. Gabriel went to university with my brother. That's how we met.'

'I'm even more intrigued. You mean that you've known him all these years and he hasn't mentioned you? At least not in my hearing.'

'Why should he mention me? We're just friends.'

Catching an expression that was almost a glower on Gabriel's handsome face, Lara sensed herself flush. Had she said the wrong thing? What else could she have said? That she was an ex-girlfriend of his? That patently wasn't true.

'So you're "just friends", are you?' Lars's tone was mockingly doubtful as his laserlike glance pinioned them both. 'Is that a new euphemism for lovers in the UK?'

'No, it isn't,' Gabriel interjected firmly, his hard jaw clenching. Out of sight, his hand folded possessively over Lara's. 'And if I tell you that Lara was only six-teen when we first met, I doubt you'd think we would have been lovers, would you?'

This time the other man's searching gaze lingered over-long on Lara, making a mental inventory of her assets almost as if she was some kind of lucrative deal he was convinced would add to his fortune.

Lowering his voice, he briefly turned his attention back to Gabriel, commenting, 'Don't tell me you weren't tempted?'

Beside her, Lara intimately sensed the silent fury and tension in her companion's body as if it were her own.

'I think we should drop the subject. don't you? Lara is my guest here and your inappropriate insinuations are making her uncomfortable. That's not acceptable.'

His ice-blue gaze swept the table. 'And that goes for all of you.'

There was a sudden marked silence and Lara wanted the floor to open up and swallow her. If anything Gabriel's warning had only increased the curiosity in the other guests' eyes. Squeezing his hand to get his attention, she felt her heart thump hard when she immediately got it. His eyes shot little sparks of tangible electricity at her.

'What is it?' he demanded.

'You don't have to defend me. I'm sure your friend didn't mean anything by what he said.'

'You know that for sure, do you?' Tugging her towards him, so that what he said would be for her ears and her ears only, he whispered, 'Number one, he's not a friend—he's a colleague, and a very ambitious and ruthless colleague. You should be aware that we're sitting at a table full of hungry sharks, my angel, and right now *you're* the bait.'

Lara shivered. As her eyes strayed across the table to the rest of the glittering company, clad in their perfect Italian suits and breathtaking haute couture, she was stunned to realise that everyone was examining her and trying to figure out exactly who she was, as if it wasn't a usual occurrence for Gabriel to bring an unknown woman to these functions with him.

Feeling her face flame self-consciously at being the centre of so much attention, she turned back to her companion. 'I need to go to the ladies' room,' she murmured.

Gabriel immediately signalled to a nearby waitress and asked her to direct her. But as he stood back and helped her to her feet Lara sensed his reluctance and frustration at having to release her even for a second.

* * *

Lara felt as if she deserved a prize for enduring one of
the most discomfiting and tense evenings of her life.
But at the end of it one thing was absolutely clear. What
she'd witnessed of the superficial and pressured life of
the New York financial 'elite' wasn't for her.

Even though it was a dream come true to be with
Gabriel, she was already longing to return home to the
simple yet satisfying day-to-day routine she was familiar with—a way of life where she didn't have to be
overly concerned about what people thought of her or
whether she was wearing the right outfit to go to dinner or to work. Even at the college library she could get
away with wearing jeans and a T-shirt.

That said, Gabriel looked nothing less than *edible* in
his flawless Italian tailoring. One of the female guests
at their table had obviously deliberately followed her
out to the loo, and had blatantly quizzed her about her
relationship with him. When Lara had frostily declined
to tell her, the other woman had immediately shared a
'no-holds barred' graphic illustration of what she'd personally like to do with him in bed.

Lara's jaw had dropped at the woman's sheer temer-
ity. It was obvious that Gabriel's warning to his assem-
bled peers not to make her feel unduly uncomfortable
was only to be adhered to as they sat round the dinner
table. Out of his sight it was open season for the sharks
to feed. Lara had quickly discovered that going to the
dinner as Gabriel's guest didn't automatically grant her
immunity from the other women who desired him and
wouldn't hesitate to tell her so.

It was a relief to return to the apartment, even though
Gabriel had been broodingly quiet on the journey home.

Inevitably her anxiety had been building because of his lack of communication, and as soon as they were alone again Lara immediately turned to him for some answers as to the reason why.

'What's wrong?' she asked as he shrugged off his suit jacket and hung it on the steel coat stand inside the door. 'I get the feeling that you're unhappy. Didn't you enjoy the dinner? Your colleagues were certainly glad to see you.'

He curled his lip. 'It may come as a surprise to you, Lara, but on Wall Street it pays to stay on good terms with the boss. With the money, as they say here. If you think that people were glad to see me simply because they love my company then you're more naïve than I thought.'

Toeing off her shoes, as was her habit when she was at home, Lara heaved an annoyed sigh.

'Do you get off on cutting me down to size, Gabriel? Does it stroke your ego to do that? Obviously it must. And anyway why *shouldn't* people be glad of your company? You can be quite pleasant when you try, though I confess that's not very—'

The final word of her little speech was unceremoniously cut off as Gabriel hauled her against his chest and devoured her lips with a hard, open-mouthed kiss. As soon as his silken tongue drove into her mouth and his hands moved down her body to lift up her skirt and touch her intimately Lara felt immediately and frighteningly powerless to deny him anything. It appalled her that she couldn't even put up a fight. But then why would she want to, she reasoned, when she loved him so much that it hurt?

'Right now I can't take it slowly,' he breathed hotly

against her mouth. 'I confess you've become irresistible to me, and I can't take it slowly because I want you
too much, but afterwards...'

Lara momentarily held her breath as she sensed his
hand slide into her panties. When his searching fingers invaded her and pushed up she gasped, her head
falling against his hard-muscled shoulder. Her senses
were instantly drowned by the heat from his body and
the seductive, sultry scent of his masculine cologne. If
he hadn't been holding her she might easily have sunk
down to the floor, because her limbs were rendered
weak as a kitten's.

'Afterwards,' he continued, his free hand caressing
the back of her neck, 'we'll take it nice and slow and
really get to know each other, find out what gives us
the most pleasure.'

Unable to reply because she was suddenly swept
away on a sea of delectation so profoundly erotic that
she couldn't speak, Lara pressed her cheek against Gabriel's pristine white shirt, registering the wild beating of his heart against her ear and wondering what
she could do to make him feel similarly swept away.

She hardly seemed to know herself when she was
with this man. All she could think about in his company was fulfilling her most carnal desires and hopefully fulfilling his, too. Had her self-enforced celibacy
all these years turned her into some kind of insatiable siren?

When she lifted her head it was to find Gabriel staring down at her with an intensity that almost stopped
her heart. 'What you do to me...' she murmured softly,
tenderly touching her hand to his cheek.

His piercing blue eyes crinkling in acknowledgement, he lifted her up into his arms as though her weight didn't even signify. Then, still holding her gaze he affirmed huskily, 'We need to go to bed. *Now.*'

CHAPTER TEN

THE FOLLOWING WEEK passed like the most fantastical dream. Whilst her days were spent sightseeing and touring the city—courtesy of Barry, Gabriel's attentive chauffeur—Lara's nights were all given over to Gabriel. On occasion he wined and dined her at wonderful restaurants, took her to the cinema or to see a show on Broadway, but whatever the entertainment or pleasure they participated in, the high point of every evening was always when they returned to Gabriel's apartment and to each other's arms.

Knowing that her short holiday was quickly coming to an end, and that soon she would be going home to England to resume her post as college librarian, Lara started to feel painfully anxious about the future of her relationship with Gabriel. Did they even *have* a future together? They had a powerful connection, certainly, and there was no disputing the fact that she loved him, but as he had noticeably avoided discussing commitment and making their association more meaningful, Lara couldn't help but be apprehensive.

She had seen first-hand how devoted he was to what he did, and how seductive it must be to be so highly regarded in the financial arena he worked in. His colleagues all seemed to view Gabriel as practically irre-placeable. But did that mean he would never consider returning to the UK and once more making it his home?

During the time Lara had spent with him in New York he had never even mentioned the family home that he'd inherited. She was wary of trying to get him to discuss it in case it stirred up the fury and despair he'd expressed when he'd read his uncle's letter, yet she knew that Gabriel would never come to terms with what had happened and start to heal his past if he never even addressed the issue.

What did he intend to do about the Regency manor house that he'd grown up in? Did he plan to sell it and not even consider going back to reside there?

If that were the case, and he stayed in New York, Lara was pretty certain she wouldn't be joining him. The elite, sophisticated lifestyle and relentlessly driven aims of the bankers and financiers to make and acquire even more money and kudos epitomised everything she and her family disliked about the pursuit of mate-rial success in the world. As her brother, Sean, used to say, 'What good is being rich if you don't do something good with your wealth to help those less privileged on the planet?'

But Lara's dilemma was more than just the fact that that particular way of living didn't chime with her per-sonal values. It had much more to do with her despair that Gabriel had never even once told her that he loved her. She had begun to suspect that he never would. Al-ready she feared their heated, passionate union would be very quickly put aside to be replaced by even more work demands and perhaps occasionally the company

of one of those 'pretty ladies' he'd mentioned that he
called upon whenever he got lonely.

Was she really so hard to love? And would he honestly prefer that lonely and ultimately empty existence
over enjoying Lara's love and devotion for the rest of
his life? Not to mention the possibility of creating a
family of their own....

Sipping at a glass of orange juice in the living room
as she waited for him to reappear that evening—he'd
got back late from work and was still getting ready so
that they could go out to dinner—Lara stared out at the
stunning New York skyline of silver and shadows and
felt unbearably sad.

Her sojourn here was rapidly coming to an end, and
as yet nothing had been resolved between them about
their relationship. This was to be her last night in the
city because tomorrow she was flying home, and so far,
aside from giving her the details of her flight, Gabriel
had hardly even mentioned it.

'Hey.'

The smoky cadence of his voice had her turning
quickly, and just in time she managed to avoid spilling
juice all over the pretty midnight blue silk dress Gabriel had bought her.

She had never sought for him to buy her gifts, and
had frequently told him so whenever he suggested it,
but when he'd told her he'd stepped out of his office
one afternoon to visit a high-end store so that he might
get her 'something pretty to wear to dinner', Lara had
been helplessly touched by his thoughtfulness. Pleased,
too. The garment was sleek and fitted, and when she'd
taken it out of the stylish carrier bag and unwrapped it

from its carefully folded tissue paper she'd been taken aback at just how perfect it was.

She shouldn't have been surprised that it fitted as though made for her, because her lover had an astute eye for the details that many men might miss—not to mention intimately knowing the lines and curves of her body. The thought that he'd committed them to memory made her blood throb and heat in anticipation of the next time they would make love.

Setting the tall glass of juice aside, she curved her lips in an affectionate smile of awe and admiration. Gabriel stood before her dressed in another flawless suit, combined with a navy silk shirt and sky blue tie. His chestnut hair was swept back off his face to reveal the carved, clean lines that she was sure Michelangelo himself would have hungered to paint or sculpt.

'Hey, yourself.'

'I see you're wearing the dress.... Stand up—let me see how it fits.'

Getting to her feet, Lara obligingly made a slow turn to show off the dress from every angle.

An array of tumultuous feelings hit Gabriel all at once. But first and foremost was the dizzying sensation of warmth that flooded his heart—flooded it like a cascading waterfall where, if you were to stand underneath it, you would scarcely be able to draw breath with the force of it.

As he stood and surveyed the bewitching combination of beauty and sensuality that was Lara, and sensed his blood start to pound with the inevitable hunger and need that always arose when she was near, he wondered if that alien feeling was love. That sense of complete and utter helplessness in the face of something that he'd always told himself he didn't want? That hitching of his heart and the weakness in his limbs whenever he caught sight of the woman he intuitively knew he would be willing to *die* for in order to keep safe? And—more than that—the feeling of devastating loss he imagined he would suffer if he were never to see her again? Surely they were all signs that pointed to him being head over heels in love with Lara?

But what followed that wondrous revelation was the dark demon of fear. Fear that he might ruin her life because he had no experience of caring for such a priceless jewel.

For so long Gabriel had held himself apart from any sensitivity or feeling around women in case he got hurt. Look what his own mother had done to him. With such a precarious introduction into the world, trust—particularly when it came to women—was surely going to be an ongoing issue for him.

His thinking ran along the lines of what if he allowed himself to get involved with someone and then got hurt so badly he would never be able to recover enough to do the one thing that he did well? That was acquiring money and status in his chosen field. At least that gave him options with regard to how he lived. And in any case, surely it was better to be rich and miserable rather than the reverse?

Mentally giving himself a shake, Gabriel turned his attention back to the dress Lara was modelling. It could indeed have been tailor-made for her exquisite form—and, being personally acquainted with just *how* exquisite that form was, he knew, with a glimmer of pride, that he had chosen so well.

'You look utterly beautiful—in fact, you're ravishing,' he told her.

'It's the dress.'

'Can't you accept a compliment for once without putting yourself down, for goodness' sake?'

As soon as the words left his lips Gabriel wanted to take them back. His thoughtless remark had made Lara's cheeks flush with embarrassed heat and he was once again reminded of his fears around loving her. In truth, he couldn't bear the idea of hurting her even *once*, let alone the many times he might thoughtlessly hurt her should they spend the rest of their lives together.

Tucking her hair behind an ear, she lifted her shoulders in a shrug. 'Perhaps I'm not very good at receiving compliments—which is why I try and deflect them with humour. It doesn't mean that I don't appreciate you saying nice things to me, Gabriel. What woman *wouldn't* want a man to tell her she looks beautiful?'

'I'm sorry I snapped at you. I guess I'm just feeling a little on edge, knowing that you're leaving tomorrow,' he admitted, his chest tightening at the thought. He went to her then and folded her into his arms. Resting his chin on the top of her head, he stroked his hand down her back and immediately sensed her quiver. 'I should kidnap you and stop you from going,' he murmured.

Moving back a little, so that she might examine him, Lara knew her luminous brown eyes couldn't hide her disquiet.

'You don't have to resort to kidnapping me to get me to stay with you, Gabriel. I'd gladly stay with you if you just simply asked.' She sighed and shook her head. 'But you *won't*, will you? Just simply ask, I mean?'

She was beginning to know him too well. 'Aren't

you looking forward to going back to England—to your family and your job…your life there?' he replied, hoping to divert her.

'Of course I am. Can I ask you something?'

Her voice had lowered softly and he guessed she was wary of upsetting him. He hated the idea that Lara felt she had to walk on eggshells around him.

Releasing her, he restlessly drove his fingers through his hair. 'What is it you want to ask?'

'Have you… Have you ever thought of coming back to England to settle? I mean, what about the house that you inherited from your family? Have you made up your mind about what you're going to do with it?'

'Yes, I have. I'll be travelling back in a few days to sign some papers. I'm sorry I didn't tell you before, but it just never seemed to be the appropriate time.'

'You're selling it, aren't you? That means you won't be coming back to settle, doesn't it?'

Gabriel swallowed hard. It was time to tell Lara the truth—the *whole* truth.

'In my uncle's letter, he stipulated that I could only inherit if I came back to live in the manor for at least six months. After that I could do what I liked with the house.'

Her eyes lit up and he saw the hope that flared in their silken depths.

'Then you *could* come back to live there? We could see each other whenever we wanted?'

'Sweetheart, as difficult as it might be for you to understand, I don't want to live in that house again. It holds too many unhappy memories for me. I'd be much better off selling it and staying here.'

The colour drained from Lara's face. 'But didn't you

just say that your uncle stipulated in his letter that you could only inherit if you lived there for six months? If you're not planning on doing that, how will you sell it? It won't be yours to sell, will it?'

'I have a very good lawyer. There are ways and means to get round the legalities.'

'I don't understand....'

Her voice faltered a little and she looked as if she might cry. Gabriel felt like the worst criminal.

'I mean, it's not as though you need the money, is it? Why not just keep the house? Keep it for your family?'

He stared at her. 'You know I don't have any family.' He ground out the words as if they might choke him. What was Lara playing at, coming out with such a thing?

'I mean that you might one day have a family of your own. That would help dispel the unhappy memories of living in the house, wouldn't it?'

'I'm happy to take risks in my working life, Lara, but not in my personal one. Don't you know that by now?'

He saw her take a nervous swallow, then slide her palms down over the pretty blue dress he'd bought her. She lifted her shimmering gaze to his.

'I suppose I do. I just hoped that, given time, you'd come to see things differently. The eternal optimist—that's me.' Her lips quirked in a self-deprecating smile. 'Shouldn't we go to dinner now? It's getting late, and I ought to try and get a good night's sleep before travelling tomorrow. I'll just go and get my jacket.'

As Lara left the room, Gabriel stared blankly ahead of him out of the window at the winking lights of the city that had helped him to make his fortune. And right then he despised himself and *it* for contributing to breaking the heart of one of the sweetest and loveliest women in the world....

They sat down on their last night together to what should have been a wonderful meal at a local Thai restaurant, but for Lara the delicious food might as well have been gruel for all the enjoyment it gave her.

She was numb from her head down to her toes. The realisation that Gabriel wasn't any nearer to changing his mind about returning to England to face the demons from his past or to consider the possibility of committing to a proper relationship with her had finally sunk in. He'd asserted that he was happy to take risks in his working life but not in his personal one. The declaration had shattered her heart because she knew it was the death knell to all her hopes and dreams where he was concerned. What else could she do now but accept his decision to continue living his life in New York without her?

'Don't you like the food I ordered for you?' As he laid his fork down by the side of his plate, Gabriel's lean, hollow-cheeked face was grim. He reached up to loosen his tie as if he suddenly couldn't bear the constriction.

Biting back the tears that precariously threatened, Lara dabbed at her lips with her napkin. 'I know you meant well, bringing me here to eat, but I'm afraid I don't have much of an appetite.'

'You should have said.'

'I didn't because you've been working all day and I didn't have anything at the apartment to cook for you. I knew you needed to eat. That's why I agreed to go out to dinner with you.'

'As usual, putting others before yourself.' Although he'd lowered his voice, the muted volume didn't disguise the disparagement in his tone.

Lara flinched. 'You make it sound like it's something you despise—to think of others, I mean. I can't help my nature, Gabriel.'

His blue eyes were as clear and cold as flawless diamonds. 'No, you can't, can you? That's why I knew it was probably a mistake to start this affair. But I'm only human and I simply couldn't resist.'

If she hadn't been trembling so hard at his words, and feared losing her balance should she attempt to stand, Lara knew she couldn't have remained sitting in her seat. For the first time ever she honestly felt she disliked the man who gazed back at her across the table.

'Is that really all you thought us being together was? An affair? Something you could take or leave? I knew you had the potential to be cruel, Gabriel, but I never guessed just *how* cruel.'

'Why? It isn't as though I haven't given you enough evidence.'

'You're right. You started giving me evidence all those years ago, when I was just sixteen.'

Lara's comment drew a disturbed frown between Gabriel's brows. 'When you were sixteen? I doubt it. You surely didn't take it seriously when I used to rib you about not having a boyfriend because you were so choosy?'

'It wasn't that. Don't you remember Sean's party? The one he threw at our house? I know you do because you talked about it that first day, when you showed up to offer your condolences for Sean. Well, that night you were flirting with me, and in my innocence I took it to

mean that you liked me. I mean *really* liked me. I foolishly told you how I felt about you....'

Lara paused. The memory was suddenly more acute
than it had ever been. The power of it made her ribs
hurt.

'I don't think it pleased you. If anything, you were
probably highly embarrassed. You told me I should look
to be with someone my own age. Then you saw that
blonde tutor from your university across the room and
you all but pushed me aside to get to her. So yes, Gabriel. I *do* know that you can be cruel.'

He shook his head. 'That was a long time ago. You
were just a kid. I wouldn't have wanted to encourage
your interest because you were my best friend's little
sister and your family's regard was important to me.'

'But feelings are feelings, no matter what age you
are, and even then mine ran deep, Gabriel. Anyway,
we're talking about what's happening *now*. What I
want to know is are you reducing what we have to the
description of a mere affair because you're trying to
protect yourself from being hurt should you commit
seriously to me? I don't understand. How can I hurt
you if you don't really let me into your life, Gabriel?'

'As hard as it might be for you to hear, Lara, I don't
need anyone in my life. My life is just fine the way it is.'

'Is that true?' Sadly shaking her head, Lara barely
knew how to proceed. Gabriel was implacable when he
erected his defences. As hard as iron. She knew that.

'It's pointless continuing this conversation.' Throwing down his napkin, he signalled for the waiter. 'I'll
only hurt you even more if we continue, and you're
going home tomorrow.'

Lara stayed in her seat and said softly, 'You're probably right. Okay. Why don't you just pay the bill and we'll go?'

'Wise decision,' he murmured, just at the same moment as the smiling waiter arrived at their table.

It truly amazed Lara how quickly she had got back into the routine of working after the long summer break. In the endless days and long, sleepless nights following her departure from Gabriel in New York she'd wondered if she'd ever find pleasure or satisfaction in the job she loved again. But as soon as she had returned to the college, and the requests and demands of the students for help with their research, she'd taken both refuge and pleasure in the familiar routine of the life she was used to.

It helped her not to dwell on Gabriel too much. She would have been utterly useless doing her job if she had.

Yet the memory of their agonising goodbye at the airport and his comment that he'd known it was a mistake to start their affair still had the power to make her cry.

The distance he'd put between them at the restaurant with his remark the night before she was due to leave had grown even wider when he'd told her he thought it best they slept in separate rooms, so that Lara could get a good night's rest before catching her flight the next day. Even though he'd been hateful at the restaurant she hadn't slept a wink. Without Gabriel in the bed next to her—the Gabriel who had been so loving and passionate—she'd felt as if an essential part of her was missing.

Although she'd told herself she didn't understand his sudden cold impulse to distance himself from her not just physically but emotionally, in truth she did understand. He'd been running away again. Not just from

Lara, but from his fear of love and all that that might mean. He simply didn't trust it in case it was taken away, just as his mother had been taken away from him when she took her own life. That was why he'd taunted Lara with his remark that their 'affair' had been a mistake. He'd been trying to push her away. He wouldn't run the risk of caring for her too much in case she ended up hurting him.

The next morning, although they'd sat at the dining table together for breakfast, Gabriel had busied himself making several calls on his cell phone that had ensured his attention was on his work and not on her.

Lara might as well have been invisible. She'd tried hard to make conversation, hoping to engage him with her heartfelt declaration that she was still going to miss him despite what he had said at the restaurant, and that it would be hard to go home knowing they might not ever see each other again.

Gabriel's handsome face had remained worryingly impassive, as though he was deliberately locking her out—locking her out of his mind and his heart—and finally, when his chauffeur had called to tell him the car was ready to take them to the airport, out of his life, too.

When he'd left her at the airport he'd hesitatingly laid his hands on her shoulders and bent his head to kiss her. Lara had tensed helplessly, hoping and praying that he was going to have a change of heart and declare he couldn't just let her disappear out of his life without making some plans for the future. But to add to her distress his parting kiss hadn't been the least bit passionate or heartfelt. They might have just been mere acquaintances. The touch of his lips had been briefly warm and perfunctory, nothing more. Then, after telling her to take care of herself, that he'd probably be in touch just as soon as he 'got his head straight', he'd turned on his heel and hadn't looked back even once as he'd exited the airport.

Back at work, despite her vow not to dwell too much on her longing for Gabriel, memories of his warm, hard body against hers, of the smiles that had tugged at her heart because they were so rare and therefore even more precious, of the sound of his voice especially before he made love to her, when he'd seductively enticed and teased her, would sneak up on her when Lara least expected it. She would wonder what he was doing and if he even gave her a second thought. Had Gabriel already replaced her in his bed with some pretty, ambitious girl who viewed him as a sure-fire ticket to success and fortune? A girl who might please him sexually but would never love him—not like *she* loved him.

'Hello, Miss Bradley. Did you have a good holiday?'

She blinked, then glanced up from the paperwork she'd been desperately trying to apply herself to before thoughts of Gabriel had intruded once again.

A tall, slim young man dressed in skinny jeans and an unironed T-shirt stood on the other side of the counter. He had a shock of sandy-coloured hair in dire need of a wash and a comb. Lara immediately relaxed. Danny Fairfax was one of the most pleasant students you could wish to meet—charming and affable, in spite of his sometimes unkempt appearance. She always made sure to make time for him when he needed help with some aspect of the research he was struggling with.

'It was fine, thanks.' She followed up this answer with an unguarded, warm smile. Danny immediately flushed beetroot-red, which endeared him to her even more. 'And I told you before to call me Lara. "Miss Bradley" makes me sound like some elderly spinster.'

His lips broke into a grin. But he quickly looked serious again. 'I'm sorry I asked if your holiday was good. I forgot that you told me your brother had recently died. Obviously you must still be grieving for him.'

The comment took Lara aback. Not just because Danny had remembered the fact but also because she realised she'd probably been thinking more about Gabriel than about Sean. Of course she still missed her brother's presence, and not a day went by when she didn't mourn him, but Gabriel was a living, breathing reality, and when she'd been with him he had reached deep down inside her and stolen both her heart and her soul. She knew Sean would understand, even give her his blessing. He had loved Gabriel, too.

Staring back into Danny's strangely still grey eyes, Lara wondered if he would ever experience the depth of love and passion that she had experienced with Gabriel. She could only pray that he wouldn't have his heart splintered and broken as hers had been.

'Yes, I'm still grieving. But losing someone like that… It still feels like they're around. You know what I mean? His presence is everywhere.' It didn't pass Lara by that she might have been talking about Gabriel.

'Yes, I do know what you mean,' Danny answered gravely. 'I lost my dad two years ago at Christmas and sometimes I hear his voice as though he's in the room with me, especially when I'm trying to work out a problem. He was from Yorkshire, and when things got tough he always used to say, "Don't let the man grind you down!" Funny how that used to help me.'

'He sounds as though he was a very wise man, your dad.'

'He was. He was the best.'

'So, Danny…' Lara purposefully switched back into work mode. It wouldn't help her to dwell on her personal sorrows too much and nor would it help Danny—although she was touched that he would share the story of his personal loss with her. It was good to know that she wasn't the only one walking around with the feeling that life had pulled the rug from under her and she might never walk on firm ground again. 'What can I do for you today?'

Gabriel had been revisiting his old bedroom. Although his initial reaction on entering it had been wary, his stomach clenched hard in readiness for the deluge of hurtful memory that would inevitably swamp him, he had been mildly surprised to see that the room was newly decorated, freshened up.

Had Richard Devenish undertaken to get a decorator in before he'd fallen ill? Why on earth had he done that? It wasn't as though he'd needed an extra room. Had he perhaps believed that his nephew would return and make the manor his home again?

Bemused, Gabriel allowed his gaze to sweep his surroundings in a preliminary search. His glance falling on the neatly arranged books in the two maplewood bookcases that he remembered from his childhood, he leant down to retrieve a first edition copy of *Brave New World* by Aldous Huxley. It had been a Christmas present from his uncle when he was just nine. He had all but devoured the book. He'd loved it so much he had even written an essay about it at school.

That year his teacher had commented in his report, *'Gabriel is a precocious reader with a highly inventive imagination that I am sure will take him far!'*

His lips nudging a bittersweet smile, he replaced the book and turned round. Janet Mullan, the housekeeper, had left the large picture windows open to let in the sunshine. The scent of stocks and roses from the garden below also drifted in delicately, filling the air with the heady summer perfume that Gabriel had always loved even as a boy.

Releasing a slow, contemplative breath, he walked to the windows to stare out at the stunning vista. He recalled thinking at that time that it wouldn't be so bad living here if he could have a few of the boys from school to come and stay with him in the holidays. But his nanny—a middle-aged lady called Margaret—had shaken her head and reminded him that his uncle had forbidden it, in case any of the valuable antiques in the house got broken.

To make up for his disappointment she'd given him a hug, ruffled his hair and said she'd take him to the local fair on the village green...perhaps he'd see some of his friends there? Well, Gabriel had gone to the fair, munched at a toffee apple and a sticky bun, palled up with a local boy and had a whale of a time, sliding down the helter-skelter and riding the carousel. That had been one of the best days of that summer, he recalled.

But sadly, events like that had been too few and far between. His taciturn uncle had grown more and more distant, seemingly preferring to stay away rather than share the house with Gabriel when he was home, and concepts like heritage and family had quickly grown to mean less and less to his nephew. The next summer holiday that Gabriel had properly enjoyed had been after his first year at university, when he had met Sean.

Inevitably, the thought of his best friend brought with it a new deluge of heartfelt memories—of Lara and the stricken look on her pretty face when he'd bade her goodbye less than warmly at the airport. It had been the hardest thing he'd ever done, and every night and day that had passed since had given him plenty of cause to regret it. It had been a cruel way to end their too-brief relationship—pretending that he didn't care how she felt. It had been the act of his life.

The truth was he cared too much. He just hadn't been able to deal with the outpouring of love and affection that he'd received from Lara. It had been a totally unfamiliar experience to have someone love him and want to be with him—not because of what he could materially provide for them but because they wanted to be with the man behind the facade Gabriel had affected all these years. The *real* Gabriel Devenish.

But why should he let Lara waste her love on him? Sooner or later she'd find out that he just wasn't worth it. In years to come, when she was married to a really decent man, she'd thank him for it.

Feeling an overwhelming sense of weariness and despair descend, he lowered himself onto the bed, put his hands behind his head, and lay down. His uncle's solicitor was waiting for him downstairs in the drawing room—waiting for Gabriel to give him his decision about what he intended to do with the house. Remembering that he'd also promised his property developer friend that he would ring him to discuss some figures regarding the potential sale of the manor, Gabriel loosed a heavy sigh and shut his eyes.

CHAPTER ELEVEN

LARA COULDN'T FATHOM what on earth was wrong with her. Yes, she'd been through the mill, losing first Sean and then Gabriel. But were those heartrending events enough to make her feel queasy and persistently light-headed, which was how she'd been feeling for several days now? She should perhaps go the doctor, but she was sure she would eventually shrug it off so steered clear of pursuing that option. Instead she determinedly focused on work, even putting in some overtime in a bid to shake herself out of whatever was ailing her.

Besides, she wasn't the only one who had lost a loved one or had her heart broken. What she should aim to do was to be more stoical. She should just endeavour to take one day at a time and somehow, some way, garner some optimism about life again.

Then one morning, as she got ready for work, Lara reached into her purse to dig out the foil packet of contraceptive pills. She immediately realised she'd picked up the previous month's packet instead of the current one. About to jettison the empty container into a nearby wicker basket, she did a double take. At the beginning of the empty rows there was one tablet remaining. How had that happened? More to the point, why hadn't she noticed it before?

Her heart started to pound as she calculated back to the week of the remaining pill. Without a doubt it was the week that she'd spent in New York with Gabriel. Six weeks had passed since then. Six weeks with no sign of a period. Lara had put the absence down to the emotional rollercoaster she'd been on, telling herself that everything would sort itself out just as soon as her emotions calmed down.

Hadn't she started to take the pill in the first place to help regulate her periods because they tended to be erratic? She shouldn't be alarmed that she'd missed one. Yet some instinct told her that she *did* perhaps need to be concerned.

Dragging her hand feverishly through her tousled dark hair, and still in her pyjamas, she sat down on the bed and let the realisation that had shockingly dawned wash over her. Wasn't it true that you had to be consistent when taking an oral contraceptive? If you missed one then you risked the inevitable. Suddenly, the reason for her queasiness, her feelings of being light-headed and her missed period became disturbingly clear. She was pregnant. Pregnant with Gabriel Devenish's baby!

It was the strangest thing, but suddenly Lara's sense of confusion and worry about her health dissipated like ice crystals beneath the sun. She would need to take a test to be absolutely sure, of course…. Touching her palm to her cheek, she sensed her skin flush warmly. A sense of joyous excitement filled her. It went racing through her blood like life-giving oxygen.

How or why she had omitted to take one of her pills no longer seemed to matter. She certainly hadn't forgotten to take one deliberately. In any case, Gabriel hadn't got in touch when he'd 'got his head straight', as he'd promised he would. He hadn't even let her know when and if he'd returned to the UK to deal with the sale of his family's manor house.

As much as it grieved her, Lara could no longer make that her driving concern. In her mind and in her heart she had left the door open for him to come back to her— of course she had. But if he didn't—and right now it didn't look as if he would—well, she would have their son or daughter to take care of, and that would in time help to ease the hurt of his desertion.

At least she hoped that it would. But whatever happened one thing was certain: she intended to be the most loving and adoring mother she could be. She might not be wealthy, but her child would be the recipient of far more important riches—her love and devotion. He or she might not have a father in their life, but that would have to be enough.

Gabriel had spent the morning with his architect, perusing and discussing the renovation plans for the manor which were already well under way. The genteel old orangery was being redesigned, along with the bedrooms, and he'd also had discussions with one of Britain's top garden designers about what could be done to make the most of the gardens.

The day the solicitor had visited the house to find out what Gabriel intended to do about it, Gabriel had made the surprising decision to fulfil the terms of the codicil to the will and live there for the six months stipulated so that he could inherit. Shortly after that he had rung his office in New York and told them he was taking a

year's sabbatical in order to decide what he wanted to
do about his future.

His decision to take a year off had dumbfounded his
employers, and they had immediately offered him a
myriad of financial temptations and seductive induce-
ments like a prestigious house in the Hamptons to get
him to rethink. Gabriel had firmly declined.

The most surprising thing of all was that when he
had come off the phone he'd felt as if a huge weight
had been lifted off his shoulders. Until that cathartic
moment he hadn't fully realised how much his work
and his drive for more success, more money and more
power had dominated his life. It certainly hadn't left
much time or space for anything else. In particular,
for the loving and committed relationship he secretly
craved but had always feared he would never be able
to sustain even if he found it.

During the past few weeks since he had returned to
the house and reread his uncle's letter—particularly the
part where he had told him of his hopes that he would
return to live at the manor and raise his children there—
Gabriel had been filled with new hope and optimism
about his future. A future quite unlike the usual picture
he had envisaged for himself.

What had helped tremendously was the fact that he
had actually started to fall in love with the house. Bit
by bit the sorrow of his childhood and his damaged past
had loosened its grip and he had started to heal.

One afternoon, whilst exploring one of the larger
bedrooms which the housekeeper was convinced must
have been his mother's, he discovered a framed photograph tucked away in a bureau. It was a picture of
his mother, Angela, holding him as a baby, and it bore

out the housekeeper's theory that the room must have been hers. There was no doubt that Angela had been a beautiful woman, with glossy dark hair and vivid blue eyes, but it wasn't just her beauty that drew the viewer in. Her smiling face exuded warmth and love in equal measures as she held her son firmly against her heart.

How she must have hated being ill and unable to look after him, Gabriel thought.

The idea jolted him.

Up until now, Angela Devenish had been an almost ghost-like figure in his mind—hardly real. As if she'd never existed at all. Now her life and the woman she had been started to fascinate him. He studied the photograph for a long time. He even took it with him into his bedroom and stood it on the dressing table so that he would see it every morning when he woke up.

But even though he had begun to make genuine inroads into seeing his mother in a different light and healing the wounds from his past, there was one face that he longed to see again more than any other. And that face was Lara's.

The only thing that had held Gabriel back from going to see her when he'd returned to the UK was the sickening memory of how he had behaved towards her when they'd parted in New York. He also couldn't forget the story of how he'd rebuffed her when she'd been just sixteen at Sean's party. She hadn't had to elucidate how hurt she must have been. It had been written all over her face.

He honestly wouldn't blame her if when she saw him again she told him to go to hell. But he hoped to God she wouldn't. Until he had made the decision to live in his family's manor so that he could inherit—not so that he might sell the property but so that he could make it his home—he hadn't known how he could legitimately approach her. All he had known was that he wanted to show Lara that he could be a better man, a truly good man—a man she could depend on.

And to do that he would have to show her evidence that he intended to stay in the country and make his life there.

If Lara agreed—and it was a big *if*—she would be an absolutely vital and crucial element in helping Gabriel create the new life he wanted. A much happier and more fulfilling life than he had ever experienced before.

Three months later...

Lara pressed her palm to the base of her spine and rubbed it. Having been on her feet since the early hours of the morning, she was so tired she could drop. Why did her tiredness and stress always seem to go straight to her back these days? she wondered.

With a jolt, she remembered that she was pregnant. The realisation still came as a shock every time she thought about it, but it had all been confirmed by her doctor so there was no more doubting. It still seemed like the most unbelievable dream.

With a wistful sigh, Lara started to go through her usual routine of shutting up shop for the day. All she could think about now was the prospect of a long and leisurely soak in the tub with some scented bubbles. That should help ease the ache in her back.

'Any plans for the evening, Lara?' her young colleague Marisa asked as she shut down her computer beside her.

'Only to have the longest, most relaxing soak in history, in a bath full of deliciously warm and sudsy water.'

'Sounds heavenly.' Marisa smiled.

'What about you? Have you any plans?'

'I'm going out for a pizza with Mark, my boyfriend.'

'You're still seeing him? I thought you two had had a big row and you had decided not to see him any more.'

Marisa's plump cheeks suffused with heat. 'Every now and again we fall out. But we quickly patch things up.' She smiled. 'He's a nice boy. I'd miss him if we weren't together. Sometimes he feels like a missing part of me I didn't know I'd lost. Do you know what I mean?'

Lara *did* know what she meant, and helplessly she felt the other girl's comment catching her off guard. Her eyes filled with tears. The thought of Gabriel and the memory of his passionate caresses and kisses was never far away. Those memories were even more poignant now that she knew she was carrying his baby. Did he ever think about her and wonder how she was doing? Did he ever miss her?

It had been neither simple nor easy to slip back into the predictable routine of the life she'd had before he'd walked in and ignited all her hopes and dreams with a fierce burning light that would never go out. So far it had been the biggest challenge of her life. Lara wondered how Gabriel would react if he knew that. It all but killed her to think he might just brush it off and put it down to experience.

'Lara?' Stepping towards her, Marisa looked alarmed to see that she was weeping. 'What's wrong, love? Do you feel sick? Do you want me to get you a glass of water?'

She suddenly sounded much older than her years,

and the younger woman's concern made Lara want to weep even more.

Touching her fingertips to the moisture that had tracked down her face and dampened her cheeks, she shook her head and forced a smile. 'No, I'll be fine, thanks. I think I just need to get out of here and go home and have that bath.'

'That's bound to help. A long hot bath is a bit of a cure-all for me, too. It's the same as having a cup of tea, isn't it? It somehow makes you feel better.'

Marisa's sage remark had the effect of making Lara want to hug her—so she did. The other girl flushed with pleasure.

'You're wise beyond your years—you know that?' Lara told her. Then, moving away, she glanced over at all the empty chairs and tables that would be full of diligent and not so diligent students again tomorrow. One thing was for certain: life went on, despite what was happening in your personal life.

Reaching for the red wool cardigan she'd hung over the back of her chair, she hurriedly pulled it on. Lifting up the heavy swathe of hair that had fallen down her back she let it fall again and shook it free. Absently glancing towards the twin glass doors of the exit, she frowned. A man dressed in a classic raincoat thrown over a dark sweatshirt and jeans was pushing them open.

Stepping inside, he took a brief inventory of his surroundings before tunnelling his fingers through his hair and moving towards them. Even if she hadn't seen his face Lara would have known that smooth athletic gait anywhere. Staring in disbelief, she found it hard to think, never mind *speak*. In fact, she suddenly felt quite faint.

'Who could that be?' Marisa whispered next to her. 'Doesn't he know that we're closed?'

'His name is Gabriel Devenish.'

Still in shock, Lara knew her voice wasn't much above a whisper. But it was almost as if she'd had to say his name out loud in order to believe that he was there and not just a figment of her imagination, or some seductive ghostly visitation from one of her nightly dreams of him.

When he stepped up to the counter and turned the vivid azure beam of his too-arresting gaze on her, a well of hurt and long-suppressed fury at his cavalier treatment rose up inside her and made her stiffen her shoulders defensively.

Lifting her chin, she looked him straight in the eye and announced, 'We're closed. If you need any help I'm afraid you'll have to come back tomorrow.'

The beautiful carved lips in front of her edged into an amused smile—a smile that unscrupulously stormed Lara's heart and turned her insides to mush.

'I'm afraid what I need can't wait until tomorrow,' he remarked, and the smoky voice and piercing eyes mercilessly imprisoned her, locked her up and threw away the key.

For a long moment she fell into a kind of trance. Then the sound of Marisa pointedly clearing her throat behind her and touching her hand to Lara's sleeve had her turning round to see what was wrong.

There was nothing amiss. The younger girl's eyes were alive with curiosity and what might have even been delight as she commented, 'I'm sorry, Lara, but I have to dash. Mark is meeting me in the car park. Take care of yourself, won't you? I'll see you tomorrow.'

'Enjoy your pizza,' Lara murmured automatically.

As the twin glass doors swung shut behind the slender blonde, her heart hammered at the realisation that she and Gabriel were alone. The impulse to do something, *anything*, to help still her nerves took hold, but Gabriel's handsome face was suddenly looking ominously serious and she couldn't help but stare. Just what did he want to say to her? Whatever it was, she was determined that she would have her say first.

'What on earth are you doing here—and how did you know where to find me? I don't recall giving you the college's address.'

'I went to see your parents,' he replied. 'Your mother told me where to find you.'

'When was this?'

'This morning.'

Lara's hand automatically shot to her abdomen. She gently rubbed it through the soft grey tunic she wore beneath her cardigan, then realised she was drawing attention to the one place she didn't want Gabriel's eyes to be drawn to.

Had her mum told him about the pregnancy? Even though she had been over the moon on hearing Lara's news about the baby, declaring it was the blessing she had been praying for, Lara was confident that she wouldn't have told him anything without checking with her first. But her insides still churned at the thought of how Gabriel would take the news.

'Why did you go to see them? Was it to collect Sean's photographs? And when did you get back to the UK? Is this another flying visit, Gabriel?'

Seeing that Lara's slender hands were gripping the edge of the fibreglass counter as if her life depended

on it, and hearing the distress in her voice, Gabriel
frowned. He hated the idea that his appearance had
upset her, even though he knew she had plenty of reason to be distressed. The need to alleviate her unhap-
piness became imperative.

'I'll explain everything in a moment. Trust me,
there's nothing to worry about. Right now all I want
to do is look at you.'

He ached with an unholy ache to take her in his arms
and kiss away every hurt, every moment of unease or
despair he had ever visited on her, but he forced himself to wait. This wasn't the moment to blunder back
into her life and just take what he wanted as if it was
his God-given right. That was the *old* Gabriel. The man
who had been too selfish and self-obsessed to know
what a gift had been bestowed on him when Lara had
surrendered her virginity and confessed that she loved
him—had *always* loved him.

'You look tired. The shadows under your eyes look
like bruises and you're far too pale. What have you been
doing to yourself? Burning the candle at both ends?'

Gabriel hadn't meant his observation to sound critical, but he saw straight away that Lara was immediately defensive—*angry*, too. Her animated reaction
confirmed it.

'What do *you* care what I've been doing? You didn't
even bother to ring me after I left New York, and nor
did you have the decency to let me know you were back
in the UK! I'm done with worrying about you, Gabriel.
I really am. I think it's time I focused my attention on
myself and my own needs.'

Her dark eyes crestfallen, she leant towards the desk

and switched off the lamp that was there. Then she opened a drawer and collected her shoulder bag.

'I'm going home now. It's been a long day.'

'We need to talk, Lara. I know you probably think I'm not worth giving the time of day to, but I want the opportunity to help change your mind about that. Did you drive here?'

'Yes, I did.'

'Then I'll follow you in my car.'

She didn't answer. With her head held high, and clutching her bag in front of her, she came round the counter and started to walk towards the exit.

Although she hadn't argued with his intention, Gabriel felt oddly hurt that she wouldn't even look at him. Instead she arranged the strap of her bag more firmly onto her shoulder and drew the sides of her long wool cardigan together as if she was cold. Almost as if needing to protect herself. Then she proceeded out of the building to the car park.

The journey back to Lara's flat was thankfully a short one. Afraid that too long a delay before they were able to talk would give her added time to mull over past events and decide she would be better off without him, Gabriel couldn't help but be anxious. She'd seemed so adamant just now that they were over. But then he remembered the times when she'd openly demonstrated how much she cared and once again hope flared inside him.

Standing beside her as she inserted the key in the lock and opened the door of the Victorian semi where she lived, he stayed silent as a reluctant Lara invited him in.

'We'll talk in the living room,' she declared, her

brown eyes issuing him with a mere cursory glance before sliding quickly away again. 'The sooner we get this over and done with, the better.'

In spite of its lofty ceiling, the room Gabriel followed Lara inside to was surprisingly cosy and welcoming. The space couldn't help but reflect the personal touches and preferences of the woman who lived there. From the small collection of family photographs that sat atop the pine bookcase and the mantelpiece to the several wooden shelves that were literally crammed with books, it was eminently clear what the occupant's priorities were.

A seriously comfortable-looking dark gold couch with an embroidered throw on the back was strewn with brightly coloured cushions, and an old Chesterfield armchair sat before an uncurtained window overlooking the garden.

'You may as well sit down.' Her tone less than inviting, Lara threw her shoulder bag down onto the couch and, with her arms folded, moved her head to indicate he take the armchair.

Murmuring 'Ladies first', Gabriel waited until his reluctant hostess had settled herself on the couch and then, shrugging off his raincoat, he folded it over the back of the venerable old armchair and sat down.

'You said you were going to explain everything?'

Her pretty face was inevitably troubled as she leant forward in her seat to study him. Sighing, Gabriel scraped his fingers through his thick dark hair and smiled. 'I will. What I want to tell you is that I decided what I wanted wasn't in New York after all, but here.'

'You mean your family's home? Have you decided to sell it?'

'I'm not just talking about the manor, Lara. Although in answer to your question I have to tell you I'm *not* intending on selling it. My plan is to live there. In fact I've been living there for the past three months now, attempting to make my peace with the past and turning the place back into a home—a *real* home.'

'You have? Oh, Gabriel, that's wonderful.'

The surprise and pleasure that shone from her beautiful dark eyes couldn't help but melt Gabriel's heart. But he hadn't finished telling her the full extent of his plans yet, and a lot depended on her answer to his next question as to whether he carried them out or not.

'The truth is, Lara...' he continued. 'The truth is it won't be a real home until you agree to marry me and come and live with me there. Will you?'

CHAPTER TWELVE

IT WASN'T THE MOST romantic thing in the world to have happen, but when the full impact of Gabriel's question hit her, Lara sensed a sudden, urgent need to be sick. Hurriedly rising to her feet, she threw him an apologetic look and ran out through the door to her bedroom's en-suite bathroom. Once there, she crouched down in front of the toilet and was violently ill even as she heard Gabriel come in behind her.

'Sweetheart, what's wrong?'

As his deeply concerned voice asked the question, he stooped down behind her and gently gathered her hair behind her head so that it wouldn't fall over her face. When she'd finished, it was to find him running some cold water into the sink and dampening a washcloth. Almost as if she was a little girl he proceeded to wipe her mouth, dabbing gently at her lips, and then he carefully helped her to her feet.

'Wait here,' he instructed, and as the familiar, warm, musky scent of his cologne besieged her senses and rendered her even weaker he briefly disappeared, to return with a glass of cold water. 'Take a good long drink,' he ordered her.

Although he patiently waited for her to finish, Lara easily sensed the concern that gripped him.

When she glanced up again Gabriel removed the glass from her trembling hands and stood it on the shelf above the sink. Then he stared at her. Many times before she had been the recipient of that intensely direct examination, but it had never been as intense as this. Disturbingly, what she saw in the depths of that glittering gaze were varying shades of anger—like the precursor to a storm—and deep, deep anguish and pain.

'What the hell is going on, Lara? You'd better tell me.'

'Haven't you guessed? Don't you know the signs?'

Suddenly overwhelmed with the situation, she shouldered past him into the bedroom. Once there, she dropped down onto the bed and brought her hands up to her face. Incredibly, Gabriel had just asked her to marry him. But was he now going to reject her because she was pregnant? She almost couldn't bear the thought. Before she knew it scalding tears were trickling down behind her palms.

Suddenly the door opened and Gabriel was there. He was staring down at her, a muscle flinching in the side of his carved cheekbone, his expression mirroring hurt disbelief.

'You're pregnant.'

It was a statement of fact, not a question. Raising her head, Lara met his accusing gaze with her heart thudding and her mouth as dry as sand. 'Yes. Yes, I am.'

'So no sooner had we parted than you found yourself another man? I thought I was getting to know you, Lara, but now I realise I didn't know you at all.'

Sounding despairing, Gabriel started to move back

towards the door, as if he had already made up his mind what he was going to do about her admission.

But then he turned and said furiously, 'You certainly didn't waste your time missing me, did you? And to think I believed you when you said you were a virgin the first time we made love. What a prize idiot I was to fall for such an unlikely story!'

With his hand on the doorknob he glared at Lara, then stalked from the room. Ice-cold fear poured through her like white-water rapids as she realised he was going to leave.

Lara jumped up and ran after him.

'Gabriel!'

She got to the living room just as he was collecting his coat from the back of the chair and she rushed forward to grab his wrist and stop him from going. Suddenly it was *her* turn to be furious.

'You *are* an idiot. Such a stupid, *stupid* idiot!' Even as the accusation left her lips a fresh bout of scalding tears rolled down her cheeks and Gabriel stared at her, clearly uncomprehending either her meaning or the reason for her distress. 'Do you honestly think I would sleep with another man when it's *you* that I love—have always loved and always will?'

His lip curled with disdain. 'But you've just admitted that you're pregnant.' He shook off her grip on his arm. 'Or are you going to try and convince me it was some kind of immaculate conception?'

Lara sucked in her breath in a bid to try and steady herself. 'Before you go any further I need to tell you—I need to tell you it's true that when we first slept together I was a virgin. I waited all these years to give up my virginity to a man I really loved because it was important to me. That man has always been you, Gabriel.' She paused to take in another steadying breath and saw the interplay of hope and uncertainty that crossed his face. 'The baby is *yours*, Gabriel,' she finished.

'What?'

'Just hear me out, will you? I fell pregnant when I forgot to take one of my contraceptive pills that week we were together in New York. I didn't do it deliberately. I would never try and trap you like that. But my head was in the clouds the whole time I spent with you—it was like a dream. I only discovered I'd missed one of my pills a few weeks after I got home. I'd been feeling nauseous and light-headed, but I put that down to being upset because I was missing you and you hadn't been in touch. I didn't even know if I would ever see you again.'

'The baby is mine?' The raincoat Gabriel was holding slid out of his hand onto the floor.

Raising her hand in an attempt to dry her tears, Lara nodded. 'I swear it. I'll show you the foil packet with the pill I didn't take still in it. You can trace it back to our week together in New York. But if you still don't believe me then I don't know how else to convince you. I foolishly thought my word and the devotion I've shown you would be enough. I don't tell lies, Gabriel. Remember I told you that once before?'

The man standing in front of her looked seriously stunned. 'Why didn't you tell me you were pregnant as soon as you found out? I would have come back straight away.'

Shrugging, Lara gave him a wobbly smile. 'I didn't want to put any pressure on you or make you feel obligated, that's why. I especially didn't want that be-

cause of the way you were when we said goodbye at
the airport. You seemed so angry, Gabriel. Angry and
distant. It was as though you resented me. I knew you
were already in turmoil because of your uncle's letter
and what he'd told you about your mother. I didn't want
to add to your worries.'

Gabriel was shaking his head as if he couldn't quite
believe what he was hearing. 'You really are unbelievable—you know that? You had every damn right in the
world to demand I come back and take up my responsibility to you and the baby. When will you learn that
you're the important one, Lara—not me?'

'Don't say that. You're very important to me, too,
Gabriel.' She followed this declaration with a puzzled
frown. 'But why didn't you tell me you'd decided to
come back and live at the manor? Were you thinking
that I would automatically expect us to take up where
we left off when you clearly had doubts about our relationship?'

'You crazy woman,' he breathed.

Fastening his hands around her slim upper arms, he
pulled her against his chest. Lara's heart went wild. As
he pushed back a stray curl where it brushed against
the side of her cheek she saw his intimate smile was
candid and unguarded as he gazed back at her, and it
rendered him even more beautiful in her eyes. That
heartrending smile suggested he'd made the decision
to reveal at last the *real* Gabriel Devenish. To reveal
the honourable and decent man behind the steely corporate facade and the much admired financial acu-
ity that he was known for. The man Lara had always
known he was.

'I didn't want to tell you I was coming back to live

at the manor until I'd taken some proper time to examine some of the hurts from my past and tried to make some headway into healing them. You didn't deserve to be with a broken man, Lara—a man who didn't know how to love anyone but himself.'

He grimaced painfully.

'And I didn't even make a very convincing job of that. I poured all my energies into my work, and my relentless desire to be the best at what I did was only because I wanted to have the admiration and praise of my peers. I was looking for validation that I was worthwhile. It wasn't even about the money. But that ambition became the most important thing in my life. A very empty and meaningless life, when all was said and done.

'Apart from being good at my job, I didn't regard myself as being good at very much at all. And I didn't have meaningful relationships because I couldn't allow myself to be close to a woman in case I was betrayed in some way—that's another reason why I directed all my attention into my work.

'And as far as doubts are concerned, I can tell you that the only doubts I had were whether I was good enough to be with an angel like you,' he continued huskily. 'I always intended on coming back for you, Lara. Was I hoping for too much when I hoped that you would want to share the rest of your life with a man like me? As I want to share my life with you?'

Lara lifted her hand to lay her palm gently against his roughened cheek. 'No,' she said earnestly. 'You weren't hoping for too much. I can't think of anything I'd like more than to share the rest of my life with you. Besides…no one else would want me if I couldn't be with you Gabriel. I'd be like an empty shell. Don't you know that you've ruined me for any other man because my body and soul belongs to you?'

A profoundly dazed look stole into the eyes that gazed back at her.

Gabriel's hands tightened as they dropped down to her hips and pulled her harder against him. 'And now you're going to have my baby. I'm going to be a father. *We* are going to be parents, with a family of our own. I can't help asking myself if I deserve to be this happy.'

'So you don't mind that we'll have a baby to take care of so early in our relationship? We can't pretend it won't be challenging.'

'We'll weather any storms that come, sweetheart,' Gabriel reassured her warmly. 'We'll weather them because together we're strong and our love won't let the challenges of life overwhelm us. Look at what we've already overcome. This baby will bring us ever closer—just you wait and see.'

His face came towards hers, but with a quick shake of her head Lara gently but firmly pushed him away. 'You have to let me go and freshen my mouth before you kiss me,' she declared. 'Then I'll let you kiss me senseless if you want!'

His carved lips quirked in an amused grin. 'That's like asking me if I need to take my next breath. If you take longer than ten seconds then I'm coming to find you—and I warn you…if you're not ready there'll be a hell of a penalty to pay.' As she smiled and walked towards the door, he added, 'And you still haven't answered my question.'

Feigning ignorance, Lara stopped and turned to examine him. 'What question might that be?'

'Will you marry me? Put me out of my misery, woman, and give me your answer. A man can only take so much before he cracks.'

Her expression softening, Lara laid her hand over her heart and then, with a graceful flourish, indicated that it was his. 'Of course I'll marry you, Gabriel. That's always been my intention—ever since Sean brought you home with him that very first time. He'll be so pleased that two of the people he loved best are going to be together, don't you think?'

It was as she turned and left the room that Gabriel finally realised fully the immense capacity to love that Lara had. Sean had possessed that capacity, too. Shaking his head, he didn't even try and stem the tears that welled in his eyes.

His head was spinning. The woman he loved had agreed to be his wife and she was pregnant with their baby. All the things Gabriel had thought would be denied him were coming true.

He already knew that his future goals didn't have anything to do with continuing to be a 'mover and shaker' on Wall Street, but were to do with being a loving husband and father, with his children growing up happy and content with two parents who adored them and who would do everything in their power to help them have a wonderful life. And they would all live together in the beautiful manor house that Gabriel had inherited from his family. Uncle Richard's heartfelt hope was going to be realised.

The architects and designers Gabriel had hired were already helping him bring his home into the twenty-first century without encroaching on the Regency

building's historic innate beauty and grace, and he
was already pleased with some of the results they had
achieved. Lara had agreed that she was, too, and the
room that had given them both the most pleasure was
the beautiful nursery—although Lara was already insisting that the baby would share their room until she
was confident that he or she was ready to sleep in a
room by themselves.

Suddenly aware that the small gathering behind
him in the glass-ceilinged conservatory had fallen into
a reverent silence, and knowing that Lara's parents
were closest to them at the front of the seated rows, he
brought his mind right back to the present and the ra-
diant and beautiful woman at his side.

Lara looked absolutely stunning in her simple but
elegant wedding gown. It was fashioned in lavender-
coloured floor-length satin and her mother, Peggy, had
helped her decide on it. It was the perfect choice for her
daughter's timeless beauty. The strapless design had a
sweetheart neckline and a beaded appliqué underneath
the bust, and the material flowed down over the waist
that five months of pregnancy had clearly but not yet
too obviously swelled.

His clasp on her slender hand tightened a little possessively as Lara lifted her shimmering dark eyes to
his. For a man who had prided himself on addressing
many corporate banquets and dinners with aplomb,
Gabriel suddenly found himself bereft of words.

Clearing his throat, he leant towards his bewitching
wife-to-be and asked in hushed tones, 'Are you ready
for this? You don't want to change your mind?'

Momentarily taken aback, Lara blinked. Then her
soft pink-painted lips curved in a loving, amused smile.

'Are you serious? To use an often used cliché, for which I won't apologise, I've been waiting for this moment all my life.'

Gabriel chuckled and claimed her lips in a briefly hungry kiss that he had no intention of apologising for, either. When he looked up again the professional celebrant who stood in front of them—a slender woman with copper-coloured hair and merry brown eyes—bestowed an indulgent smile upon them and reprimanded him teasingly.

'You're meant to kiss the bride when I pronounce that you're man and wife, Mr Devenish, *not* before!'

Unable to resist, Gabriel remarked, 'No offence, but nobody tells me when I can and can't kiss the woman I love—the woman I adore more than life itself.'

Briefly stunned into silence, the celebrant bestowed another smile on him. Then, her gaze encompassing both him and Lara, she said, 'Shall we proceed with the ceremony now?'

Unable to stop himself from having the last word, Gabriel twined his fingers with Lara's and answered, 'Trust me, I'm as anxious to get the ceremony under way and make this amazing woman my wife as you are!'

There was a delighted ripple of laughter from behind them at that declaration, and a gently respectful round of applause. As for Lara—she glanced up at the handsome blue-eyed man at her side, dressed in a flawless midnight blue tuxedo, and offered up a silent prayer of thanks for her great good fortune.

Then the voice of her brother stole into her mind, saying, *'I always told you to go for what you wanted in life, and that if you wanted it enough you would get it...remember?'*

Swallowing back her tears, Lara murmured under her breath, 'Yes, Sean, I remember—and you were right. Thank you.'

* * * * *

BILLIONAIRE BOSS, M.D.

OLIVIA GATES

One

"Lili…look alive! The boss man himself is about to arrive."

Liliana Accardi swung away from the microscope to impale her coworker with a glare, his rhyming—whether he meant it or not—annoying her.

But it was just as well he'd interrupted her. Instead of the gray-scaled cells she was supposed to be studying, she'd been seeing only red. Ever since she'd heard the news that would end all her professional and scientific dreams. No way was she rushing off to go stand in line while said new "boss man" inspected them like a shepherd inspected his newly acquired flock.

Brian Saunders raised his hands in a "don't kill the messenger" gesture. "I just think you should come, if only to get firsthand word on the direction of his management. Maybe he'll allow you to carry on with your work, after all."

"Yeah, sure. From what I've read about him since I started my morning with the delightful news of his takeover, Antonio Balducci rules his empire with a steel fist. He'll never allow me independence."

Brian spread his arms. "You know me, I never say never." At her hardening glare, he grinned. "I'm in the same hijacked boat as you. I just decided to deal with my captivity and go on the journey with a different attitude."

She huffed, deflating in her chair.

Brian was right. He was just another victim of the tsunami takeover. She should save her wrath for their new boss.

But Balducci wouldn't be *her* boss for long. Not if he insisted on sweeping years' worth of work and results under the rug and forcing them to dance to his profit-hungry tune.

Despite a medical degree, two master's degrees and lucrative offers, she'd spent years at Biomedical Innovation Lab with a salary that barely paid the bills. All to do marginalized but necessary research.

Until Balducci Research and Development opened its bottomless maw and swallowed them whole. They now sloshed deep in its belly among other chomped-off acquisitions.

What most galled her was the humiliating speed with which everything had been initiated and finalized. The commercialized global whale, a major tentacle of the

Black Castle Enterprises leviathan, had assimilated them in mere hours.

Antonio Balducci, the billionaire celebrity surgeon, had tossed a hundred million dollars their way—chump change for him—and once again proved that money was the most powerful incentive on earth.

"Uh-oh." Brian took a step back as he spoke. "You've got that look on your face."

She frowned. "What look?"

"The one you get when you've decided to go to war."

She huffed a chuckle, half amused, half embarrassed. "I didn't realize I was *that* easy to read. After all the years I spent battling my verbal incontinence, thanks for letting me know I've only developed the mental and emotional variety."

An indulgent smile lit up Brian's genial face. "You're just straightforward and spontaneous."

She rolled her eyes. "Which are the PC words for unrestrained and blunt."

"And it's something everyone is thankful for."

She groaned. "You mean it's not only you as my best friend who can see through me? Everyone else can read me like a ten-foot neon sign?"

Brian's grin was appeasement itself. "And they love you for it. In a world full of pretense and games, you're a rarity and an incredible relief. Not to mention extremely cute."

"An outspoken five-year-old is cute. A transparent thirty-one-year-old is not."

Brian wrapped an arm around her shoulder and gave her an affectionate squeeze. "You'll be cute when you're a hundred and thirty-one." He pulled her up. "Now let's go meet our new boss. I have a feeling this won't be as bad as you think."

Taking off her lab coat, she tossed him a challenging glance. "I bet you it's worse."

"You're on." He never could resist a challenge. "If I'm right, you go on a date with one of the restless bachelors that plague my serenely married existence."

Unable to resist Brian's infectious good cheer any longer, a smile spread Lili's lips. All nine of Brian's brothers and brothers-in-law were either single or divorced. He and his wife, Darla, were always trying to set them up.

"But if I'm right," Lili said, "you strike me off your list of possible bachelordom cures. I'm the last woman on earth you should consider for such a task, anyway."

"I know, because you'll never get married. You've told me a hundred times." He grinned knowingly. "All the women who turn out to be the best wives say that. Including Darla."

Lili stifled a scoff. "You're comparing me to Darla, the paragon of domesticity and motherhood, and a savvy businesswoman to boot, when I can barely manage a single life that consists of work, exercise, sleep, study, rinse and repeat?"

"Details, details." Brian winked as he held the door open for her. "You could well be twins where it counts."

She shook her head, but let him have the last word. She was nothing like Darla or any other woman born with the ability to conduct intimate relationships or nurture families. Like her mother. And she'd long been at peace with that.

So she was confident she'd win their bet, and at least one good thing would come out of their current mess. Brian would finally stop trying to shove her into his version of a fulfilling existence.

As she passed him on her way out of the lab, she swept it in one last regretful look.

If things went according to her projections, as she was certain they would, this would be the last time she saw it.

Their new boss was late.

As she sat in her usual seat halfway down the conference table, Lili fumed.

Either Balducci had met his demise—and they couldn't possibly be that lucky—or he didn't consider them worthy of his legendary punctuality. And that boded even worse for them than she'd expected.

Her bleary gaze scanned the room. All thirty of the BIL employees were there and unlike her, they'd all clearly run back home to dress for the occasion, leaving only her in an appropriately drab-as-her-mood outfit. Also unlike her, they seemed relieved, even excited at the takeover. Even hating this as much as she did, Lili realized why. She had been feeling the toll of the obstacles they'd had to tackle continuously to do what other better-funded labs did in a fraction of the time. But to her, setbacks, false starts and near misses were an expected part of scientific endeavor. It seemed her attitude hadn't been shared by the others as she'd thought, and she was the only one with a purely negative stance on the takeover. And a hostile one toward the man behind it.

Everyone else was awed by the very mention of the legendary Dr. Antonio Balducci. The buzz she was sensing wasn't only over any favorable expectations with him at the helm, but also over the opportunity of meeting him in the flesh. The ladies especially looked aflutter at the prospect. From her online research of him, she grudgingly conceded their reaction was the normal one, not hers.

Since she reserved her curiosity for scientific matters, she'd barely known a thing about him before she'd heard the news. After she had, she'd gone through the stages of shock, denial and fury, and through everything she could find on him on the net.

To her surprise, she found three parallels with him from the first thing she read. Like her, he was a doctor, and he'd been born to an Italian father and was an only child. But that was where their similarities ended.

He was an American now, naturalized three years ago, while she was an American through her mother. Both his parents were long dead, while her own mother had died only a year ago, and her father who had never existed in her life, had recently—and to her continuing surprise, very enthusiastically—reentered it.

Pulling her thoughts away from that development, she turned them to the man at hand.

Not much was known about Antonio Balducci's early life. He was raised in Austria, his mother's homeland, where he became fluent in six languages and where he lived until he graduated from medical school. It was only about eight years ago that information about him, staggering in quantity and quality, had started pouring in.

That was when he'd shot onto the world scene, an awe-inspiring figure whose success in every field he entered was phenomenal. Being a founding member of the global juggernaut Black Castle Enterprises was meticulously documented, as well as his founding of the conglomerate's medical R & D business—the arm of his empire that had taken over her beloved lab.

Adding to his lure for the media was his effect on the females of the species. Women went nuts over him like they did over music and soccer legends like Presley and Beckham. If she'd thought his effect a media exaggeration, she was seeing empirical evidence of his irresistibility to women right before her eyes. And that was before he actually arrived.

But all that wasn't what he was best known for. Most of his fame stemmed from being sought after by the world's elite to perform or even consult on their rejuvenations. But his *biggest* achievement was being hailed as a trauma and reconstructive surgical god whose work bordered on magic.

She ground her teeth together. The only magic she thought Balducci practiced was the black kind. To her, he was the capricious force who was pulverizing everything she'd worked for, just because he could.

And the damned man dared be late for her destruction!

Suddenly conversation was cut off as if someone had

hit Stop. She looked up and saw all eyes glued to the doorway behind her. That meant…

She swung around to catch the moment when the man who'd quashed her ambitions bulldozed into her territory. And it was her turn to feel she'd been caught in a stasis field.

As everything decelerated to a standstill, a mental protest went off inside her mind.

No one should be all that, and look like that, too. Is there no fairness in this world?

Gaping and unable to do anything about it, she stared at the figure in the doorway. In a slate-gray suit that molded to a body that belonged to a world-class athlete, not a surgeon and entrepreneur, Antonio Balducci dwarfed the room with his physical and personal presence.

While viewing his photos online, she'd dismissed the possibility that he looked that good in real life, believing he'd had his photos touched up or he'd achieved his perfection surgically.

But even across a packed room, she knew neither of that was true. If anything, the photos had downplayed his looks. And she could discern surgical interventions from a mile away and she had no doubt whatsoever that every one of Antonio Balducci's jaw-dropping assets was authentic.

At forty, the man had skin that looked like an alloy of polished copper and bronze. The tensile medium was pulled tight over a masterpiece of bone structure. Her fingers itched to indulge in a much-neglected pastime and sketch its every detail: the leonine forehead, the patrician nose, the slashing cheekbones, the powerful jaw and cleft chin.

After transferring the framework of his unique face to paper, she'd linger over every hair framing his majestic head, the most robust mass of raven silk she'd ever seen. But among all those wonders, two things transfixed her. The wide, sculpted lips bowed in a mysterious quirk. And his eyes.

Apart from their amazing shape and startling blueness, it was what they conveyed that sent her heartbeat into disarray. Contrary to the opacity of his smile, his gaze radiated an amalgam of expressions. Amusement and austerity. Curiosity and superiority. Astuteness and calculation. And a dozen other things she couldn't decide on.

Those were the eyes of a scientist. But equally they were the eyes of a conqueror.

Which probably summed him up just right.

As he walked into room, déjà vu struck her.

Among his photos, one in particular had arrested her. A rare shot of him and his partners in Black Castle Enterprises.

They'd been captured as they'd exited their opulent New York headquarters en masse. It was an unrehearsed shot that was far more hard-hitting than any posed shot could have been, and it had earned its photographer instant fame.

The photo had captured their essence in such starkness that when it was published, Black Castle stock prices spiked to unheard-of levels. The men looked like a pantheon of warrior gods who'd descended to earth

in the guise of ultramodern businessmen. The array of
sheer male power and beauty in that photo was breathtaking. It had clearly robbed the whole world of breath.

Yet even among those gods among men, Antonio
had stood out.

Not only had his brand of gorgeousness thrummed
the chords of her specific taste, something else had
fascinated her on a fundamental level. Though they
were all extraordinary, she'd felt he had an edge over
the other men. Even in the remoteness of a photo she
felt he had the coolest head, the most deliberate mind.
Even in her fury, that had appealed to her so fiercely
she'd found herself saving the photo for leisurely in-
spection at a later date, maybe even as material for a
future illustration.

And here he was in the impossibly perfect flesh, the
epitome of splendor and sangfroid.

She wouldn't be surprised if he belonged to some
next-step-in-evolution elite who'd eliminated all human
frailties and imperfections and who operated on pure,
merciless intellect.

He now stopped at the table and leaned his six-foot-
plus frame to flatten his palms on its shining surface.

Seething with renewed resentment at his effect on
her, she followed his serene gaze as it swept the room.
From the chain reaction she felt going off around her,
he seemed to be making eye contact with everyone.
Everyone but her. His gaze skipped over her as if she
were a blank space.

After the momentary consternation of being passed
over, she was relieved. If his mere presence provoked

those reactions in her, she didn't want to find out what she'd feel if that all-seeing gaze bored into her.

Once he'd had them holding their breath, he inclined his head. "Thanks for accommodating me at such short notice. I'm glad you could all make it."

Man, that voice. If everything about him weren't too much already, that darkest vocal spell would have been bad enough on its own. Making it even worse was an ephemeral accent that intertwined through its meticulous articulation, deepening its impact.

As murmured responses rustled around the room, he straightened to his towering height.

"I don't want to hold you up, especially those of you whose schedule is nine to five, so I'll get right to the point of my visit." A perfectly timed dramatic pause. "I hope you're as optimistic as I am about the new state of affairs, and will find working under the Balducci umbrella a rewarding experience, scientifically and financially."

He spread a prompting smile around the room and Lili saw everyone grin back at him like hypnotized fools.

Without taking his eyes off the assembly, he gestured to someone she realized had been behind him all along. The shorter man in turn directed four people behind him to come forward. They had piles of folders, which they passed around the room. When it was her turn to receive one, she stared down at the inch-thick glossy volume graced with Balducci's distinctive serpent logo.

"In your hands is comprehensive info on Balducci's operations," he explained. "As well as the mission statement for its new merger with your facility." Merger, huh? Big of him to call his incursion that. "Until you read everything in detail, let me give you a brief summation.

"I founded Balducci R & D to furnish the world with visionary medical solutions. A dynamic, adventurous and fast-paced researching, manufacturing and distribution organization specializing in state-of-the-art products and technologies in a number of leading medical fields. My aim remains to provide the medical community with unparalleled clinical products that set the trend in medicine. For six years, Balducci has been the primary supplier, to hospitals, clinics and research institutions, of advanced medical solutions in a variety of fields. With a constantly growing global team of the best the world has to offer in their disciplines, which I'm proud for you to be a part of now, we provide exceptional value, service and support much above the industry standard. And we achieve the highest customer retention rates in every market we currently dominate. But there are new frontiers I aim to conquer." Yeah, just what she'd figured. "And this is where you come in."

Everyone sat up, taking even closer notice. The man really had masterful timing and delivery.

When he'd made sure everyone was hanging on his every breath, he went on, "I don't need to tell you that your team is composed of some of the most avant-garde researchers of our time. I have no doubt you're well aware of your individual and collective worth. I certainly am best equipped to know it. I'm still suffering from the very sizable hole in my assets it took to acquire your services."

As chuckles of pleasure spread through the room, Lili's hackles rose higher. What was wrong with her colleagues? They were proud they had a price? Sure, he pretended "acquiring their services" had taken a toll on him, but they all knew this was untrue. The man was worth over a dozen *billion* dollars!

Then he spoke again, dousing her new spurt of irritation.

"The methods and results you've contributed to the medical community working with limited funding and resources is nothing short of astounding. Each and every one of you is exactly the kind of unique-approach, enterprising scientist that Balducci covets. As you'll see from the documents you have in your possession now, each of you has been assigned to a project I believe you're most suited for, where you'll have anything you could possibly want to make progress in it, and hopefully reach a breakthrough. And let me be clear. By anything, I do mean *anything*. My assistants will be available to provide any of your needs. But my own door is always open if what you need is too ambitious, as I hope all your work with me will be."

By the time he finished, she was gaping again.

The man was overpowering. Velvet over steel over an enigma. Not only the most magnificent male she'd ever seen, but the most persuasive, too.

What he'd outlined was every scientist's fairy tale come true. Unlimited resources to be as adventurous as they wished, caring only about the work, while funding and feasibility were being taken care of by dedicated experts with access to bottomless pockets and powered by limitless ambition. His.

He'd almost convinced even her. Almost.

But if she had to fight his hypnosis with all she had, she had no doubt the others were already in his thrall. A darting glance noted the glassy eyes of those who no longer questioned that his decreed path was the one to tread. Even Brian had a budding hero-worship expression on his face.

"That would all be well and good, *if* you were offering to fund our projects, not yours."

It wasn't until everyone swung to gape at her as if she'd thrown a grenade on the table that she realized she'd spoken.

And she did it again, without intending to.

"In your R & D career, you've consistently ignored basic research, what has produced centuries of history-changing breakthroughs, spawned whole industries and disciplines in medicine. You've also ignored the kind of research we do, of untrendy ailments that don't provoke public or market interest. You've overlooked necessary research for a jumble of popular, feel-good, cash-cow fields like the cosmetic and weight-loss industries."

The elusive smile that had been hovering on his lips suddenly froze.

All her blood followed suit.

Her heart thudding, she wished for some cosmic rewind button so she could erase what she'd just said.

Why had she spoken at all? She'd already found out her worst-case scenario would come to pass and they'd be herded wherever he wished. She didn't do posturing confrontations. She knew her power, or rather, lack thereof. So why hadn't she kept her big mouth shut and just tendered her resignation in silence?

Before she could draw another breath into her constricted lungs, he turned his head in her direction and impaled her on the lasers he had for eyes.

And all she could think was…uh-oh.

Two

Lili's heart plummeted as the world emptied of everything but this overwhelming entity who had her in his crosshairs.

Before she obeyed the flight mechanisms that screamed for her to run, tossing a "Don't bother firing me, I quit" over her shoulder, Antonio Balducci started talking, pinning her down even more.

"As my reconstructive surgeries do incorporate an aesthetic element, I do invest in the development and manufacture of all aesthetic disciplines and products."

His voice. That perfectly modulated melody of cultured lethality. A glacial sound of hair-raising beauty. Pouring all over her like a freezing/searing deluge.

Oh, crap. She hadn't thought this through. Hadn't

thought at all. That bitter outburst had just…well, burst out of her. What if he got verbally combative?

She'd flay him right back, that was what. Before she ran.

But before she snatched the next breath, still trans-fixing her with that impossibly blue stare, he went on, serene and far more menacing because of it, "As you'll see from the info I provided, only twenty percent of my operations focus on the 'popular, feel-good, cash-cow' side of my specialty."

Whoa. He was quoting what she'd said. When she'd thought he'd only realized she'd been talking—and criti-cizing him openly—just before her tirade ended.

But he hadn't only heard her, he'd memorized what she'd said. He'd even *sounded* like her when he'd quoted her. She had a feeling he could recite everything she'd said word for word. Which shouldn't surprise her. It only substantiated her theory of him being some sort of post–human being.

His eyes bored into her, making her feel he'd drilled a hole into her skull and was probing her brain. "The re-maining eighty percent of my operations revolve around the more relevant sides of my field of interest, and those of others. Problem is those don't generate media cov-erage or capture the market's imagination. This is just the state of the world. I didn't invent it."

"No, you just exploit it."

At her volley, he tilted his head, as if plunging deeper into her mind. Then those chiseled lips twitched and her stuttering heart burst into a stumbling gallop.

"The pursuit of luxury products tends to trump necessary ones and 'cash cows' are such for a reason. Alas, human beings will be human beings. I assure you, I have no role in their condition. So what would you have me do? Not provide them with what they wish for? Judge their foibles and let someone else reap the benefits of catering to them? Benefits I eventually put to uses you might deem to approve of?"

Was he teasing her? Nah. He couldn't be.

"And aesthetic concerns are not frivolous luxuries. No matter how *you* view them, they do greatly affect people's psychological and mental health. I don't morally grade what people need or consider worth paying for. Who's to say that products that reverse the signs of aging aren't as important to a substantial percentage of people as depression treatment? And would you view me and my business any kinder if you knew I also research the latter? And am involved in actual aging reversal research, too?"

Okay, he *was* teasing her. Poking fun at her, more like, making her criticism sound misinformed and holier-than-thou, or at the very least naive. And seeming to draw appreciation from everyone in the room while at it, adding to the unhealthy awe he'd already garnered.

He only made her feel like a hedgehog with its bristles standing on end. Mostly because she found her own lips twitching, too.

So, the man had a sense of humor. Had he come complete with it, or had he had it grafted as another weapon in his overflowing arsenal? Or did he realize the benefits of manipulating lesser beings with the illusion of ease and indulgence, and had a subroutine written into his program that he could activate at will?

"Among the commendable-by-your-standards investments I can afford to make with the profits of not-so-commendable ones, there are ones in my own field. Restoring functionality, for instance. Thanks to the money-generating machines, I can invest heavily into integrated prosthetics, microsurgery appliances and research, scar prevention and treatment, and lately, muscle and nerve tissue regeneration. *That* endeavor will be the main focus of this facility in our collaboration. I'm not even putting a limit to the budget for this one. Whatever it takes to reach a breakthrough, I'll provide the resources."

Then just as he'd given her his undiluted attention, he took it away, making her feel as if he'd taken the chair and the ground beneath it right out from under her.

Before she realized she had a response to his rebuttal, she found herself sitting up, her pose confrontational, her tone even more challenging. "Well, it's all quite laudable, I'm sure, that—while not advancing basic science as only someone of your clout and resources can—you invest in advancing your field. But 'this facility' already has its own array of 'commendable' projects under way, and it would be a loss that can't be measured in money if we shelved them to head in the direction where you point us. Just because you acquired our services doesn't mean you can cancel all our efforts, or should dictate which breakthrough is worth benefiting from our expertise backed by your unlimited funds and clout."

This time everyone in the room turned to stab her on the pointy edge of their disapproval. The canny man had already won them over to his side, promising them shiny new projects, not to mention endless means to frolic in the land of scientific possibilities to their hearts' content.

This time, Balducci didn't give her the courtesy of a response. His argument had been designed to win her over, or at least chastise her. From her renewed attack he must have decided further response wouldn't make a difference. As the epitome of pragmatism someone of his success must be, he'd decided she wasn't worth the extra effort. He wouldn't waste more time on a dissenting cog now that he was certain he had the rest of the machine wagging its components awaiting his directives.

Turning his attention to the rest, he directed everyone to read the folder carefully. Everyone's roles and projects for the next year were spelled out to the last detail. Tomorrow would be the first working day under the new management, and he would be available at the provided email or phone number for any questions, concerns or minor adjustments. Any major suggestions would be discussed in the next general meeting. He closed by thanking everyone in such a way as to have them swooning all over again before he dismissed the assembly.

Everyone rose to shuffle around him, waiting their turn to catch his eye or shake his hand. Lili cursed them for the limpets they'd turned into, and cursed him for turning them into such. Still, she was thankful for the milling crowd that gave her the cover under which to escape. Snatching her bag up, leaving the folder behind, she rose. Head down, giving him the widest berth she could, she made a beeline for the door. To her dismay, he was making short work of everyone, and those he'd dismissed were already squeezing out of the room, hindering her escape. She barely curbed the urge to push through them and forced herself to take her turn walking out. Still she bristled at the censure and pity in their oblique gazes, but mostly at *his* disconcerting vibe at her back.

In minutes, she burst out into LA's summer afternoon. She usually hated the transition from the beloved seclusion of her lab and the building's controlled climate to the hot, humid bustle of the sprawling city. But now she was relieved to be out of what had become a place she'd hate to set foot in again. The place that was now Antonio Balducci's.

She'd reached her Mazda in the parking lot when she felt as if an arrow had lodged between her shoulder blades.

It was his voice. Calling her.

What the hell!

Though her hand froze in midair with the remote, her thoughts streaked ahead. Did she dread him so much, like a kid dreads the headmaster singling her out, that she was imagining it? Even if he had called her, he must be here only to get his car, too.

In the next millisecond her analytical mind negated that theory. Antonio Balducci wouldn't use public parking. He wouldn't have driven himself here in the

first place. One of those people who followed in his
wake like efficient phantoms must be his chauffeur.
He couldn't have just stumbled on her. Which meant he
must have pursued her specifically, and very quickly.
Which made even less sense than any other theory.

As her mind burned rubber, his voice carried to her
on the warm, moist breeze again, the very sound of
forbearance.

"Dr. Accardi, I'd appreciate a word."

She swung around, her face scrunching against the
declining sun in a scowl. "What for?"

She groaned at how petulant and aggressive she
sounded. But this guy tripped all her wires. Watching him approach her like a sleek panther sent them
haywire. He was so big he made the parking lot claustrophobic, so unhurried he made her feel cornered, so
unearthly gorgeous he made her every nerve ache.

When he stopped two feet away, he siphoned the
air from the world. Harsh sunlight struck deepest blue
and indigo off his raven hair—which she realized had
a smattering of silver at the temples—and threw his
every feature in sharp relief, intensifying his beauty.
She was sure she looked horrible in such unforgiving
lighting, but Dr. Paragon here? He was even more perfect at such total exposure.

As the word *exposure* dragged her mind places it
didn't want to go, she yanked it back and squinted way
up at him even from her five-foot-eight height. She mentally kicked herself for not having her sunglasses as a
barrier to hide behind, as protection against his all-seeing
gaze. But since she always went home long after sun-

down, frequently not at all, she rarely packed them. As if they would have been an extra burden in her mobile home of a tote bag. But that was what she was—always ready for all possibilities in her work, and the personification of unpreparedness in her personal life. Which she now was in such a close encounter with the monolith before her.

Just as she thought he'd stare down at her until he melted her at his feet, he raised his hand, making her notice the folder he'd been holding all the time.

"I brought you this," he said. "You must have forgotten it."

He followed her to give her the folder she'd left behind?

Her mind raced to decipher him and his actions as her senses crackled with his nearness. When she spoke, she sounded exasperated, even if she was more so with herself. "No, I haven't forgotten it."

"So you left it on purpose."

"Apart from omission or commission, are there any other reasons I could have left it behind?"

One corner of his lips lifted in acknowledgment of her chastising logic, intensifying his already staggering effect. She hated to think how he'd look outright smiling or laughing.

"My apologies for the redundant comment. Will asking about the reason you did leave it meet with the same exasperation?"

She exhaled, trying to find the civil, easygoing person inside her who was generally in the driver's seat... and failing. "From what I read about you, and from the evidence of your achievements and power, you possess an unchartable IQ. I'm sure you need none of it to work out the reason I did."

"Indeed. Your motivation is quite clear. It was a material rejection to underscore your verbal one. I had just hoped it was a simple oversight on your part."

"And since you now know it wasn't, if this will be all…"

His forward movement cut off her backward one, along with her air supply again. "Actually, it won't be all. Bringing you the folder was incidental to the main reason I sought you out." He employed another of those pauses he used like weapons, making her bate whatever breath was left in her lungs. "I'd like to further discuss your objections to my policies."

She gaped up at him. That was the last thing she would have thought he'd say, or want. Not that she could actually think with him so near. She could only react.

Not finding any appropriate reaction, the first thing that surfaced in her mind was another accusation. "You said you didn't want to hold us up."

He gave a conceding tilt of his head that made his hair rearrange itself into another pattern of perfection. She could swear she heard the silk swish and sigh.

"I did make it clear I meant those who have a nine-to-five schedule. You're not one of those. In fact, you're the only one who almost makes this place your home."

She stared into his spellbinding eyes as he stared back with the same intentness.

How did he know that?

How? Because the man had a level of intelligence and efficiency she'd never before encountered. It stood to reason he'd researched the staff before he'd acquired them. Though she'd thought they'd be too insignificant for him individually, she had to revise that opinion. To reach his level of success he couldn't be a detached leader who left details to others. He had to be hands-on. Nothing and no one was too trivial or below his notice.

She wouldn't be surprised if he had invasive info on everyone who held or would hold any position in his businesses...and had memorized it, too. Thinking that disconcerted her on a primal level. Even if there wasn't much about her to know, just that he did know it put her at an even bigger disadvantage, if that was even possible.

"Nothing to go back home to?"

His quiet question surprised an unfiltered answer from her. "There never really was."

Her dismay deepened at the contemplative cast that came over his gaze. She'd exposed herself even more, and she held him accountable for it, him with his damned hypnotic power.

But her consternation was swept away by the surge of memories. Memories of growing up with only her mother, who moved her around so much following her medical career she'd never stayed long enough in one place to form real friendships. Only when Lili had entered medical school herself had her mother finally settled in LA, just before she fell prey to early-onset Alzheimer's. Lili had gone back to live with her, before being forced to put her in a home for four years before her death a year ago. Her mother's house remained a place to crash when she wasn't working. Being a workaholic was what saved her from feeling lonely. It was the only other thing she'd inherited from her mother. Hopefully. Home had always been wherever she worked. This lab had been her home for the past three years. Her haven. Until *he* happened.

"There you go again."

"There I go what again?"

His lips spread wider. The ground beneath her tilted. "Using me as target practice for your poison-laced glances."

Choking on the heart that his smile yanked into her throat, she shrugged. "They're just dipped in heavy tranquilizers. Or loaded with fifty thousand volts."

At that, he did something she'd dreaded in theory, but had thought would never come to pass in reality. Not in her presence.

He threw his head back and laughed.

And his laughter was…horrible. It did terrible things to her insides, had her hormones rushing in torrents in her system.

Great. Just great. Just when she discovered she had those kinds of hormones after all, they had to be activated by him of all men. And in broad daylight. When he was laughing his magnificent head off at her, no less.

To make things worse, one big, elegant hand rose to wipe his left cheek. He'd laughed so hard, it had wrung a tear from his eye. Fantastic.

But what was really worth marveling at was how

moisture smeared his hewn flesh. Her thoughts caught fire imagining him drenched in exertion, during or after he'd—

Shaking away the sensual images only lodged them deeper into her brain. Her tongue tingled with until-now unknown urges—the sudden longing to drag him down to her, so she could trace that cheekbone, taste his virility. Only his hand combing back the hair that had fallen over his forehead distracted her from those idiotic impulses. The hand of the virtuoso surgeon he was, powerful, graceful, skillful…in every possible way, no doubt—

For God's sake, stop. *Stop noticing his every detail and getting arrhythmia over each one!*

But in the absence of others, she had no buffer against his sheer charisma and sensual power—both of which she was certain he didn't even mean to exercise on her. A man like him must have them on all the time on auto. She'd never even thought men like him existed outside of legends and fairy tales.

After she'd become a jumbled mess, he sobered, the wattage of his smile dazzling her.

"So you don't want me dead, just incapacitated."

She fidgeted, her tote getting heavier by the second. "Ideally, long enough to remove you from my path. I want you gone from my world, not the one at large."

"That's big of you."

Nerves jangling at the outright teasing she could no longer mistake, she sighed. "When it doesn't come to my lab—yours now—I do recognize that, even if it's to your humongous advantage, you are a formidable force for good."

His eyebrows shot up. "Considering your views of me back there it's unexpected to hear you admit that."

"I'm a surprise a second. To myself most of all today. I sure didn't mean to say any of the things I said back there."

"So you didn't mean them?"

"I said I didn't mean to *say* them."

"So you did mean them."

"Can't mean anything more, in the context of my own concerns." She shot him a defiant glance, this man who'd detained her because he could do anything he wanted and have the world bend over backward to accommodate him. "You're sadly misguided if you think you'll get an apology or a retraction."

"You've given me both when you deigned to recognize my worth to the world."

"Still doesn't change the fact that I wish I had the power to make you disappear."

He shook his head, his grin widening, wreaking more havoc with her already compromised nerves.

"What do you find so funny now?" she mumbled sullenly.

"Not funny, delightful. You're definitely not the first person to wish to eliminate me, but you're the first to tell me so to my face."

"Hey, watch your terminology. You go around using words like *poison-laced* and *eliminate*, and if something ever befalls you, I'm a prime suspect. I only wish to be rid of your disruption. All I want is to go back to work tomorrow to the news that you've withdrawn your bid and let us be."

"And if a way presented itself for you to make this happen?"

"I wouldn't hesitate."

He gave another chuckle. "It doesn't seem you were handed discretion at the cosmic assembly line. Are you this blunt with everyone?"

Noticing the watchfulness that entered his gaze at this question, getting the feeling that he somehow didn't relish the idea, she shrugged a shoulder. "Not since I was a kid. Or at least I thought so, until just before you arrived and Brian told me I'm transparent. I thought it was only my expressions that everyone could read, that I wasn't as incontinent verbally, then you started your hypnotic session and I felt my colleagues being assimilated into your hive mind, and I…well, any tact I thought I cultivated evaporated."

"You don't like this about yourself." It was a statement, not a question. "You should. In fact, you should continue being as outspoken about the grievance you have with me. I have a feeling it goes beyond objecting to the change in course I'm proposing."

She almost snorted. "Proposing? You mean dictating. And you think that's not enough for me to consider you and your takeover the worst thing that could happen to this place?"

"I didn't get the impression anyone else shared that unfavorable opinion."

This time, she did snort. "Of course, you didn't. You must be surprised there was even one dissenting voice."

Her blood frothed again at how her colleagues had succumbed to him without even a fight. "You know very
well the effect you have on people."

"I only noticed the inflammatory one I had on you."

"Yeah, well, I guess I'm the mad scientist type."

"Aren't you all supposed to be that?"

She exhaled. "I thought so. But the promise of open-
ended coddling proved irresistible to my colleagues."

"But not to you."

Her shoulders hunched with futility. "Yeah."

The blue of his eyes seemed to intensify. "Why?
What makes you so resistant? Why is the promise of
everything you've ever dreamed of at your fingertips
not as alluring to you?"

"I told you why in agonizing detail and you already
know I hate redundancy. Especially after you took such
pleasure in deconstructing my argument and having
the last word."

"I don't remember I had the last word."

"You didn't bother to have it. You just ignored mine."

"I chose not to engage you again in front of everyone, decided to do so in private. As I am doing now."

"You shouldn't have. I have nothing more to say."

"So do you only take exception to leaving your own
project behind?"

"I take exception to being forced to."

"Your results won't evaporate if you shelve them
for a while."

"I see no reason to while I'm making progress."

"There are many reasons, scientific and financial.

You'll also gain expertise working on my projects, your own work would eventually benefit."

"If you think I need expertise you shouldn't want me working on your projects."

"I meant added expertise. I wouldn't have paid all that money if I thought you were anything but the best."

She waved his placating response away. "You didn't pay anything for me. That hundred million—"

"*Two* hundred million. Half of which is funding for phase one of all the projects I have planned for you."

She forced her open mouth closed. "What's a hundred million dollars more, huh? But whatever you paid was for our collective services and obedience, probably for the rest of our lives. Now that you've found one troublemaking apple in your bushel, you can always toss it out."

"I have no intention of tossing you out."

"Well, I intend to jump out of the cart myself."

His eyes narrowed. "You're contemplating quitting?"

"I'm done contemplating."

His expression went blank. But though there was nothing to read in it anymore, she felt she was getting the first real glimpse of what he hid beneath the polished exterior of the genius surgeon and suave businessman. Something lurked below his placid surface, something more sharp-edged than his state-of-the-art scalpels. *Someone* utterly ruthless. No, more. Someone lethal.

Which was stupid. Whatever else he was, this man was a healer. He didn't end lives, he saved them. All these feverish thoughts must be the sun frying her brain. Or was it such intense and close exposure to him?

Then he spoke again, sending her every hair standing on end. "It's clear contemplation has nothing to do with your decision. I wouldn't even call such a knee-jerk reaction one."

He again sounded like when he'd been addressing their assembly, making her realize how deliberate and calculated he had been in comparison to how he'd been talking to her now. He had been out to subdue and mesmerize everyone. He was trying to make her bow to his will now.

Well, he should have realized by now that his tried and true methods only backfired with her.

Bent on walking away this time, she stood as tall as she could. "Call it what you like. I quit, Dr. Balducci. I'm sure my loss will be nothing more than a negligible annoyance, since BIL is chock-full of those who will ecstatically do your bidding."

"You can't quit, Dr. Accardi."

"Because the lump sum you paid included my price? Just a sec…" She took the bag off her shoulder, rummaged for her wallet, pulled the money she found and stuck the bills out to him.

"What's that supposed to be?"

Extending her hand as close as she dared get to him, she met his glowering with her own. "I don't know what the going rate per head was, but taking into account the premises and everything else, I'm sure I didn't cost you more than that."

His eyes fell to the notes before he raised them to her, full of mockery. "I assure you, you cost me much more than that."

She refused to lower her hand. "You let me know exactly what I cost you, and I'll pay for my freedom in installments. Consider this the first one."

As he realized she wasn't joking, his gaze clashed with hers as if to make her cower before him. She was sure such a glare had brought many adversaries to their knees. Tough, it was going to let him down this time. Even if she felt he'd set her on fire if she held his stare any longer.

A second before she averted her own eyes, he suddenly looked down at the money. He plucked three hundred-dollar bills from the bunch before he raised his eyes again and almost knocked her flat on her back with the mischief filling them.

"Now you really can't quit."

She gaped at his wicked grin. "What?"

"You just paid me for shares in your facility. Now you have to stay and run the place with me. Or for me."

Before another thought could fire in her stalled brain, he turned and strode away.

Out of nowhere, a sleek black limo slithered soundlessly up to him.

Before he got in, he turned to her with a mock salute and said, "See you tomorrow, partner."

Three

Antonio caught himself grinning again and again all the way back to his mansion in Holmby Hills.

Shaking his head for the umpteenth time since he'd left Liliana Accardi gaping at him as if he'd grown a spiked tail and leather wings and taken flight, he again wondered what the hell had happened in that parking lot. Actually, what the hell had happened since she'd blasted him in that meeting room.

This wasn't what he'd envisioned at all. Not after everything had gone according to plan. At first.

He'd made the bid on the lab, knowing he'd find no resistance. He'd finalized everything in record time before moving to the next phase—conquering his new subordinates. He'd done that, too, with more acceptance

OLIVIA GATES   41

than his best projections, thanks to his long-perfected methods of making people do his bidding.

He'd started practicing his influence from childhood when he'd been in the clutches of The Organization, which had taken him and hundreds of children to turn them into lethal mercenaries. Even among his brotherhood, as unyielding as they were, he'd enjoyed a unique position of power. While Phantom—Numair now—had been the leader everyone deferred to, it had been Antonio everyone trusted to have the most levelheaded opinion. When he'd become their medical expert, they'd trusted him with their very lives.

He'd taken that skill into the outside world after they'd escaped The Organization. Normal people had been no match for the sway he'd honed with some of the world's most shrewd and lethal people. He'd plowed through the worlds of medicine and business like a laser, being described by rivals and allies alike as irresistible and unstoppable. Not that he reached his goals through aggression or intimidation. He relied on persuasion and manipulation, so no one had a reason to fight him and every reason to succumb to him.

Among his brothers, he was the one who had an equally close and friction-free relationship with all. Yet he'd allowed not even them beyond the serene facade he'd refined.

They believed it was Wildcard—or Ivan Konstantinov as he now called himself—who knew Antonio fully, as he'd been closest to him since childhood. But Antonio hadn't even let Ivan in on everything he'd been through or everything he was. He hadn't told Ivan anything he was doing or planning now.

While the others had searched for their families, sought reunion with them and/or revenge on those who'd stolen them away, Ivan, who'd come to The Organization old enough to know his family, had elected not to contact his family once he'd been out. Antonio had elected not to bother with either finding his origins or seeking revenge. Or so he'd told his brothers. In reality, he'd found out everything about his family.

What he'd learned had made him think The Organization had done him a favor by abducting him. His Italian aristocracy family put its members through hell for appearances' sake, which they enforced at any expense, even abandoning or destroying any of them who threatened their traditions and standing.

As they had him.

His mother's pregnancy when she was seventeen had threatened their image. Her inappropriate lover had been dealt with, while she'd been taken away to avoid the scandal. The same day she'd given birth to him, he'd been given to an orphanage, from which he'd been culled by The Organization less than four years later. Up until that day he'd lived hoping his "real family" would find him.

It turned out he'd been better off with The Organization than in the Accardis' sterile, cold-blooded environment where relationships were warped and members turned into shells of human beings. At least The Organization had let him pursue his true inclinations, what had made him who he was. It had been there he'd forged stronger-than-blood ties with his brothers, nothing like the pathological ones his family shared.

He'd at first decided to ignore the existence of the family that had wronged him so irretrievably. But after three of his brothers had found their roots and reunited with their own families, he'd begun to feel restless until he'd realized that he was being eaten alive with the need to even the score.

And to do that, he had to destroy the Accardis. Starting with his mother.

Agreeing to or at least accepting her family's crime, she hadn't attempted to search for him, had moved on instead and gotten married three times. She'd had legitimate offspring with each of her husbands as well as adopted children. The oldest was a man five years younger than him, the youngest a girl of twelve, making his crop of half siblings no less than six.

He'd planned to infiltrate the family anonymously, to exact up close and personal retribution on those who'd had a hand in his abandonment.

But the elitist snobs hadn't opened up to him, not even with the bait of vital financial relief. Getting close to this family could be through the only way they allowed.

Through blood. Through a member.

After a thorough analysis of the extended family, he'd zeroed in on one member. Liliana Accardi.

Liliana was the daughter of Alberto Accardi, his mother's third cousin. Her American mother had escaped Italy and the poisonous Accardi family when Liliana was only one and run back to the States. But after her mother's death last year, the only child, family-less

Liliana had started to reestablish relations with her father. The man who hadn't bothered to see his daughter after he'd granted her mother a lucrative divorce was now eager to welcome her into his life. Surprisingly, the rest of the Accardis seemed as enthusiastic to invite her into the family. That had added to her potential use to Antonio.

Being a fellow doctor was another thing that had made her his best choice. And the fact that she'd graduated at the top of her class, but had ended up in a minor nonprofit lab battling impossible odds. Her quixotic tendencies had only made him consider her an even easier target. Everything else about her from looks to personal history had made her the most surefire as well as most tolerable vehicle for his needs.

He'd decided to approach her in a professional setting, bait her, snare her, then through her, enter the family, exact punishment from within, then walk away when they'd all paid, each to the exact measure he'd decide they deserved.

As for Liliana, she'd been wronged, too, if on an infinitely smaller scale. Though he'd despised her for seeking the family who'd driven her mother away and made Liliana grow up alone, to court their favor and inclusion, he'd intended to be lenient with her. *If* she provided him with a smooth ride to his life's most anticipated surgery, that of excising the petrified heart of the family who'd thrown him away like so much garbage.

He'd had no doubt she'd fall at his feet like all subordinates, like all women. The plan was simple. He'd make a proposal she'd grab at. After all, it would make a much more convincing entry into her family if she was delirious at her phenomenal luck. Then when he broke it off, if she'd benefited him—and if she didn't turn out to be another soulless Accardi or a greedy female—he'd compensate her handsomely.

Then he'd entered that meeting room, delivered his opening speech, and though he'd had the expected deference and delight from everyone else, he'd gotten none of the usual fluttering anticipation and adulation from her. Instead, she'd left him in no doubt of her reaction to his takeover, nor of her opinion of him.

From then on, everything had gone off the rails.

After his first surprise at her impassioned attack on his methods, history and person, he'd tried to overpower her, herd her back to his scripted pathway. Just as he'd thought he'd put her in the place where he needed her to stay, she'd retaliated with a more incontrovertible accusation.

Everything in him had surged to engage her full-on. But that would have been fodder for gossip and would have put him in a defensive position—something he'd never let himself be in. That had been when he'd realized he'd miscalculated.

The woman he'd thought would fall into his palm like a ripe plum had turned out to be a prickly pear.

A change of strategy had been in order.

But for the first time in memory, he couldn't come up with a course of action but to dismiss her. So he'd let her final words hang there in the conference room without a rebuttal from him. That confrontation had ended with the score of Liliana Accardi one, him nothing.

He had decided to resume her conquest the next day, after he'd upgraded his plan. But he'd itched with impatience, all his senses trained on her, the only one of the staff to avoid him. He'd pretended he hadn't noticed her as she'd kept her distance on her way out, when in truth he'd noticed nothing but her.

At one point, when she'd been closest to him, his resolve to ignore her had almost broken down. But he'd managed to let her walk out without doing something stupid.

Then he'd noticed the folder.

He'd realized adjusting his plan might be for nothing. This contrary woman might not be giving him another day. She'd forced him to pursue her there and then.

He'd still been certain that once he had her one-on-one, he'd bring her back in line. But the more he'd tried, the more she'd forced him to improvise, and the more he had, the further away from his desired results he'd gotten.

Not only hadn't he managed to overwhelm her, she'd taken him by surprise again and again. He'd found himself reacting without the least premeditation, something he never did. Then he'd found himself guffawing like a fool. He hadn't meant to laugh, but her unfiltered responses had been so unexpected and droll, she'd been the one to overpower his control and intent.

Not that his unprecedented spontaneity had earned him any leniency. Her disapproval and resistance had only increased until she'd swung the wrecking ball of her "I quit" right into him.

And she'd meant it. He'd been certain she had.

Just as he'd thought he was down to coercion, she'd done that most ridiculous thing, offering him the money she had on her. After his initial perplexity, it had been like a light had burst inside him, illuminating the tunnel of dwindling options she'd squeezed him in. How to end this impasse on a high note. His solution, not to mention its effect on her when he'd declared it, had brightened his mood in a way he hadn't felt in…ever.

Suddenly, the grin stretching his lips since he'd left her in that parking lot froze.

He might have decided to change the dynamics of dealing with her, but if he'd learned anything about Liliana Accardi so far, it was that she cared nothing about his power or wealth or what she could gain from them. To her, he was nothing but the invader who'd stormed into and defiled what she considered her home.

His parting shot might have been the worst thing he could have said. That defiant creature could now be working herself into a lather, more determined than ever not to return to the lab.

When the limo stopped, his mood was blacker than it had ever been, even during his worst days in The Organization.

Seething in uncharacteristic exasperation, he heaved out of the car and strode inside his mansion, thunderclouds roiling through his veins.

Damn that Liliana Accardi.

He'd picked her as the easy-to-tame lab rat, and she'd turned out to be an impossible-to-curb hellcat.

He had no time for a struggle with her. She wasn't

even his target, just a means to an end. But instead of
a solution, she'd turned out to be an insoluble problem.

If she insisted on defying him, he'd let her quit. But
he'd make sure she'd find no other job in the country.
Hell, on earth. She'd either work for him or she could
go flip burgers. He'd put her in her place, doing exactly
what he thought her good for. Then he'd search for a
more amenable member of the Accardis as his bridge
into that accursed family.

It was only an hour later, under the beating needles
of a punishing jet shower, when he found himself stroking a painfully hard erection to an explosive climax to
the memory of the mutinous passion in Liliana's eyes,
that he realized his plan was inapplicable.

Logic said he should consider her a lost cause. But
this volcanic lust she'd provoked in him—more inexplicable because it was for her being, not her body, which
he hadn't even properly seen—made it impossible for
him to walk away from her or let her walk away from
him. It was the last thing he'd thought would happen,
but he *wanted* that aggravating, uncontrollable rebel.

It no longer mattered to him why he'd wanted to tame
and acquire her in the first place. All that mattered to
him now was that he did. For his own pleasure.

He'd never done anything for his own pleasure.

High time he did. And Liliana Accardi, that intrac-
table creature, the first one to ever defy and spurn him,
was the perfect place to start.

Lili ended the phone call with Brian and pinched
the bridge of her nose, hard.

She didn't need this. Not after the night she'd had.

After Antonio Balducci had left her feeling punch-drunk, she'd driven home, garnering way more honks from disgruntled drivers than she usually did. She'd never gotten used to driving in LA. Never gotten used to living in that house. All she could think of was it was time to let it all go. Let her mother's memory and everything she'd built in this city go.

That was all she could think when she could focus on anything but Antonio Balducci. When every word he'd said to her, every look, every inflection of his voice and peal of his laughter hadn't been revolving in her mind like a mini tornado.

She'd arrived at the house exhausted in a way she hadn't been since her mother's final days. But her fatigue hadn't been soaked with despondence, but with jittery restlessness.

Antonio had messed her up but good. And he'd known it. He'd almost skipped away knowing he'd shut her up and had the last word this time.

If she'd surprised him with her resistance, he'd shocked her with his response.

See you tomorrow, partner.

Indeed!

When she'd finally fallen asleep, she'd fallen into a turbulent realm filled with heart-hammering glimpses and whispers and touches. All of him.

She'd woken up burning and wet, sure he'd meant to invade her dreams. She'd never squirmed for release like that, but had drawn the line at seeking it. He could rule her subconscious, but she was damned if she'd con-

sciously give him that power over her, even if only she
would know about it.

At least that was what she'd told herself until she'd
sought the relief of a hot bath and ended up bringing
herself to an unprecedented orgasm to his memory.

Damn him.

She'd been still trembling with aftershocks when
Brian had called her. Antonio had asked him to let her
know their first management meeting was at two sharp.

At Brian's rabid curiosity, she'd said Antonio was
just messing with her, as punishment for daring not to
prostrate herself at his feet, like they'd all done. She
doubted Brian bought that. Even when she believed it
to be the truth.

She'd underestimated Antonio's need for control.
He'd pursued her to lasso her back when she'd dared be
the only one who didn't roll over and expose her belly.
She'd struggled against his inexorable influence, trying
to make him consider her a troublemaker not worth the
effort it would take to subjugate her, to maintain his no
doubt pristine dominance record. That had only backfired, judging by his parting shot.

Even then, she'd really thought she didn't have to
worry about him anymore. He might be obsessive when
it came to getting his way, but she was certain he was
too busy to bother with his employees again, especially
rebellious ones. She'd thought he'd walk away and forget all about her, or remember her only as a weird creature who'd afforded him passing amusement. She'd been
secure—and oppressively let down—that she'd never
see him again.

Then Brian had called.

Antonio hadn't been joking. Or maybe he had been, and he hadn't finished yanking her chain yet. It appeared she entertained him, and it was equally obvious he hadn't had enough of her diversion yet.

Problem was, she had to oblige him.

He was the one to give her the end-of-service releases, recommendations and payments. As much as she would have loved to not look back, she needed all that to be able to leave and survive until she found a new job.

After dressing in her most funereal outfit, she pulled her unruly hair—which seemed to have more red in its auburn depths to go with her mood—in a severe bun. Forgoing even the little makeup she usually wore, she winced at her reflection.

Now that she was aware how she looked to others, she could see that everything she felt was emblazoned on her face. Aversion, aggression, anticipation and, dammit, arousal.

She shouldn't have given in to the urge to seek release. It had done nothing but inflame her more. Her body throbbed like an exposed nerve, every movement triggering an avalanche of responses. Now sexual awareness was stamped all over her.

Hoping the drive to the lab would dampen her condition, she cursed herself, Antonio and the whole world and headed there. It felt like she was about to sever a chunk of herself and leave it behind. But she had to do it.

She'd try to continue her work elsewhere. If she couldn't, whatever she decided to do then would be her choice, not his. That it would be a choice he'd forced her into would still be better than being forced to do what he wanted now.

Arriving at the lab, she realized from everyone's unusually zippy behavior that he was there. Probably setting up his boss area for whenever he came to inspect. No doubt he was also expecting her to obey his directive. The rat had gotten to her through her best friend so he'd corner her.

Well, it hadn't worked. It was 4:00 p.m. already, and when he got the confrontation he wished for after she'd gathered her stuff, she'd make sure it would be their last face-off.

As she headed to her lab, she noticed everyone was looking at her differently, with incredulousness and something else...a new kind of courtesy, perhaps? The only explanation was that he'd taken his joke too far, had told everyone what he'd told her yesterday.

Annoyance with all of them, especially with him, mushroomed as she pushed into her lab...and felt as if her brain had hit a brick wall.

Antonio sat at her desk. His gaze collided with hers at once, as if he'd been waiting for her to walk in.

"Is this how late you'll be coming in from now on?"

Every nerve in her body fired at the combo of his jaw-dropping beauty and his teasing remonstration.

Before she could consider a comeback, he uncoiled to his formidable height, approached in that indolent predator's prowl, his lips twisting. "I didn't expect you to change to partner mode that quickly. But then you never do anything I expect. I like it. Immensely."

Forcing herself to move as he came to a stop before her, she unhooked her backpack and circumvented him. Without looking back at him, she started emptying her station, every nerve jangling in alarm as he came closer.

"Are you doing what I think you're doing?" When she didn't answer him, he harrumphed. "I enjoy your unexpectedness up to a point. That point is when you use it to deprive me of it. This, Dr. Accardi, I won't sanction."

Packing her last article, she yanked the zipper closed, then looked up. Though she'd braced herself, she felt gut-punched to behold his gorgeousness up close, now smoldering hotter with disapproving authority. Forcing steadiness into her stance, she pulled an envelope from her backpack's outer pocket, and thrust it out at him.

It was déjà vu when he glowered at it, but when he raised his eyes, there was no questioning. He knew what that was.

"I'm not accepting your resignation, Dr. Accardi." His lips crooked into that smile that had her insides liquefying. "Not to mention it would take far more than a piece of paper now to terminate our partnership."

Grinding her teeth at the throbbing between her legs, she thrust her other hand palm-up at him. This time, he raised a questioning eyebrow, making her want to yank that regal head down and bite that perfect wing of provocation.

"My three hundred dollars, please."

"Buying back your shares?" At her nod, he laughed, and her legs almost gave out. "You think your money spent a whole night with me and remained the same?"

Images bombarded her, of spending a whole night with him and being changed forever. Even if he hadn't meant for her to think that, she did. The man was sex personified. She had to face the fact that she'd walk out of here, never to see him again, and would forever pleasure herself to his memory.

Gritting her teeth, she kept her hand outstretched. "My money, please. This is no longer remotely funny."

"It's the most fun I've ever had. And I don't have your money on me. I don't walk around with three hundred thousand dollars in my pockets."

Her mouth dropped open. "Not even you can multiply stock by a factor of a thousand overnight!"

"You'd be very impressed by what I can do over the course of one night." Her blood boiled over before he added, "But you're right. I was exaggerating. Your money is now around thirty thousand dollars. Still don't have that much on me."

"Keep it, capital and investment. Consider it my contribution to whatever good science you develop."

She had to get away from him. If she succumbed to him in any way, the damages he'd cause her would be worse than his wiping out three years of her work. This man could end her peace of mind. Could turn her into one of those women who groveled at his feet. It was getting harder with every breath to resist his spell and it wouldn't take him long to cast it fully over her. And while others seemed thrilled to be enthralled, it would destroy her.

But when she tried to walk around him, he blocked her, mischief frolicking in his eyes.

Stopping, she clutched her backpack harder. "Listen, Dr. Balducci. Enough, okay? I don't want to work for you, and I sure as hell am not your partner. Accept my resignation and give me what I ask for in this letter. I only ask for my rights."

"I don't care what you think your rights are." He silenced her protest by stepping closer, until the heat of his body and breath singed her. "I don't need to read this letter to know that you make a habit of shortchanging yourself. I, on the other hand, offer you what you really deserve."

That had her heart stuttering. "I only deserve to be left alone to continue my work. I never asked for anything more."

"And if I consider granting you this?"

And *that* had her heart skipping like a pebble over water. "Y-you would?"

"I would. On the condition that you become my partner."

She coughed a mirthless laugh. "I'm not even partner material for an ice-cream stand. I know nothing about running a business. If you're doing this to stop me from leaving for some reason only you'll ever know, I assure you, you don't need to bribe me with any bogus executive position I have no wish for and would be useless at. I'm probably the only person you'll ever meet who considers such a promotion a terrible fate and not a reward. But I'll gladly stay if you let me continue my work."

"So you're fine with me as your boss? You'd stay in spite of all your vigorous objections to me and my methods?"

"As long as you leave me alone, professionally and personally, I don't care if you're developing immunizations to sunlight for vampires and to silver for werewolves."

His lips split in such an exuberant smile, dazzling her with a flash of white teeth and searing charisma.

She was trying not to hyperventilate when he made it impossible, reaching out and slipping the backpack off her shoulder, his long, strong, capable fingers sliding against her flesh, making her core clench with violent need.

"Until we come to a new agreement," he said, "put your personal effects back where they belong."

She clung to the backpack as if to a life raft. "What new agreement? We didn't have an old one."

"Then we'll make a brand-new one from scratch."

With the utmost gentleness, he insisted on tugging the backpack out of her white-knuckled grip.

Letting it go felt as if she were lowering her last shield against him.

After placing it on her workstation, he faced her with a grin that had her swaying like a building in an earthquake. He leaned his hip on the desk, folded his arms over his expansive chest.

"Now that that's taken care of, there's something else I require."

"What's that?" she croaked.

"You. For dinner."

Four

"You want to have me for dinner?"

Lili hated that she'd squeaked. This man kept yanking at her composure. It was a matter of time before he snapped it.

"I meant I want to take you to dinner."

Her insides tightened more at his forbearing tone. "My IQ might be selective, but even I got that. Don't be—"

"—redundant? Yes, I know how you hate that." His gaze took on a new level of intensity. "But the other meaning is also right. Though I'd rather have you for dessert."

More convinced he'd decided to go all out having fun at her expense, she hissed, "Spare me the clichés, Dr. Balducci. And stop looking at me like that."

"Like what? Like you're the most fascinating thing I've ever seen? How can I, when you are?"

"That's what you tell yourself about the people you toy with? That they had it coming, being who they are?" She shook her head as his smile faltered. "But that's not how you're looking at me. At least, it's not how you're making me feel."

Every trace of levity left his face, avidness replacing it. "How am I making you feel? Tell me."

"You make me feel as if you're probing my every last thought."

His lips quirked, the smile back in his gaze. "Why would I do that when you wallop me over the head with everything that comes to your mind the moment it does?"

"It's what I've been asking myself, too, wondering why you bother. But you probably do it automatically. I think you go around scanning people to their molecular level and archiving your findings for future exploitation."

His eyes sobered. "So you don't think I do it for future reference, but for exploitation."

"Actually, I don't think it's only exploitation you're after, but flat-out mind control. You're not probing my thoughts, but trying to herd them where you want them to go. I can feel your mental tentacles trying to steer my brain."

His laugh was louder and longer this time. "Your unflattering opinion of me is devolving into sinister depths."

"I'm sure you don't care about anyone's opinion of you."

"I care about yours." The way he'd said that, his baritone caressing her inside and out… "Stop thinking it's your obligation to fight me on everything." His voice dipped another octave, making her very marrow vibrate. "Accept my dinner invitation, Dr. Accardi. I promise I won't eat you. No matter how tempted I am to do so."

Truth was, it was she who was tempted. To succumb to his persuasion. All she wanted was to say yes, to everything he was asking of her. Come what may.

She kneaded a throbbing temple, as if to stem her fast-dwindling common sense and willpower. "I don't know what's going on inside that convoluted mind of yours, Dr. Balducci, and I really don't want to know. But whatever it is, I know one thing. What you're doing here? It's a terrible idea."

His eyebrows shot up in imperious query. "It is? Why?"

Though she was certain he knew, she'd spell it out. She'd give him whatever would make him leave her be, spare her the tumult of his inexplicable interest.

"First, you're you and I'm me. Second, you're my boss, until you accept my resignation. I'm against mixing professional and personal stuff. It always has catastrophic consequences, even when the professional situation is ideal, not as problematic and hostile as ours."

"I have zero problems with you professionally. And the last thing I am is hostile. I'm the very opposite."

"So I'm the hostile party. My bad."

His smile widened. "I like your hostility. A lot."

"Yeah, you find it hilarious."

"Tut-tut. I object to your insinuations that I'm having fun at your expense."

"I'm insinuating nothing. You *are* having a ball."

"That I definitely am. You tickle my humor like no one else. I say that without malice or condescension— just the opposite. Like you, I say only what I mean."

"Really? I doubt that—about as much as I doubt my ability to grow fur in winter." That earned her another heart-palpitating chuckle that she did her best to ignore. "If you said only what you mean, I don't think many in your path would remain alive."

"So you're saying I'm tactful, even merciful?"

"Tactful? Maybe, but for your own ends only. Merciful? Sure. And I'm a flying manta ray."

A guffaw exploded from him, seeming to take him by as much surprise as it did her.

His hand pressed his chest as if laughing hurt him. Which it might, since he must be exercising muscles long petrified from lack of use. She had a feeling not much amused him.

His other hand wiped at his eyes. "How does your mind come up with these things? Wait, don't answer. Mad scientist brain at work. And I thought I was one myself before meeting you. Turns out I'm too unimaginative to be one." When she groaned at his self-deprecation, his hands rose in a placating gesture. Then he leveled his hypnotic gaze on her, his lips still twitching, as if unable to stop smiling. "So if it's dubious I'm tactful, and certain I'm not merciful, what do you think I am?"

"You're inexorably diplomatic and inhumanly charismatic. And you wield both traits like weapons of mass manipulation. Not that I fault you for that. That *is* the best way of dealing with underlings for the best outcome. Why cultivate resentments and enemies among lesser beings when you can as easily foster worship and recruit willing slaves?"

"My diplomacy and charisma aren't getting me any worship or acquiring me any slaves in this room. They seem to work in reverse on you."

"Yeah, contrary to my norm, my reactions to you seem the total opposite of everyone else."

"So it's only me who has that effect on you." His eyes flared with something scalding...and smug?

Really? He craved ego-inflating strokes from her? He didn't get enough from everyone else?

Well, she wasn't contributing to the severity of his self-aggrandizing syndrome. And she wasn't letting him keep on trying to break through her barriers.

"*So* since it's clear you won't give me what I came here for, I'll leave you to your manipulation games with your new horde of worshipping followers. But do take this still. Consider it a souvenir."

Pushing the envelope in his hand, she skirted him to retrieve her backpack. She rushed to the door, forcing herself not to take a last look at him, praying she'd make it out without stumbling. She was almost out when his rich voice had goose bumps storming all over her.

"What did you mean before when you said, 'You're you and I'm me'? What are we exactly?"

She waited until she was outside the door, safe

enough to turn to him. Beholding his majesty for the last time, she suppressed a pang of regret and sighed.

"We're two different species."

Antonio watched Liliana Accardi disappear, battling the urge to hurtle after her, to drag her back, preferably thrown over his shoulder, swearing and scratching.

After he managed to get himself under control, he shook his head.

And he'd thought he'd already been beyond intrigued coming here. Now, after she'd defied him again, lambasted him as no one had ever dared to, then walked out on him like no one had done before, his condition had worsened exponentially.

He was hooked. For the first time in...ever.

All through this latest confrontation, he'd kept seeing himself capturing those lush lips, shoving her back onto that workstation she'd cleared, and having his way with her. All the way. Repeatedly.

He'd gotten hard the moment she'd walked in, and remained painfully so, even now. Even when he hadn't guessed what her body looked like under those drab clothes she wore like a camouflage. For the first time physical attributes didn't count to him. Coveting her essential self—something he'd never thought possible—took his arousal to a level he'd never experienced.

He stared down at the envelope she'd foisted on him. To think he'd set this up thinking she'd be just a conduit. A means to an end.

But it had taken her only one confrontation to derail his meticulous plan. Not only was she the only to ever outright challenge him, but when he'd added the extra pressure of personal interest, the point when other women would have buckled breathlessly, she'd become even more resistant.

Amazing.

She hadn't even bothered considering his invitation. An invitation he'd never issued before, and that other women would kill for. She'd just scoffed it off and walked away. She would have done so without looking back if he hadn't asked her another question. She'd stopped only long enough to give him her final verdict.

We're two different species.

Shaking his head again, he headed back to her workstation, sat down in her chair. Though it was uncomfortable and creaky, it was the only place he wanted to be right now. It made him feel closer to her somehow. He'd take that comfort until he had the woman herself close once again.

If he even managed it.

That was another first. To be uncertain he could win someone over.

After a moment of grappling with this added complication, he tore open her resignation letter.

The wording was appropriate, yet it revealed her unbending spirit, that indomitable spark that fueled her unique persona. Yet with every letter, something tightened more behind his rib cage.

She was asking for far less than she deserved. Than the least contributor in this lab he'd acquired to be near her deserved.

He'd been right. This woman had no idea of her worth.

How had this happened? Why had she come to think this was her due? Who had made her feel worth so little?

Her life was an open book with very few lines, so there could be only two culprits. Her father was the foremost perpetrator. Knowing he'd let her grow up without caring to establish any relationship with her must have formed the early views of her self-worth. Her mother hadn't been the epitome of parenthood, either. She'd been a severely dysfunctional woman who had no right to limit her daughter to her very questionable care. After Liliana's early childhood, she'd become consumed in her work before falling prey to a debilitating mental disorder, repeating her husband's abandonment, albeit in different ways.

It explained a lot about Liliana. Those abandoned as children grappled with not only trust issues, but with sometimes crippling feelings of worthlessness all their lives. He knew that all too well, having been a discarded child himself.

But he'd been lucky. Unbelievably, The Organization had been a better place for a child to grow up than the biological family Liliana had been unlucky enough to be born to.

That meant his approach today had been another miscalculation. He'd thought if he showed her that his interest had become personal, it would soften her. When it had only made her more adamant, he'd thought she'd been alarmed at how fast he was moving, because of his reputation as an indiscriminating female magnet, which he'd cultivated to serve his purposes.

But it wasn't only this part of his public persona that repelled her. It was how she perceived all of him. And how she perceived herself in comparison.

Like no other woman he'd met, she was actually put off by his wealth and power. To her he was a taker, like her father, someone immersed in his own needs and greeds, who cared nothing about the devastation he left behind.

Then came the part concerning herself.

If she didn't value herself, as was evident from that letter, it stood to reason that she was unable to understand his interest in her. So she'd assigned him the most unsavory motive she could think of. That he was toying with her for his cruel entertainment.

What irony, that she suspected his manipulation when he'd already relinquished it.

He could just hear his brothers saying this turnabout only served him right, in punishment for his initial plan to use her. Not that they hadn't done the same in their day. At least Rafael and Numair. They had both initiated their relationships with the women who'd become their wives with self-serving motives.

Not that he wanted to end up with a wife. He just wanted to experience and satisfy those unprecedented urges this spitfire provoked in him. And he would pursue her to the ends of the earth till he did.

He probed those new motivations more deeply. Was he feeling this way only because she defied him and pulverized his plans and expectations?

The internal interrogation ended before it started.

No. That was what had lured him in initially. But he'd stayed and kept going deeper because of *her*. She was a conundrum. A genius in her field, she was also so insightful she'd sensed things about him that no one had before. And she kept none of her insights to herself. Yet with all her brilliance, she was socially awkward, had reclusive tendencies. But what had him at the mercy of this unknown and unstoppable compulsion was that inside that steel shell of resolve and resistance, he felt such vulnerable, untried softness.

It was *that* that made him want to eat her up.

But his need to break down the insulating walls she'd erected around herself, what she kept raising higher around him, was more than desire. More than his dominance demanding she bow to him like everyone did. It actually...dismayed him, what she thought of him. Because it was unnervingly accurate. She saw him more clearly than anyone, even Ivan.

He was suddenly no longer feeling self-satisfied being who he was. Now he actually felt the urge to change, so he could improve her opinion of him.

If anything had ever disturbed him, it was *that* thought.

Could he be getting soft and stupid like his brothers? Behind the suave front he'd meticulously created, he'd always been the one with steel-enforced nerves and diamond-coated insides. Not even this unpredictable fireball could change that...could she?

Of course she couldn't.

And when he got her to succumb—and he definitely

would—not only would he remain unchanged, it would still serve his original cause. There'd at least be that, once his desire for her dissipated.

But then, he couldn't even imagine it doing so. From the aroused condition he remained in just thinking of her, it seemed his need for her wouldn't fade easily or soon.

Which suited him. He had all the time in the world.

He would savor her capture and her devouring, slowly, thoroughly, as he'd never done anything in his life.

Lili woke up very late. It had been another restless night filled with outlandish, feverish dreams starring Antonio Balducci.

She'd woken up with a hammering heart and a cramping core. She'd felt so needy that she'd barely refrained from relieving the throbbing between her legs in the shower.

Getting out in record time before she succumbed to temptation and ended up feeling only worse, she eyed the pajamas she'd decided to spend the day in, shrugged listlessly and headed to the kitchen in her bathrobe instead. She needed sugar. Lots of it. She'd bought giant triple chocolate chip muffins last night. Two for breakfast sounded about right. It wouldn't compensate for the loss of her job and security, but it would make her feel better nonetheless. Hopefully.

Flopping on the couch in front of the TV, she decided she'd binge-watch every single episode of every sitcom she liked. If that meant she'd sit there with only kitchen and bathroom breaks for the next month, so be it.

By the fourth episode of her favorite show, she found herself actually watching and not replaying her confrontations with Antonio in a never-ending loop. Soon she was chuckling, then laughing, then reciting the lines that had become engraved in pop culture. She was singing a jingle alongside one of her favorite characters at the top of her lungs when the bell rang.

Her raucousness came to a halt as her eyes darted to the wall clock. At 1:00 p.m. on a Wednesday, the few neighbors in her gated community who ever came knocking knew she'd be at work.

It had to be one of them checking out the inexplicable noises. Or the mailman leaving something she'd forgotten she'd ordered online, as usual.

Coming to this conclusion, she turned the volume down, subdued her hair and tightened the belt of the two-sizes-too-big bathrobe. Failing to locate her slippers, she pattered barefoot to the door.

She pulled it open, eyes down looking for a package. Instead, they fell on a pair of big shoes. Polished, handmade ones.

Her eyes trailed up, over endless legs, a lean abdomen, a door-wide chest and shoulders, all encased in darkness that seemed to absorb the sunlight like a black hole.

"You're sitting at home watching sitcoms and causing a neighborhood-wide alert, when you should be in your lab advancing medical science?"

Lili blinked, for a moment believing the colossus she was staring at was an apparition. Perhaps she'd been thinking of him so obsessively she'd actually conjured him.

Not that even her fevered imagination could replicate him. Antonio Balducci was really on her doorstep,
glowing like a gilded god in the afternoon sun, perfect
in ways that she hadn't known possible and that should
be outlawed.

And there she stood in front of this vision of grandeur, the hair she hadn't combed a riot of tangles, no
doubt looking like a freckled porcupine drowning in
its parent's garment.

When she continued to gape at him, he folded his
arms over his chest, his gaze mock-severe. "May I remind you that you didn't ask permission to take the
day off?"

His reprimand finally snapped her out of her stupor.
"May I remind you that I tendered my resignation?"

His majestic head jerked up in dismissal, presenting
her with an even better view of his formidable jaw and
cleft chin. "You may also remember it was categorically rejected."

She tossed her head back, too, attempting to emulate
his haughtiness. "I needed you to approve my resignation only so you'd provide me with my end-of-service
benefits. Your approval is unneeded if I relinquish them.
Which I did. So I can do what I want. And I'm doing
exactly that. Sleeping in and watching TV."

He gave such a pout, it was a wonder she didn't jump
him to bite those maddening lips. "I hate to burst your
bubble, but a rejected resignation only means you still
work for me."

"No, it means I give up all the rights that come with
an accepted resignation."

"Accepted resignations don't only come with benefits. They come with recommendation letters—"

She cut in. "I'll do without those, too."

He continued as if she hadn't interrupted him. "—endless severance forms to fill and to sign—"

She butted in again. "I'll do that sometime next week."

That made him stop, his gaze merrily roaming her, his lips twitching on the verge of ending his not-so-convincing stern act.

Yeah, tell her about how ridiculous she looked.

"Won't you invite me in?"

"No."

Her immediate answer gained her an equally swift "Why?"

"Because of all of the above."

His eyes twinkled in the sunlight, a more crystalline and intense blue than she'd ever seen. "It's not good for your health to hold a grudge."

"Oh, it's very cathartic to do so, for a limited time. I've allowed myself a week of hurling curses your way."

As his lips lost the fight and broke into a smile, the image burst in her mind of a lightning bolt striking him in that perfect ass. And she burst out laughing.

His eyes narrowed as he examined her. "Are you drunk, Dr. Accardi?"

"What if I am?" she spluttered. "I can't get a ticket riding my couch."

Without warning, he crossed her threshold.

A thousand alarms rang in her head. "Hey, you can't do that. I haven't invited you in."

He walked her back into her foyer, his advance slow, smooth, a sweep of power and seduction, the very opposite of her ungainly stumbling.

"Like a vampire, you mean?"

"I wouldn't be surprised if you were one."

"Then I would have certainly developed that anti-sun vaccine you mentioned before." He took another step closer. "I would have also developed a no-invitation-needed immunization."

Another few steps back had her thudding against something hard. The archway of the great room. Her heart bobbed in her throat as he bent his head closer and inhaled deeply, his eyes watching her intently.

"You smell of…you."

The way he said that, it was as if he were bracing himself against some sharp ache. His velvet groan was the darkest she'd heard his voice.

Trying not to let the shudder that traversed her body rattle it visibly, she smirked. "Thanks for the news flash. And here I always thought I smelled of someone else."

"Do you have any idea how you smell?"

"As long as I don't smell bad, who cares?"

"If you don't know who, I won't tell you. Yet." He lowered his head, closed his eyes and drew another deep inhalation. "I know now that defiance and dry wit and fearlessness have scents. Hot and sweet and bright." Before she decided if she'd swoon or not, he added, "You also smell of ginger and orange." He'd pinpointed the scents in her shampoo and conditioner. His eyes opened, heavy and hooded, filled with so much she couldn't understand but that still seared her to the marrow. "And chocolate."

Gulping, she nodded. "Yeah, I've overdosed on triple chocolate chip muffins."

"Sounds great. Smells better. Offer me some."

"What makes you think I have any left? Should I refresh your memory about the definition of *overdosed*?"

He gave her a perfect Bela Lugosi leer. "Should you be haggling with a hungry vampire who's doing you the courtesy of settling for chocolate instead of blood?"

"The hungry vampire will take the blood anyway, so I'm at least saving the chocolate."

Shaking his head in gesture of surrender, he laughed. Peal after peal of debilitating male amusement. That thick, corded neck jutting from his open black silk shirt was the closest it had been to her lips. It was so tempting, as if inviting her to reach up and sink her teeth—

Dammit. Get away!

Though he wasn't really crowding her, she sucked in her stomach as she squeezed out from between him and the wall. Grabbing the remote, she turned off the TV, then swung back to him. He'd followed her, was facing her across the couch.

"How about we dispense with the comic relief and get to the reason for your home invasion?"

"I came to resolve the issue that made you skip work today."

"For the last time, I skipped nothing. I quit."

"Yes, I got that the first time you said it. I'm here to tell you quitting isn't an option."

"It's my only option. You gave me ultimatums—"

"I offered you alternatives."

"—and I rejected them. So I was back to square one—working on your project and having mine swept aside."

He shook his head. "You keep making assumptions of what I think or what I'll do, and they're consistently inaccurate."

"What's inaccurate in all I said?"

"Only the most relevant part. Your assumption that I wasn't open to compromise. Which I certainly was. You pushed, I countered and our negotiations were just starting when you took off."

"There was nothing more to negotiate."

"There's always more. Nothing is ever final."

"I thought with you everything is."

His gaze swept her from head to toe and back, swathing her in fire. "I thought so, too. But I'm learning that was because I never found a worthy challenger."

"Me? Yeah, right."

"I will cure you of that self-deprecation yet. For now, I'm here to tell you that you can have your project back, with all the logistical support and financial backing I would have offered you to work on mine. I ask for nothing in return."

Her mouth fell open but nothing came out.

It was only on the third attempt that she croaked, "So what's the catch?"

"You're *assuming* again."

"Just spit it out. The one thing I can't handle is surprises. I have to know what I'm walking into while I'm still a thousand miles away."

His eyes gleamed with approval. "A control freak, I see."

"Takes one to know one. But then again, I'm just a wannabe who has nothing to show for my obsessive proclivities. You're the real deal with the billions to prove it."

"Again, you shortchange yourself." He frowned for a moment before he exhaled. "There's no catch, Dr. Accardi. Your pressure tactics worked."

"What pressure tactics?"

His huff was incredulous. "Seems it's not only me who does things on autopilot. You flat-out bulldozed me."

"I was only struggling not to let you bulldoze me."

"And your struggle was so ferocious you upended the tables. It took me a while to realize I was beaten, since it never happened before. But there's a first time for everything. So here I am, coming with a white flag. If there's one thing I ask, it's that you promise you'll separate our professional and personal interactions from now on."

"We have no personal interactions."

"Something I aim to rectify, starting now, over lunch."

"What is it with you and meals?"

"We do have to eat. We'll eat together."

It was her turn to shake her head, disbelief coursing through her. She'd expected him to consider her a pest, to dismiss her and spare her his disconcerting focus. But not only had he come after her again, but the more obnoxious she was, the more patient and persuasive he grew.

But for whatever reason he was doing this, there was only so much temptation she could withstand.

Clinging to the last vestiges of sanity, she exhaled. "You must be in dire need of amusement. But let's say I accept, how about something quick? Coffee? Here?"

He shook his head, unmovable. "Lunch. Out."

"I'll give you a muffin."

His laugh rang out again, and she could swear all of her mother's crystal still distributed around the living area where she'd left them sang in response.

He was still chuckling when he persisted, "Lunch. A leisurely one. So clear your agenda."

"What agenda? I'm unemployed now."

"You're no such thing. We're celebrating your triumphant return to your lab. This is nonnegotiable, Liliana."

Her heart somersaulted. It didn't matter that it was impossible. It did. Then it attempted to burst out of her chest.

At her distressed cough, he covered the distance between them urgently, held her by the arms, solicitous, singeing her even through the thick terry cloth.

"Are you all right?" When she nodded and tried to step away, he followed, hands tightening on her arms. "Liliana…"

"Lili." It was too much hearing him say her full name, making it an overpowering spell. "If you're no longer calling me Dr. Accardi, then call me Lili like everyone else."

An eyebrow rose imperiously. "You're Liliana to me

and I will always call you that. That is also nonnegotiable."

Stepping back so she could breathe again, she raised her hands. "Okay, okay, call me whatever you want. I will call you whatever I want, too."

"And what's that?"

"I didn't mean to your face."

His guffaw was more delighted than ever. "And what will you call me outside of your internal rants?"

"I'd rather not call you at all."

He took her arm again, steered her toward the ground-floor bedroom where she slept. "Call me anything you want. I eagerly anticipate whatever you come up with. Now go dress."

"I haven't said I'll go out to lunch with you."

"You will."

"Is this the billionaire's entitlement or the surgeon's god complex, or were you just born an overbearing brat?"

He whooped in laughter again. "You'll get a chance to find out over lunch. Now go put on something nice."

She yanked her arm from his grip. "I don't have something nice. Not by your standards."

"Anything that doesn't smother you in layers of cloth."

"I don't have that, either."

"Anything not hideous. I'm sure you can manage that."

"This bathrobe isn't hideous. Would you settle for that?"

"I would. Would you?"

She should go out with him in her bathrobe and bare feet and see if he'd still take her to lunch.

Her thoughts paused before she huffed in resignation, threw her hands up and headed to her bedroom.

She'd bet he wouldn't bat an eyelid. If she even stripped naked it wouldn't deter him. Or maybe *that* would change his mind about taking her out and he'd—

Oh, shut up. He'd nothing. All this was probably him conducting some experiment, and he considered her the perfect test subject.

After that lunch, and after he was sure she'd go back to work, she doubted she'd see him again. Even had he been interested in her *that* way, Antonio Balducci had perfected the art of the one-night—or the one-outing— stand.

So what would one lunch hurt, anyway? She should actually make the most of it.

It would be her first and last chance with him.

Five

She'd worn something nice.

As nice as she could manage from a wardrobe designed for a life that had no social or romantic components.

Not that she'd thought it was nice when she'd put on the dark green sleeveless above-knee dress with matching three-inch sandals.

That verdict was his.

When she'd come out of her bedroom, flushed because he'd been across from her door when she was totally naked, he was watching the same sitcom episode she had been when he'd arrived.

He'd thrown his head back like a lazy feline, then had said one word. *Nice.*

The word itself was innocuous enough. It had been

the way he'd looked at her and the way he'd said it, that lethal gaze and that purr of bone-liquefying seduction, that had swept her in flames of longing.

Not that she thought that was his objective. Seducing her was too far-fetched a motive behind everything he'd done so far. Her amusement factor remained the most probable reason.

She reeled all over again at the cascade of events that had led her to this point, where she was sitting beside him in his luxurious Lamborghini.

When he'd found her eyeing everything as if she feared touching it, he'd only said that he always bought Italian-made cars, as a nod to his heritage—which she shared. Knowing he was trying to disprove her "different species" comment without tackling it head-on, she'd countered that he found this car appealing not because of its country of origin but its million-dollar price tag. He'd only sighed about her continued gross misjudgments and, with a wiggle of an eyebrow, *under*-estimates.

Feeling it would be obnoxious to criticize his personal spending habits, she'd instead questioned the absence of his limo and chauffeur. His response had been yet another blow to her equilibrium. That he hadn't been about to pick her up for their first lunch together with another man around.

Another woman would have been flattered out of her mind, with all sorts of ludicrous hopes soaring. *Her* response had been to stress what self-preservation dictated this should be—their first *and* last lunch together.

He'd given her an enigmatic look and let her statement stand. Either he agreed, or he'd let her say whatever she wanted because he knew he'd get his way in the end anyway.

Now she stole another glance at his sonnet-worthy profile as he negotiated a stretch of unruly traffic in downtown LA. Questions spun faster inside her mind.

What exactly was his way? What could he want with her? It couldn't be her as a woman that he was after. Could it?

Okay, so she was pretty enough, in what people called an unusual way. She'd had lots of interest from good-looking and successful guys. It had been her who'd been uninterested. A romance, or even a hookup, with all promised upsides, hadn't been worth the consequences she'd obsessively calculated.

But in comparison, *any* guy was a straggly tomcat to this majestic lion beside her. Whatever her attractions to men, she couldn't be up to *his* standards, not when he waded among the rare beauties of the world and didn't give even them the time of day.

That brought her back to her one plausible theory. That she entertained him like none had ever done, intrigued him because she hadn't fallen at his feet, and was still challenging him with every breath. Even as she melted inside.

"We're here."

His deep drawl jerked her out of her musings as he brought the car to a smooth stop. He sprang from the low-slung car fluidly, then rushed around to help her out. Her exit from the car was nowhere as seamless as his, his boost compromising her balance more, landing her against his unyielding strength.

He steadied her, that disturbing intimacy flaring in his eyes, and every primal urge in her fiercely wished she could remain engulfed in his heat and dominance and security.

As her ingrained aloofness kicked in and she stepped away from his support, a valet rushed to take the car away. Assorted other men in formal suits—she counted six—descended from two cars and stood at varying distances, clearly his bodyguards.

Following the trajectory of her gaze, Antonio sighed as he guided her over the curb to wide marble stairs. "That's my partner Richard being overprotective. He's Black Castle Enterprises' security specialist, and his men follow us every second, till we die. If it's up to him, we never will."

Something dreadful lurched inside her at the thought of such an indomitable being dying.

His gaze stilled on her face, as if he'd felt the intensity of her reaction and was probing her mind for its cause. "I hope it's not bothering you."

She blinked up at him as they ascended the stairs toward an ornately carved mahogany double door. "Why should it?"

"Because you're out with a man who allegedly needs that much protection. Not a comforting thought, I'm sure."

That was what he'd thought had dismayed her?

Not that she could fault his inaccuracy. She'd given

him no reason to think she'd be disturbed at the thought of his death. But she was, jarringly so.

"When we try to make him lay off, Richard tells us we're lucky he posts guards at that distance. It's pointless arguing with him when his only alternative is 24/7 surveillance much closer up."

"He has a good reason for his vigilance," she murmured. "You're too high-profile. You're as recognizable as any Hollywood celebrity, and much more influential. There must be many people whose lives would be easier with you out of the way."

She fought not to clutch his arm in reflex protection as two doormen opened the doors for them. She hoped he'd tell her that she watched too many action movies, that paranoid prophylactic measures were merely part of his partner's job.

As if diagnosing her anxiety right this time, his gaze gentled. "As you so keenly observed before, I never make enemies. I also make sure it's in everyone's best interest to keep me around and healthy. I'm in no danger whatsoever."

"Really?"

His smile broke out again, brightening her mood at once after the sharp dip it had taken. "Really."

Believing him, she exhaled her pent-up breath. "But the valet is *your* man. You wouldn't trust someone you haven't picked and vetted yourself with that car of yours."

His eyes glowed, though with what she couldn't diagnose. Whatever it was, a girl could get addicted to it, could get lost in it, and be lost without it.

"*That's* the mind I wanted working on my projects."

"An hour ago you considered that that mind jumps to rash and unsubstantiated assumptions."

"Only when it comes to my motives. We did agree I invert your thought process. How about you try to keep it upright from now on?"

"I don't do it on purpose, you know. But I'll try for the duration of lunch. Should be easier when I'm busy eating."

He swept an arm forward to usher her inside. "Then by all means, let's eat."

The restaurant he'd chosen turned out to be a place she hadn't known existed in the city she'd lived in for the past eight years. Inside a building she'd passed a hundred times before.

On the outside, it looked like any other upscale building in LA. On the inside, it made any other grand place she'd ever been inside look shabby. It wasn't only the old-world, aristocratic luxury, but the very atmosphere radiated mystery and exclusivity. She kept expecting to see James Bond and his gallery of villains walking through the hyper-real setting.

But then, next to the god who led her deeper into his domain, every other larger-than-life character, real or fictional, would fade to nothing.

As they made their way deeper into what had to be a club of some sort, everyone in their path, each clearly hailing from a world of extreme breeding and wealth, exclaimed reverential greetings. Some actually bowed.

And she'd thought the Italian clan she belonged to by birth, who'd recently burst into her existence, was the epitome of elitism. But Antonio's affluence, not to mention the awe he commanded, far surpassed the Accardis.

Not that wealth or power were of any interest to her. Her family's or his. The only reason she was debating entering her father's world was so she would have the family she'd never had. As for Antonio, the trappings of fame and fortune actually detracted from the far more impressive man cloaked in them.

With a hand on the small of her back, he led her into a ballroom-sized room with only one table for two in the center, exquisitely set in silk, silver and crystal. Her mind boggled at what it took to empty such a place and reserve it exclusively, at such short notice. If he didn't keep it perpetually reserved for himself, that was.

He'd just sat down opposite her when her phone vibrated with a loud buzz in her purse. Still jangling from Antonio's gossamer touches as he'd seated her, she almost jumped.

His hand rose in pure graciousness, permitting her to take the call, but his eyes remained fixed on her, letting her know he'd give her no privacy.

Getting the phone out, she fumbled it in unsteady hands, mumbled her chagrin at him, and herself, under her breath. It came out louder than she'd intended, since it elicited a blinding flash of his teeth.

She reeled in her runaway reactions, groaning as she saw the caller ID. Not the best time to talk to the *other* man who caused her emotional upheavals.

The moment she croaked a hello, her father's voice burst into her ear. "*Mia bella* Lilianissima, how are you, *tesoro*?"

Lili winced. Her father's over-the-top enthusiasm never ceased to jar her. It was weird he'd be so vocally eager after a lifetime of not even acknowledging her existence. It was even more unsettling after her mother's detached treatment, and the fact that Lili had been raised to think her father and the whole Accardi clan had ice water running in their blue-blooded veins. Recently, everything had been one contradiction after the other.

She took a breath and steadied her voice before she spoke. "I'm fine, Alberto. How are you?"

"*Tesoro*, when will you start calling me Padre or Daddy?"

She licked her lips, Antonio's vigilance intensifying her nervousness. "Maybe one day I can manage Father…"

"Then make that day today, *tesoro. Per favore!*"

"Uh, listen, Albe… Father…" She paused as her father celebrated her capitulation on the other end with another deluge of endearments. "I'd love to talk, really, but I'm at lunch with…an associate." Antonio's eyes glowed with something that made the electricity surging through her system spike. "I'll call you when I get home. Or tomorrow. With our time difference it must be already very late for you."

"I'm not in Venice, *tesoro*. I'm in New York City. Among the reasons I'm calling you is to tell you all the US-based Accardis are anxious to meet you. They're holding a reception in your honor in our main ancestral home here."

She almost blurted out a refusal. Not that she expected such an event to be unpleasant. So far every Accardi her father had introduced to her had been gracious and welcoming. Either her mother had falsely advertised the family in order to explain why they never had anything to do with them, or they were accommodating her father's fervent desire to include her in their exclusive ranks. Up till now, though, she'd met the Accardis one or two at a time. The idea of meeting them en masse was enough to give her performance anxiety.

"Is this weekend good for you?"

"No." The response came out far sharper than she'd intended. Biting her tongue, she tried again. "I…have work to do."

"On the weekend?"

Her gaze again clashed with Antonio's watchful one, then saw the satisfaction there. Her blood heated to the point where she felt steam rising off her body.

"Our lab has been taken over, and our new taskmaster has turned things upside down. I'm behind in my schedule because of his antics, and I have no idea when I'll get caught up."

Antonio's grin became as wide as she'd ever seen it as he beckoned to a waiter bearing champagne chilling in an ice-filled antique silver bucket.

Narrowing her eyes, she moved to end the call. One turmoil-inducing man at a time was her limit.

"Please let them know I'm unavailable this weekend before they put any plans in motion. When I sort out my stuff here, we'll discuss this further, okay?"

"*Certamente, tesoro.* Call me whenever it's convenient for you. Don't worry about the time difference or any other considerations. Wake me up, interrupt my meetings, anything at all. Talking to you is far more important than anything else. I have a lifetime of un-made calls I need to make up for."

To that she grumbled something vague around the lump that suddenly filled her throat and ended the call.

As she put her phone away, struggling to swallow through the tightness, Antonio poured champagne in her crystal flute and handed it to her.

"Your father?"

She grimaced. "Rhetorical questions fall under my redundancy ban. My father was so loud you must have heard his every word. And you heard me call him Fa-ther."

He also no doubt knew everything about her per-sonal life, such as it was. Who her father was and that she'd grown up without him must have been the first things in the dossier he must have on her as he had on everyone in his employ. He probably knew the recent developments, too. He just wanted her to elaborate with her own version of details and updates.

At his unrepentant, probing stare, she sighed. "Yeah. My father. Long-absent and recently very much pres-ent. Therefore the extreme enthusiasm. He'll cool off, eventually. But for now I'm the daughter he reconnected with, all grown-up minus the hassle of years of teeth-ing, tantrums and teenage angst."

That still, strange expression on his face deepened before he exhaled. "This is another thing that proves we're not two different species at all."

"What? That I happen to have an Italian father, too?"

"And that you grew up without said father."

"You…" Suddenly the lump was back in her throat. It was ridiculous, when she'd never really considered herself unfortunate, but imagining the boy Antonio had been growing up fatherless…hurt.

It was clear *he* wasn't going to elaborate. Which was fine by her. Though curiosity burned inside her, she didn't want to learn anything that would make her stupidly ache more on his behalf.

To assuage the pain she suffered now, she gulped a big mouthful of silky champagne. "That sort of barely puts us in the same genus."

He toasted her with his flute. "At least it's a step up the ladder toward us occupying the same evolutionary status." Taking a sip, he put his glass down. "But we do share far more than that. We're both doctors—"

"Who've trodden diametrically different paths, have opposing approaches, and reached incomparable results."

Undeterred, he continued as if she hadn't interrupted him in this volleying rhythm between them they seem to have perfected. "We're both unyielding—"

"Yeah, that's why I'm sitting here having lunch with you in this top secret hideout for billionaires and spies and not watching my sitcoms as I wanted."

"And that's why you made me bow to your demands without any of my own objectives realized in return."

Her lips twisted. "So you say."

"So it *is*. This round is all yours." He beckoned to the maître d' without taking his gaze off her, a new heat entering his eyes. "But don't think you're going to win every time."

His warning made it sound as if their interactions would continue beyond this lunch, or her going back to work.

A thrill of disbelief, dread and expectation buzzed through her all during their ordering process.

As soon as the maître d' left, Antonio sat forward, his eyes growing somber, worsening her condition. "There's just one thing I'm confused about."

She took another sip to relieve her drying mouth. "You get confused like mortals?"

His smile didn't reach his eyes this time. "No, I don't, actually. But you affect me in unprecedented ways. You confuse the hell out of me. Therefore my inability to understand how you would seek the father who abandoned you. I have firsthand knowledge of how you can do without anything or anyone. Not to mention how unforgiving you are."

"You describe me like *such* a well-rounded sociopath."

"I describe myself, too. More things we have in common."

"Things of which I have a drop while you have an ocean." She fell silent until the waiters placed soup in front of them and left. "But you're right, as usual. I had no intention of seeking him out. I lived my life without him and his family, and I never wished to change that. It took him months of persistence after my mother's death until I finally agreed to see him."

That earlier strangeness returned, deeper now, as if

that piece of information disturbed him. Which made no sense.

Suddenly famished, for food or other things, she sought the refuge of the soup and changed the subject.

For the rest of what turned out to be the most incredible meal she'd ever had, they talked about so many other things, never again broaching anything personal.

After lunch he insisted on taking her to another place for coffee. Another place where he was treated like a god, and where she almost felt it was sacrilegious for her to be. And again, the place had only them.

She finally had to comment. "You emptied the restaurant at your exclusive club, and this place, too, for only us, didn't you?" He only nodded. "Why? Do you have something against eating in other people's presence?"

"I ate in yours quite successfully, as I recall." He leaned back in his seat, regarding her with that intentness she'd come to expect but would never get used to. "I wanted you to relax without intrusions or distractions."

"I *am* known for being around human beings without any adverse reactions." She shook her head, picked up her cappuccino cup, the finest china she'd ever touched. "But you're way stronger than I am. Apart from the evident ways."

"Care to explain that statement?"

"You can stomach all this over-the-top luxury and sycophancy. I wouldn't be able to, even on an occasional basis. It's actually one of the reasons I'm so reluctant to get any deeper into my father's life. Like you, he lives in a rarefied world where I can't belong."

Antonio stared at Liliana and again felt everything spinning even further out of his control.

He'd orchestrated that lunch to give her a taste of what it would be like to be with a man of his caliber. Though his money and power had no effect on her when her research hung in the balance, he'd thought when she was made their beneficiary on a personal level, it would be different.

But the more he immersed her in its benefits, the more repulsed she was by the evidence of his status. She'd made sideway remarks through the past hours, but now she'd come right out and said it. Being in such surroundings, getting the treatment only limitless wealth bought, disturbed, not dazzled, her.

Taking another sip of cappuccino, she shrugged. "To each his own, of course, but I don't see why you need to exercise your power in such ways."

He gritted his teeth on another unknown sensation. Chagrin. "Maybe I was trying to impress you."

A not-too-delicate snort made her put down her cup before she spilled its contents. "You thought this would impress me? Have you met me?" She sat forward, her eyes wide and earnest. "You know what *really* impresses me? It's that if you were stripped of all your financial assets right this second, with that brain of yours, filled with all your knowledge and experience, with those hands that perform miracles on a regular basis, your worth wouldn't be affected. Anything you lost, you'd re-create, bigger and better, because luck and circumstances played no role when you first created it. So no, this—" she swept a hand around "—doesn't impress me. If anything, all this glitter and bustle doesn't become you, actually taints your true value. Without any of those trappings, it's you on your own, your gifts and abilities, that's invaluable."

Something swelled inside his chest until he couldn't breathe. So he didn't, let himself succumb to those whiskey eyes as they penetrated him to his core with their absolute truthfulness.

No one besides his brothers had ever treated him without artifice. But their candor had been nothing like this. It was indescribable being exposed to hers. Her ruthless bluntness at once slapped him for being a pathetic show-off and bestowed on him the most validating evaluation of his life.

He got adulation wherever he went, but no one had ever told him anything like that. That his intrinsic value remained unchanged without everything he'd achieved or acquired. It was what he'd told himself since he'd escaped The Organization. That his abilities would bring him success, would amass fortune and power, would re-create them if he ever lost them. But only Liliana had ever expressed that exact same belief in him.

And she did so when she still considered him an antagonist. She was fair enough that she'd give even an enemy his full due.

She raised her cup to her lips. "Though I commented because you dragged me to this creepily empty seven-star establishment, I hope you don't always feel the need to flaunt your wealth and impose your worth on the world. I assure you you're the last man on earth who needs to do that."

He finally exhaled his pent-up breath. "I'll be sure to make a note of that."

So not only had he failed to impress her, she'd ended up counseling him.

To make things worse, he'd totally lost track of time. Six hours had passed, when he'd intended to tantalize her for only a couple of hours and leave her wanting more, so next time she'd be more eager, or at least, less resistant.

But he'd been incapable of ending the most enchanting day he'd ever had, the most exhilarating duel he'd ever waged. He'd been swept on the tide of their affinity, the hunger that had been building inside him demanding more of her. It now craved all of her. Now, not later.

She pushed her cappuccino cup away. "Was that leisurely enough for you?"

"Not quite."

"C'mon, you said lunch, and it's now time for dinner."

"Then you have dinner. At a place of your choosing."

"You think it's possible for me to eat anything else? I can barely breathe. But you're a big boy who needs his nutrition, so you go ahead. I'll walk back home." She tapped her slightly curved belly through that dress whose color made her skin glow and her hair and eyes sparkle with red and gold fires. "I can sure use a long, hard walk."

"So we'll walk together. Then I'll drive you home."

She started to object and he cut her off. "You don't think I'd let you go back home on your own, do you?"

"Why not? I've been doing it since I was a kid."

"You're not doing it on my watch." Before she could say anything else, he was on his feet, his hand extended to her.

Though she grumbled that he was an entitled chauvinist, she gave him her hand. It was all he could do not to yank her by it, slam her against his aching body and drink her dissension dry.

As they stepped out into the night, the warm, humid ocean breeze was so strong it swept her curls across his face. He groaned, getting another whiff of her scent, which had almost had him pouncing on her back in her house. His hardness had long crossed from painful to agonizing.

Giving in, he reached out to catch those locks. He'd send his plans of taking it slow to hell, would capture her by that lush cascade of silk, push her against the nearest building and devour her.

But she aborted his feverish intentions, pulling her locks away, one from between his lips. And their hands touched. Jerking hers away as if he'd electrocuted her, she mumbled that her hair came alive in the wind, produced a clip from her purse and secured her rioting hair in an improvised updo.

Triumphantly declaring the problem contained, she starting walking. It took him a moment to get his stiff legs to fall into step with her. His breath had clogged in his chest so hard again he had to force himself to breathe.

That tightness increased all through their two-hour walk down the bustling streets. As did his enjoyment.

They argued, agreed, bickered and shared companionable silences. He even got her to laugh many times, once so hard she shed tears.

Getting her to lower her guard enough with him, then to respond to his wit and teasing so unreservedly, was the most rewarding thing he'd ever done.

Then to his dismay, she said that her feet were starting to hurt, being so unused to heels. He should have considered this, at least realized her discomfort when she'd slowed down. Not only had he been inconsiderate but now their walk had to end.

He offered to carry her so they could go on, and she laughed it off, thinking he was joking, which he wasn't. He called Paolo to deliver his car, and she took her sandals off while they waited, so he did scoop her up. No matter how much she spluttered for him to put her down, he insisted he wasn't letting her stand barefoot in the street.

Once driving, every cell of his body on fire, he kept wondering how he'd prolong the drive and his time with her.

He didn't want this night to end.

Then he felt her looking at him. At the next light he turned to her, found her gaze fixed on him with what looked like distressed embarrassment.

The tightness he was getting used to feeling around her returned in full force. "What's wrong?"

Her lips twisted. "Just that you went to great lengths

to show me a good time and I was only a rude jackass in return."

"You only said what you thought without filters."

"Which is the definition of rudeness. I played back our whole outing and I realized you've been nothing but gracious while I've been obnoxious. At first I was so on purpose, but then I decided to stop, and I was still downright offensive."

"You were no such thing. You even paid me the biggest compliment anyone ever has. To everyone I *am* my success and power and money. You're the only one who ever thought I am the one who gives worth to my achievements and assets." Those wide eyes he never wanted to stop staring into grew larger. He gritted his teeth as he had to turn back to the road and drive again. "And even if you've been rude, I would have deserved it, since you consider I've coerced you into this outing."

"You didn't. I know I could have said no. But I did want to come. And I did enjoy everything, because I was with you. You're the best company I've ever had."

His gaze swung to her, caught her expression as she'd said these unbelievable statements.

Had he ever thought her anything less than the most perfect thing he'd ever seen? Was that how she truly felt? Could he be that lucky?

And whatever remained of his premeditation snapped. "I don't want to drive you home, Liliana. Come with me to mine."

The moment the words were out, he wanted to kick himself.

This was the last thing he should have said. He'd

barely gotten her to trust him enough to enjoy being with him and to admit it. And he had to go and crash through her limits like an overeager teenager.

Now she wouldn't only refuse, she'd swat him back to persona non grata status. Women usually played demure at this point, so men wouldn't think them easy. But *her* refusal would be the most legitimate response ever.

Amidst the fury of self-disgust, he almost missed her answer. Braking too abruptly at the light, jerking her in her seat, he turned to her, disbelieving.

"What did you say?" he rasped.

Looking up at him without the slightest trace of guile, she repeated what he hadn't believed he'd heard her say.

"I said okay."

Entering Antonio's sprawling mansion a fraught half hour after he'd asked her to go home with him, Lili still wondered if she was having another wish-fulfillment dream. One far more detailed and realistic…and outrageously ambitious. She kept wondering if she'd wake up any moment now.

But the dream continued, tangible, all-encompassing, like his heat at her back, his aura intoxicating her like the champagne had failed to. Everything was way over the top.

Problem was, it was really happening. He'd asked her to come home with him and she'd accepted. In embarrassing speed and eagerness.

"Would you like a drink?"

She swung around at his quiet question, almost losing her balance, and found him watching her with the most unreadable glance he'd leveled on her so far. Every fiber in her body quivered. He'd been almost silent since she'd said okay. Now the way he regarded her... What was he thinking?

To give herself space, to figure out what to feel or do, she nodded. With an even more disturbing glance, he nodded back as his powerful hand loosened his tie and undid a button as if they were suddenly suffocating him. Her dry throat convulsed as she watched him turn away, cross the lavish, ultramasculine great room to a wet bar at its end, his every movement sheer poetry of grace and control.

Her mind raced as he prepared their drinks, every now and then saying something that only necessitated monosyllabic responses from her.

She was now convinced he was interested in her. As a woman. Also known as sexually. While she could tell him he couldn't have picked a worse candidate for such interest, she doubted he'd listen. His intense fixation on her had only grown at her attempts to dissuade him from coming closer.

Maybe because he could talk to her, or she jogged his jaded senses, or she was a type he'd never encountered. Whatever the reason, he was interested.

But *interest* was too mild a word, insultingly so, to describe what he provoked in her.

She *craved* him.

When she'd never wanted anyone. Or anything, for that matter. Besides scientific discovery. Not that she'd ever felt anything this out of control for science.

Still, mere craving didn't describe her feelings now. Every last component of her being was aroused. Her mind, her senses, her body. She was in an uproar. For him. Only ever him.

But while his interest had grown directly proportionate to her resistance, since she'd stopped resisting him back there in his car, something had changed. He'd been almost...subdued.

Had he regretted inviting her here the moment she'd agreed? Had he only done so because, based on her behavior so far, he'd fully expected her to decline? Was he already losing interest now that she'd suddenly stopped providing him with the only things that had attracted him to her, resistance and surprises?

This probably explained the way he was behaving now.

Even if it didn't, she knew if she capitulated and joined his worshipping hordes, he *would* lose interest in her and move on. Sooner would be better than later. The longer she was exposed to him, the more severe the havoc he'd leave in his wake.

That led her to one possible decision. She'd give him what he expected as his right from all mortal beings.

He was sauntering back now with the drinks, as if he were postponing reaching her as much as he could. Stopping two steps away, when he'd always kept only one between them, he brooded down at her as he handed her a glass.

Gulping down agitation and regret, she took it. Then she reached for his glass, too. His eyes widened as he unclasped the glass and let her take it. Trembling in earnest now, she put the glasses down on a nearby coffee table.

His expression was perplexed when she straightened. It became stunned when she covered the space he'd kept between them, then reached up and pulled the tie he'd fully undone right off.

Dropping it to the ground, she lowered her eyes, unable to take the brunt of his blazing eyes this close up, or his disappointment that she'd turned out to be like every other woman he'd ever met. Squeezing her eyes shut, she did what she'd been aching to do since she'd laid eyes on him.

Sliding her hand beneath his shirt, she longingly glided her shaking, prickling hand over his hot, hard flesh.

Six

Antonio felt his mind short-circuiting.

Liliana. She was touching him. Igniting him into an uproar. Shocking him into paralysis.

This wasn't even among the things he'd expected or hoped for. He'd planned to court her, to break down her resistance in stages. But with a single "okay," she'd thrown everything out of whack. He felt like he'd been pushing with all his strength against an immovable object when suddenly all resistance was removed. He found himself hurtling with unstoppable momentum, falling flat on his face.

He'd still been struggling to adjust his thinking, and his actions accordingly as he'd handed her that drink, when she'd thrown him for a loop again by taking his, too, then proceeding to whisk off his tie. As the silk had hissed against his neck, as if relieved to part with his shirt, he'd frozen, his every sense converged on her eyes, trying to fathom from her expression what the hell had been going on.

But they'd been turbid with so many emotions. He *thought* he'd seen shyness, uncertainty, resignation, recklessness…and hunger, before she'd closed them as if to escape his analysis. Not that he could have been certain of anything. His mind had been a tangled mess by then.

And that was before she'd *touched* him.

Now a small, delicate hand slid beneath his shirt, as if searching for his heart. He felt as if she'd found it, taken hold of it. It was the only explanation for why it boomed in erratic thunder, when it had always remained steady in emergencies and under literal fire.

Her touch was like nothing he'd ever felt. It was like *he'd* never been touched before, and her tentative softness was his first exposure to human contact, to sensual stimulation. Sensations he'd never felt before exploded within him, detonating every single barrier inside him. The last dam was his control.

He was no longer in command of his thoughts or reactions, nor did he want to be. Of its own accord, his hand clamped her wrist, stopping the torment of her touch. Her eyes jerked open and up, alarm and mortification spreading in their gold depths. And his last thread of restraint snapped.

A primal rumble surging from his depths, he did what he'd wanted to do every second of the past three days. He yanked her against his body, hard. He growled something incoherent at the music of her cry, enveloping her in his arms and crushing her against him.

For one suspended moment, their gazes merged. Hers was at once stunned and surrendering. His heart felt as if it would explode if he didn't possess those lips that spilled those mind-melting sounds of submission.

"Antonio…"

He swooped down, his open mouth swallowing her gasp as he drove his tongue between her lips and plumbed her depths. The taste and scent of her, both overpowering aphrodisiacs, made him growl again and again as he feasted on her.

Opening to him, letting him all the way inside her, she whimpered, squirmed. He gave her what she was wordlessly begging for, deepening his possession, every glide against her moist silkiness, every thrust inside her fragrant deliciousness pouring fuel on his fire. Mindless with the need to devour her, to invade her, he hauled her up into his arms and strode to his bedroom with her curled up against him.

He flung himself down on the bed, taking her on top of him. She cried out as she impacted him, then again as he reversed their positions, taking her yielding, trembling body underneath him. His hands were almost rough in his haste to push her dress up and open her thighs. He groaned at the feel of her velvet firmness filling his hands. Lodging himself between her splayed smoothness, he rose on his knees to take off his jacket and shirt, tearing the latter in his haste.

Her eyes grew heavier as he exposed himself, her

body undulating its plea beneath him, her voice quavering as she gasped his name between fractured breaths.

With pants still on, he slid over her again, undoing her hair's improvised confinement, driving trembling hands into her thick tresses, his gaze feverishly roaming her flushed face. That face, that essence, had taken control of his desires and fantasies from the instant he'd seen her. Now he'd take her body. He'd possess it until she wept with pleasure.

Her eyes glittered with molten gold then overflowed. He jackknifed up, gaping at her as tears spilled down her hectic cheeks in pale tracks. His thought just now had been metaphorical, but she was shedding tears for real.

She was that aroused? As aroused as he was?

Triumph and hunger raged through him like wildfire. He should be shocked at their ferocity. But he reveled in feeling out of control for the first time in his life.

"Antonio, please…"

Her tearful plea, her body buzzing beneath him with a need as brutal as his own, undid whatever sanity he had left.

He fell on her like a starving predator, his lips wrenching at hers, his tongue driving inside her as he ground himself against her.

Suddenly she was heaving beneath him, her moans becoming strangled shrieks.

It was only when her cries in his mouth turned to whimpers and her body melted limply beneath his that realization trickled through his fury of arousal.

Had she…climaxed?

Struggling to stop grinding against her, he raised himself on shaking arms, found her staring at him from slit lids, panting through swollen lips, her body nerveless.

She *had* orgasmed. Before he got her naked, before he took her, just from him emulating the act of possession. She lay beneath him, boneless, the sight and scent of her satisfaction maddening him more. Her eyes told him release had only left her hungrier, readier for his invasion.

But he'd already been jarred out of his fugue. And what he realized he'd been about to do horrified him. He would have taken her without preliminaries. Without protection. He had none here. He'd never had a woman in this house, let alone this bed, had never intended to have one here.

He could pleasure her again, but he was in too precarious a condition. If he'd lost his mind from one touch, if he continued touching her, he'd get her naked, would end up buried inside her, would ride her until she climaxed around him, wouldn't be able to stop until he spilled deep inside her womb. It would be an irretrievable step that would spoil everything.

Among all the inhuman tests he'd been exposed to and had always passed with flying colors, raising himself off her now, ending this, was the hardest thing he'd ever done.

Her hands clung weakly to him, trying to coax him back to her. He'd never resisted anything so overwhelming.

But he managed to. Rising from the bed, keeping his

eyes off her so he wouldn't launch himself back at her, he strode to his dressing room and replaced the shirt he'd shredded before he strode back out to her.

His heart almost stopped when he found the bed empty. Exploding into a run, he only slowed down when he found her in the foyer, retrieving the purse she'd left on a table there.

"Liliana…"

His voice sounded as if it issued through gravel, which he felt filled his throat. Slowly, she turned to him, her face for the very first time totally unreadable. She said nothing.

"I'm sorry I pounced on you like that. It wasn't why I invited you here."

"I know. I'm the one who invited it."

Her exoneration was yet another unexpected blow that ratcheted his upheaval.

Feeling that anything he said now would make the situation worse somehow, he exhaled in frustration. "Maybe it's better if I take you home now."

Her eyes the darkest he'd seen them, she shook her head. "It's better if you don't. I'll call a cab."

He needed to argue, to convince her to let him see her home. Maybe he'd find something sane to say on the way to right the course of events that had devolved into this stilted mess. But he knew in his condition he'd only compound his mistakes.

Deciding to let her go, and to stay away from her until he got his act together, he exhaled. "I'll get Paolo to take you home." At her nod of consent, he reached for the intercom. "He lives on the premises, so he'll bring the car to the front door in a couple of minutes."

Without meeting his eyes, she again nodded, turned away and walked to the door. In seconds, she was gone.

He didn't know how long he remained rooted, staring at the door through which she'd disappeared. All he could see was how she'd looked as she'd walked away. Steady yet subdued, the energy and fire he'd always seen and felt in her every step now gone, as if something had been extinguished inside her.

Collapsing on the nearest seat, he pitched forward, burying his face in shaking hands.

What had he done?

"Won't you finally tell me what you did?"

Lili winced as Brian walked into her lab. His mood was so bright, she felt like closing her eyes to avoid its glare.

"I've been letting you get away with not telling me long enough," he said, "but after this morning, I can't wait any longer."

Yeah. Because this morning Antonio had sent a decree down his chain of command that everyone in the lab had their choice of project, whether it was one of his, their original ones or a new endeavor. Not only that, but if anyone saw fit to work on several projects simultaneously, they would be given all logistical and financial support. For scientists, who were always tied up in endless financial red tape, to be given such free rein was a dream.

"For God's sake, Lili, you have to tell me," Brian

urged. "The only things I don't tell you are things you certainly don't want to hear."

She returned her eyes to her laptop to escape his merriment and curiosity. But she no longer saw the data she'd just inputted, what she believed was her first breakthrough, which had caused the first lift in her spirit in the last two weeks. The two weeks since she'd last seen Antonio.

"For the last time, Brian," she mumbled. "I didn't do anything. The man just reconsidered."

"*After* you gave him all of your mind, not just a piece of it." Brian perched his hip on her desk. "But I thought that only made him give *you* back your research. Judging from today's developments, you must have done more."

"Unless I've developed some sort of long-distance mind control, I can't see how I could have. I haven't seen the man since the day I came back to work."

The day after her magical time with Antonio came to a disastrous end.

Brian regarded her as if he was deciding whether she was telling the truth. Then his grin widened even more. "Seems you didn't have to do more. That initial dose you gave him worked like a vaccine. Its effect intensified as time went by, until he developed full immunity, or in this case, empathy with your own views."

"Botched scientific metaphor aside, it's so nice to be likened to attenuated or dead microorganisms."

"I'm likening you to the tiny busters who save lives, like you've saved ours."

Slumping back in her chair, she exhaled. "Don't exaggerate. I didn't do anything. And what lives? You were all gung ho about joining his projects."

"I myself would have worked on anything that kept me employed and serving the cause of science. But this? This is what I became a scientist hoping to do one day. This is the beginning of a life I never thought I'd be able to live. And whatever you say, I know I have you to thank for it."

"Fine. Believe whatever you want and leave me in my own version of reality, where everything is the absolute opposite of what you insinuate about my effect on Antonio Balducci."

Brain sobered when he realized she was barely reining in her agitation. "Have I put my foot in it?"

"Down to the knee joint."

Dismay flared in his eyes. "Don't tell me you've…"

"Fallen for him" went unspoken. And "been rebuffed" was also concluded.

"Man, Lili! Granted, the guy is a god, and all the women and half the men around here are swooning over him, but you of all women… I thought you'd be immune."

"Well, you thought wrong."

His gaze switched from disconcerted to solicitous in a heartbeat. "You know the last thing I want to do is step on your toes, but I know how you bottle stuff up, and how you always feel better when you talk to me about it."

"Not this time, Brian, so just drop it, okay?" His persistence had helped her once before, after her mother's death, when he'd finally gotten her to unburden herself.

But knowing it wouldn't help this time, she changed the subject. "But since you're so eager to listen to me, do you have an hour? I think I'm onto something big here and I want your opinion."

Her diversion tactic worked, since scientific curiosity was the only thing that could take Brian's mind off just about anything. And for the next two hours she showed him her latest findings and he corroborated her every hope. By the time he left her, they were both certain she'd just broken through to the next level in her research.

Though this was huge, and she was beyond thrilled, that excitement didn't carry to the rest of her being. Most of her remained a prisoner to the memory of that night with Antonio.

That night, after his driver had taken her home, she'd collapsed in bed, shaking like a leaf with both mortification and arousal.

Instead of dreaming of him, she'd stayed awake all night, her mind filled with memories of the mindless minutes when she'd offered herself to him, when he'd almost taken her. His every touch and look and breath had replayed over and over, burning her with their vividness and her humiliation. She'd been so on fire for him, it had only taken him a few thrusts through their clothes for her to climax.

While it had stunned her, since she'd never reached release so easily, so violently, it had shocked him more. Maybe even alarmed or disgusted him. For what kind of woman would go off like that from just a few kisses and grinds? He must have figured he'd terribly miscalculated, and the iceberg he'd thought he'd enjoy melting had turned out to be a powder keg that would end up blowing up in his face.

She couldn't blame him that he hadn't wanted to be anywhere near her after that. He'd torn his gaze away from her pleading eyes and himself from her clinging arms, rushing to put clothes on to show her there'd be no further intimacies. Not that she'd been about to wait for him to come back to tell her that. She'd tried to run out of his mansion without seeing him again. But he'd caught up with her before she could, and though he'd tried to be considerate, what he'd said, how he'd looked at her, had been an even worse blow. Besides his obvious dismay and regret, it had seemed as if he'd...pitied her.

She hadn't closed her eyes till morning after that night, agonizing over whether to continue her earlier plan of leaving California, or going back to the lab he'd promised she could return to on her terms.

She'd ended up going back to work. A major part of her decision had been the hope that she'd see him again. She'd kept envisioning scenarios of how he'd come and what she'd say, in apology, or at least in an attempt to excuse or explain her actions. Anything to take them back to where they'd been before she'd touched him and spoiled everything.

That first day back in the lab, she'd kept expecting Antonio to walk in at any moment, kept jumping at any movement or sound, imagining she'd heard his voice or caught a glimpse of him.

But he hadn't come. Not that day, not since.

With each passing day, she'd been torn more among

shame, longing and despondency. Antonio had disappeared from her life as she'd known he would, only sooner and under far worse circumstances. She'd been right. All he'd needed was her capitulation. Once he'd had it, and so resoundingly, he'd lost interest. He must have even been horrified by her extreme reaction. He might have even feared he could have set himself up for a *Fatal Attraction* scenario.

It mortified her that she wouldn't be able to tell him he had nothing to worry about from her, or that she would always cherish whatever time she'd had with him. If that sounded pathetic, as it probably was, she didn't care. It was true. Being with him had been the most intense experience of her life. It pained her that what would always be a precious memory to her would be a distasteful one to him.

It also dismayed her that he'd disappeared before she could thank him. For going above and beyond in giving her everything she'd thought she'd never have, and thereby enabling her to reach the next level in her research. And he'd done that even after her accusations and suspicions and nastiness, then her reversal into a sex-starved maniac.

If she let him know through his deputies what she hoped to do, she feared he'd assign her some unsavory motivation. Even knowing she'd never see him again, the thought of losing his admiration, his respect, hurt the most.

"Are you busy?"

That voice. *His* voice.

In the split second before she looked up, she was certain she'd find nothing there. She'd jumped at too many phantom sounds and images of him before.

But this time, her gaze didn't land on nothingness. It collided with the too-real, too-magnificent sight of Antonio Balducci.

He was really there. Peeking around her lab's door, only his head and part of his shoulders visible. As if he was ready to retreat if she said yes, she was busy.

The world dimmed, and for the first time she knew how it was possible to faint with a brutal surge of emotions. Shock, elation, trepidation and a dozen other contradictory things.

Had he come to see her? Or was he here inspecting the status of her research, thanks to his generosity? Oh, and, by the way, to put things straight with her?

"I can come back later if you prefer."

His baritone reverberated in her very being, shaking her out of her paralysis. She rose unsteadily. "No. Actually you're just the person I wanted to see."

"I am?"

"Yes, yes, I...wanted to tell you a couple of things."

Walking in and closing the door behind him, he straightened to his daunting height, this carefulness of the last time he'd faced her, almost a wariness, still permeating his body language.

Man, she'd really managed to scare him. Was he worried she might jump his bones or something?

Circling him as far away as possible, she linked her hands behind her back. "I was going to make a formal proposal and send it to you up the chain, but since you're here..."

"You don't need to do that when you need more funds or resources for your research."

"It isn't for my research." She inhaled a bolstering breath. "I've taken a comprehensive look at your… folder, and I owe you an apology. The research you wanted me to helm is right up my alley and I find it very ambitious and exciting. If I reorganize my schedule to make a timetable that would have me working on both projects simultaneously, it is completely doable, with your resources and support in place. So if you'd still like me on the project, count me in."

"Actually, I no longer want you on it."

Her heart plummeted yet again with the validation of her worst fears, that her value to him had been negated by that foolish episode. It felt like a physical blow that almost rocked her on her feet.

Struggling not to choke on the lump that expanded in her throat, she waved her hand in dismissal. "Never mind, then. It was just an idea." Then an even worse thought detonated in her mind. "If…if you don't want me here at all, I understand. You still have my resignation, and you can approve it any time you—"

"Stop." His admonition was exasperated, almost pained. "Stop jumping to conclusions about me and what I mean. I don't want you on my project because I don't want your efforts and focus divided. I want them on your own work, where you're making remarkable progress."

He did? And he knew that? How?

"But when you conclude your work successfully, if you're still interested in any of my projects, there's nothing I want more than to have the benefit of your vision and expertise." He paused, exhaled, the searing blue of his eyes suddenly darkening. "But I'm not here to talk about work."

The heart that had been expanding with his every word felt as if it shriveled again. He was here to clear that personal land mine that now existed between him and an employee he wanted to keep.

She nodded. "I understand."

"I doubt you do."

"You must want to talk about that night two weeks ago. That's the other thing I'd hoped to talk to you about. I want you to forget that embarrassing episode ever happened, and be sure nothing like that will ever happen again. Just chalk it up to pathetic inexperience and let it go at that, okay?

As if he hadn't heard a word she'd said, his gaze focused on her eyes with such intensity, she felt them misting.

"Do you know why I've stayed away these two weeks?" he asked quietly.

She forced everything in her to go still, refusing to jump to more conclusions, especially ones laden with false hopes. She'd already accepted that he'd streak through her life like a meteor, affording her a brief blaze of splendor before he disappeared. She should be thankful he'd hurtled on before he'd done more damage. She should cling to the shield of resignation, even if every cell in her body still popped with the electricity of anticipation.

When she said nothing, Antonio answered his own

question. "I retreated to give you space, to reassess the damages I caused when I pursued you, besieged you, forced you out of your comfort zone and into what you might come to regret."

That was why he'd stayed away? Not for the horrible, degrading reasons she'd been torturing herself with?

"But there was another reason, too."

Her heart hit Pause, dreading his next words.

"I had to rethink everything I'd intended for this lab, to make decisions that would benefit everyone the most, by letting them resume their work or make their own choices, with my adjustments." He started walking closer, the gaze fixed on her filling with so much she couldn't bring herself to believe. "I had to prove to you, and to myself, that I can do what you can approve of, can be someone you can truly value and admire. You made me reconsider everything I do, professionally and personally."

By the time he was close enough for her to reach out and touch him again, she was ready to collapse at his feet. And that was before he made his closing statement.

"And that's why I'm here now. To tell you I want to hit a restart button with you. At your pace, on your terms."

Antonio had never dreaded anything in his life, a life filled with horrors and dangers and catastrophes. Not really.

But he dreaded Liliana's answer. He didn't know what he'd do if she rejected him.

Could he just walk away? How, when the thought

of losing her sent him straight out of his ordered, controlled mind?

For two weeks he'd forced himself to stay away, until he could provide her with tangible proof of what she meant to him, how she'd changed him. That time apart from her had been almost more than he could bear. He'd spent every moment struggling not to charge after her, to carry her back to his bed and keep her there until he'd branded her, made her unable to walk away from him ever again.

But first he had to prove to her he could become a man she could trust and respect for his ability to change, to do the right thing, not only a man she could admire for his abilities or lust after for his body and the unstoppable chemistry they shared.

Waiting for her verdict as if it would decide his fate, believing it would, he struggled to keep his expression from betraying the upheaval inside him. The last thing he needed was to scare her off with the intensity of his need.

"Why?"

After every scenario he'd played out in his head, she managed to surprise him yet again with that one-word question for an answer. She neither jumped on his offer, nor made him grovel some more, nor rejected him outright.

"You'll have to help me here, Liliana. Why what exactly?"

"Why me? Really? Now that the element of my surprise, my novelty, is gone, not to mention my resistance?

When I never considered those reasons enough for you to pursue me in the first place?"

His heart contracted with an emotion he'd never bothered with. Shame. But also wonder, that she was so attuned to him she'd sensed his early ulterior motive. This *was* his punishment for harboring those intentions, to have them resonate in her psyche, tainting her view of his motives when they no longer existed. When he now just wanted her.

Those eyes that filled his every waking and sleeping second probed his, filled with the candor and strength and vulnerability he'd become addicted to. "If you don't have specific reasons why you want me, then just tell me. Tell me what you expect from me, what you wish from being with me. I also want to know all the possible outcomes."

His head spinning, he blinked. "Outcomes?"

"Yes, like what to expect when you lose interest, how you intend to handle the eventual end of whatever we start." Her shoulders lifted in a self-conscious shrug. "I told you I can't handle uncertainty or afford upheavals."

Her scientific approach to his offer, insisting on analyzing his motives and charting a probable course for their relationship, was at once endearing and stunning. But what oppressed him was her expectation of worst-case scenarios.

"You mean you'd accept being with me even when you expect it to be a limited and finite liaison?"

She gave him such a look, as if he'd just said the most ridiculous thing, as if it was impossible for her to expect anything else, either from him or for herself.

Then she laughed, the sound mirthless. "I think any-one who enters a liaison without such expectation is just courting disaster. But I do want you so intensely that I'd take whatever is being offered, as long as I know what it is. I just need to go in knowing what to expect. That's all I ask. Total honesty."

His heart twisted with another feeling he'd never suffered from. Guilt. Total honesty was the one thing he couldn't offer her. He couldn't come clean about his initial plot to use her to get close to the Accardi fam-ily. He doubted even her pragmatic nature could forgive that. Even if it did, he feared her spontaneity with him wouldn't survive the revelation.

But he couldn't bear that she thought herself his in-ferior, that she expected nothing but impermanence and limitations as her due.

Itching to shake her out of those beliefs, he took her by the shoulders, groaning with the pleasure of her re-sponse, of touching her again.

"I'll say this once more and never again, Liliana. You are not only absolutely wrong in how you value your-self, but you appallingly underestimate my desire for you. I've *never* wanted anything like I want you. As for why I do, let me enlighten you. I want you because of *everything* you are. Every single thing about you fasci-nates me, elates me, inflames me. I adore your candor, and your wit leaves me with the bends. Your mind de-lights me and everything else about you, every gesture and breath and inch, makes me want to devour you. I'm the one who worries that once you come closer, it might be you who loses interest."

To say she looked incredulous was as accurate as saying she was reticent. But those eyes he'd been lost without flared with renewed life with his every word. Now their blaze made him almost give up any pretense of control.

But it was she who mattered here, and he had to make her feel secure. "All this doesn't only equalize our positions, Liliana, it makes me the supplicant. As such, I have no expectations. It's you who'll state your terms, set your parameters and every other thing you wish for in our intimacies."

Growing excitement glinted in her eyes. "What if I make outrageous demands?"

"I will welcome anything." His lips twisted as he surveyed the caring and generosity filling her expression, what he knew made up most of her being. "Though I doubt you'd ask for anything. You don't have a selfish or greedy cell in your body."

"I don't know about that, but I'd never make any demands. I want you free of obligations, for they have no place between us. I want you, and if you want me, for me, I'll be with you. Until it no longer makes you and therefore me happy." He started to object, furious that her insecurity about him hadn't been appeased, but she overrode him. "What I want to renegotiate is our professional situation. As my boss…"

He groaned his frustration at her evasion. "Will you please forget that? I'm no longer your boss. I gave you back full control over your work."

"Did you do that only to please me? To remove the obstacle of the boss/employee dynamic between us?"

He shook his head. "I do want to please you, Liliana, and remove all barriers between us, but I would have found another way to do so if I didn't believe your work held more merit than mine, given that you're so much further ahead in your research. I only attempted to force you to relinquish it initially as a demonstration of dominance. But not only am I now giving you absolute autonomy, I'm here to turn the whole lab over to you."

She staggered back. "Holy one-eighty, Antonio."

He caught her closer again, needing to convince her. "That's how you make me feel, Liliana. Like nothing I ever cared about matters anymore. Nothing but you, but us, matters to me now."

"Even so, you don't toss a two hundred-million-dollar lab at me to prove it. I told you I'm not partner material, and you want to make me director?"

"Even if you lack management skills, your scientific knowledge and your insight into your colleagues make you perfect for the job. I'll provide you with support staff who'll deal with the executive and financial issues. But in every other way, you'll make a far better boss than I can be for this place."

"Okay, time-out." She held her hands in the famous gesture. "You're clearly suffering from an extreme case of U-turn. So it's up to me to moderate you until you level out." He reached out to her hands, but she grabbed his instead. "Now listen, Antonio. I'm not taking this carte blanche or any other offer you come up with. And that's final. I only wanted to reach a common ground where both my goals and your interests could be met. I wish nothing more than to realize them both in a way that's the most beneficial for everyone."

As he looked into her earnest eyes, it was at this moment that Antonio realized something monumental.

What he felt for her.

Exactly what his brothers described they felt for their soul mates.

Love.

Seven

Love.

The word echoed in Antonio's mind as he stared at Liliana, who continued to detail how the common professional ground she was suggesting would work.

It had to be love. It *was*. This pure, limitless emotion.

But how? When he'd been in her presence only a handful of times? When he'd lived his life believing he didn't even have a heart?

But as he looked into her eyes and saw clear to her soul, saw what had delighted and spellbound him from the first, he knew.

Time was irrelevant. And he now did have a heart.

Liliana had planted one inside him.

Totally at peace with the discovery of its creation, and ecstatic about its captivity in Liliana's kind hands, he swept her in his arms and silenced her with everything that was bursting in his newly forged heart.

She melted into his kiss, not reciprocating, just yielding to him, letting him do whatever he wanted to her. That communicated how much she wanted him to possess her far more than if she'd gone wild in response.

He tore his lips from hers. "If you don't want me to take you right now, you'd better stop that."

Her long, thick lashes rose languidly, revealing passion-filled eyes that almost made him drag her down on the ground and take her there and then. "I'm not doing anything."

Pushing her back against the nearest wall, he pinned her there with his full weight, needing to imprint her with his body. "Exactly. Your surrender is sending me berserk."

"Yes, please."

"Liliana…" Her name erupted from his chest as he hitched her legs around his hips. His tongue plunged inside her open mouth, swallowing her gasps and eliciting more as he drove his hardness against her core through their clothes. "Will you come for me again?"

"Antonio…" She arched against the wall, making a fuller offer of herself.

Feeling her precious flesh burning in his hands, he quickened his cadence, the need to see her coming apart for him again riding him harder with each thrust.

"Do you know what it did to me when I felt you climaxing under me that night?" Her moans fractured, the flush staining her cheeks deepening before she buried her face in his chest. An incredulous laugh escaped him. "Are you shy?"

Suddenly she wriggled in his arms until she made him put her back on her feet, her eyes downcast. "I thought you were horrified… I thought that was why…"

A deeper wave of color surged over her face and neck. He cupped her jaw, made her look at him. "Why I stopped? I did that only because feeling you heave and tremble beneath me, realizing that I aroused you so much I drove you to orgasm even before taking you, snapped my control for the first time in my life."

She regarded him with a mixture of self-consciousness and disbelief. "You didn't seem out of control at all."

"It must be my surgeon facade. But if I'd remained near you one more minute, I would have taken you. Without protection. And I knew you'd let me."

Her eyes widened in realization and admission, proving he'd been right. She *would* have let him. She wanted him inside her without barriers, branding her with his pleasure. As he would, soon.

"I had to get away from you since I had no more control and your every touch and breath and glance had me at breaking point."

A keen escaped her as she crushed herself to him, silently demanding he stop holding back.

Unable to even contemplate it anymore, he pressed her to the wall again. He was devouring her whimpers, undulating feverishly against her when a one-note buzz jolted through them both.

His phone. The line he kept for his brothers.

Dammit.

Setting her down but unable to stop caressing her, he gestured an apology as he pulled the phone out.

It was an integral part of their brotherhood's pact, to answer a call from a brother at once. They'd depended on one another to survive, then to escape, then to conquer the world. A brother's call trumped everything. They never called one another on those special lines unless it was something serious. As the group's doctor, he'd gotten many of those calls.

Then came the last couple of years. Since then he'd gotten calls that were serious only in his brothers' eyes. After all, they considered any twinge their wives or children suffered the end of the world.

But this was Ivan. He wasn't married and would never be if all remained right with the world. Ivan had never called him on this line. Not once.

His heart thudding in mounting trepidation, he pushed the answer button. "Ivan?"

"Tonio, I'm landing in LA in half an hour. I need you and your best surgical team ready. Code Whiteout."

Code Whiteout meant he needed Antonio's secret surgical facility, where he had a special team on standby and where he treated injuries they needed kept below law enforcement's radar.

He gritted his teeth at the agitation he felt cracking his best friend's usual Siberian composure. "Tell me."

"A...friend and his sister. They were gunned down. I have a team stabilizing them. I need you to put them back together."

"I'll meet you there."

Ivan ended the call without another word. Antonio turned to Liliana, found she'd walked away to give him privacy.

He rushed after her, caught her in a ferocious hug. "I have to go, *mi amore*. Emergency surgery."

She almost jumped at his endearment, her eyes flooding with such exquisite delight. "Of course."

"Do you know how I hate leaving you now?"

"If it's as much as I hate you leaving, I pity you fiercely." Her smile wobbled as she caressed his cheek. "But duty calls. To both of us. I'd better get back to work before the bright ideas I was working on evaporate." He hugged her again as if afraid *she* somehow would. Seeming to read his paranoia right, she grinned. "I'll be right here when you're done."

"From the preliminary report, I don't foresee being done for the next twelve hours. If that."

"Then I'll see you whenever you can see me." She brushed his hair back, her touch soothing and bolstering.

He got out his keys, pressed them into her hand. "I'll text you my security codes and Paolo's number. He'll pick you up from your house after you get what you need. I want you there when I get home."

Her eyes made him this promise, and so many more, all of which he knew she'd keep no matter what. Then she stood on tiptoes and kissed him, giving him a glimpse of the ecstasy they'd share.

Before he grabbed her again, she stepped out of his arms, turned him around and marched him to the door. "The sooner you're gone, the sooner you'll be back to me."

As he stepped outside her lab, his heart lurched. Leaving her felt like leaving behind a vital part of himself.

"I'll be home as soon as I can."

"Oh, no, you're not rushing a surgery on my account. I'll be there no matter how late you are. And if you're not home by tomorrow morning, you know where to find me. Now, shoo."

At her grin, he groaned and turned away, forcing himself not to look back. He'd be late if he did, and Ivan would kill him. He'd do his job then rush home to her.

The anticipation kept him flying high all the way to his secret facility on the fringes of LA. It was only when he was entering it that he realized something.

When he'd given Liliana his keys, he'd been asking her to move in with him. He'd texted her nonstop on the way, but from her answers it was clear she thought he wanted her there only tonight. Even thinking that, she'd taken the keys happily. It pained him all over again that she didn't have any expectations, was truly content with anything he offered.

It made him wonder how such unconditional passion was possible, and how he of all people was on its receiving end.

But even if he didn't deserve it yet, he would.

He would deserve *her*.

It was 2:00 a.m. by the time he finished the surgeries.

It would have been much longer if he'd had to perform trauma repair and reconstruction on both patients. But by the time he had them on his table, he'd known one of them would not make it. Ivan's friend. The sister was critical but could survive with a liver transplant. Her brother was a tissue match for her and Antonio could harvest his liver, which had been one of the few things remaining intact in him. Ivan, who'd been watching everything in the gallery, had told him to do *anything* to save her. Which he had.

Letting his team take her to the ICU now, he tore his bloody scrubs off and stepped out of the OR. Ivan was right at the door, looking like he'd go on a rampage at any moment.

"Sorry about your…friend." Antonio wouldn't ask for details. Ivan would tell him if he wanted him to know. "I trust you know who did this to them?"

Ivan's usually forbidding face turned positively demonic. "They're already dead."

That was quick, even for Ivan. But then, no one could hide from him. Ivan had always traced the untraceable. But being the lord of the cyber world wasn't where his talents ended. His business rivals called him Ivan the Terrible, unsuspecting that Ivan was literally lethal. He was as accomplished an assassin as any of their other brothers.

"She will be fine, won't she?"

Antonio exhaled, rubbing his stiff neck. Ten hours of operating on Ivan's mystery woman had been extra grueling, mostly because of Ivan's volcanic agitation. Antonio did everything he could for all his patients, but when one of his brothers was involved, the stakes were almost unmanageable. Something he didn't relish while having a human life under his scalpel.

"She will be. But even after I discharge her, it'll be a long road to recovery. Does she have anyone to take care of her?"

"She has me."

Antonio went still. Coming from Ivan, this was major.

It *could* be duty driving him, or a debt he owed his dead friend. But Antonio felt this went far beyond that. Though Ivan had never intimated that he'd ever cared for a woman, Antonio felt this one was important to him. Very important. In a way no woman had ever been.

This was either a relationship Ivan had chosen not to tell him about, or it was a new development, as intense and life-changing as his situation with Liliana.

And if this weren't such a grim occasion, Antonio would have told him about her, would have joked about the brothers falling like dominoes one after the other.

But if Ivan felt about this woman like Antonio did for Liliana, what had happened to her, what was still ahead of her, must be killing him. While he had so much joy to look forward to with Liliana starting tonight, Ivan could only watch the woman he cared about struggle for her life.

Feeling guilty that he was the happiest he'd ever been while Ivan suffered his worst pain, Antonio grabbed him by the shoulders. "She *will* be fine, Ivan. She's strong, and you brought her to me in the best condition possible. I believe her brother was lost at the scene, and it was only your efforts that kept his systems going till you got him here. It's the only reason his organs were viable, making the transplant possible. It was you who saved her."

Ivan avoided his eye, kept his downcast under the blackest frown Antonio had ever seen as he turned away. But not before Antonio saw what felt like a blow to the solar plexus. His iceberg of a friend's eyes filling with tears.

Knowing Ivan wouldn't want him to acknowledge his upheaval, he followed him in silence to the ICU's observation area.

He stood behind him, felt agony radiating off him as he watched his mystery woman being hooked to monitors and drips.

"I'm a phone call away, Ivan."

Back rigid, breathing strident, Ivan only nodded.

Knowing he could do no more for now, Antonio exhaled at the unaccustomed feeling of helplessness and walked away.

An hour later, Antonio entered his mansion. It was dim and quiet. But he knew Liliana was there. She'd texted him, and so had Paolo the moment she'd gone inside safely.

He walked through the foyer into the great room and found her there on the couch, her hair streaming off its edge in a cascade of curls. She was sound asleep.

He approached her soundlessly and looked down at her. With his best friend's ordeal reverberating in his being, seeing her there, whole and irreplaceable, had a storm of emotions raging inside him. He wanted to wake her up, lose himself inside her, hide her within himself. And none of it was about lust. It was about passion and protection. Tenderness and togetherness.

And everything he'd never shared with or offered another human being.

Unable to keep away anymore, he bent to pick her up. The moment he touched her, she opened her eyes. They penetrated him to his very recesses with their instant welcome. As she tried to sit up, he scooped her up and pressed her head to his shoulder.

"Shh, *cuore mio*, don't wake up."

She nestled deeper into his hold, her lips moving against his thundering heart as she spoke. "I was just dreaming of you…as usual."

"Then continue dreaming, *mi amore*."

He carried her to his bed, their bed now, wondering again that he was using Italian.

He'd learned the language in The Organization, perfecting it before he had English. They always taught every child his mother tongue, so they'd use him in missions involving his country or countrymen. But he'd never spoken it outside of those times.

Liliana made him speak it. He wanted to lavish on her the passionate endearments unique to the language he should have grown up speaking. Somehow, only they felt right to express what he felt for her.

Reaching his bed, he placed her lovingly on it before remotely parting the drapes, letting the moonlight in. He started to undress her, and she stirred again. She caught his hands, embarrassment staining her cheeks in the silver light.

He kissed her, pushed her back gently, crooning encouragement and praise to her as his hands roamed her body, and she melted back again, letting him do anything he pleased. And it did please him, beyond words, to get rid of every barrier, to finally see that body that had inflamed his though it had always been obscured.

And she was divine. Smooth and strong and sinuous, in the exact proportions he'd just discovered translated into his personal definition of perfection.

She watched him throughout, hanging on his reactions. He didn't leave it to her deductions. He told her exactly what he thought. Then he started undressing himself, reveling in the awed, voracious look that possessed her face. If there was ever a reward for the years he'd spent training and maintaining his physique, it was *that* look. He was already addicted to it. Then he removed the last of his clothing, letting her see just how hard her beauty and her hunger made him.

At the sight of his erection, she gasped and sank back deeper in the bed, as if she already felt it invading her, pinning her to the mattress. She licked her lips, those lips he wanted nothing more than to feel around his hardness.

But that would come later. Now he needed to reassure himself that she was safe with him. That she was his to cherish, to protect.

Getting into bed beside her, he pulled her into his burning body. He groaned in unison with her long moan, aching and relieved, as their flesh touched without barriers for the first time. Then, gradually, he felt her tension dissipate in the serenity of deep sleep.

He watched her, at peace in his arms, for as long as he could, before he too succumbed. To the first true rest of his life.

* * *

He woke up to unknown yet breathtaking sensations. Silk and velvet sweeping all over his body.

Liliana was trailing her hands and hair and lips over him, caressing and kissing and delighting in him.

The light beyond his closed lids said it was around sunset. He'd never slept that long. Nor had he ever slept with anyone present except his brothers. He'd certainly never fallen asleep with a woman in the same bed. Not once in his life.

He kept his eyes closed for as long as he could bear, to savor her worshipping, his heart drumming to a slow, hungry rhythm.

Then he couldn't take it anymore. In the same second he opened his eyes, he reached for her, swept her around and beneath him. This time, there would be no stopping him.

"Antonio."

The way she made his name sound like an aching plea. For him. For everything with him.

He took her lips. A thousand volts crackled between them, unleashing everything inside him in a tidal wave.

Maddened by the immediacy of her surrender, he captured her lower lip in a growling bite, stilling its tremors, attempting to moderate his passion. But she made it impossible when she parted her lips wider for his invasion, and her taste inundated him.

Such unimaginable sweetness. And the perfume of her breath, the sensory overload of her feel. Everything about her was a hallucinogen that pounded through his system, snapping the tethers of his sanity.

Her whimpers urged him to intensify his possession. His hands shook with urgency as he wrapped her legs around his hips, rose to revel in the overpowering sight she made trembling in his arms.

"Tell me, *mi amore*. Tell me you need me to take you."

Her answer was only squeezing her eyes in languorous acquiescence.

"I will take everything you have, Liliana, devour everything you are and give you all of me. Is this what you want? What you need? Now? And from now on?"

Lili heard Antonio as if from the depths of a dream.

Everything that had happened since he'd come to her yesterday making his offer of himself, on her terms, felt like one.

But in her wildest fantasies, she wouldn't have dared hope for Antonio to feel the same sweeping desire for her, or to succumb to it, let alone as quickly as she had.

But he did. He had. And once again he was demanding her confession and consent. He was holding back to make certain she craved his invasion and sanctioned his ferocity.

Oh, how she did. Even if the power of his dominance, the starkness of his lust, staggered her. She might have come to his mansion, let him take her to his bed, might have been so bold as to wake the sleeping tiger, but now as she lay beneath him, waiting to be devoured, a storm of agitated desire overwhelmed her.

Her heart plunged into arrhythmia and she felt as if her every cell swelled, screamed for his possession.

Almost swooning with need, she gazed up at him as he loomed above her, the fiery palette of the horizon framing his magnificent body, setting his beauty ablaze. His eyes looked filled with tempests, precariously checked. He was giving her one last chance to dictate the terms of her surrender before he devastated her.

Feeling she'd die if he didn't she told him, "Take all of me, give me your all. Do everything to me, Antonio...*everything.* I need it all."

Raking her body in fierce greed, he bared his teeth on a soft snarl as he cupped her breasts in hands that trembled, kneaded them as if they were the most amazing things he'd ever felt. Then he bent and took one nipple in the damp furnace of his mouth, squeezing a shriek out of her. She unraveled with every nip and suck, each with the exact pressure and intensity to extract maximum pleasure. He layered sensation upon sensation until she felt inundated.

She was shaking out of control when he slid down her body, painting her with caresses and licks until he stilled an inch from her core, his breath on her making her feel she'd spontaneously combust.

He lit her fuse when he spoke, his voice a ragged, bass growl. *"Perfetto, bellezza, magnifica."*

As if everything about him weren't overkill already, he had to go speak Italian. It made her writhe.

"Antonio, *please...*"

"Si, amore, I will please you...always and forever."

He pressed his face to her thighs, his lips opening over her quivering flesh like a starving man who didn't know where to start his feast. Her fingers convulsed in his silky hair, pressed him to her flesh, unable to handle the stimulation, yet needing even more.

He dragged a hand between her thighs, electrifying her as the heel of his thumb brushed open her outer lips. Her undulations became feverish, her pleas a litany till he dipped a finger between her molten lips, stopping at her entrance.

"I dreamed of you like this from that first day, open to me, letting me possess and pleasure you."

He spread her legs, placed them over his shoulders, opening her core to him fully. Her moans became keens, sharpening, gasping.

He inhaled her, rumbling like a lion at the scent of his female in heat, as she was. He blew a gust of sensation over the knot where her nerves gathered. Her hips rose to him, a plea escaping her lips. It became a shriek when he finally, slowly, slid a finger inside her and she came, pleasure slamming through her in desperate surges.

He'd again made her climax with one touch.

Among the aftershocks, she felt his finger inside her, pumping, beckoning at her inner trigger. Her gasp tore through her lungs as his tongue joined in, circling her bud. Each glide and graze and pull and thrust made her need ignite again as if she hadn't just had the most intense orgasm of her life.

Soon she was sobbing, bucking again, opening herself fully to his double assault until he had her quaking and screaming with an even more violent release.

She tumbled from the explosive peak, drained, stupefied.

From the depth of drugged satiation, her heavy gaze sought his in the receding sunset. His eyes glowed azure, heavy with hunger and satisfaction.

"From now on you're on my menu every single day," he whispered. "I'm already addicted to your taste and your pleasure."

Something squeezed inside her until it became almost painful. It flabbergasted her to recognize it as an even fiercer arousal. Her satisfaction had lasted a minute and now she was even hungrier. No, she felt something else she'd never felt before. Empty. As if a void inside her was growing, demanding to be filled. By him. Only ever him.

"Don't indulge your addiction now." She barely recognized her voice, sultry with hunger, hoarse from her cries. "If you don't give me yourself right now, I might implode."

All lightness drained from his eyes as he squeezed her mound possessively, the ferocious conqueror flaring back to life. "And you will have me. I'll ride you to ecstasy until you can't beg for more."

His sensual threat filled her with nervous anticipation. Her heart went haywire as he slid back up over her, sowed kisses over her from her mound to her face, before he withdrew to look down at her.

His exhalation was ragged. "Do you realize how incredible you are?" As she mumbled something between dismissal and embarrassment, he persisted. "Don't you *see* how incredible I find you?"

He rose above her, displaying the full measure of his sculpted perfection. She struggled to her elbows, her mouth watering, her hands stinging, with the need to explore him, revel in him.

But he wasn't inviting her to witness or examine his splendor, but demonstrating her effect on him. Glimpsing his manhood in the semidarkness last night had filled her sleep with sexual torment. It was why she hadn't been able to keep her hands off him when she'd woken up, though she hadn't dared remove the sheet he tented even in sleep. Now she forced her gaze down… and was again awestruck at the size and beauty of him.

What if she couldn't accommodate him? Please him?

His muscles bunched as he reached down to the floor, picked up the pants he'd discarded and produced a foil packet. He was ready this time. Last time he hadn't been, which meant he didn't have women here. That was such a momentous realization, it made this even more incredible than it already was.

Then holding her eyes in such promise, he tore the packet open.

She almost came again just watching him sheath himself.

"Now I take you, *mi amore*. And you take me."

Though she shook with agitation, she whimpered, "Yes…yes, please."

She received him in trembling arms as he came down over her. She cried out at how her softness cushioned his hardness.

Perfect. No, sublime.

Pushing her legs wider apart, his eyes solicitous, tempestuous, he bathed himself in her readiness in slow strokes from bud to opening, driving her to desperation before he growled and finally sank inside her in one long, fierce thrust.

A red-hot lance of pain had the world flickering out for long moments, squeezing a cry from her very depths, before other sensations surged back in a rush, none she'd ever felt before. Fullness, completion.

Her eyes fluttered open to find him turned to stone on top of her, his eyes wild with worry.

"You're a... You were a... It's your first time!"

Quivering inside and out, the last thing she wanted was to talk, her mind unraveling with the feel of him filling her. But she had to answer his strangled exclamation. "You do remember me saying I was pathetically inexperienced, don't you?"

His distress ebbed, tenderness replacing it. "Oh, yes, I do. *Dio mio*, you're a surprise a second. Make that a shock a second. I didn't think you meant...*that*."

"What else did you think I meant?"

"I didn't think. I basically *can't* think around you."

Then he started withdrawing from her depths, making her feel he was turning her inside out.

"No!" She clung to him with her arms and legs, tried to drag him back inside her. "Don't go. Don't stop."

Throwing his head back, he squeezed his eyes. "I'm only trying not to lose my mind here, *mi amore*, in consideration of your...state of inexperience. Don't make it impossible." He opened his eyes. "I'd only stop if you wanted me to."

Emptiness threatening to engulf her, she thrust her hips upward, impaling herself on his massive girth, uncaring about the chafing pain, even needing it. "I'd die if you stopped."

His groan was pained, as if she'd hurt him, too. "Stopping would probably finish me, as well. For real."

She thrust up again, crying out as he stretched her, the sensation making her delirious.

His hand combed through her hair, dragged her down by its tether to the mattress, pinning her there. Her heart shook her like an earthquake as she crushed herself against him. "Don't hold back. I love the way you feel inside me. I *love* it. Fill me, hurt me until you make it better."

"*Si, amore*, I'll make it so much better." He cupped her hips in both hands, tilted them into a cradle for his own, then slowly thrust inside her to the hilt.

It was beyond overwhelming, being full of him. The reality, the meaning and carnality of it, rocked her essence.

He withdrew again, and she cried out at the unbearable loss, urged him to sink back into her. He resisted her pleas, taking his time, resting at her entrance before he thrust back inside her. Then again, and again. Slow, measured, making her cry out hot gusts of passion and open herself wider with every plunge.

Holding her gaze, he watched her intently, avidly, adjusting his movements to her every moan and grimace, waiting for pleasure to fully submerge the pain. He kept her at a fever pitch, caressing her all over, sucking her breasts, draining her lips, raining wonder over her. "*Perfetto, amore*, inside and out. Everything about you is perfect."

Her body soon rewarded his patience and expertise. It gushed readiness and pleasure over him, demanding everything he could give her.

"Antonio, I need everything now, please."

"*Si, bellezza*, everything." His groan reverberated in her mouth as he drove his tongue inside her to his plunging rhythm, quickening both.

Everything within her tightened unbearably, her depths rippling around him, reaching for that elusive something, something way beyond orgasm, nothing she'd ever attained, but that she felt she'd perish if she didn't have now.

No longer coherent, she begged him, over and over. "Please, Antonio, please."

But he understood, knew she couldn't bear the buildup anymore. "*Si, amore, ora.* Now I give you all the pleasure this divine body of yours can withstand."

Tilting her up toward him, he hammered inside her with a force and cadence that rattled the whole world, dismantled her every cell. He breached her to her womb on each plunge until he detonated the coil of desperation in her deepest recess.

Convulsions tore through her, clamping her inner muscles around him as her insides splintered with pleasure too agonizing to register, then to bear, then to bear having it end.

But it didn't end. It went on and on as he gave her more and more, until finally she cried out with his each jarring thrust.

Then came a moment she'd replay in her memory forever. The sight of him as he climaxed inside her.

Her orgasm intensified as he threw his head back to bellow his own pleasure. He fed her convulsions with his, his release so fierce she felt it through the barrier, making her sob with the need to feel its hot surges filling her.

Whimpering as he continued to move within her, completing her pleasure, her domination, she was helpless to do anything but let the enormity of his first possession drag her into oblivion.

Eight

An eternity later, Lili surged back into her body, realizing what had brought her back. Antonio was moving, starting to leave her body.

Unable to bear separation, she clung to him. He pressed soothing kisses to her eyes and lips, murmuring reassurance in that voice that strummed everything in her as he swept her around, careful to remain inside her. Then she was lying on top of him, satiated in ways she couldn't have imagined, reverberating with the magnitude of the experience and in perfect peace for the first time in her life.

When her heart stopped thundering enough to let her breathe, she raised a wobbling head. "Is it…always like that?"

His eyes looked as dazed as she felt, and his lips

twitched. "It's never been like that for me. Everything with you is always a first."

"You're telling me that's not why people make such a fuss about sex? Because it's that…that…" No description could do what had happened between them justice.

"In my experience, 'sex' has absolutely nothing in common with what we just had. This was…magic."

Her body began to throb all over again. "It was for me."

"You have nothing to compare it to, but I do, so I know how magical it was, and what made it so." Before she could infer the meaning of his confession he added, "It's because I love you."

She bolted upright, gaping down at him.

He started withdrawing from her depths carefully as he sat up, too. In spite of her paralysis, her moan echoed his groan at the burn of separation. Her gaze remained meshed with his as he looked at her as if she were the one thing he lived for.

"I realized it yesterday. That all those overwhelming feelings I feel for you are love."

She collapsed on the bed in a daze, could do nothing but watch him as he rose to discard the condom. Then he came back to tower over her, godlike, still fully engorged, a frown of uncertainty creeping over his face.

"I can see this comes as a shock."

Her heart stumbling, eyes stinging, she could only choke, "That's the understatement of our era."

"Is it a good or bad shock?"

He seemed actually worried. Very worried. *Really?*

It was the only thing she could say out loud. "Are you for real? Is that even a question?"

His shoulders rose and fell. "I've learned to never assume anything with you. You never react in any way I expect. I also realize this could seem too quick—"

"You think?" She felt caught in a hurricane of disbelief and jubilation that uprooted her very existence. "It's been less than a week."

"It's been *three* weeks."

"Two of which you didn't even see me."

"Because I was on a mission to be worthy of you and your trust and respect. And I did see you. I was watching you."

Her mouth dropped open. "You were?"

His grin was sheepish. "I practically stalked you. At home, at work. Before you ask how, I…have my ways."

She struggled up to her elbow, incredulousness mushrooming inside her. "I'm sure you have. But even so…"

Lowering himself to the bed, he stretched out beside her, gathering her along his hot, hard body. "I've always made life-and-death decisions in seconds. Taking three weeks to conclude that I love you is a glacial pace for me. I took that long only because the decision to love you for the rest of my life is way more weighty than any life-and-death issue I've ever dealt with."

She shook her head. How could all this be happening?

His large hand cupped her head. "Do you know why I came back to you when I did?"

"Because you completed that quest you thought would make you worthy of me?"

"You think it took me two whole weeks to do that? Everything was in place in two days."

She blinked dazedly. "So why?"

"I was waiting for you."

"To do what? Seek you out?"

"No, to reach your breakthrough. I knew you were close when I first acquired the lab, and that when you used the resources I put at your disposal, you'd no doubt reach it. I didn't want to come back before you did. I wanted you to have this achievement you so deserve, before I distracted the hell out of you."

That was tremendous. Unbelievable. But... "If you came the next day and explained that I didn't put you off and you didn't fear I'd boil your rabbit, I wouldn't have agonized over you with every breath. I might have even reached that breakthrough sooner."

His frown was spectacular. "Dammit. Everything I do because of you or for you backfires right in my face."

She caressed his cheek placatingly. "With an end result that's far better than any plan could have projected. Look at where I am now with my work, how ecstatic everyone is that you bought the lab. Look at me lying here with you, after you've given me absolute pleasure and so much more I never dreamed I'd have, and are now telling me that you...you..." A strangled cry escaped her as she buried her face into his chest, tears pouring from the depths of her soul. "This is... you are...too much. Way more than my heart can withstand or contain."

"You are impossible for my heart to withstand or contain, too. What I feel for you is so intense, I feel I would go mad if you don't reciprocate."

"Oh God, I do, Antonio. I *love* you. I think from the first moment I saw you. But I never thought you could love me back."

"You captured me from that first moment, too. I know myself, and I can promise you one thing—I'll love you more every day. I only hope you never think I love you too much."

She surged into him, shaking, tears flowing, unable to talk or breathe anymore. Her heart was overflowing. He soothed her, caressed her all over, sucking her lips, her nipples, lavishing the most amazing endearments and praise on her until she wrapped herself around him, undulated against him.

"Take me again, Antonio."

His laugh was distressed as he unclasped her thighs from around his waist. "You might think you're ready for another round, but trust me, you're not." He laid her back gently, his gaze scorching her all over before returning to her eyes, filled such sensual indulgence her core cramped with need. "So...never before, eh?"

Feeling free to show him everything in her heart and how wanton he made her, she rubbed her nipples against his rock-hard chest. "Apart from...uh...self-help, no. Why bother, when it wasn't you?"

His gaze went supernova as he crushed her to him, then her lips beneath his.

When he let her breathe again, she felt self-conscious

again. "So you're not wondering how I reached this age without having sex? You don't find it…"

"Pathetic?" he repeated her earlier description of her inexperience. "What's pathetic is how ferociously glad I am that you didn't." He pressed into her, his arousal undiminished, his body buzzing with vitality and dominance and lust. "And I don't find it strange at all, now that I know you. You don't do anything unless it satisfies your meticulous, exacting mind, and I am only proud and grateful I'm the one who does. After you made me work my ass off for it, of course."

He understood. And appreciated. Her heart swelled with thankfulness, even as it still quaked with the enormity of knowing he loved her back.

She caressed his hewn cheek, letting him see everything inside her. "I never wanted anyone, never considered anyone worth the trouble. But even when I thought you were unattainable and knew you would be trouble of unimaginable magnitude, I wanted you. I craved you, in any way, for any length of time, no matter the price. Or I thought I craved you. After this…cataclysm, I'm addicted to you."

After another smothering, devouring kiss, he withdrew. "It's merciful you are, since I'm beyond addicted to you. It's also lifesaving for those men you didn't bother with. If you had, I would have gone hunting them."

She burst out laughing. "Now I've got an image emblazoned forever in my mind. You in a loincloth, chasing poor, inferior men, clubbing them over the head and throwing them in a pile."

His smile was predatory. "*Si, amore*, laugh at the caveman your love has made of me."

Arching with an unbearable surge of delight and desire, she opened for his erection, needing him back inside her. "Go caveman all over me, please."

His pupils flared in warning. "I'm barely holding him back, so behave. You're too sore now."

"But I want you to let him loose. Make me almost die of pleasure again, Antonio."

Groaning as if in pain, he thrust against her. "From the first time you cut me up with that tongue of yours, I knew. That under the guise of the prim, contentious scientist there was a woman I wanted desperately. But even I wasn't ambitious enough to hope I'd find this, the most perfect, uninhibited sex goddess. You almost killed me with pleasure, too."

"Then take us to the edge of mortality again, *please*."

"Command me, *amore*. You only have to breathe, to just be, and I would literally die for you."

Before her mind could wrap around those earth-shaking words, he rose over her, opened her wide around his hips and slid his hardness between the molten lips of her core. He nudged her nub and the world vanished in a burst of pleasure.

It came so quickly, a boil in her blood, a tightening in depths that now knew exactly how to unfurl and undo her. She opened herself for him, knowing he would only pleasure her this way, undulating faster against him until another orgasm, different yet still magnificent, tore through her.

He pinned her down as she came, gliding his shaft

against her quivering flesh in the exact pressure and rhythm to drain her of every spark her body needed to discharge.

After she slumped in quivering fulfillment, he rose between her spread legs and pumped himself to a roaring climax.

Watching him take his pleasure over her trembling body, the body he now owned, was mesmerizing. It was the most flagrantly erotic sight she'd ever witnessed, and the most profoundly fulfilling emotion she'd ever felt.

Pulling her to his body, he mingled their sweat and pleasure and heartbeats, surrounding her in his love and cherishing, dragging her into a realm of safety and contentment.

When next she woke up, it was to Antonio's caresses.

He was wiping her down with something wet and warm. Moaning, she opened her eyes to find him bent over her in dim, golden light, a being out of a fable, cosseting and worshipping her. Joy surged on a tremulous smile as she sought his eyes, only for it to be aborted at the sight of the disturbed expression in their depths.

That had her scrambling up, her heart shedding its languor, starting to drum painfully. "What's wrong, Antonio?"

He exhaled, continued to rub her stomach. "I was watching you sleeping so trustingly in my arms...and I kept wondering how you feel the same for me. Or how you'd continue to."

She stopped his hand. "Where is this coming from?"

Extricating his hand from her grip, he threw the hand towel aside squeezed his eyes shut briefly. "Apart from my…partners, I never had any relationship of any sort with anyone."

This was all? She poked her elbow in his side, inviting him to grin back at her. "Same here."

"You're nowhere near the same, *mi amore.*"

"Of course I'm not. You're unique."

He shook his head. "It's you who are. While having more money and power than almost anyone doesn't mean I'm anywhere near your level."

"I already told you I don't factor your money and power in your uniqueness. The man you are beneath the trappings, the force of nature who achieved such success, who saves lives and puts bodies back together like no one else can, who turns everything he touches into the best it can be…that's the man I love."

"*Dio mio, dea mia.* You're far more than I ever imagined anyone could be. You're far better than I deserve."

She scrambled up to her knees, caught his hot face in trembling hands. "Why, my love? Why do you feel that way? When you said you feared I'd be the one to lose interest, I thought you were being gallant. But you meant it, didn't you?"

He nodded. "It scares me like nothing has before, that one day you'll look inside me and hate what you see."

This was more serious than she'd first imagined. And it needed to be resolved, at once.

She sat back on her heels, feeling it was the most natural thing to be naked with him in every sense of the word.

"When you told me you grew up without your father, too, I thought I saw scars beyond your perfect, placid facade and I hoped they'd been long healed. But now I feel this goes far deeper than growing up fatherless like me, that you suffered way more hardships and injustices and abuse than anything I can imagine. And it makes me even more proud of you and in awe of what you attained in spite of it all."

"What if you're right, and there's way more to me that you can dream of in your worst nightmares? What if it's so terrible that if you knew, it would send you away screaming?"

"You're not hypothesizing, are you? You're really afraid I can't handle the truth." His eyes went bleak, overwhelming her with the need to unburden him. She pressed her hands to his heart, needing to absorb his pain. "This damage I feel inside you…it goes beyond a physical or psychological ordeal. You've…done things. Ugly things." His gaze faltered, and it felt as if his last reluctance gave way, letting her plunge deep. And she felt she was reading everything inside him, dragging out every festering darkness. Her voice shook as she put what she saw into words. "You were involved in… violence. You used your skills in cold-blooded and lethal ways. Even to…kill."

She bated her breath as his eyes widened, stunned.

Then all the fire that had ever been there was extinguished and he only said, "Yes."

Ever since Antonio had realized he wanted Liliana, he'd broken out in cold sweat just thinking how it would hurt her if she ever learned she'd initially been a tool in his plan of revenge, even if he hadn't and would never act on it.

Though he couldn't come clean about it, ever, he needed to be honest with her any other way he could. He'd already started by opening up about his feelings. Now he needed to go further, all the way, and open up about himself.

His surface was as perfect and placid as she'd said. But he was anything but inside. Not even his brothers knew of the wreckage inside him. But *she'd* seen it. She'd said it made her proud of him that he'd become what he was in spite of what he'd been through. But though she'd somehow seen what no one else had even guessed at, she still couldn't even guess at the specifics.

What if he told her all the things he'd done as a slave of The Organization, what he'd had to do to gain his freedom, and it horrified her? What if she thought him too damaged, beyond redemption, and ran for her life?

But he owed her the whole truth. He'd keep from her only what might hurt her feelings or damage her trust in him. What didn't apply to them anymore anyway, and never would.

More than anything he wanted to make her promise she'd never leave him no matter what she learned, but he couldn't do that. She'd give him her pledge, and she'd keep it, even if she hated it and him. She was that noble, that kind. No, she had to have total freedom to act in her own best interests. Even if it meant leaving him behind. Even if he couldn't survive without her.

Needing to put some distance between them so he

wouldn't weaken, he pulled away from her, rose to fetch his pants.

As he came back to stand over her, she pulled the sheet over herself, as if she feared she couldn't face whatever he'd say in the vulnerability of nakedness. It made him hate himself more for causing her even a moment's uncertainty or anxiety.

Holding her suddenly fragile gaze, praying she wouldn't end up hating him, he said, "Though I'd give anything for you not to know, you need to know. What I am, what I've done. I'll abide by whatever decision you make once you know everything."

And he exposed all the horrors of his past, what not even his brothers knew. The only thing he left out was the identity of the family who'd discarded him.

All through his confession, what most agonized him were the brutal emotions that ravaged her, from shock to horror to denial to desolation. He couldn't stop to analyze each one so he could go on.

When he was done, he stood before her, unable to believe he'd finally unburdened himself, shaking with the discharge of a lifetime of torment and rage that he'd suppressed under layers of steely discipline. But what truly shook him was dreading the reason behind her weeping.

Before he could bring himself to ask, she scrambled off the bed and launched herself at him so explosively, she made him stumble and fall.

He barely caught himself before he crashed flat on the ground, cushioning her on top of him as she rained copious tears and frenzied kisses all over him. She sobbed so hard he was terrified she'd do herself real damage.

He frantically tried to soothe her. "*Mi amore*, please, nothing is worth your tears. I beg you, don't cry."

She shook her head and cried harder, but he finally understood what she was reiterating in her incoherent sobbing.

"My love, my love, I'm sorry, I'm so sorry, so sorry…" *This was all for him.*

His one-of-a-kind, magnanimous firecracker was breaking her own heart on his behalf.

He crushed her to him, trying to defuse her upheaval. "*Mi amore*, it's all in the past. I just needed you to know."

She struggled out of his hold and rose above him, her eyes reddened, her lips quaking. "And I'd give anything, *everything*, if I could undo it all, make you unsuffer every single second."

He caught her face, stilled its shuddering. "You have. Just telling you, just that it didn't matter to you, worked like an antidote to the poison I had in my system. I can now leave it all behind where it can't touch me, or us, again. Just loving you erases it all, makes up for it a hundred times over."

Her sobs lessened as he talked, stroked her hair, pressed her to his chest.

With her upheaval fading, she spoke against his flesh. "You know what's driving me insane right now? Besides being unable to go after those who hurt you and making them suffer a far worse hell than the one they put you through? It's that I had such a ridiculously easy life compared to you. I can't even share your ordeals except in my imagination. And I *hate* it!"

He went still beneath her. His heart had expanded until he wondered if it would burst. Not a bad way to go, he thought. If he didn't want to live forever. To be with Liliana.

"*Mi amore, sposami.* Marry me."

His words echoed in absolute silence.

They'd both stopped breathing. The very world stopped turning.

Then both their chests emptied on ragged moans as she raised an unsteady head to look down at him, flabbergasted.

And everything poured out of him. "I never had a heart, but you created one inside me. A heart that was made to love you, that can't survive without you. So if you want me alive, you'll have to say yes."

She burst into tears again. "God, Antonio, yes...*yes*. But..."

"No buts."

"I was just going to say—but I think you should slow down, take more time to think about this. After you do—"

His lips silenced hers. "I can't slow down, and I won't think about it. I want nothing else but you. I now realize everything in my life has been leading up to this. This moment. This union. You." He took her in another compulsive kiss. "So never say 'but' again."

"Even if I say that no word remains after what you said 'but' yes?"

"You can say anything, as long as it ends in yes."

And for the rest of the night, she said almost nothing but yes. She whimpered, whispered and screamed it. She said yes to him, to them, and to everything their future together would bring.

"You have to tell us, Lili."

Lili turned to the redhead who regarded her with such warm curiosity. Scarlett Kuroshiro, the wife of Raiden, one of Antonio's brothers, was unearthly beautiful. Her husband, who sat beside her, clearly as besotted with her as she appeared to be with him, was Japanese by birth and as gorgeous as she was in his own way. But what truly amazed Lili was their year-old baby daughter, who mixed them both into an incredible mixture. Their adopted children, five of them from four to eight years old, were all playing on the grounds of Antonio's mansion with the other brothers' kids and their nannies.

"Yes, you have to." That was Jenan, another brother's wife, the guy who looked like a genie. Sheikh Numair Al Aswad, the brotherhood's leader. Jenan looked like she'd walked out of *Arabian Nights* herself, and actually *was* a princess. "We must know what you did to Antonio," she said. "What superpowers do you have?"

Lili smirked. "This coming from the pantheon of gods and goddesses Antonio has for brothers and sisters."

Everyone laughed. They'd been laughing every time she'd said anything. It was either that Antonio had given them strict orders to be super delighted with her every word, or that her brand of humor tickled them as much as it did him.

"It's fate." Rafael, the youngest brother, a Brazilian and another juggernaut, hugged his wife, Eliana, into his side tighter. "So our brotherhood would be blessed by the duet of Eliana and Liliana."

Eliana looked adoringly up at her husband before she winked at Lili. "I somehow don't think fate conspired such a perfect match just so your brotherhood would have wives with rhyming names. Besides, I'm Ellie and she's Lili."

"No."

"No."

Both Antonio and Rafael spoke in unison, each vehemently refusing his mate's nickname.

Eliana sighed, giving Lili a we're-in-this-together look. "You're Liliana and never Lili to Antonio, right?"

Lili wiggled one eyebrow at Antonio. "Yeah, and he has exclusive rights to it. So y'all better call me Lili if you want to remain on your doctor's good side."

"It's clear to *me* why Antonio is falling over himself to marry you." That was Richard Graves. Not Antonio's brother, but his partner, the one who smothered them all in security measures, who used to be Rafael's handler. The Brit was the perfect combination of suave and grit, a Bond/Lancelot hybrid. His hand laced with Isabella's, his wife and a surgeon herself, his body touching hers from shoulder to calf, as if he couldn't be away from her. It was weird, since the guy looked as cold as a cobra. "You're a combination I didn't think existed, but exactly what would bowl him over. You must have mowed him down without even trying."

"That she did." Antonio laughed, looking down at her adoringly. "I'm down for the count. For life."

"That's what you guys do. Even those who resist their fate for years." Isabella pinched Richard, who growled and buried a kiss in her neck. She giggled, looking at Lili. "When they give in and give you their hearts, it's yours forever. They'd conquer the world for you, live and die for you. They're a bit scary, but each of them is one-of-a-kind and we can't think how we lived before them."

Richard squeezed his wife tighter as the other women fervently corroborated her statements and their husbands hugged them closer, too.

Lili looked up at Antonio, as usual finding his heart in his eyes, the heart he said he'd grown to love her with.

Pulling him down, she murmured against his lips, "I have no idea at all how."

She surfaced from his drowning kiss to the hoots and claps of the couples, and the disgusted groans of Jakob Wolff, the guy who looked like a Viking marauder, and the only single brother around.

Antonio had just told them about his proposal last night. The ladies had insisted on meeting her at once, and the men had made their wishes come true without delay. They'd all converged on LA from wherever they'd been in the world, arriving at Antonio's mansion one after the other. By the time they'd started arriving, Antonio had told her everything about their previous and current personas, and she'd memorized all the info.

The only one who was missing was Ivan Konstantinov, Antonio's best friend. But he certainly wouldn't have left the side of the woman Antonio had saved that first night she and Antonio were together. Antonio had told her they were missing another brother, but that she wouldn't be seeing him. He'd left their brotherhood six years ago, vowing never to return. It seemed it had been an unspeakable falling-out, since Antonio, who'd so far shared the most horrendous stuff with her, wouldn't say a word about why "Cypher" had left them.

Antonio had wanted their wedding to be three days from now, a whopping week after he'd proposed. But she'd convinced him it was either forgo a wedding completely, or if he wanted an actual party, they needed at least a month. Adamant that there was no way he wasn't giving her a wedding, and reluctant about what he called an unbearable delay, he'd succumbed and set the date.

The evening proceeded in escalating mirth and harmony. Those juggernauts—who between them could rule the world and did to a great degree—and their gorgeous mates promised to be available at all times to help with the wedding preparations. Lili was so delighted with them all, his "family", she kept thanking him for rounding them up for this impromptu engagement party, and thanking them for coming and for being this fantastic.

Everything was so amazing it made her feel she'd plunged into another level of the fairy tale she'd been living with Antonio since that day he'd changed her life. And every now and then one incredulous question floated in her mind.

Could anything in this world be that perfect?

Nine

"My father called again yesterday."

The razor in Antonio's hand stilled over his left cheek. The eyes that had been promising her another session of devastation in the mirror, clean-shaven this time, emptied.

Next second he refocused on shaving, grunting something vague.

Her heart slumped a notch in her chest.

His reaction to the subject of her father and her family was the only thing that marred the perfection they'd been sharing so far.

Her father had been after her to set a date for that reception the Accardis wanted to hold in her honor. When he heard of her engagement, and to whom, his cajoling had become persistence. He couldn't wait to meet her fiancé.

And she couldn't wait for Antonio to meet him, too. Now that she'd been included in Antonio's family, her reluctance to establish a relationship with her father and the Accardis had evaporated. She now wanted to attend the party in which she would meet her long-lost family.

But though Antonio was always eager to do everything with her or for her, joining her for that party wasn't a foregone conclusion. As he'd just proven again.

She tried again. "He's really eager to meet you, and he's hoping I can give him a final answer about the Accardi reception."

Next moment, her heart lodged in her throat. At the shocking burst of wrath and revulsion she saw reflected at her in his eyes.

He suppressed his reaction at once. But she'd seen it.

This was far worse than she'd first thought. It was like this lethal persona that lived within him had surged to the surface. And it had been positively murderous.

Feeling close to tears for thoughtlessly causing him this flare-up, she squeezed her eyes shut and turned to leave the bathroom. "Please, forget it. I shouldn't have brought this up."

"No." She heard the razor clatter in the marble sink, and then the sound of his hurried, powerful footsteps a second before his hands clamped her shoulders and turned her to him. "*Dio mio, mi amore*, no. You should always tell me everything. Everything you want to do, anything on your mind. Always. I beg your forgiveness if I made you feel you can't talk to me about this."

A tear trickled down her cheek, inciting a vicious string of self-abusing expletives from him.

Furious with herself, she wiped it away, pointed at the moisture. "This is for *you*. I hate that I didn't take a hint, cornered you into letting your anger surface. I know how you hate your harsh side, what it takes to curb it so perfectly, to maintain your inner peace. I hate that it's only on my account that you can fall prey again to such aggressive emotions."

Clad in only low-riding black silk pajama bottoms, he scooped her up in his arms, his erection lodging in her quivering belly. "Well, you'll have to live with the fact that I would give up all the peace in existence for the savage emotions you inspire in me, along with the sublime ones. You'll have to make your peace with the fact that I can happily kill for you, not only die for you."

Melting in his hold as he swept her up and carried her to bed, she wrapped her legs around his waist. "Since I'd rather you live for me, thank you very much, let's forget I brought up my father and my family. You probably think I'm stupid to consider accepting his advances. You must consider they more or less did to me what your family did to you."

He started to speak, then clamped his lips. Because she'd put her finger on the truth and he wasn't about to say she didn't. He always told her the truth.

As he came to half lie over her, she cupped his cheek and reveled in his beauty, this god among men who desired her so completely, who was unbelievably hers. "I understand how your anger toward your family extends to mine, and it's totally justified. I wouldn't have considered being anywhere near my father or any of the Accardis on my own. But he's been trying so hard, I wanted to give him a chance before I decide whether to have him in my life. I didn't want unresolved bitterness lurking anywhere if I could work it out. The best I expected was that my family would be a once-a-year presence in my life, and my father would be a peripheral one.

"But that was before I realized how forcefully you feel about this. *Nothing* is worth making you suffer the least discomfort. You, and our lives together, are the only things that matter to me. I *did* mean it when I said let's just forget about this."

Antonio stared down at his woman, the woman he'd been falling deeper in love with each passing second.

Every time she'd mentioned her father and their joint family, his agitation had built. Though he now considered whatever debt they owed him paid a million times over just for being the reason he'd met Liliana, he abhorred their very existence. He never wanted to see any of them, not to punish them or to have anything to do with them. But the idea that they were trying to enter her life, when they were bound to taint it, made his loathing mount. He'd destroy them all before he let them cause her the least heartache.

But she needed closure and now, because she considered only him and his feelings, she was dismissing that need.

And there was no way he'd deprive her of anything at all. He'd swallow his hatred, hell, he'd swallow molten steel if it provided her with peace. On the off chance that her father and his family brought her a measure of contentment, he'd even tolerate them. He'd be there for her, with her, at every event, honoring her and showing them she had a lethal protector in him. Just in case any of them thought to show their true colors.

He gathered her closer, delighting in her feel, her love. "We'll forget nothing. I'm going to meet your father, and we're going to New York to meet your family." Anxiety flared again in her reddened eyes. He caught her lips in a cherishing kiss, aborting her protest. "We'll do everything that might provide you with even a remote possibility of well-being, always. And that, *mi amore*, is that."

Flying to New York on Antonio's private jet, Lili felt she'd plunged deeper into the parallel universe she'd stumbled into since the day he'd entered her life.

The Accardis had set the reception for the very next weekend, two days after Antonio had insisted they accept their invitation. The haste had to be her father's doing, no doubt. But this meant that the first time Antonio met him would be at the reception.

All the way, Antonio had placated her worries about his aversion to her family. He assured her if she enjoyed knowing them, he'd be lenient and might even consider liking them. After all, she made him so happy he could forgive any past transgressions and afford to be magnanimous like her. That had reassured her, until they entered the Accardi family mansion.

Now she felt something writhing inside him. Something dark and vicious.

Before she told him she would leave if he didn't want to be here after all, her father came rushing toward them as soon as they crossed the mansion's threshold.

In the seconds before he reached them, his smile as wide as humanly possible, Lili noticed something for the first time. Her father and Antonio looked alike. Apart from the size and age difference—Antonio was much bigger, and her father had wrinkles and silver hair—the two men shared the same bone structure and skin tone. If she'd seen them on the streets, she would have thought them relatives. In fact, if someone saw the three of them, with her looking like her mother, people would have thought it was Antonio who was her father's son.

"*Mia bella Lilianissima*, you're here!"

Feeling Antonio going rigid beside her, she stood with a wooden smile, awkwardly letting her father hug her.

Thankfully, he did so more briefly than in the few times she'd seen him. For now he had a distraction in Antonio.

"Dr. Balducci, a hundred welcomes to Casa Accardi."

"One would do, Signore Accardi." Antonio took her father's extended hand after a telling hesitation, as if he loathed touching him. He still managed a courteous nod, for her sake.

Oblivious to Antonio's aversion, her father enfolded Antonio's hand in both of his fervently. "I'm beyond delighted about your and Lili's engagement. Only the best man is worthy of her, and that's what I hear you are. And an Italian, too. It's just perfection. Everything is coming together in the exact perfect way that my incomparable daughter deserves."

As if he'd reached his limit, Antonio withdrew his hand from her father's grip. "Liliana is beyond incomparable, and deserves only the best of everything. Which I'll make sure she gets, now and forever."

Antonio's words sounded like a warning. He was telling her father he'd better be on his best behavior with her, or else.

Her nerves jangled at Antonio's barely veiled threat. Regardless of whether her father deserved it for his past behavior, she'd hoped her fiancé would offer him that leniency he'd talked about. It was clear Antonio wouldn't offer any until her father proved himself. Which she was sure Antonio wouldn't make easy.

Not that her father noticed any subscript in Antonio's words. He now led them to the open doors at the end of the expansive entrance hall, from which the sounds of music and conversation were emanating. "Between us, we're going to make sure of that, Dr. Balducci." Her father looked at him expectantly. "Can I call you Antonio?"

"If you wish." That was said in the tone of "don't you dare." Antonio looked so forbidding it was only thanks to her father's enthusiastic obliviousness that he hadn't turned to stone. Then his voice plunged into the subzero domain. "I understand you had no contact with Liliana as she grew up. Now, in your new eagerness to know her, I keep wondering what could possibly explain the years of absence and silence."

Her father stopped, looking as if Antonio had just handed him the best gift he'd ever had. "I'm *so* glad you asked! I tried to explain to Lili when I contacted her after Luanne's death. But she always insisted what was past was past."

Yeah. She hadn't wanted to hear his reasons. She could establish some kind of relationship with him not knowing them. But if she knew them and found them pathetic or unacceptable, she wouldn't be able to go forward in any kind of relationship with him.

Her father clamped her and Antonio's arms. "Come, please. This can't be told with dozens of nosy Accardis around."

Her father rushed them to an old-fashioned smoking room filled with burgundy leather chesterfields, Persian rugs and dark wood paneling. Though everything was authentic and antique, it showed the weight of time and clearly hadn't had any recent maintenance. Though the three-hundred-year-old mansion was imposing, it wasn't in the prime condition she'd expected from such an elite family.

After her father sat them down side by side, he stood before them as if to give the performance he'd been waiting for all his life.

Then he began. "Luanne was glorious, very much like you, my beloved Lili, at least in looks and in her brilliant mind. Unorthodox, independent, a trailblazer. I fell in love with her on sight in Saint Mark's Basilica, as I believe she did with me. She told me she was the only child of a single mother who also worked in the medical field, that all she'd known since childhood had been academic endeavor and excellence."

So she'd been living her mother's life. Until Antonio.

"She'd just finished her medical residency and was about to start her fellowship when she discovered she hadn't actually lived yet. So before she plunged into her hospital work she'd decided to take two years to roam the world. Italy was her first stop.

"We spent every minute together for two weeks until she said she was heading north. I was besotted with her, but knew I'd never see her again if she left, so I proposed. She was stunned, refused on the spot, left the next day. So I followed her, all over Europe. My mother and uncles were enraged. I'd just taken my father's place in the family law firm, which I'd trained all my life to do, and I left them in the lurch. Then Luanne finally succumbed and we got married in France, but when we went home, no one was happy. Not only had my desertion caused the firm irredeemable losses, but I was supposed to marry to benefit the family. But I wanted none of that. I told them I wouldn't take my father's place permanently, that I wanted to leave and be with Luanne and the baby we knew by then we'd made. You, my darling girl."

Her throat tightening with every word, she leaned closer into Antonio, who intensified his hold on her as if protecting her from her father's revelations.

Her father went on, his gaze looking backward in time. "My mother told me Luanne wasn't wife material, would make a terrible mother, that I'd destroy my life and yours if I remained with her. Luanne hated my mother, too, hated all the Accardis and their elitism, hated being in Venice, and in what she called a moldy dwelling fit only for monsters and ghosts.

"When our stay in Venice lengthened and Luanne gave birth to you while I took care of the problems my absence caused, she started believing I'd never stand up for myself or for you, that I'd remain under my family's boot forever. To prove that only she and you mattered, I set a date for when I'd leave it all behind and go back with her to the States.

"At first, she was ecstatic. But as your first birthday neared and I was getting ready to leave, she began asking me what I would do there while she worked. Stay home and raise you? I knew nothing but the law, but I wouldn't be able to continue that in the States. My family threatened to disown me if I left them again, which would have left me penniless, but I didn't care. Then on your first birthday, Luanne told me she no longer wanted me, that I was suffocating her, that she wanted me and my family out of her life. Out of yours, too.

"I was convinced she was suffering from prolonged and severe postpartum depression. I told her so and she broke down. She wept and wept and begged me to let her go. My heart broke, but I couldn't reach her. I could only say that whatever happened between us, I would remain your father. I had rights to you, and you had a right to me. Her misery deepened as she asked how I would be your father across continents. What would it do to you, always waiting for a father who'd come only when my family let me go? How many times a year would that be and for how long? I insisted I'd manage something regular, but she thought it would only keep her and you in purgatory forever.

"After I failed to soothe her and her health declined, I was forced to grant her a divorce, but I gave her all the money I had. I wanted her to buy a beautiful house in an upscale neighborhood, to have enough money to bring you up in luxury, so she never had to work too hard and could be with you more. Problem was, only a portion of the money was mine. The rest was family funds. I thought I'd manage paying it back before anyone found out, but they did.

"They went after her for the money and things escalated. I was helpless to stop it from spiraling into an ugly legal fight. During the proceedings, my family even tried to get custody of you, claiming she was unbalanced. That was when she told me she never wanted to see me again, that she'd already told you I didn't want to see you, and that my family were horrible people who wanted to throw you out on the streets. I still came regularly through the years, trying to see you, but she wouldn't let me. She said you were stable and hardworking and the last thing you needed was the upheaval of my erratic presence and the influence of my evil family.

"By the time you became an adult and I could approach you without her consent, you'd had too many years without knowing me. I knew she'd turn it into a fight over you, causing you the upheaval she said she protected you from. I felt I already failed you, so... I gave up.

"When she became ill, I installed a lump sum in a

new account in her name, asked her attorney and bank to let you think it was a backup plan she always had, and gave you full control of it, so her care didn't burden you, at least financially. *Dio mio, figlia mia*, my daughter, I wanted to be there for you, but I didn't know what to say. I didn't want to blame her for anything in her condition. But the moment I heard of her death, I had to try again. She wasn't there to be hurt if your opinion of her changed, or for you to be torn between us. And…here we are."

It all added up. Knowing her mother, Lili accepted this as a plausible explanation. It shed a new, understandable light on the Accardis and a favorable one on her father.

Before she could get any words past the vise gripping her throat, her father bent over her, taking her hands in his. "I don't ask that you forgive me for not fighting harder to be your father. I only hope you'll give me the chance to be in your life now, in any way. Like your future groom, I believe you deserve only the best, and I hope you'll give me the privilege of doing my best to provide you with it."

And she found herself in his arms, hugging him and being hugged by him, the father she'd never had, but would now have for as long as life allowed them.

After her father deluged her in apologies, and obtained her promise to let him into her life, she turned to Antonio. He was on his feet, muscles bunched, gaze pinned on them.

Unable to read his expression, she reached out to him. He at once claimed her to his side, wincing down at her. "*Mi amore*, your tears kill me, even ones of happiness."

Blubbering a laugh, she wrapped her arms around him. "You'll have to withstand those. It's not every day that I get my father back." She met his turbulent gaze and smiled, asking him silently for his blessing.

As he took her trembling lips, he murmured against them for her ears only. "He can call me Antonio."

Whooping with delight, she invited her father closer, hugging him with her other arm. "You can call him Antonio."

Realizing the significance of that, her father poured jubilation all over them. After getting confirmations that they'd make use of him in their wedding preparations, and anything else, for life, he led them back to where the Accardis awaited them en masse.

Entering the ballroom tucked into Antonio's protection, Lili boggled at the number of polished elites who queued to introduce themselves.

Not that she thought their regard had anything to do with her. They were here at her father's demand, to make a grand gesture in his atonement campaign. But all the awe everyone exhibited was on Antonio's behalf.

The night blurred from then on. The only thing she registered clearly was Antonio's simmering intensity. He might have sanctioned her father's story and had acquitted him of being a cold-blooded deserter, but it was clear the Accardis hadn't passed his test.

Then suddenly, the unease she felt in Antonio spiked to something else. Something darker.

Trying to understand why, she paid extra attention

to the people who'd just come forward, but she found nothing different about them.

Before she could probe the situation further, her father pulled her away while Antonio remained held back by the newcomers.

As she greeted two more of her father's cousins twice removed, her focus remained on Antonio as he frowned at those who thronged around him. Then one of the two men said something to her that made her give him her full attention.

"You'll go down in the annals of our family history as the one who saved us all, Lili." At her incomprehension, he elaborated, "As you may know, our family businesses are intertwined, and over a year ago, some bad stock market decisions led to a domino effect in all our holdings. Dr. Balducci, through his Black Castle division, offered to bail us out, saving us from the impasse—that has since regretfully worsened—in return for acquiring our major ancestral assets."

The other man nodded. "We two were the ones charged with conveying the family's decision to turn down his offer. The damned family rules dictate those assets stay within the family at any cost. I can't tell you how relieved everyone is now that we can finally accept his offer, since he *will* be family shortly."

"*If* his offer is still on the table," said the other man.

The first man winked at her. "If it isn't, we're sure you, dear Lili, can convince him to put it back there."

As her father exclaimed that he'd never heard of this, Lili's gaze sought out Antonio again, her mind spinning. He'd never mentioned it. So maybe he hadn't been involved and it had been his brokers trolling for acquisitions?

No, there was no way he wouldn't be in charge of every offer issuing from his organization. So why hadn't he told her about this aborted transaction involving her family? Could it have slipped his mind? That was again something she found impossible to believe. Nothing slipped Antonio's mind.

Could part of his tension around her family be on account of the thwarted deal? And it continued in part because he didn't know yet that it would go through? Did he know their engagement would provide a solution to this deadlock?

Whoa. It seemed she could still slide back into insecurity. She thought she'd stopped wondering why Antonio wanted to marry her, stopped looking for reasons besides that he loved her.

But this deal certainly couldn't be even a contributing reason. The financial benefit would all be her family's in their current bind. At best, the acquisitions could have only minor value to him compared with his other assets.

Dismissing her absurd thoughts, she concluded her side meeting, laughingly promising the two men to put in a good word for them with Antonio.

As she rejoined him, his mind seemed to be elsewhere as he received her, his gaze leaving her whenever anyone came to talk to them to fix on one certain part of the ballroom. She followed it and saw the same relatives who'd first made him tense up.

By the time he asked her if she didn't mind leaving, she'd had enough tension for one night and eagerly agreed.

Her unease lingered until the moment they entered their hotel suite. Then he swept her up in his arms, threw her down on the bed and took her with an even more ferocious hunger than ever before. Flesh on flesh, he melted her disquiet and bound her deeper under his spell.

In the next week, her family members competed to invite them to their homes.

Antonio gave her carte blanche to accept all invitations, though it meant flying all over the country. His brotherhood family had taken up the slack in the arrangements for their wedding and kept them apprised of all developments, so they could afford the time to get to know hers better.

As the visits started, a new discomfort crept over her. Though he seemed willing to know everyone for her sake, and she was grateful since there were some members she liked and wished to know better, she soon noticed his focus was on one woman. One of those he'd tensed around during the reception. She'd become a common denominator in all the gatherings.

Sofia Accardi.

Sofia, her father's third cousin, was in her late fifties, but looked like a great mid-forties. She oozed charisma and distinction and she seemed intensely interested in Antonio. Her children—her daughters especially—were present on most occasions, flocking around him like moths to the flame.

Then Sofia invited them to her home, despite it being in the midst of a major renovation. When Lili said they'd come later when the work was done, the woman was insistent. It was Antonio who ended the debate, accepting the invitation.

It was insidious—the feeling Lili had that Antonio had consented to every invitation so far only so it wouldn't look strange when they accepted Sofia's. The woman he'd remained stilted around all week.

Now as the day progressed at Sofia's estate, everything Lili felt from Antonio intensified her suspicions.

Sofia *did* provoke something inside him. Something volcanic in intensity. Could it be…attraction? Lust? Worse?

Sofia, though older, was incredibly beautiful and voluptuous, a very sensual woman who was known as a man-eater, having gone through three husbands and uncounted lovers. Lili, in her relative inexperience, felt decidedly lacking compared to the woman who was more on his level than she would ever be.

After dinner, while she was trapped in conversation with Sofia's daughters, Antonio, who'd said almost nothing to her all evening, walked out of the family room. And her agitation boiled over.

She couldn't wait until they left. She had to find him, ask him, now. If he was having second thoughts of any sort, this was the time to come clean.

As she excused herself, she realized it wasn't only Antonio who was unaccounted for. Sofia, too, had disappeared.

Feeling like her whole world was sinking under her

feet, she went in search of them through the immense house.

The areas under renovation were barricaded, so that left only the private quarters. The bedrooms. Nowhere a guest like Antonio would be. It couldn't...he *wouldn't*...

Suddenly she heard his voice. An emotion-filled growl.

It was followed by a husky, pleading moan. Sofia's.

Her heart almost uprooted itself in her chest and every muscle trembled as she stepped through a door she hadn't noticed was ajar in the dimness of the corridor, one a barricade announced off-limits.

The room inside was pitch-dark, but its French windows opened to a terrace, from which their voices emanated.

Then she saw them.

In the lights coming from the garden, under the canopy of a starlit night, Antonio stood like a monolith with his back almost to her as Sofia hugged him frantically.

Then slowly, as if he couldn't resist anymore, his arms wrapped around her.

Ten

Lili froze.

The sight in front of her… Antonio, with another woman…

There was nothing. No more air. No more heartbeats.

Then the woman's lament pierced her like a bullet. "You have to believe me, Antonio. I never wanted to give you up."

The agony the words contained lodged like an ax in her chest.

They…they had a previous affair? And Antonio still felt that fiercely for her? Still loved her? But he'd said *she* was his first love. He'd said he'd grown a heart to love *her*.

Antonio pushed Sofia away on a butchered groan, as if tearing himself from her arms hurt him, badly. The sound of his torment made Lili shrivel.

Had he been with her only because he'd thought Sofia had abandoned him? Because he couldn't have her? And now that he evidently could, he was fighting his desire for her?

But Lili didn't want him honor-bound or obligated. If he didn't love and desire her as completely as she did him, she only wished him to have what he wanted. If that was no longer her, she had to set him free. Now. *Now.*

Before she could force her numb legs to move, Sofia started sobbing, and what she said robbed Lili of all power, made her sag to her knees.

"I held you only once after my C-section when I was still drowsy from anesthesia. You were the most perfect baby boy."

Sofia was...was...*his mother.*

"When I fully came to, my family had sent you away. I threatened to kill myself if they didn't return you but they told me it was too late, that an undisclosed adopter took you. I went mad. I tried to commit suicide." She extended her hands to him so he could see the scars she still bore. "After I was saved, I knew I'd been stupid, since I couldn't find you if I died. But there seemed no way to find anything about you, and I fell into a deep depression. Three years later I met my first husband, and he promised to help me find you. But his investigations only discovered that my parents and uncle had lied, that they'd put you in an orphanage. When Mark found out which one, I eloped with him and we went to the orphanage. But you were no longer there and we couldn't find your trail. I drove myself insane imagining you'd fallen into the worst of hands."

A vicious huff crackled from Antonio. "You can't even imagine the kind of hands I fell into. They make slave traders look like Good Samaritans."

The sob that tore through Sofia sounded as if it had ripped her apart inside. She reached her hands out to him.

"Don't." He pulled away, as if her touch would burn him. "I don't need your pity or your guilt. As you can see, I far more than survived."

She tried to approach again before her hands fell to her sides, defeated. "You're right. I can't even imagine what you went through, or how you conquered your horrific beginnings and then the world. I can only tell you my side, how I lived with the trauma of your loss, of imagining your fate." A sob choked her, soaked her voice in tears. "But I did always feel you were out there, alive, strong. Then I saw a photo of you in a magazine and felt that I knew you. Then I saw you face-to-face and felt the connection between us. Your half siblings felt it, too, even if they couldn't imagine what drew them to you like that. I thought I was crazy, but the way you looked at me, at them, made me hope you felt it, too. But today, I just *knew* who you are, and that you know who I am. I felt you didn't want me to acknowledge our relationship. But I had to do it. Had to tell you I recognized you, that losing you tore a hole in my soul that nothing has ever mended, not even having more children, or adopting two boys who reminded me of you. My father and uncle died years ago, and my mother is now senile, but I still curse them every day as I did for the past forty years, for what they did to you and to me."

This time, when she reached for him, he let her cling to his arms. She looked up at him, her eyes beseeching. "I know I can never undo what's been done to you. I can't do *anything…*" Another harsh sob escaped her throat. "Nothing but hope that you'll let me know you, and maybe one day, in some way, I'll make it up to you."

Lili was a mess of tremors. Sofia's impassioned confession shook her far more than her father's had. To imagine what some of those Accardis—his family like they were hers—had cost him, was beyond endurance.

Then he finally spoke, his voice darker than the night. "When I discovered what your family did to me, what I thought you agreed to, I planned to exact punishment, on you and on the whole family whose rules dictate throwing away unwanted children. I wanted to buy your ancestral assets, lure you all into a merger with the promise of saving you from bankruptcy, so I'd end up in control of your very lives, before I took my time destroying you, each in the way you deserve. But even in their desperation, the Accardis rejected my life raft because, of all the irony, I wasn't 'family'."

The realization hit Lili so hard she felt her head would burst with it. What she'd always felt but couldn't even guess at. The reason he'd approached her in the first place.

He'd needed an in into the family.

It had been her.

That was why he'd pursued her, why he'd proposed to her.

It all made sense now. He'd never loved her. Never even wanted her. He'd only wanted revenge. She'd been nothing but his means to his lifelong retribution.

The blow of realization was so brutal it interrupted her very heartbeats.

"But now after you told me how—"

Antonio's words were suddenly cut off as he tensed and turned to look in Lili's direction.

There was no way he could see her in the darkness. And she hadn't made a sound. She couldn't move, couldn't even breathe.

"Liliana?"

He did feel her. Or it was her devastation he felt. Now she realized that everything between them had been a lie.

Suffocating, feeling she'd rather die than face him now, she scrambled up, stumbling as she ran back out of the room.

"Liliana!"

His shout punched her between the shoulder blades, intensifying her desperation.

She had to escape him, escape the agony. But she couldn't pass through the others on her way out. She had to find another exit.

Spilling into the next barricaded room, which must open onto the same wraparound veranda leading to the garden, she rushed to open the closed French doors, growing frantic as his thundering footsteps drew closer, his shout begging her to stop another lash propelling her forward, making her more frantic.

Then everything happened at once. Sofia's shrill warning, Antonio roaring, and she was falling.

Pain exploded, sharp and searing, tearing through her midriff. A simultaneous agony splintered through her thigh, almost fracturing her awareness.

Then she was on her back, staring up at the stars as they blurred, the night darkening around her.

The whoosh of blood in her ears receded, only to be replaced by Antonio's frenzy as he begged her not to move.

Not that she could. Even drawing enough oxygen not to pass out was excruciating. She lay there, paralyzed with pain, watching his massive silhouette, an avenging angel jumping down a steep drop to crouch over her.

Vaguely, she realized the veranda she'd tried to escape through wasn't there. She'd fallen through its skeleton, getting stabbed on the way down by protruding concrete-reinforcing steel bars. From the agony now emanating from her left side, she realized she must have damaged some internal organs. Probably her spleen, intestines, maybe a kidney. Her left femur was also fractured. Muscle damage was a given, maybe nerve damage, too.

She couldn't see Antonio's face, could only hear his strident breathing as he swept her in the bright beam of a flashlight.

Then she heard the tremor of dread in his voice as he pressed down on her side. He'd assessed her injuries and was applying pressure to slow the bleeding. "I'm here, *mi amore*, I've got you. Just don't move."

"*Dio mio, dio mio*, is she…?"

Without looking up, he hissed, "Leave *now*, Sofia. Tell no one."

Sofia's gasp at Antonio's harshness carried to Lili's wavering consciousness, but the woman complied, disappearing from Lili's field of vision. Then Antonio started talking, barking sharp, concise orders. To Paolo, to fetch his medical kit from the limo. To his pilot, to get a helicopter. To the medical center, to prepare his OR.

Working at top efficiency, Antonio, the miracle worker who put people back together, had everything ready in minutes to reconstruct her. After he'd broken her, torn her apart.

He bent over her, raining frantic kisses all over her face. "You're going to be okay, *mi amore*, I promise."

She tried to cringe away. "You…shouldn't…"

"Don't talk. Just let me take care of you."

"You shouldn't…" Her teeth clattered, more with desolation than with blood loss or pain. "…have done… this to me…"

A groan escaped him, his shudder transmitting to her trembling body. "Whatever you heard, whatever you understood, whatever you think I did, you're wrong, *mi amore*, I swear."

Tears oozed out of her very soul. "I…loved…you…"

"And I worship you. You're everything to me. *Everything.*"

All light faded, taking his image with it as blackness sucked her under. "I—I think…it's better…this way…"

As she slipped away, she wished it would be forever. So she wouldn't live knowing she'd never had him, or with the agony that would never go away.

* * *

Antonio watched Liliana's eyes flutter closed, felt her bloodied body going limp and still, and went mad.

His roar almost tore out the heart that had been exploding with every beat since he'd watched her plunge into that jagged maw of concrete and steel.

He'd done this to her. This was his fault. All of it.

She was lying here, torn and broken, because he'd lied to her. Because he'd overridden her disinclination and accepted his mother's invitation. Because she must have picked up on his weirdness, because he'd left her behind without explanation, making her follow him, hear what had made her escape him so desperately through the house they shouldn't have been in.

If he lost her…

No. He'd *never* lose her. He *would* save her. He'd pay his very life and far more to restore her, body and heart.

But before he could do anything, he had to suppress the insanity of terror and the violence of self-hatred. He had to go through his perfected motions. Everything he'd ever learned, every skill he'd acquired, every bit of experience he'd accumulated through the long years of slavery and struggle and success, had all been for this moment.

Everything he was had been made for her. Everything he could do, he'd learned to save her.

From the injuries he'd caused her.

Antonio raced against time in a crazed fast-forward, spiraling through all levels of hell.

In what seemed like minutes, he'd flown Liliana to his nearest medical center where he'd had to cut her open, literally this time, so he could mend her. He'd poured all his expertise, all his being, into saving her. It had driven him insane, not only the extent of her injuries and the reason she'd sustained them, but the feeling that she was resisting his efforts. He might have been unhinged with terror and guilt, but he did feel as if she wanted him to fail.

It had been when she'd flatlined, when there'd been no medical reason anymore that she should, that he'd become sure.

She'd wanted to die.

In the horrific lifetime until he'd managed to restart her heart, he'd known. If he'd failed, his heart would have stopped seconds after hers.

Now she lay in the ICU, just like Ivan's mystery woman had three weeks ago. But the latter had fought to survive. He could feel Liliana still fighting to escape. He'd hurt her so much, it was as if she didn't want to wake up to face the agony.

Some of her last words revolved in his mind again, hacking it to pieces. *You shouldn't have done this to me. I loved you.*

He'd been a coward, avoiding a confession that could have caused a passing crisis, a pain he could have healed. He'd been self-deluding, thinking she wouldn't pick up on the turmoil that racked him every time he saw his mother. Liliana had always felt he'd been hiding something, but because of his evasions, when she'd overheard him, she'd concluded the worst. What had once been the truth.

And it had destroyed her.

Sagging to his knees beside her bed, he let the tears he'd never shed before pour out of his very soul.

"You're my life, *mi amore*. I can't and won't live without you. I beg you, don't punish me by harming yourself."

In response, her vitals only grew more erratic.

Exploding to his feet, he rummaged for medications, roaring for his assistants to prepare emergency resuscitation.

Just as he was about to inject the cocktail into her drip, a deep voice broke over him.

"I don't think she needs that."

He swung around to blast whoever was interfering, then rocked on his feet with the aborted aggression when he saw Ivan.

His head nurse was scurrying away. Had she fetched Ivan to deal with him? He sure would have blasted her, as he'd done every member of his medical team all night.

Ivan approached him as if he were approaching a wounded tiger. "I know she doesn't need that because you never second-guess yourself, never up your meds. You get it right the first time. Always."

"But it's *Liliana*. And I doubt I'm even sane anymore."

Ivan's hand clamped his, forced it down. "Come with me, Tonio."

He glared at his friend through his tears. "She needs—"

"She needs you to leave her alone for now." Ivan dragged him away, his pull inexorable in Antonio's shaken state. "You told me…*she* would feel me in her sleep, and it would give her strength, make her fight. When she woke up, she told me it was true. Now your lady feels you, too, and to me it looks like your presence distresses her. You might be the very thing compromising her survival."

It killed Antonio to admit this had to be the explanation. There was no medical reason why Liliana shouldn't be stable.

Letting Ivan tug him to the observation area, he sagged down, his gaze pinned on Liliana's inert figure and inanimate face. He plummeted into a deeper hell of guilt and desperation.

It was only when Ivan's assessment proved right and Liliana's vitals stabilized that he finally choked out, "How did you know? How did you come?"

"Paolo called me, and I called the others. As for how…she insisted she is stable, can spare me for hours and told me to go to you. If it had been a choice between being by her side or yours…"

"You would have chosen her." Antonio looked back at Liliana. "I'd choose her, too, over anything or anyone. Starting with myself."

Just then, his brothers and their mates began arriving.

It wasn't long before he told them to go away. His sanity was hanging by a thread, and their empathy, their every bolstering word, the very sight of them together, was about to snap it.

Finally, they reluctantly left, with Ivan promising he'd keep them updated. He told Ivan his presence wasn't helping anymore, to leave, too, but the icy Russian just ignored him.

As the last of his brothers disappeared from view, Ivan turned to him. "I take it from your condition, and her unconscious reaction to your presence, this isn't just an accident?"

Suddenly feeling the crushing need to share everything with his oldest and closest friend, Antonio told Ivan everything.

After he fell silent, Ivan's gaze grew contemplative. "This is good for you, you know?" Anger exploded inside Antonio, making him lunge to grab Ivan by the lapels. Ivan crushed his hands in the vise of his, forcing him to listen. "You were always too serene, too untouchable. I always knew this meant what's inside you was even more nightmarish than any of us. And this woman has reached inside you and dragged out your chaos, so she could dispel it. She also released every emotion you never thought yourself capable of."

"She created them. And I am the reason she's lying there. Because I lied to her, because she thinks I never loved her."

Ivan shrugged. "But you'll prove you do, and that you had some stupidly noble reason for hiding what you hid from her. But even if she thinks you don't love her now, I suspect deep down she feels that you do, since she's found the perfect method to brutally punish you."

"I'd take any punishment but this." His eyes burned with more tears.

"But this is what she's choosing, even unconsciously, hurting you by showing you how you hurt her. So you'll take it, until she believes you've had enough, until *you* believe you've atoned. Then if everything the brothers say about her and what she feels for you is true, she'll take you back."

Antonio didn't even dare hope it would be that easy, or that it would come to pass at all. But somehow Ivan's prophecy stopped the spiral of madness. He couldn't have Liliana wake up to find him totally deranged.

And she *would* wake up. He'd transplant his very life into her if that was what it took. He would have her whole again at any price.

For the next two days as Liliana remained asleep, Antonio discovered that hell was bottomless.

He'd forced himself to heed Ivan's theory that her deterioration was directly proportionate to his proximity. Though despondent, he'd watched her from afar, every second he could.

On the third day she woke up while one of his assistants was tending her. He watched every nuance of her return to consciousness, then awareness, feeling as if he were waiting for a verdict of life or death.

Her lashes fluttered open, a hand jerking when she found herself hooked up to drips and monitors. Her whole body tensed before slumping back, realization replacing confusion on her face.

Through the open mike where he'd listened to her

every breath, he heard his nurse explaining her condition and reassuring her. Liliana only listened, but as his assistant finished checking her, she said something he couldn't hear in her ear.

A minute later his assistant came out and, with a wide smile, told him he'd pulled off another miracle. Liliana was far better than expected after such an extensive surgery.

And she'd asked to see him.

Afraid to breathe, to hope, he didn't know when he'd moved, but he found himself standing over Liliana.

She spoke without raising her eyes, her voice hoarse from intubation, chafing his every nerve ending. "Thank you for saving my life. Even if you no longer need me."

He must have misheard her. She couldn't have said... "What?"

Her eyes rose to him now, but they were no longer hers, but a stranger's. "Since you've revealed yourself to your mother, I'm sure you can now enter my—your family to destroy it from within on your own."

He didn't know how he remained standing. He'd thought there could be no more pain than what he'd suffered in the past three days. He'd known nothing.

This, what she believed, was true agony.

"*Per Dio*, am I that big a monster in your eyes now?"

"You're a vigilante, and you do what needs to be done to achieve your goal no matter the price. You're also a surgeon and you save patients regardless of their value to you."

"You think I considered you just another patient?"

he choked out, unable to believe how horrible it had all become.

"It's a fact you no longer need me."

"I will need you, and only you, till my dying breath."

Her gaze emptied more. "You probably didn't wish it to end this way. I do realize you must feel bad about my injuries—"

He cut across her mutilating words. "I don't feel bad, Liliana, I feel devastated."

"You shouldn't. I'm responsible for what happened to me. I barged into clearly labeled danger zones, repeatedly."

Both the under-construction site, and his life.

He gritted his teeth against the mounting pain. "What devastates me is that I destroyed your faith in me, in yourself, so completely. And it's why you almost…almost…"

"But I didn't die, thanks to you." She surveyed his agitation with a blank look, as lifeless as her voice. "And I do understand your need for exacting retribution on the family that threw you away. If only you'd told me in the beginning, I'd have helped you, if only for the possibility you'd find a peaceful and just resolution, and you wouldn't have needed to go to these lengths to use me as your stealth weapon."

"You must believe me, *mi amore*. Whatever I intended to do, I abandoned it all after I first saw you. I wanted only you since."

As if she hadn't heard him, she went on, "But now that you discovered you've misjudged your mother even worse than I have my father, I hope you'll reconsider your revenge. The guilty ones are either dead or as good as. And I doubt no one else, no matter their faults, deserves your wrath. I hope you won't destroy everyone indiscriminately for the crimes of some of their own. And that you'll give your mother the chance she hoped for."

It agonized him more that even in her own devastation she was thinking of others.

He dropped to his knees beside her, his hand trembling as he took hers. "I avoided even talking about your family, not only because none of them mattered anymore, but because I was afraid they'd hurt you. I only agreed to meet them when I realized how much you needed to settle their issue, and to be there to protect you from them. It turned out the only one I needed to protect you from was myself. And I failed. I failed you."

"I failed myself. And now I'll have the scars to remind me never to do so again."

Before he took her hand to his lips, she pulled it away with surprising strength, as if she could no longer bear his touch. She turned her head away, closing her eyes. Her dry eyes.

It was as if she had nothing left to say to him. As if she had nothing left inside her.

He remained on his knees beside her as depletion claimed her again, at last learning the meaning of helplessness.

During the next two weeks, as Liliana recuperated, Antonio never left the center, always hovering around, trying again and again to get her to talk to him. But after that time when she'd first woken up, she'd given him nothing but silence. His presence seemed to plunge her into deepening despondency.

Everyone kept telling him to let her bounce back from the trauma, that she was hurt that much because she loved him as fiercely and that he'd eventually heal her with his love. But the days had passed and Liliana seemed to be drawing further into herself.

And today he couldn't bear it anymore. He'd just entered her room, said he would stand there beside her bed, no matter how long it took, until she talked to him again.

Then she finally did, and shattered his heart.

Eyes no longer distant, raw, ravished, she looked up at him, her pain and betrayal skewering him to his vitals. "You lied to me, Antonio, when all I ever asked of you was honesty. Even if you've developed feelings for me, everything that you said or did, everything that happened between us, is tainted by this lie. Now I can't trust or feel again. My emotions, my faith, like the body you've put back together, have been damaged and will remain scarred."

Before he could swear to her that he'd wait forever for her to heal, that he'd erase her scars, she sat up, swung her good leg followed by her casted leg over the side of the bed. "There's no more medical reason for me to remain here. I want you to discharge me."

All he wanted to do was rave and rant and keep her there until she gave him another chance.

But he couldn't press her more in her fragile state.

"I will. But please, Liliana, whatever you think of me or however you feel now, *please*, come back with me to our place, let me take care of you as you recuperate."

She shook her head, and for the first time since her accident tears started to fall. He hated himself more with every track of moisture that stained her pale cheeks.

He wished *she'd* rave and rant. Her subdued misery was so much worse than any passionate display that would have given him hope he could revive her emotions.

All he could do now was stop hurting her more, let her go and hope she'd heal enough one day to let him in again. Pray that she wouldn't shut him out like her mother had her father, for the rest of her life.

The day that should have been their wedding day came and went in total silence from Liliana.

She hadn't gone back to Antonio's mansion. And she hadn't returned to the lab.

He was hailed as the leading expert of mending catastrophic injuries, but he'd injured the one person he needed to live, an injury he was helpless to heal.

It was during one of the surgeries he now buried himself in that he realized the truth.

It didn't matter that he healed her so she'd come back to him. It mattered that she healed for herself, so she could resume her life, her work. He and what he felt were of no consequence.

Only she mattered.

And because only she did, if her emotional health depended on letting her go, he would.

Even if it destroyed him.

Eleven

Three months after the accident, though Lili had fully recovered physically, she hadn't gone back to work.

Among those who regularly came visiting, Brian had been the one who kept persistently trying to convince her to do so. She'd insisted right back that she'd decided to take all her missed vacations at once.

Ever since Antonio had discharged her and sent her back to LA on his private jet, she'd left the house only for follow-ups and the intensive physiotherapy Antonio had scheduled for her, both performed by others under his command.

She hadn't seen or heard from him since.

At times, longing for him made her unable to breathe.

Her father, whom she'd told a severely edited version of the truth, had been adamant it meant she'd healed enough to believe in Antonio's love again. But she knew missing him had nothing to do with being over the trauma. Missing him, with every breath, had always been her default.

As for his love, after being dedicated to her after the accident, he had been silent since he'd discharged her. Whatever he'd felt for her, it seemed she'd pushed him away so hard he'd given up on her.

She couldn't heed her father's fervent advice to contact him. She couldn't impose on him if he'd moved on.

She was indulging in what had become an obsession, driving herself insane again wondering if he'd ever really loved her and if she'd killed his love, or if he'd discovered he didn't feel enough for her after all, when her doorbell rang.

Since everyone called before passing by, the hope that it was Antonio propelled her to the door the fastest she'd moved since the accident.

But it wasn't him on her doorstep. It was Sofia Accardi.

After exchanging a long stare, Lili stunned and disappointed, Sofia discomfited and tentative, Lili invited her in. Questions flooded her mind, all about Antonio. Instead of asking them, she awkwardly offered Sofia something to drink.

Over a cup of tea, Sofia finally started talking. "I would have come earlier, but Antonio said you needed space."

Was that what he thought? Was that why he hadn't attempted to contact her?

"He also said you're healed completely."

"I…am." Physically, at least. "Antonio is a virtuoso. Even my scars are negligible, and fading every day."

An exquisite smile adorned the woman's gorgeous face, which now Lili could see was an older, feminine version of Antonio's. "His scars are fading, too. He's been letting me and his siblings closer, and it's been… indescribable. I always felt my baby had survived, had grown strong and special, but Antonio surpasses my every fantasy."

As he surpassed Lili's. So much so it was why she'd always felt she couldn't possibly deserve his love.

Sofia went on. "He told me you asked him to give me a chance. So I owe you the happiness of having my son back." Her smile faded as she continued. "But he abhors many members of the family for being of the same school of thought that led my parents to deprive me of him, and toss him into the nightmarish fate he still won't tell me about. These people owe you their *lives*, since you're the one who stayed his hand."

She'd had that much influence on him? Or had he just considered none worth the trouble of revenge?

Whatever the reason, she took joy in knowing that he was letting go of his bitterness and rage, letting his family heal him, accepting the love he deserved. If her role in his life had been to get him to this point, it was enough for her. She wanted him happy, even if she'd never be again.

Sofia reached for one of her hands. "But I'm really here to express how sorry I am for everything that happened since I insisted you visit me when my house was such a mess. Antonio explained why overhearing us upset you so much, but he said nothing further. I feel so guilty."

Lili put her other hand on top of hers. "Listen, Sofia, the renovation was barricaded, and I stupidly barged inside it. I was an idiot to overreact and run away in the first place. You have nothing to feel guilty about."

Tears glittered in the woman's eyes. "Even so, I felt terrible, and so helpless watching everything come apart. Your wedding…"

Unable to hear another word about their aborted wedding, she interrupted Sofia. "That's another thing that was all my doing. But I'm only happy that I brought you and Antonio back together."

"If only I could do the same." Sofia hugged her. "I would have loved to have you as a daughter-in-law."

Stunned by the woman's display of affection, distressed that her words meant Sofia thought a reunion with Antonio wasn't in the cards, she numbly hugged her back. "I would have loved to have you as a mother-in-law, too."

From then on and until Sofia left, they diverted the conversation to less stressful areas. When she took her leave Sofia made Lili promise to keep in touch.

As she closed the door behind her, Lili felt a new friend had entered her life. But what would that matter if she'd couldn't bear having her in it, if she only reminded her she'd lost Antonio?

Would her very life matter if she had?

And she could no longer bear not knowing.

She had to let *him* tell her. If there was still a chance, or if she should just surrender to despair.

* * *

The decision to approach Antonio was easier made than executed. All morning, fear held her back. Uncertainty, which she'd always been unable to handle, was now what kept her going. Because part of uncertainty was hope. If she killed the hope that she had a chance with Antonio, her life wouldn't be worth living.

But she not only couldn't go on not knowing for sure either way, but something terrible roiled inside her, prodding her to seek him out today. Right *now*. It wasn't the usual longing that gnawed at her. It was something ferocious that demanded action.

Just as she was about to leave the house to go to his medical center where she knew he was every day, her cell phone vibrated.

It was a number she didn't know.

Heart hammering, hoping against hope that it was him, she answered. The deep, dark voice that poured into her ear almost had her pile in a heap on the ground.

Because it wasn't Antonio.

It took her a second to recognize the voice. Jakob Wolff.

"Hello, Lili, it's Jakob. I have Ivan with me and we were wondering if you could see us."

Trembling with worry, she croaked, "Of course. When and where?"

"Right now. We're parked right outside."

"Oh. Oh! Please, come right in."

Tripping in her haste, she rushed to the door, opening it in time to see the two men step out of an imposing Rolls Royce. Breath bated, she watched these two who were an intimate part of Antonio's life walk up to her door.

Inviting them in, leading them where she'd had Sofia just yesterday, Lili and Ivan were soon immersed in their first face-to-face meeting. He seemed as curious about her as she was about him. Until recently, Ivan had been the closest person in the world to Antonio. If they'd gone through with the wedding, Ivan would have been his best man, would have become the brother she never had.

Suddenly Jakob sat forward, making Lili aware of his presence again, and of his impatience. "We're not here for chitchat."

Ivan sighed, nodded, got a dossier out of his briefcase, handed it to her. "Indeed. We're here to give you this."

Confusion deepening, she took it from him, and at his prodding, opened it and read.

With each line, each page, her shock deepened.

These were legal documents. Written in extensive, meticulous terms. Turning over Antonio's R & D empire to her.

When she finally raised flabbergasted eyes to them, Jakob's lips curled in disgusted disapproval. "Antonio believes you're better equipped to benefit the world with what he's built. He also believes you'd probably want to segregate it from Black Castle and become your own independent business, which he believes would be best for you and for your nonprofit policies and pursuits."

"If you're wondering what he'd do instead," Ivan said, watching her closely as if to document her reaction, "he'll turn full-time to what he's best at. Surgery. But he says he'll now emulate you, direct his skills and resources to nonprofit work. But as a surgeon, that would take him into the field of humanitarian work. He's already organized his first mission."

Lili stared from one man to the other, as if they'd suddenly laugh and tell her it was all an elaborate joke.

But from their grimness and their clear dismay at their brother's bequest, and mostly from the wording in those papers, which she knew was Antonio's, this was real.

"Needless to say," Ivan said, "we are extremely disturbed by his decision. We know no one could ever replace him, but since it's you, the others have empowered us to extend you an offer. We will accommodate anything you wish, if you agree to keep the division part of our joint business."

She could only stare at them, totally numb.

Jakob added, "He also said you'd have qualms on account of having no financial or management skills, but he assures you everything will be run by his deputies, while you orchestrate the scientific direction of the organization. He himself will always be available to you as a consultant whenever you wish."

And it was as if a dam burst inside her, making her blurt out, "Is he insane?"

Ivan nodded with another sigh. "Bonkers."

"It gets worse." Jakob produced another file from his own briefcase. "These are the deeds to his mansion in LA, his penthouse in New York City, his best jet, and assorted assets and holdings with a collective net worth I couldn't stomach registering."

She felt as if she'd been caught in an explosion, and the shock waves were widening, tearing down everything.

All she could finally manage was a whisper. "I—I don't get it."

"Don't you?" Jakob tilted his head, a contemptuous edge creeping into his steel-hued gaze, making him look pretty sinister. "From where I'm sitting, you seem to have gotten everything you could have wanted and way more."

She shook her head, shell-shocked. "I only want him."

"Now *that's* priceless." Jakob scoffed. "You dare say that, when you put the man through a hell far worse than all his ordeals combined?"

Ivan frowned. "Jakob's right on this one. According to Antonio you had every right to punish him, but I kept hoping you'd stop your punishment before you finished him. When you went past even that, I wondered what kind of succubus could do that to him. Then I saw you and I don't get it. You're filled with marshmallows and rainbows. How could you do this to him?"

"I didn't do anything," she cried out. "How could I punish him when I thought what he felt for me was... *nothing* like what I felt for him? When he left me alone after he discharged me, and I thought he'd realized he was better off without me, as I always thought he would be?"

Ivan's eyes narrowed before they shot wide. "That's

it. That's my answer. You're really *that* insecure, aren't you?"

A shudder of misery shook her. "Only when it comes to him."

Ivan huffed mirthlessly. "Then, boy, are you two even. He's totally, explosively, inventively irrational when it comes to you, too. The man has been punishing himself for hurting you far more brutally than any of our abusers ever did."

"The only thing that hurt me was thinking he didn't…didn't…"

"Didn't love you?" Ivan supplied for her. "If he loved you any more he'd be downright dangerous. As it is, I think he is, very much so, to himself. All this…" Ivan flicked a hand at all the paperwork. "Signing his life away to you? Going to put bodies back together in the most dangerous war zone he could find? He might not be doing it consciously, but I know him. He's given up on you, and he can't face life without you, so like a missile on its last burst of fuel, he's trying to go out with a bang."

The horror of Ivan's analysis and prophecy froze the blood in her arteries.

Then she exploded, pouncing on the two men, shoving the folders at them and dragging them up. "You have to stop him!"

Jakob's gaze became contemptuous. "You think we didn't try? After the number you did on him, he's been like an automaton with no course-correction function left."

Anger broke through her distress. She grabbed Jakob's arm, shaking him. "Aren't all of you all-powerful? *Do* something!"

Still probing her, Jakob remained unperturbed by her agitation. "Antonio instructed us to give you all this after he left for his mission."

The world spun, made her stagger back. "He—he already left?"

Jakob steadied her, his gaze no longer accusing. "Not exactly, but that was another instruction. Not to tell you when he left or where he went."

Ivan took her arm, turned her to him. "And that's actually why we're here now. To tell you he's leaving tonight. Because we're not the ones who're all-powerful here. You are. The only one who can stop him is you."

Lili believed Ivan and Jakob would never talk to her again.

Not after she'd blasted them for wasting all that time testing her and not telling her about Antonio's plans right away.

She'd also drafted them for a ride to his mansion, where they said he'd be, packing and emptying it for her possession. On the way, with Antonio's phone shut off, going mad thinking she'd be too late, she'd piled more and more invective on their sullen, silent heads.

Now they both turned to glare at her as she spilled out of the car at Antonio's door.

Before they drove off in a shower of gravel, Jakob shouted from his window, "You broke him, now you fix him."

Lili rushed to the front door. Climbing steps was still awkward for her, but she took them two at a time.

She entered the mansion to total silence, and dread almost chomped her in half. Was she too late? She'd failed to intercept him before he disappeared out of reach, maybe forever?

Terror mushroomed out of her on a scream. *"Antonio!"*

Footsteps exploded from the direction of the bedroom, which had been theirs once. They thundered before abruptly stopping. And then Antonio appeared across the great room.

He froze, just like she did.

But even across the distance his eyes told her everything, explained everything, put to rest everything that had been driving her insane.

He did share her heartache and misery, felt her same desperation and pain. But his agony seemed to have broken him. Her invulnerable Antonio. She'd done this to him.

Would he leave still because she'd hurt him beyond repair?

Suffocating with dread, all she could say was, "I love you. Please forgive me. Don't go." Then everything turned black.

"Liliana!"

Antonio exploded into a run and caught her before she hit the ground in a dead faint. After a frenzied exam proved she was physically fine, he rushed her to his bed. The bed he hadn't come near since she'd left him.

Though he knew from his obsessive follow-up of her condition that she was perfectly healed, she looked so spent and fragile. Just like he'd felt…until he'd heard her screaming his name, seen her standing there, her eyes open to him again, showing him into the depths of her soul. Until she'd said she loved him and asked him not to go.

Holding her made him feel as if the heart that had been ripped out of his body was restored. Feeling her warm and whole and *there*, he felt that the life that had oozed out of him every second since he'd lost her was returning. She was here to revive him, to give him another lease on life.

She came to with a gasp, her eyes frantic before she saw him. Then she came apart, clinging to him, a quaking, weeping mass.

Her sobs tore him up inside. "Don't go, please. Don't leave me. Don't leave me anything of yours. I want you, only ever you…please…"

His lips silenced her agony, his tears mingling with hers. "And I want only you. I wanted to leave everything behind when I thought you could no longer want me back."

She wrenched at his neck, his chest with trembling lips, soaking his flesh with her tears, covering it with the worship he'd withered without. "I'll stop wanting you when I stop breathing. Probably not even then."

Before he succumbed to the need to reclaim her, he had to know one thing for sure.

He rose above her, holding her precious face in his trembling hands. "Do you forgive me, *mi amore*? Re-

ally forgive me, for how I once planned to use you? I don't want the least doubt or bitterness lurking in your heart. That's what you said that day I let you go—that's why I couldn't persist anymore. I felt I could overcome your pain, but I would never erase your mistrust. And I couldn't do that to you. So do you really believe that I loved you from the beginning, and that I did change for you?"

She burst out in another weeping jag, dragging him down to her and deluging him with kisses and tears. "I believe you. I'll always believe you."

After the storm had abated, she drew back to look at him with such earnestness. "But I want you to promise me that if you ever feel any differently, you will tell me. You must never hide anything from me again, whether you're afraid it would hurt me, or know for sure it would."

"I take it this is a two-way street? If you ever stop feeling the same as you do right now, you'll tell me?"

"Since I'll never stop loving you, the only thing I'll confess is that I'm loving you more."

"But if for some unimaginable reason you stop loving me?"

She rose, her eyes telling him everything he needed to breathe again, to live again. "I'll always tell you the whole truth. You know I'm incapable of saying anything else."

"I know." His groan exorcised the last of his tension. Then he let her push him on his back, reveling in her beauty and honesty and openness, all the treasures he'd thought he would never be blessed with again, in the absoluteness of her love, which he'd thought he'd destroyed. "It's why I was in such despair. I knew you would never exaggerate to punish me, so I truly thought I'd lost you forever."

"I would have remained yours forever even if I never found my way back to you."

"And what good would that have done me?" he exclaimed.

She took his lips in a deep, devouring kiss before she pulled back, a grin lighting up her beauty. "I'd already found my way back to you. When your brothers arrived to give me your insane bequest and tell me of your crazy plans, I—"

He heaved up, his whole body tensing. "Those bastards! I'm going to strangle each and every one of them. I told them not to—" Then it hit him. "What am I saying? It's because they disobeyed me that you're here in my arms again."

"Actually, it isn't. That's what I was trying to say. I was coming to you when they came knocking." She looped her arms around his neck. "It seems I felt you were going to do something drastic, and I reached my limit at the same time you did."

"Even if you hadn't, and you decided much later to call me back, I would have come running."

"If I'd missed you, you would have come back to find your brothers roasted." At his incomprehension, she grinned sheepishly. "They put me through their elaborate tests to determine if I'd been manipulating you into giving me what you left me. It almost made me too late to stop you. If it had, I would have turned into a fire-breathing dragon."

A guffaw escaped him, the world suddenly bright and limitless again. "That must have been Jakob and Ivan. No other brother who got his wife's seal of approval on you would have *dared* suspect you of any ulterior motives."

"Yeah, it was Starsky and Hutch." As another laugh burst out of him, she clung to him again, her shudder shaking through him. "Promise me that whatever humanitarian missions you undertake won't be in areas of active conflict. If you don't want to kill me with worry."

Taking her down, he covered her, pressed into her, as if he wanted to absorb her into his being. "I'd never put myself in harm's way when you need me."

Her fingers convulsed in his hair as she pulled his head up, her eyes fierce with conviction. "The whole world needs you, alive and well and being the irreplaceable force for good that you are. And this brings me to your bequest. All I'll ever need from you is your heart, your trust, your appreciation. But only you can direct everything you've built and achieved."

"You do have a better scientific mind than me."

"My mind and whatever else I have are at your service always. It will be an honor, a privilege and a pleasure to work with you in any capacity. But only you know how to bring everything together, to create and grow the best businesses that are beneficial to the world. You must take everything back." She suddenly chuckled, her golden eyes gleaming. "If you only saw your brothers imagining me filling your shoes, you wouldn't have had the heart to suggest it. Holmes and Watson were having little heart attacks at the very thought."

His laughter rang out with hers, until they were both almost in tears all over again.

Then merriment turned to passion, then to desperation and they were tearing each other's clothes off, competing to give more pleasure, to drag the other deeper into oblivion.

After repeated storms, full domination and surrender, Antonio rose above her and finally touched the places he'd avoided all night. Her faint scars. As he traced them, tears blinded him.

At her gasp, he raised his gaze, found her own eyes streaming again. She realized how he felt.

He still needed to put his feelings into words. "Those moments when your lifeblood bathed my hands as I struggled to stem it, when I was forced to cut into your flesh to save your precious life, when I felt you fighting me so you could let go... I'll never heal from them."

Hers sobs fractured her breath, her words. "I'm sorry, so sorry."

Wiping at his eyes, he smiled with everything in him. "Never be sorry for anything. Just like you made me a new man who has no rage or darkness, who can be ecstatically in love, who can be a son and a brother, you've probably absolved me from every sin I've ever committed. This punishment is enough to take care of all of them. I only wish you didn't have to get hurt so I'd be punished. It's a catch-22 really, since I can only be hurt through you."

Her dawning grin caught on another sob. "I hate being your Achilles' heel."

He hugged her again. "But I love having you as my only vulnerability. I can't live without you being everything to me. My strength and weakness, my joy and agony, my desire and dread."

"You're all that to me and everything else and it's... enormous."

Heart swelling with gratitude, he nodded sagely. "Humongous."

They shared another moment of total communion, before they laughed again. Their mirth caught fire again and they were again surrendering to the power of their bottomless passion and hunger.

Afterward she lay satiated in his arms, wondering what she'd ever done in her life to deserve him.

As if he'd heard her thoughts, he turned her face to him, his words sounding like an irrevocable pledge.

"The heart that grew inside me from the first moment I saw you is yours forever because you gave it life. You changed my perspective and priorities. You made me let go of my anger against my family even before I met them. It's because of you that I gave them and myself a chance, why I have them back in my life now. You're the reason I *have* a life, not just a race for more achievements and acquisitions. You're the reason I want to live forever."

The tears that came so easily to her now flowed again, ones of bliss this time. "Maybe immortality should be my new research, then. I've been eyeing gene therapy for longevity for a while now."

"If anyone could find its secret, it's you." He gathered her tighter, his expression becoming adamant. "And it *is* you who's more qualified scientifically to run the research division, while I want to give back to the world now. And that's another reason I'm yours. Until I met you, I took what I thought life owed me, and I gave back only strategically, to increase my profits. But now that I've found you, now that you love me, the world has given me far more than I can ever deserve. Now I have to create balance, give back everything I can so that I can continue to deserve having the miracle of you and your love."

Drowning in his love, in relief and gratitude, she took hold of the hands that had given her her life back, took them to her lips as she gave him her own pledge.

"And I only want the privilege of sharing your exceptional journey. You have all of me—the heart that grew to love you, the body you awakened and owned and saved, the soul that became whole only when you healed it, and everything else that I am. They're all yours, my love. Now and forever."

* * * * *

COMING SOON!

We really hope you enjoyed reading this book. If you're looking for more romance, be sure to head to the shops when new books are available on

Thursday
14th June

LET'S TALK
Romance

For exclusive extracts, competitions
and special offers, find us online:

f facebook.com/millsandboon

◎ @millsandboonuk

🐦 @millsandboon

Or get in touch on 0844 844 1351*

For all the latest titles coming soon, visit
millsandboon.co.uk/nextmonth